The Perfect Mistake

Copyright © 2023 Olivia Hayle

All rights reserved. No part of this publication may be distributed or transmitted without the prior consent of the publisher, except in the case of brief quotations embodied in articles or reviews.

All characters and events depicted in this book are entirely fictitious. Any similarity to actual events or persons, living or dead, is purely coincidental.

The following story contains mature themes, strong language, and explicit scenes, and is intended for mature readers.

Edited by Andie Edwards of Beyond the Proof
Proofread by Shannon Shacka
Cover character art by Vic Grey of @bloodwrit
Cover Typography and background by Cormar Covers

www.oliviahayle.com

To everyone who has watched their dreams die and been forced to find new ones. There can be something liberating about the first option disappearing… and realizing you can now be anyone and anything you want.

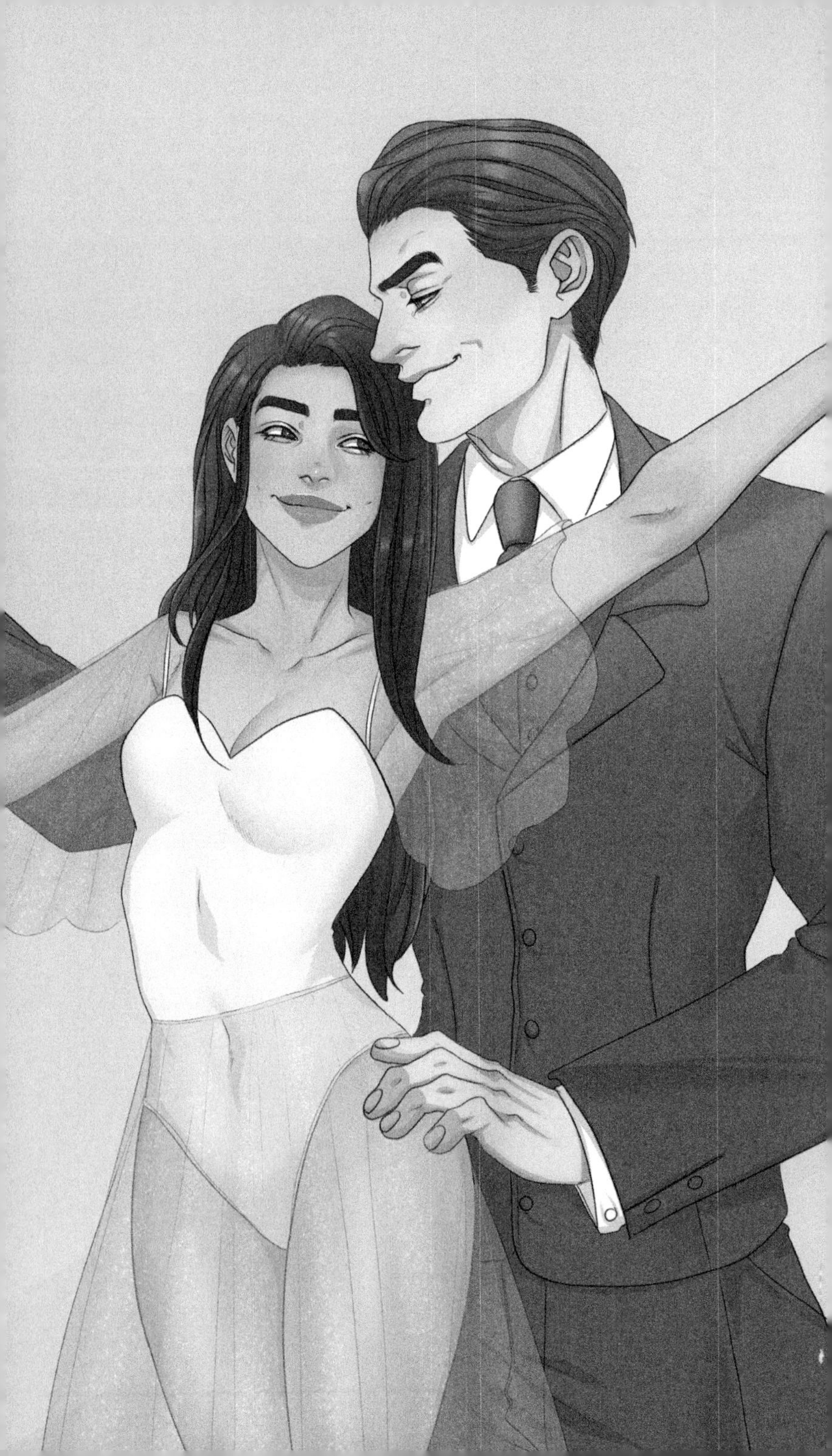

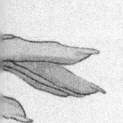

CHAPTER 1
ISABEL

I walk through the dance studio on quiet feet. My pointe shoes are laced up tightly, and they make no sound against the well-worn hardwood floor. Thousands of dancers have walked these halls for over a century. All of them suffering the same things I am today. The pain, the fatigue, the rivalries, the ambitions.

The injuries.

I pass by an open door where a group of ballet dancers are warming up and shooting the shit. Irina is in her splits, her curly brown hair teased back into a firm ballet bun. The new prima ballerina. Matt, Beth, and Simone are smiling around her, but I know the latter two must be burning up inside. Irina is young to be the prima ballerina, and she's new in the role. This fall will be her first season dancing in the position everyone covets.

Even me. Now I know that dream is at least six months—if not a year—away, even if it wasn't for Irina. *If ever*, a voice whispers in my head.

I walk down the corridor to the unassuming wooden door at the end. It doesn't even have a name on it, or a title, but that doesn't matter. Everyone at the New York Ballet Company knows and respects this door. We all fear it.

I knock.

"Yes," she says.

I push it open and enter Ms. Moore's office. She's sitting behind her desk, perusing a list of dancers, her gray hair swept up in a strict chignon. Her wrinkles are soft around her eyes, but they are the only soft thing about her.

"Ah. Isabel. Good."

I close the door behind me. "You wanted to talk to me?"

"Yes." She takes off her reading glasses and knots her hands together on the table. "I spoke to the physician yesterday about your hip."

My stomach sinks. "Yes, he says that—"

"You need to rest, if you're to ever dance again."

I nod. It's safer than speaking, even though every part of me wants to protest. "I can continue like I've been doing," I say. "Cutting my training in half to ensure I'm able to perform on show nights. I can do this. I promise. It'll be enough to heal."

Her eyes pierce. "We create art on that stage every single night. Can you create art?"

"Yes," I say. It's what I've been working my entire life for. Over two decades, every early morning and late night, every time my feet bled or my muscles ached. It's the only thing that has ever mattered.

"I can't keep an injured performer in the troupe in hopes she'll recover. You know this, Isabel. I need to slot a new dancer into rehearsals to get her up to par." She looks down at her list, at her sharp and neat handwriting, and I know she already has a shortlist of girls who will replace me. Might be looking at it right now.

"I'll get better."

"That's what they all say." She sighs, and something seems to soften around her mouth. It's the first time I've ever seen that particular expression on Ms. Moore's face. It's terrifying. "Isabel, you're out. For your own good. Injuries happen and, sooner or later, every ballerina's career ends. Mine ended almost twenty-five years ago. You'll survive it."

Survive it? Every career ends, but not mine. *Not yet.* I'm only twenty-five. I was planning on doing this until I was thirty at the very least, or thirty-five. It's extraordinary but not unheard of to dance at forty.

Twenty-five?

"No, all I need is rest," I protest. If I can take a week off, I can come back—"

Moore looks up at me. "Isabel," she says. "The decision has been made. Antoine agreed with me, and he'll work you out of the choreography effective immediately. I'll be in touch about the logistics, your severance package... and look, if you feel completely healed in six months, come back for a meeting with the physician. If he gives you the green light, we can have a conversation."

I take a few steps back toward the door. Everything feels numb. My legs. My brain. My heart. Her words sound empty. It's not an opening, it's a parting gift. It's pity.

"Okay," I say.

She looks back down at her papers, preparing for tonight's performance, and that's it. I'm out. I'm done.

She's wielded her scythe again, but this time, I'm the one on the receiving end and not the one consoling.

Numbed limbs carry me down the corridor I've walked so often. The building that the New York Ballet Academy calls home is old—one of the finest in the city—with the top floors designated entirely just for us. For the principal dancers of the premier Ballet Company. One of the best in the country.

I've worked so hard to be a dancer here. To climb the ladder, to build a career, and to grow the skills to one day become a prima ballerina. It's my home.

I hurry past a group of dancers stretching out. I don't stop to talk to them. It wouldn't surprise me if they saw this coming; if one of those girls in there might replace me...

For all the talk of us being a family, we're a deeply dysfunctional one. I've seen what happens when ballerinas leave. Hugs are exchanged, *we'll need to keep in touch—you're welcome back anytime* spoken, but, inevitably, we never see the person who left again.

They disappear.

They might still live in the city, but they might as well have moved to a different country.

And the annoying thing is, walking like this, my hip doesn't hurt at all. But as soon as I start to dance, as I stretch and kick, it will start to. Being a ballet dancer means being in pain, and I've pushed through my fair share over the years. This shouldn't be any different. I should be able to overcome this just as easily as I've done before.

My failure feels like a knife through my chest.

I take the stairs instead of the elevator out of habit. *Laziness is the enemy of perfection,* drilled into me since I was a kid. Not that I need to now. I can be as lazy as I want. Moore's offer of having a talk in six months when I'm healed feels mostly for show. I've rarely seen top-level professional ballerinas make a successful return from that long of a break. This sport, this *art,* is competitive to a fault. For every dancer that falls, there are three waiting to take their place.

I stop on the fourth floor. It's reserved for the kids' classes, and those don't start until later in the day. The halls are deserted now. I walk past the open doors of empty studios. The smooth maple wood floors, the giant mirrors, and the barres.

Once upon a time, I was one of the kids that would soon fill up these rooms.

I walk into a dusty studio. It's easy to remember this particular one. I'd spent an intense season dancing here with

Madame Novik, the first teacher to make me cry. I had danced my little heart out in here at nine years old.

A glance in the mirror reveals my present. I'm neither short nor tall. Long black hair in a ponytail down my back. A leotard the same olive color as my skin, and a short lycra skirt made for movement. Tights. Pointe shoes.

Dark eyes and a flat mouth.

I can't imagine never dancing here again. The thought won't slot into my brain, a puzzle piece that won't fit. I sway, watching my movements in the mirror. *Lines, think about your lines. Keep your head up. Weight on the working leg. Rotate. Double-time.* I spin and twist up en pointe, observing my reflection.

It feels good. It feels right. I *know* how to do this, regardless of what Moore and Antoine might have decided. It's what I was born to do.

I dance toward the large windows in the back of the studio and the sunlight streaming in through them. It's warm against my face. I pirouette, and pirouette again, spinning faster than I should without being properly warmed up.

I jump, and pain flares through my leg. I welcome it. The damn thing. *Hurt me even more.* This time I embrace it. I might as well blow the whole hip out if I can't dance anymore. No need to be cautious any longer, to save my strengths for evening performances.

I don't follow any choreography. I string together movements I know like the back of my hand, and feel the numbness give way to devastation.

There's no music, but I feel like I can hear it all the same, like a fading melody drifting faintly through the studio. A few simple arabesques with brisés, movements that are ingrained in the very fibers of my muscles.

I dance faster. My legs extend, toes point, arms held tight with every muscle strained. Sweat starts to bead on my forehead, and the twinge in my hip grows stronger. Soon it's impossible to ignore, to push away, to lock in the drawer where I keep most of my bodily aches.

But I don't stop dancing.

Not when my body is begging me to cease. Not when my hip feels like it's on fire. Maybe that's what I've been doing wrong. I've been listening, when all I need to do is work through it. Push harder.

My cheeks feel wet, and my chest aches, but I don't stop. Another pirouette and a kick. And another. And another.

There's a knife-like pain in my right hip, and I falter halfway through the spin. My balance is off, and I hit the ground without any of the grace I've been told to always show.

The fall hurts, but not as much as my hip. And nothing throbs like the burning feeling inside my chest, the sensation that's hot on my cheeks. I swipe them and find that I'm crying.

Heavy footsteps echo in the silent dance studio, and a hand lands on my shoulder.

"Isabel? Are you okay?"

The voice is familiar. I look up to see a man in a suit, looking down at me with a serious expression. His thick brown hair is cut short, his jaw clean-shaven, and his hazel eyes steely. Faint lines fan around his eyes and mar his forehead, but they only make him look more distinguished.

Surprise cuts clean through my pain. There's no logical reason for him to be here. For his hand to be on my shoulder. This man doesn't just *show up* in places. He's one of the most important men in the city. He's also my best friend's older brother, fifteen years my senior.

"Alec?"

CHAPTER 2
ALEC

Mac pulls the car to a stop outside the New York Ballet Academy. It's in Midtown, an innocuous stone building, with trees flanking the entrance.

"Idle or park?" Mac asks me.

I want to answer *idle*. This should be a quick errand, but judging by the firm *noes* my assistant has been getting, it might take a while.

"Park," I say and get out of the car. I button my suit jacket as I walk into the Dance Academy and prepare for a fight.

My daughter wants to start ballet.

It's her latest obsession, and after a week of trying to get her into dance lessons at the school my assistant says is the best in New York, we've gotten nowhere. They don't take students midterm, classes are full, and—if she's a beginner—she'll have to start with the other freshies in January…

They've run us through with excuses. But I'm good at finding ways around obstacles. People always want something, and most of the time it's money. There are very few individuals who won't ask *how high* if you're willing to pay them to jump.

The lobby of the Dance Academy smells like sun-warmed

dust and something else, something like pine or tiger balm. A receptionist gives me a bored look. It's a young guy, couldn't be more than nineteen, with a wiry build.

"I'm looking for the head of the kids' classes," I tell him.

"Down the hall on the fourth floor," he says and flips the page of a magazine.

I take the stairs and emerge in a corridor that looks exactly like the lobby. Worn wooden floors and the scent of... *is that pine?* hangs even stronger in the air here.

I head past the half-open doors to empty studios. It's lunchtime. If this is New York's largest school for children interested in ballet, no wonder it's deserted at this hour. They're in school, just like Willa, who will surely ask me about ballet lessons tonight. Again.

When she decides she wants something, she's ruthlessly determined. It's one of my favorite things about her.

I hear the patter of movement inside a studio. Footfalls against the floor, rhythmic and soft. Someone's dancing. I glance toward the sound as I walk past.

And stop short.

A solo ballerina is dancing in an otherwise vacant studio, leaping through the beams of sunlight flooding the room. She spins, faster than should be possible, her leg rising and falling.

It's... mesmerizing.

She springs across the floor, her long black ponytail swishing in the air behind her. She's dressed in tights, a short skirt, and a skintight top. A ballerina's outfit. It makes her look elongated and tall, like the twirling ballerina on top of my sister's jewelry case, all those years ago. Connie would take it out so often that the melody still lingers in my mind.

The dancer's slim arms move fluidly, but there's muscle beneath her skin. Still, it looks effortless. Like she's flying or swimming through the air. She kicks her leg up, and for a brief second, it's perpendicular to her torso.

I catch sight of the woman's profile.

It's Isabel.

What? My hand tightens at my side, and I know I should leave, but I can't. What are the odds? She's my sister's best friend, and I've met her a few times over the years, but not once have I seen her like this.

Connie must have mentioned that Isabel is a ballerina. But I hadn't known it was... *this.* She's dancing like this is her passion as much as her profession.

Her movements speed up, accentuate, and I know I should walk away. This moment feels private. Dancing alone in a studio, without music.

But I can't move.

There's a focus on her craft that I can feel, even out here in the hallway. She's pouring everything she is into her motions. In all the times I'd briefly met her... I hadn't known she could do this. Become a living flame, the embodiment of grace.

I'd noticed Isabel's beauty the first time I met her, outside Connie's apartment, years ago. She was Connie's neighbor and then became her friend. Young, only in her twenties. She'd always been full of shy smiles and polite manners. Big, dark eyes. Long hair. I shouldn't have noticed back then. But I did.

Like this, she's incandescent.

She spins, faster and faster and faster. My eyes track the graceful movement of her leg, kicking out around her as she twists. I've never seen anything like it.

Halfway through a turn, her standing leg gives out.

Isabel collapses to the floor like a house of cards folding onto itself, suddenly and quietly. She hits the wooden surface with a soft thump, her shoulders hunching over. There's a faint moan from her prone body.

I move before I can think.

"Isabel?" I put a hand on her shoulder. It's bare beneath my hand. "Are you okay?"

She looks up. There's a look of dull pain in her eyes, and a tear runs down her cheek. Her mouth opens in surprise. "Alec?"

"What happened?"

"My hip, it's... I haven't been... What are you doing here?"

"Should I get someone? Do you need help?"

"No, no, I just need to sit for a little bit." She straightens, but her leg remains beneath her, folded over. She quickly wipes her tears. "Shoot."

"Let me call for help."

A feeble chuckle escapes her. "Don't bother."

I let my hand drop from her shoulder. "It's your hip?"

"Yeah. I have a hip labral tear... It doesn't like when I dance too much." She's suddenly composed again, blinking up at me. Too composed. The hurt must be great, but I know all about not wanting to show pain.

I reach down a hand. "Can you stand?"

She gazes at my palm for a long moment before putting her own in it. Her skin is soft, her fingers slender. I grip them tight and gently pull her to her feet.

Isabel gives a low sigh of pain. "Darn."

"There must be a medic here, or some kind of physician. You work here, right?"

"Yeah." She looks down at her hand, still gripped tightly in mine. *Right.* I release it. "But I was leaving for the day. I should probably just go home and rest."

"Good. The Greystone is pretty far. How are you getting there?"

"I bike." She shakes her head, blinking a few rapid times. "Sorry, but why are you here?"

"I was visiting the director of the junior ballet classes."

"Magda? Why?"

"My daughter wants to start dancing here."

"Oh," Isabel says. Then her eyes widen. "But the training season has already started…"

"Yes. Exactly." I see the understanding in her eyes and I wonder how far it extends. I have the papers in my bag for a very generous Connovan sponsorship for underprivileged dancers, ready to use if the junior director refuses to enroll my daughter.

All you have to do is tell them how high, and people will jump, I think.

"Willa wants to dance?" Isabel asks.

I look down at her. "Yeah."

"Sorry, but Connie talks about her niece and nephew from time to time." She takes a step toward the door, but it's halting. "This is a good school. I danced here as a kid, too."

"You did?"

"Mm-hmm. They're pretty strict about the term start dates." She shrugs. "Strict about everything, really."

Maybe that's exactly what my daughter needs. We head to the exit, and with every step, Isabel tenses. It's nearly imperceptible, but I catch it.

I frown at her. "You can't bike home."

She pauses by the door frame. "Of course I can."

"You're hurt."

The dark eyes flash with something akin to protest. But then she sighs. "Yeah. So?"

I turn toward the elevator. "Come on. I have a car outside."

"Alec, I can't—"

"Yes, you can."

She starts walking beside me down the corridor. "I need my bike, so I might as well just ride it home."

"We'll fit it into the car." I have no idea how, but Mac will figure it out.

Isabel shakes her head. There's something unsettling about

walking next to her in her outfit. The times we've met, she's always been in jeans. Shirts. Normal clothing. Not this ballerina getup that leaves much of her bare, with so much skin on display.

I didn't need to add this imagery to the things I've already noticed about her.

"No, I can't accept that," she protests.

"Connie would kill me if I don't help you," I say.

Her lips curve. "Yeah, that's probably true."

"Which means you're the one doing me a favor."

Isabel looks up at me. There's a question in her eyes and something else. Curiosity maybe? But then she nods. "Okay, thanks. I'll go get my things."

"I'll wait downstairs."

She disappears through another door, and before it swings shut, I spot rows of lockers. Of course. I lean against the wall and text Mac to bring the car around. While I wait, I open my emails and see the deluge that has flooded in during my brief absence from the office.

The London acquisition hasn't gone through. Our Chief Financial Officer wants an urgent meeting. Confirmation from my assistant about the jet we'd chartered for the executive team next week.

I scroll through all the messages, marking them *read*, when the door opens again. Isabel comes out carrying a giant backpack, her face set in grim lines. She's thrown on a sweater and sneakers, leaving her long legs still exposed to view.

The bag dwarfs her slight form.

"Let me take that."

I must have sounded gruffer than I realize, because she hesitates. But then she nods and lets me grab the monstrosity from her. It's heavy. "You bike with this?"

"Not every day," she says. "I had more stuff to take home today. Clothes to… wash."

We walk in silence down to the elevator. I don't think we've ever spoken as much as we have today. In my mind,

I'm still seeing her twirl in that empty studio. *To think she'd been able to do that all along.* The few times we've met, it's been…

Uncomfortable. Electric. Dangerous.

Every chance encounter, I've found myself far too aware of her. Of her expressions, her smiles, her words.

We ride down in the tiny elevator. She's quiet, but when I glance down, I see her wipe her cheek. Is she crying again?

Fuck.

She walks ahead of me through the lobby. "I'll get my bike."

"I'll wait by the curb with the car," I say and watch her retreat quickly down the steps to the sidewalk. She heads toward the bike rack while wiping her face with the back of her left hand.

It must be her hip. I've heard of the pain dancers experience. Injuries, fractures… Is she hurting that much right now? I frown at her back, thinking through what solutions I have.

Mac pulls the Bentley to the curb and steps out. "Sir?" he asks, looking down at the hiking backpack I'm holding.

"Put this in the back," I tell him. "Do we have space for a bike?"

He frowns but doesn't question it. "Yes, if we fold down one of the seats."

"Let's do it."

I join Isabel by the rack. "You okay?"

She finishes unlocking her bike and gives me a wide smile. Her eyes glitter but her cheeks are dry. "Yes, feeling better already. Sure the bike will fit?"

"Yes. Look, I can take you to a doctor's office instead."

"No, no. I'll be fine. I just need rest." Her smile remains in place. "Trust me, this isn't the first time the hip has acted up."

Mac and I lift her bike and wedge it into the trunk. "To the Greystone," I tell him.

He nods and pulls out into the busy traffic. Isabel and I

don't talk until the car finally arrives at her building. It's familiar, located on a street I've visited often enough while Connie still lived here, too.

Mac lifts her bike out, and I move to assist when Isabel puts a hand on my forearm. "Alec," she says.

I pause. "Yes?"

"Thank you. Truly." Her smile has softened, and her eyes don't shine with tears anymore. "I really appreciate this."

I clear my throat. "Anything for a friend of Connie's."

Mac and I help her into the lobby of the Greystone with her bike and bag. We both watch as the elevator doors close behind her, and she disappears from view. The sight of her dancing stays with me, but so do her tears. The vision of her crying lodges in my chest uncomfortably, a memory I know I won't be able to shake.

My throat feels too tight, and I undo the top button to pull my collar loose. *Inconvenient,* I think and know it to be true. But knowing it won't stop the attraction.

It's not until the car pulls away from the Greystone Building that I realize I never did talk to the junior ballet director about my daughter's classes.

CHAPTER 3
ISABEL

I stare at the letter that arrived in my mailbox a few days ago. After opening the envelope, I'd left the papers on my two-seater couch, unfolded and poised to strike like a cobra.

I expected this would come, just not this soon. It's been just over a week since I left the Company, with all the contents of my locker in my backpack and a throbbing hip. Ice packs and rest had taken care of the pain, but now that I'm out of a job, my injury is far from my most pressing issue.

I've lived in my little one-bedroom apartment for six years. It's one of several properties around New York that's sublet to the New York Ballet on ninety-nine-year lease agreements. A remnant of former times, when wealthy patrons showed support for the art by offering affordable residences to ballet principals in their newly built properties. I bet whoever commissioned the Greystone has their name on the small golden plaque in the hall of the New York Dance Academy.

When I joined the corps, I was allotted a place to stay at a comped rent. For six years I've paid what in New York City can only be called a nominal fee.

I should have cherished it more while it lasted.

My phone vibrates against the wooden top of my coffee table. Once. Twice. Three times. The group chat with my younger siblings has been blowing up all morning, which isn't unusual for them. My silence is, though. I haven't told anyone about being released from the Company. Just stayed holed up in the tiny, rent-controlled apartment I'm about to lose.

I haven't even been able to relax by reading. My Kindle lies next to my phone, just as unused. There's been no escape from the single, all-consuming question. *What the hell am I supposed to do now?*

There's a knock on my door and a cheery "Hello! You in?"

I startle off the couch. It sounds like Connie. But she hasn't lived in the Greystone for months, not since she married her nemesis turned soulmate.

For a second, I consider not answering her. Pretending I'm not in.

But then her voice rings out again. "Isabel? I've got beignets!"

"Coming!" I push myself off the couch and open my door. Connie is a glowing vision in the outside hallway. Her auburn hair is up in a ponytail, and her cheeks are flushed.

Her smile dies when she sees me. "You okay?"

"Not really."

"Shit," she says and holds up a paper bag. "Should I get more beignets?"

"How many did you bring?"

"Three. I had four, but I ate one on the way."

I push the door further ajar, letting her in. "It'll do."

It's a Sunday, but she looks just as put together as she does when heading to work. Trenchcoat and boots, and a winking emerald on her ring finger. "I figured something was up when you canceled yoga yesterday. I had to come by anyway, to look over the final details about my old apartment, and... Isabel?"

I sigh. "Yeah. Sorry. It's... it's just been a really long week."

"I can see that," she says cautiously and puts the bag of beignets down in front of me. "So. What can I do to help?"

"I'm not dancing anymore."

Her expression goes slack. "Your hip? I thought it was getting better."

"Not fast enough for my artistic director or the head of the Company, though."

She sits down at my kitchen table, her eyes serious. "Tell me what happened."

So I do, curled up on the chair across from her. I'm still in my workout leggings. I've lived in them for days, spending every morning going through my hour-and-a-half-long stretching routine. Some habits die hard.

Halfway through my tale, I start to cry. I don't mean to. I haven't all week, not since I lost my composure in front of Alec. But telling someone about it, having to hear my own voice out loud... It hits me differently.

"Oh Isa, I'm so sorry," Connie says. "You know what? Screw the people in charge at the Company. If they can't see what an asset you are to the team and just give you some time to recuperate, then it's their loss."

That makes me chuckle through the tears, because it's so blatantly inaccurate. At any moment, at least three prospects are waiting to take a single dancer's place. It's cutthroat and competitive. I'm not an asset. *They're* the asset.

"I don't know what to do," I say. "I have no other marketable skills. None. I've dedicated my *entire* life to this. Every waking moment." I grab the letter, and it crumples in my hand. "And now I have to move out."

Connie's eyes widen. "*What?*"

After I explain it to her, she looks thoughtful. "Damn, I

wish I hadn't sold my apartment when I did. You'd have been more than welcome to stay there."

"Thanks," I say. It would have helped, but I'm glad it's not an option. Connie and I are great friends, but we come from different worlds. As a Connovan, she grew up in a radically different part of New York than I did. Same city, a whole other world. Being homeless is not a problem any Connovan will ever face. And unless one of them makes a disastrous financial decision, that will be true for all future Connovans, too.

"We have spare bedrooms," Connie says earnestly. "You can always stay with me and Gabriel."

"Thank you," I murmur.

"Honestly. It wouldn't be a problem at all. The opposite, really."

I wipe my cheeks. "Thanks."

Her slight smile turns into a frown. "Alec mentioned that he saw you last week. That your hip was... that you were in pain. Maybe it's a good thi—"

"He mentioned it?" I ask. That's surprising. I hadn't thought he would... Then again, I know almost nothing about Alec Connovan. Nothing more than there's something about him that has always intrigued me... made me want to impress him, somehow. Understand him. But he has never struck me as the talkative kind.

"Yes." She leans back on the couch. "At the Dance Academy. I'm sorry I didn't realize how much your hip has been bothering you. We don't have to continue yoga."

"It's fine"

"It's not. I'm sorry, Isabel." Her smile turns determined and her eyes fierce. "But don't worry. We'll figure something out, I promise."

"Yeah," I say. I'm sure I will. But whatever it is, it won't change the fact that my greatest dream has just died.

It's hard to imagine if anything will ever replace it.

CHAPTER 4
ALEC

The text that ruins my day isn't long. Four sentences in total—innocent in tone and infuriating in their message.

I'm handing in my notice of resignation, effective immediately. I've also been in contact with the agency. Your children are lovely, but I can't provide what Willa needs. Have a good day.

Riley had lasted three weeks. Highly recommended by the childcare agency, with a master's degree in child psychology and six years of experience, and Willa had broken her in less than a month.

I rub a hand over my forehead. This can't continue. The agency will run out of qualified nannies, and I'll run out of patience. Whichever comes first, and right now, it feels like I might be the factor that blows up.

For fuck's sake.

I'd spoken to her just the other day about this. Being needlessly difficult isn't nice. Antagonizing nannies isn't nice. Driving them away is…really fucking inconvenient for Daddy.

There is something reluctantly admirable about Willa's dedication to this. And I already know that when I ask my daughter about Riley quitting, she'll look at me like an angel with big hazel eyes and soft brown hair, and tell me she doesn't have a clue about what happened. *Riley was really nice, Daddy. I promise. I'm sorry she left.*

Mm-hmm.

Right.

I open my online calendar. Meetings take up the rest of my day. There's that late-night gala tomorrow night—the one I was supposed to give a keynote address at. And an early staff meeting on Thursday…

All things that will need to be rearranged until I have a new nanny. Apologetic emails of withdrawal sent by my staff, meetings pushed back to next week, and deals put on pause. I switch screens to a chat with my assistant. At least that's someone who's working out well. For the first time in months, I'm dealing with a competent aide.

It's depressingly hard to find people who take pride in their work.

There's a sharp knock on my door, and before I can type, my assistant fires off a message.

Constance outside your door for your check-in.

I glance down at my watch, and yeah, my sister is on time. I'm the one off-schedule due to Riley's text. I hit a button, and the door to my office swings open. My sister walks in. She looks focused, a folder of papers under her right arm.

"Hey," she says and pulls out a chair in front of my desk. Then she frowns. "Bad news? Is it about Nate's acquisition in London?"

I shouldn't be this easy to read. "No."

"Right. Anything I can help with?"

The response should be another obvious *no*, leaving it that. But as I toss my phone onto the desk, something compels me to tell her the truth. Maybe it's all the shit we went through just a few months ago. "My latest nanny just quit."

A small smile curves her lips. "No way."

"Yes. Glad you find it amusing."

Her smile widens. "Sorry. It sucks, of course. But this is… What is Willa doing? She's nothing but amazing whenever I see her."

"Yeah, well, she likes *you*."

Connie's eyes soften. "What are you going to do?"

"Cancel most of my plans and start interviewing replacements. That'll take at least a week, too, if not longer." I rub the back of my neck. A tension headache is setting in at my temples. Great. I'll have to ask my housekeeper to help with babysitting duties, and that's on top of her already long days running the apartment and cooking meals.

"Do you have to go through the whole vetting process?"

I give Connie a withering glare. "I won't leave my children with a random stranger."

"Of course not, that's not what I'm suggesting… Just that, is a written test and a physical exam really necessary?"

"I have never asked for either."

"Just about," she says. Then her face lights up. "Okay, I have an idea. It's a unique solution to this problem, but I think it would work."

I lean back in my chair. "All right. Tell me what it is, so I can dismiss it."

"Promise you'll let me finish." She taps her nails against the folder of papers with rhythmic precision. "You know my friend Isabel."

Surprise ripples through me, but I mask it behind a tight expression. That name is the last one I would have expected to come up in this conversation. She seems to be everywhere lately. At the studio… And in thoughts my mind has entertained since seeing her last week. The memory of her dancing in the sunlight intruded at the most inopportune times.

I cross my arms over my chest. "What about her?"

"Her injury means she can no longer dance. At least not for the next few months, so she's in the market for a job."

Ah. Maybe that's what she had cried about. Not just the injury, but the realization she wouldn't be dancing again. Judging by what I've seen, that's a fucking travesty.

But I shake my head. "I only hire live-in nannies."

"I don't think that will be a problem for her at all," Connie says.

"I doubt she has the right expertise. You know I only hire people with a lot of experience in childcare. Isabel is a dancer."

"She has two younger siblings, so she has experience," Connie says. "She's also the calmest and most responsible person I know. Willa wants to learn ballet, right? Isabel can teach her. She might be the only nanny Willa will tolerate."

It makes a modicum of sense. Even I can see that.

But it should still be a non-starter. Accepting this option will invite trouble of the worst kind, into my home. Getting thoughts of her out of my head will be impossible if she's sleeping a few rooms down from me.

The suggestion shouldn't appeal to me.

It shouldn't.

"She's your friend," I say. "Since when do we mix business and pleasure?"

That stumps Connie for a moment. She leans back, eyes thoughtful. But then she nods. "That's a good thing, here, since I can vouch for her. But it's not like the *two of you* are friends. Your relationship will be strictly professional. It's the perfect solution," Connie says.

The image of Isabel dancing flashes through my mind again. The way she'd felt in my arms as I pulled her to her feet. Her tear-filled brown eyes. Her soft voice.

The final argument isn't one I can articulate. Not to anyone, and especially not to my little sister. I can barely do so to myself. *She will be a temptation. A beautiful, intriguing temptation who's been beguiling me for years.*

But I've met beautiful women before, and it's never thrown me off. It won't now. Not when it's a woman far too young for me, my sister's best friend, and an employee. I've never been a slave to my emotions, and I'm not about to start now.

Not to mention, I'm not looking for any kind of personal entanglement. My wife died five years ago, and if there's one thing I've learned, it's that relationships are costly. When they inevitably end, they'll take everything out of you. Your peace, your sanity, your happiness… and your heart.

Resolve hardens my spine into steel.

"Call her," I say. "Can she be here for an interview this afternoon?"

My sister smiles and reaches for her phone. "On it."

Odds are Isabel won't last more than a week anyway. What's the worst that can happen?

CHAPTER 5
ISABEL

Contron is intimidating.

It belongs to a world I don't live in. Cutthroat, sure, I'm used to that. High-stakes, yes, I know that well. But the large skyscraper in front of me bearing the name of Connie's family company is a far cry from a dance studio or a stage in front of a welcoming audience. It's cold steel and brutal glass shapes, and it's the headquarters of a business empire.

I take a deep breath and walk into the lobby.

When Connie had called about interviewing for Alec, the *no* hovered on the tip of my tongue. How could I become his employee? How could I walk into a room and not feel the charged current rip through me, like it always does when he's around, and answer questions about my job experience?

But the truth is a raw, uncomfortable thing. I need an income. I need a place to stay. And more than anything, I need something to do. The past week without hours of ballet practice had nearly driven me mad. I can't take more weeks like that.

I haven't stood still for years, and doing so now would break me.

So I keep moving. Straight toward the lone receptionist seated behind a desk in the vast, steel lobby. The Contron logo looms large behind her on the wall.

To the right are the electronic gates, with the elevators beyond the security perimeter. I watch as a few men in suits walk by carrying lunch bowls and swiping their access cards to gain entrance.

The receptionist looks up at me. "Hello. Can I help you?"

"Yes, I'm here to see Alec Connovan?"

A smile curves her lips. It's not a particularly nice one. "Sorry, you're here to see the CEO?"

"Yes."

"And who called this meeting?"

"He did. Well, I got the information from Connie."

"And that would be Constance Connovan?" the receptionist asks slowly. "Do you have an invitation email or a letter?"

I shift from one foot to the other. "No, it was over the phone. I'm a friend of Connie's."

She's still smiling, her lips pulled into a mocking curl. But she reaches for her phone. "I'll call up. And who shall I say is here to see the CEO?"

"Isabel Morales."

"Right. Excellent. You can have a seat."

Sitting down on the pristine white sofa in the lobby feels awkward. About as awkward as my black jeans and brown teddy jacket among this sea of suits. I couldn't be more out of place if I tried.

What was I thinking, agreeing to this?

Alec. It's the painfully simple answer. He's always been impossible to overlook. Whatever the attraction is, it's hard to put into words, but that's what I've felt from the very first time he glanced at me. His hazel eyes had been hard in the hallway outside of Connie's apartment. His hair messy. Later, I learned that it's never messy.

I shoot Connie a text.

> Isabel: Hey. I'm downstairs in your lobby, but can't get through the security gates.

It takes five minutes before she walks out of the elevator and through the biometric gate. She's a vision of professionalism in her gray slacks and white silk shirt, and her auburn hair is in a bun.

Connie smiles when she sees me. "Isabel," she says and pulls me in for a hug. "Thanks for coming by on such short notice."

People are watching us. Curious glances are thrown our way by passersby returning from their lunch breaks... and an outright stare from the receptionist.

I've never seen people react to her like that before. She's always been Connie—my friend in yoga class and at dinners out or at home.

"Come, this way..." She swipes her card, and we cross the security gate. An elevator opens and she walks straight inside. I notice other people hanging back, choosing another car. Does she realize how much deference people here give her?

Judging by the smile on her face, I bet she doesn't. It makes me love her more. I want to tell her how impressive she is, but I file it away for a later conversation.

"Alec is grateful that you could come in. I know he might not say it, but he is," she assures.

"You said kids' nanny quit? Just today?"

"Yes, and it's not the first time." She nudges my shoulder. "My niece is... spirited. I hope you don't mind a tough crowd."

That makes me chuckle for the first time in days. "I've been dancing for a tough crowd all my life."

"I figured," she says. "You might be bendy, but you don't break."

Maybe not, even if it feels like I've come awfully close to snapping this past week. We stride through the office landscape of the top floor; down multiple hallways, each as bland as the one before it. Finally, we reach a man sitting at a desk to the right of a large wooden door with CEO emblazoned in gold letters upon its hefty surface.

I feel a little stunned by my surroundings. At the Dance Academy, everything was old. Worn in, like a pair of used ballet flats. Grants were rare and hard to come by. Every penny went into production, not into the superficial scenery. Here, money is in every single line of the building. In the expensive decor and the glossy paint on the walls.

"Sorry, I have to leave you here," Connie says with an apologetic smile. "I have a video meeting with a supplier in Japan starting… now. Text me when you're done, okay? Maybe we can have lunch."

"Yeah, sounds good."

She disappears, and I'm left alone in front of the CEO's office. His assistant glances at me briefly before pressing a button on his keyboard. The large door swings open, but there's no one on the other side of the threshold.

"Come in," a voice says.

I swallow my nerves and step into Alec's office.

He's sitting behind a giant glass desk. Windows blanket the wall behind him, opening up to the cityscape beyond. Large built-in bookshelves to his left hold row upon row of books, drawings, and the occasional framed certificate.

"Hi," I say.

His gaze is impossible to read. "Hello. Have a seat."

I sink onto the chair in front of his desk. Cross my legs and clear my throat. "So, I heard you're in the market for a new nanny?"

"Yes. Connie was the one who suggested you, actually." His mouth turns into a faint frown. "Your injury. What happened after the other day?"

"It's better," I say. "Thanks for driving me home."

"But you're not dancing anymore."

I've lived with that reality for a full week so far. One week, compared to years of living with a dream. It hurts to hear it phrased so plainly.

"No, I'm not. At least not until I'm fully healed."

He nods and leans back in his chair. His thick brown hair is cut fairly short and neatly brushed back. "Why do you think you'd be a good nanny?"

And now I'm in a job interview. I take a deep breath, slipping into the audition process. It's one I've been through many times before. "I like kids. I have two younger siblings—twins—and they were definitely a handful. When I was growing up, I often helped my mother take care of them. Once I got older, I babysat them. I'm also disciplined and responsible, thanks to years of following strict workout routines. And I'm great at learning on the job."

He nods once, resting his hands on the desk in front of him. My eyes linger on the steepled gesture. The backs of his hands are broad; long fingers with square knuckles. They're large hands.

"Isabel," he says, and my gaze snaps back up to his. "My daughter can be challenging. She has decided she would rather have no babysitter at all. But she's eight, so that's out of the question."

I smile. "She's rebellious, then."

"At times. From what I've heard, she can be harsh to a nanny." His eyes turn assessing. "Can you handle that?"

The frank question makes me want to chuckle. The things I've endured from ballet teachers would make non-dancers flinch. I've been slapped, berated, poked and prodded, and screamed at in front of my peers until I bawled. It took a few years, but now I can have an instructor yell inches away from my face and I will not move a muscle.

"I can handle that," I say.

"Good. The position is live-in."

"Yes, Connie mentioned." My voice sounds remarkably steady, even if the idea of residing in the same space as Alec sets my insides on fire. Nerves make my chest tight.

"I sometimes need to leave early, and there are evenings when I'm not back until late," he explains. He doesn't look happy, either. But then again, I've never even seen him smile. He's always stern. In control. *Restrained.* "You'll have help. My housekeeper Katja is there from midday to dinner time. Mac, my driver, knows all the pickup routines at school and extracurriculars. You'll get my private number to use if anything happens. Here's the rundown."

He pushes a stack of papers across the desk, and I flip through them. The notes are meticulous. Names and ages of the kids, their favorite meals, preferences, nicknames, and the locations of Alec's home and his children's school…

My stomach drops. This isn't a little babysitting gig like I had in high school. This is much, much bigger. And the man across from me doesn't suffer fools.

"I also have a contract. Please look it over, and if you're pleased with the salary offer, go ahead and sign."

I accept another stack of papers. "When do you want me to start?"

"Is tomorrow too soon?"

"No."

"All right." His jaw flexes. "And Isabel, I know you're Connie's friend…"

The sound of my name in his deep voice shouldn't be that pleasant. It really, really shouldn't. "I know, but I promise that won't affect this. I can be professional."

"Good," he says. And then, like it's an afterthought: "So can I."

That almost makes me smile. *As if he's ever anything but.* Alec glances down at the heavy watch on his wrist. "I took this meeting in between the existing ones. I have to go."

"Of course." I stand and grip the mountain of paperwork. "I'll get back to you as soon as possible with the signed contract."

He extends his hand across the table. I meet it with my own, and his long fingers close over mine. We shake once, twice, three times. A warm tingle travels up my arm.

"Thank you," Alec says. His voice is cordial, but his eyes on mine are intense. I can't read them. Maybe he's wondering if he just made a mistake.

As I walk out of his office, arm still tingling from contact with his, I can't help but wonder the very same.

Admiring him from afar was one thing.

Living with him will be something very different.

CHAPTER 6
ISABEL

The legendary St. Regis prep school is located in an ornate stone building on the Upper East Side. Trees line the street outside the wrought iron fence that ensures the grounds stay protected. Beyond the gate, I spot the large copper bell that must ring when classes begin. Extravagance is everywhere—the landscaping, the structures, the athletic fields. The campus is so large and so popular among the city's elite that, in the past century, it has become a premier kindergarten to grade twelve institution to send their sons and daughters. No child should have to leave the warm embrace of a school where a tuition fee is more than my annual salary.

Right now, the schoolyard is empty. But it won't be in five minutes. There's already a row of cars down the street, and parents or nannies linger on the sidewalk, in time for pickup to get underway.

Yesterday, I was interviewed by Alec in his office. Today, I'm picking up his children. Things have gone dizzyingly fast, and if it wasn't for the comprehensive brief he'd given me, I would be feeling completely unprepared.

The car behind me is Alec's. With dark-tinted windows,

the black Bentley blends in amid the fleet of similar vehicles. Alec's driver is named Mac, and he's standing beside me with his giant arms crossed over his chest.

He must be in his fifties, bald and bearded. Everything about him makes Mac seem less like a driver and more like a bodyguard.

"They'll be out soon," he says calmly.

I nod and hoist my bag higher up on my shoulder. There's a list in the brief, and I run through it in my head. *Double-check that Sam has his backpack (he often forgets). Ensure Willa gets a snack. If there are no after-school activities, go directly home.*

"And they know there's a new nanny here today?" I ask. Alec had already assured me the kids would be informed, but I have to confirm again.

Mac nods. "They spoke about it in the car this morning."

Good.

Great.

Not nervous at all.

It's been ages since I babysat. I must have been seventeen or eighteen at the time. Now, I'm twenty-five. Lots of things have changed since then.

The bell rings, and the doors of the school open. Uniformed children pour out en masse. The smallest come first, and I crane my neck to look for Sam. He's in kindergarten, and I should be able to spot him...

"He's the one with the giant blue backpack," Mac says. "To the left."

Oh. There he is, with a mop of auburn hair so similar to Connie's, and yes, a too-big backpack. His uniform consists of navy shorts and a light-blue button-down. He looks like a little scout.

He's talking to a friend as they head toward the gate. *Showtime.* I move through the crowd.

"Sam?" I ask with a smile. "Hey. I'm here with Mac to pick you up."

He looks up at me with hazel eyes and a mouth that's shaped like an O. For a second, it's hard to imagine he's Alec's son. He's all soft cheeks and round glasses.

"Okay," he says and falls in step beside me.

Well, that was easy. "I'm Isabel. It's nice to meet you."

He nods and then he sees Mac. His legs speed up until he reaches the driver.

"Hey, buddy," Mac says and holds up a hand. They high-five. "Got your homework?"

Right. They do this every single day.

Sam gets into the car without protest and happily accepts the granola bar I give him, per the instructions in the brief.

Willa's next. I recognize her the second she comes out of the school. She's wearing a plaid skirt and white button-down like all the other girls, and her brown hair is in a ponytail. She's talking to a few other girls her age, and they're walking close, heads bent together as they chat.

I wave *hello*.

She spots me. Her eyes are unreadable before she turns back to her friends. It's another five minutes before she walks toward Mac and me.

"Hi, Willa," I say. "I'm Isabel. I'm—"

"The new nanny. I know." She steps past me.

"That's right. I'm a friend of your aunt Connie."

Willa looks at me with a blank expression. "Really?"

"Yes, really. We've been neighbors for years."

"What does she look like?"

"Your aunt? She's got hair like your little brother's, she's a bit taller than I am, and has green eyes."

Willa doesn't acknowledge my response. "Have you met my dad?"

"Yes, several times. I saw him just yesterday at his office."

She frowns, and for a second, I think she's about to say something else, but she just turns on her heel and walks to the car. The kids don't seem to have a problem picking out which black car is theirs.

The drive back to Alec's apartment is uneventful. Sam talks to Mac in happy tones, telling him stories from his day that only occasionally actually make sense. Willa looks out the window while sitting perfectly still.

I wonder how many times they've done this. Had a new nanny walk into their life and pick them up from school.

It's not a long car ride to my new home. I'd been there before heading to do pickup and familiarized myself with the layout and the look of the place. It's a large Upper East Side apartment not far from the Greystone. The beautiful building has both a doorman and a concierge. The apartment itself... well... It's huge, for one, and some might say that size doesn't matter, but in New York City, real estate is one of the few things where it does.

Every square foot is another display of wealth.

After Mac drops us off, Sam leaves his backpack in the entryway and runs straight to the kitchen where Katja is preparing snacks. Willa sits down at the kitchen table and pointedly ignores me.

I stand in the doorway and have absolutely no idea what to do.

None.

Katja seems amazing, but her job is to cook food and prepare lunches for tomorrow, not to mention keep the apartment clean and do laundry. My job is the kids. Entertain them. Educate them. Help them with homework.

I sit down opposite Willa.

"Are you doing homework?"

She doesn't answer me.

I peer over the table and catch a hint of the book she's opened. English homework, it seems like. We sit in silence for a few long minutes. It's not just that she is focused—doing her thing—her silence feels very pointed, and her eyes are glued to the pages.

I wonder if it's a front of some sort. *Look, I don't need a nanny.*

Fine.

I fill a glass of water and set it in before her, but otherwise leave her alone. Then I head to the kitchen island where Sam is chatting happily with Katja, who is preparing a ton of veggies.

Sam looks over as I approach. "This is Isabel. She's our new nanny," he says loudly.

Katja smiles at me. Her curly blonde hair is gathered into a low ponytail, and her expression is polite. "Yes, we've met earlier, actually."

"Oh," Sam says. He takes another apple slice and chews slowly. "Okay. I'm going to play now."

"You do that. Do you want your apple slices with you?"

"Yes." Katja hands him the bowl, and he scampers off toward his bedroom.

I breathe out a sigh. "Are they always this... independent?"

She shrugs and turns back to her chopping board. "Yes, mostly. But that doesn't mean they don't still need guidance. Sam often has big projects in kindergarten and he forgets schoolwork easily. Willa is... well, she doesn't need much help with the school part. She's great at that."

I glance to where Willa is sitting at the kitchen table, her head bent. She looks engrossed in her work, but I suspect she's listening to every word.

"I bet they both are," I say. "Their dad told me wonderful things about them."

Willa's pen falters slightly. *Yeah. Definitely listening.*

"When is he coming home tonight?" I ask.

"Oh, I forgot to mention this to you earlier. Here," Katja says, wiping her hands on a towel and walking over to the fridge. A tablet is stuck magnetically to the door. "We have a copy of his schedule here that his assistant keeps updated. Let's see… Alec will be home at six tonight. In time for dinner with the kids."

"Great," I say. That leaves me three hours. "Thank you for being so welcoming, too. I can imagine it's been hard for you and also Mac with such a high turnover of nannies…"

Katja's polite expression softens into something more genuine, and she sighs gently. "It's been challenging, yeah. But I have a good feeling about you."

That makes me smile back. "Thank you."

The next three hours pass with remarkable unremarkableness. Willa makes it clear—through ignoring—that she doesn't want anything to do with me. I respect that. Maybe that's step one in her process of vetting a new nanny, and if so, I won't interfere.

Sam is much simpler. He's happy to have a captive audience to explain his plastic building creations and his stories from school. I sit cross-legged on the carpeted floor of his bedroom and listen to all of it. He's helpful when I ask him about his school projects, too, and even grabs the instructions for an assignment from his backpack. It's a crumpled-up piece of paper.

Everything seems to shift once Alec arrives home.

It's like the household had held its breath in anticipation, and all of it whooshes out when the front door opens. Willa leaves the book she'd been coloring in and rushes to the entryway. Sam follows at a more leisurely pace, but he makes sure to grab the ship he'd been building to show his father.

I linger in the hallway behind them.

Alec is standing by the console table, undoing his cufflinks and dropping them into a small dish. He looks impossibly tall next to both of his children.

They're talking over one another.

"Daddy, look, I made a ship. The big one."

"We had gymnastics today, and I was second best in class."

Alec ruffles Sam's hair and smiles at Willa. "That's great, honey."

"Daddy!"

"Yes, that's a very cool ship. Is it like the one we saw in the harbor a few weeks ago?" He asks and shrugs out of his suit jacket. Something about the scene feels far too domestic for my eyes. I'm not meant to see Alec Connovan like this. No one is, except his closest circle. And I'm certainly not in it.

But I can't look away, either.

The sternness I've always seen on his features is still there, but it's lessened. I don't know if this is his mask… or if it's the truth.

He listens to his kids speak with a focused expression and starts to roll up the sleeves of his light-blue shirt. Inch after inch, his large hands working in turn on folding up the fabric.

It's hard not to imagine those hands… No. I can handle this attraction. So what if he's tall, broad-shouldered, and handsome? It doesn't matter that his age makes him distinguished or that his stern calm radiates something I've been craving for longer than I can admit.

I've danced until my feet bled. This kind of discomfort should be nothing at all.

Alec glances around the room like he's looking for something. His gaze halts when it lands on me.

He pauses mid-sleeve roll.

"Isabel," he says. His eyes rake over my body in the quickest of flashes, and I resist the urge to cross my arms over my chest. Maybe my jeans and sweater aren't appropriate nanny-wear for the Connovan household? But there had been no mention of a uniform in the brief.

"Hey," I say.

His expression grows tense. "Has everything gone all right?"

"Yes, absolutely. Without a hitch."

Alec nods once and looks back down at his kids. He gestures toward the dinner table. "I want you two to have a seat. Katja is almost done with dinner."

Willa dances backward to the table. Her demeanor has done a complete one-eighty in the five minutes Alec's been home. "Okay."

"I'll be there soon," he says and crosses the space toward me. Over his shoulder I see Willa shooting me a venomous look.

His voice lowers. "Hey."

"Hi," I murmur.

"I'm going to eat with the kids," he says. "You're free for the rest of the night, but I'd like to speak with you. Do you mind waiting?"

"No, not at all."

"Good," he says. This close and this *undone,* I catch the scent of his cologne. "Have you seen your rooms?"

"Not yet," I say. There hadn't been time earlier between the quick introduction to Katja and needing to head to St. Regis for pickup.

"They're down that hall, to the left. Past the playroom. Check them out, and I'll join you shortly."

I nod. "Sounds good."

Out in the living room, I can hear Sam singing a tune and Katja's hushed voice. Cutlery scrapes against plates. Alec leaves without another word, and I'm left to wander down to my rooms. He spoke of plural. I peek into the playroom as I pass, and while it's a normal-size bedroom, it's a veritable treasure trove of toys. A makeshift teepee in the corner holds a pantheon of stuffed animals. Tiger, hippo, snake, horse. I continue on to find an ajar door at the end of the hall.

I push it open.

It's like a one-bedroom apartment. An open-concept layout, sure, but it's large enough to have a queen bed in the corner, a sofa in the middle, and a kitchenette on the other side. Not a shitty one, either. Here you can actually cook.

Two large windows overlooking the courtyard.

This is nothing like babysitting my neighbors' kids for fifteen dollars an hour when I was seventeen. This is high-level, professional shit. I wonder if I'm the least experienced nanny Alec has ever hired and immediately regret the thought. I don't even want to think about it. Maybe the others were teaching his kids foreign languages and how to express their emotions in a healthy manner, and provided weekly progress reports.

I sink onto the two-seater couch. The room is tasteful, beige, and beautiful. If other nannies have lived here, they haven't left their mark. Maybe that's what we're meant to do. Flow in and out of the Connovan family unit without leaving a trace.

It takes Alec thirty minutes to join me. I hear his footsteps first, hard treads against the hardwood. The door opens and he's silhouetted in the frame, his shape sharp against the light.

"Hi," I say. "This is a beautiful room."

He strides inside. "It'll do?"

"Yes, absolutely."

"When can you move in?"

"Tomorrow?" I ask. The sooner I leave the Greystone, the better. There's no shortage of dancers who want the apartment, and I don't want a call from Moore.

"That works," he says. His jaw looks tense, though, and he glances from me to the bed in the corner. Maybe he's starting to rethink the whole thing. *Who is she, really? Why did I hire her?*

Maybe I should rise or offer him a seat beside me. But neither option seems right, not with him looking straight at me and giving not a single inch of ground.

He's always been hard to read.

"I signed the contract," I say instead. "I emailed your office, but I brought it today, too. Would you like a copy?"

"Keep it for your own records." His mouth turns down in the faintest of frowns. "Your injury. It won't be aggravated by this job?"

"It'll be all right."

"Handling kids isn't exactly easy on the body," he says.

I shake my head a bit too rapidly. "Trust me, it's far easier than dancing on pointe for hours a day."

A ghost of amusement flickers in his eyes. "Right. I shouldn't underestimate you."

"You can, if you'd like," I say. "Just know that you'll be proven wrong."

"Consider me warned," he says. Then, he clears his throat, and the flicker of amusement dies. "You'll have your rooms to yourself. The kids know not to bother you when you're in here, unless I'm away on business trips. At those times, they might come to you at night if they need anything. I try to be home as much as I can, but there are at least a few evenings and early mornings a week when I'm gone."

"Of course. That makes sense."

"My kids come first. Your job is to always make sure they're taken care of and appropriately stimulated, and that they don't fight. If you can't do it, you will be let go, effective immediately. Doesn't matter that you're Connie's friend."

"I understand," I say. "They're your kids. Of course."

"The common areas are—"

"Off-limits. I understand," I say. "Trust me, I won't be a bother."

He shakes his head. Runs a hand along the back of his neck. "Free to use."

"Oh." Even when he's home? Somehow that strikes me as unlikely. He seems like a man who guards his privacy fiercely. While we might be living in the same apartment, I suspect I won't be getting any glimpses of the man behind the mask.

"How was Willa today?" he asks.

"She wasn't a problem at all. I think she's evaluating me, but she kept to herself."

"Good. Let me know if that changes."

How bad could an eight-year-old get? I think. But I just nod. "Of course."

There's a beat of silence between us, and then another. I force a smile to my face. "Where do you sleep?"

"My bedroom is in the opposite hall," he says. The kids' bedrooms are between us, then.

He turns toward the door, but pauses with his large hand on the frame. "Welcome, Isabel."

My chest tightens at the sound of him saying my name. "Thank you… Alec."

CHAPTER 7
ISABEL

My mother's voice is a flurry of rapidly intermingled Spanish and English, and tinged with worry. I listen to her through my headphones and continue unpacking the clothes I'd brought to my new home. Good thing my previous place has been a furnished rental. All I own could be packed in two suitcases and a large IKEA bag. My bike in tow, and here I am, living in Alec Connovan's multimillion-dollar condo.

"Maybe you should focus on healing instead," Mom says. "So you can rejoin the ballet in a few months."

"Mom, I have to earn money."

"Move back home, then. You can give ballet classes to the kids in the area."

That makes me chuckle. "I don't think a single one would be interested. This is a good solution, Mom. It's stable. At least until I get my hip in order."

"I don't know this man," she says firmly. "He could be anyone. And living with him? It's not safe."

I sigh. "He's Connie's brother, Mom. You know Connie. You've *met* Connie."

"So? I don't care if he's the Pope's own brother. He can still be sleazy."

"He isn't," I say. Not even a little bit, not once in the years I've known him. *Unfortunately.*

Her disapproval bothers me. It always has. But this week has brought plenty of lows already, and it seems like my quota is met. Mom's tone of voice rolls right off my back.

Telling her and Dad that I'd been cut from the Company had been the hardest part of the week. I'd done it in a text to Mom, knowing that she would spread the news like wildfire in a matter of hours. It had saved me a lot of difficult conversations.

"Come to dinner on Sunday," she says. "Sebastian and Elena will be there. Your cousin, too. You need to be with family right now."

Yes, where everyone will have a thousand questions. My siblings have already been blowing up my phone, and it'll be even worse in person.

"Maybe. I don't know my schedule yet," I say. "I'll have to double-check."

I can hear a frown in her voice. "Your new employer doesn't own you."

"Of course, he doesn't."

"You need to get weekends off."

"I got none when I was dancing." A sigh escapes me. "I have to go, Mom. Tell Dad I love him."

"You won't tell your mom?"

I roll my eyes. "Love you, Mom. Bye."

I'm left alone in the large emptiness of my suite. The bed is comfortable, the dresser holds all my clothes, and I've already filled the mini fridge with my favorite snacks.

It doesn't take me long to unpack the rest. Especially since I left the suitcase with my workout and ballet clothes untouched in the corner.

No use for those anymore.

My hip is already better after a week without training. I hate that the rest is the answer and that my body is betraying me. I hate that I fell in love with ballet when I was five.

And I also hate that my body aches with longing for the routine. Every night, I still dance it in my head before I fall asleep, keeping the count with my finger against the bed cover.

I wonder who's dancing my part now.

Has anyone considered texting me about how I'm feeling? Irina, the prima ballerina, would never. But maybe Simone or Beth?

I survey the room. My new home. Thank God for it. As awkward as it is working for Alec Connovan, at least I have something to do.

I'd probably lose my mind if I didn't.

Keeping to the schedule, I leave the apartment, taking the elevator down to the garage where Mac is waiting by the car. From a distance, he looks distinctly intimidating. Arms crossed over his bulky frame, and tattoos creeping up his neck. But he smiles when he sees me.

"Day two," he says.

Pickup goes just as smoothly as yesterday. Sam is happily oblivious to the world around him, and Willa gives me the silent treatment. This time, though, I'm handed a note in the car about Sam's upcoming project for show and tell in three weeks.

Three weeks feels like a lifetime from now.

Just as yesterday, the same thing happens when we make it home. Snacks, homework, and play. Willa takes a seat at the kitchen table and unfolds her book with wane movements.

I consider joining her. But her stiff frame speaks volumes. *Don't you even dare.*

As I'm headed toward Sam, she speaks up. "You said you knew my aunt," she states. "I haven't heard about you."

"Yes, we've been friends for a few years."

"Hmm. My dad told me you were a ballerina." Her voice is heavy with disbelief.

"I am, yeah. I've danced since I was Sam's age. I've been performing with the New York Ballet."

"Well, not now. Now you're a nanny."

I grit my teeth. She's still speaking without looking at me, her voice dismissive. It's not hard to imagine why other nannies have struggled.

"Yes. I injured my hip quite badly and it needs rest before I can perform again."

That makes her turn. Hazel eyes sweep appraisingly over my form. "You look fine," she says.

It doesn't sound like a compliment.

"It mostly bothers me when I dance. Not so much when I walk around normally." I take a step closer. "What homework are you doing today?"

Her eyes are unreadable. They're so like her fathers. "None of your business."

Whoah. She's like a kitten with her hackles raised.

I smile at her. "Gotcha. I like doing my work alone, too. I heard that you're really good at math."

"Yeah."

"I know you've had a ton of nannies, too. Four, just in the last year, right?" I say. Katja had filled me in. She's worked as their housekeeper for years. One of the few people Willa likes, it seems. "It must be annoying to have new people come and go all the time."

Willa doesn't say anything, but she's looking at me.

"We can get acquainted with one another slowly. I won't push," I say. "And if you ever want to learn some ballet, you just let me know. I think it could be fun. I'll go chat with Sam now about his homework assignment and let you work on yours."

She watches me walk out of the room. I release the breath I've been holding as soon as I'm out in the hallway. My younger siblings had been very different from Willa, but I remember how important it was to talk to them as if they were adults.

After all, I'd come into *her* life. She already knows all the routines and requirements. The last thing we need is me trying to assert some kind of dominance here.

Maybe that's what the other nannies had done.

Sam and I talk for a bit before I notice the stack of games in the corner. It takes a little coaxing, but when he realizes I genuinely want to play, he grabs his favorite board game.

"Should we ask Willa to join us?"

Sam looks down at the box for a long moment. "Okay," he says and runs out of his room to where Willa is. We find her done with her homework, lying on the couch, coloring in a book.

"Play with us," Sam says and throws himself down on the thick carpet. "Come on."

I sit cross-legged down beside him and remove the box's lid. "You guys are going to win. I have no idea how to play this game."

That doesn't convince Willa. Sam and I play two straight rounds, and he giggles every time I pretend to place a tile in the wrong spot. Thank God for Sam. He seems to wake up every day and choose happiness.

Willa pretends not to watch us.

That's how Alec finds us. He comes home earlier than expected, walking into the apartment. "Hey guys," he says. He pauses by the kitchen table, looking at Willa's homework. There's an air of distraction around him.

Willa sits up on the couch to watch him.

I raise my voice. "We're playing a board game. Want to join us?"

Alec looks over, eyebrows raised. I'm sure he'll say *no*. But then he looks at Sam focusing on the game board so hard that a furrow has appeared between the light brows.

"Sure," he says. "Give me a minute."

It takes Willa fifteen seconds to abandon her careless attitude and sit down across from Sam and me. "You're doing that wrong," she tells me, but barely finishes the sentence before she looks over her shoulder at where her dad is shrugging out of his suit jacket.

I shift to the side to make room for Alec. He folds his long legs and sits down with a faint groan. It's a deep sound, slightly husky. His shoulder brushes mine. "So, who's winning?"

"I am!" Sam exclaims.

"I'm definitely not," I say and finger my little labyrinth pieces. "No beginner's luck here."

Alec's voice lowers. "Nicely played," he murmurs.

I smile in his direction. Yeah, so maybe I'm not playing at the top of my game.

He grabs his pieces with a practiced ease that suggests he's played this before. "I need to talk to you after dinner. About next week's schedule. I have to travel for a few days."

"Yeah, of course," I say. I meet his hazel gaze for a few seconds too long. "Come knock on my door?"

"I will," he says.

"Come on! It's your turn, Dad!" Sam complains.

Alec smiles. "All right, let me see…"

I don't think I've ever seen Alec's smile before. It's a small, curved thing, but it warms the stern features of his face. The smile looks unused. Something he rarely brings out of storage.

We play a few rounds. Willa is chatty, engaged, and almost boisterous. She and Alec are slightly competitive, while Sam is mostly focused on collecting as many pieces as possible and trying to cheat.

I reach for the dice at the same time Alec does. Our hands brush, his palm against the back of mine. His skin is warm.

I pull my hand back. "Sorry."

"No, it was your turn." He glances at me with amusement glowing in his eyes. It's hard to look away when he is like this. "I guess I'm just too eager to win."

"Does winning come with a prize?"

"My eagerness would be less embarrassing if it did."

That makes me smile. "We can create one to protect your ego."

"That," he says, his eyes dipping down to my lips, "would be even worse."

Across the game board, Willa's voice is sharp. "Come on, let's play. Or we eat dinner."

Alec clears his throat and hands me the dice. "Your turn," he murmurs.

Maybe it is, but that doesn't help me feel in control. Not dancing anymore might be good for my hip, but being around this man on a daily basis will be terrible for my health.

CHAPTER 8
ALEC

Time is a weird thing.

Somewhere over the years, the days started to feel like weeks, and the weeks like months, even though they all flew by faster than I could blink. It was the worst kind of paradox. I didn't savor the minutes or treasure the hours. I barely even noticed their passing until it was time for another New Year's Eve, another birthday, and yet another anniversary of Victoria's death.

It felt like she died yesterday, *and* like she'd been gone a decade. Some days I needed to look at a photo to remember her face, and at other times, I could see her in every one of Willa's features.

Time is a *terrible* thing.

The only thing I know for sure is that I never have enough of it. Not to be everywhere I want to, or fulfill all the tasks I need to.

Tonight, I didn't make bedtime with the kids. Isabel had to solve that one on her own for the first time. Sam could be impossible to coax into bed once he has a project he wants to finish, and while Willa is more pliant about it, she could decide to do a million different things before bed.

Isabel… The first week has gone better than expected. I'd asked both my kids about her, and, while Sam hadn't said much, he'd been nonplussed. Willa thought Isabel was too quiet and asked me, twice, if she was a *real* ballerina. It was still better feedback than she'd given about a nanny in a long time. I wondered how much of that was influenced by Isabel being a friend of Willa's aunt.

I get into the elevator and type in the passcode to send it straight up to my floor. It moves at a slow, steady pace, and I run a hand over my face. The exhaustion feels bone-deep.

Tonight hadn't gone well.

Even that might be an understatement. Connie's recent marriage to a Thompson had set the entire family unit reeling. My father had taken it… well, *hard* is to put it mildly.

I unlock the front door and find the hallway empty and dark. It's almost ten, and both kids should long since be in bed. The quietness is an encouraging sign. She's gotten them to sleep, then.

Soft voices carry from the living room.

I follow the sound. It's the TV. A show, where people are walking around, chatting. Isabel is sitting curled up on the couch. She's wearing a pair of shorts and a T-shirt. Her long, thick hair is in a braid down her back.

Her profile is illuminated by the faint glow of the screen.

Fuck.

Her beauty is unmistakable like this, and it impacts me so much more seeing her in my home. Now her beauty is all I can see.

She turns and then straightens in her seat. Her face softens into a smile that makes my chest tighten. "Oh! Hi. I'm sorry, I didn't hear you come home."

"That's okay." My voice sounds gruff. I head to the bar cart in the corner and grab one of the tumblers, filling it with whiskey. The night has been long already, with two of these at my father's, and I shouldn't have a third. But I need to do something about the coiling agitation I'm feeling.

None of the other nannies have ever caused this. They were employees. I spoke to them about the kids, the practicalities, and they reported to me. And none of them ever sat on my couch in tiny shorts and a braid that would look good wrapped around my—

What the hell is wrong with me?

"I'll turn off the TV," she says. "Sorry, I wanted to be closer to the kids' rooms in case they woke up again. You know, before you got home."

"Don't worry about it," I say again. "What are you watching?"

She sinks back on the couch. "Um, *Gilmore Girls*."

"I don't know what that is."

"It's a TV show. About a mother and a daughter who live in this small, idyllic New England town."

I grip my glass and walk closer to the couch. Her voice has the same calming, soft tenor it always has. *She even talks gracefully*, I think. Just like she dances. I can see her moving in my mind's eye, in the emptiness of that dance studio, with nothing but sunlight illuminating her form. "Tell me more," I prompt.

Her dark eyebrows rise. "About the show?"

"Yes."

"Okay. It has a large cast of side characters, including the mom's parents. They're rich and traditional while she's not, so there's constant conflict there. And then, there are men, of course."

"Men," I repeat. There's a space beside her on the couch, but that's a line I shouldn't cross. I take another sip of my drink instead.

She turns to me and nods, a smile on her lips. "Yeah. Both the mom and the daughter have love interests. They're both young—the mom was a teen mother. So there's a lot of intrigue. Fans can be Team Jess, or Team Logan, or… I can't imagine you really want to hear about this."

"I don't. But it's nice to—" I cut off, and clear my throat. *Hear you talk?* Seriously, what is my problem? Everything, apparently, since I go against my better instincts for a second time.

I sit down next to her on the couch. "So, you like this show?"

"Yeah. I've watched it before, but it's nice to rewatch." She's looking at me, but I keep my eyes on the screen. Take another sip of my drink.

We sit in silence for a few long minutes.

"How did tonight go?" she asks gently.

I want to avoid the question. Glancing down at the whiskey in my hand, I hate myself for pouring it. Things shouldn't get to me anymore. I don't have time to feel.

"As good as it could've."

"Family dinner…, right?" There's a faint smile in her voice. "Sorry. I spoke to Connie this morning."

The two of them being friends is going to complicate things. I always knew that, and I still hired Isabel. But I need to make sure I never forget it. "Yeah." I twist the glass around. "The wedding party is soon."

"This weekend," Isabel agrees. "I take it 'Operation: Convince Dad' hasn't gone well."

That makes me scoff. "That's what Connie called it?"

"Um, I might have said that." Her voice is tentative. "So, not good, huh? I'm sorry."

It's said so earnestly that I glance over at her. Isabel's dark-brown eyes are steady on mine, waiting. She knows most of the story already. Connie married the son of Contron's biggest competitor. He's involved in his family business. Connie works for us.

Our father took it as a very particular kind of betrayal.

"No," I say. "It didn't go great. My dad still considers

Connie's husband a... Nevermind. He won't say it to either of their faces, of course, but attending their wedding party is more than he's willing to do."

My voice has hardened by the end of that statement. He's being obstinate, recalcitrant, incompassionate.

He's being everything he taught us to be, and I hate him for it.

"So he won't come," Isabel says. "Not the end of the world, just like I've told Connie."

I glance at her. "It's not that easy."

"Oh, of course, it's not easy. But it is simple. He has a choice, if he wants to be a part of his children's lives," she says. Then, her voice lowers. "Sorry. I know he's your father, too. It's just... I've spoken to Connie about this before."

I lift my glass to my lips. "I bet you have. I don't even want to imagine what you've heard about me."

"All terrible things," she says.

Is she teasing? The whiskey is warm down my throat, and I relish the burn. Try to focus on it instead of the need that won't go away, but that I have to ignore. *She's not for me.* "Good. I hope you believed them all."

She chuckles. "Of course not."

"You should," I say, and I mean it. On the screen, a large group of people are meeting in a town square. It looks painfully staged, a set that's too pretty to be real. Maybe that's the draw of the show. They've made nosy neighbors and small towns something quaint. "So. Did you grow up in a place like that? Is that why you like it?"

"I grew up in Brooklyn."

"Ah. So very similar."

She laughs again. It's a small, genuine sound, and I like it far too much. "There was definitely a lot of gossiping neighbors, but that's the only similarity."

Not a lot of men, then? The question hovers on the tip of my tongue, but I swallow it back. "I bet you have a lot of stories to tell, then."

She crosses her legs over. There's a lot of smooth skin on display, her legs leanly muscled. I focus on the screen instead. "My mother is the keeper of all the stories, even if she's only a semi-reliable source of information. She has a habit of mixing up people's names and not particularly caring if she gets the details right."

"Huh. Sounds dangerous."

"Oh, it can be. My little sister once said that our mom was the ultimate misinformation spreader. "

"You have siblings," I say. She had mentioned that in my office.

On the screen, the mother and daughter pair are sitting in a diner. The table between them is filled with an obscene amount of food.

"Yeah. Twin siblings, actually. They're five years younger than me."

"Mm-hmm. So they're what, nineteen?"

"Twenty," she says.

So, she's twenty-five, then. I knew she was younger than Connie, but not by how much. *Twenty-five.* That makes me fifteen years older.

I take another long pull of whiskey. "And have either of your siblings married your family's archnemesis recently?"

Isabel laughs again. The sound washes over me. "I don't think we have an archnemesis. That's for you Connovans, not for the rest of us. My father has a petty feud with the guy who runs the dry cleaner's across the street, but that's it."

"And you're not planning on marrying him."

"No. He's fifty-something. And already married."

"Right," I say. "Wise move."

She chuckles and reaches for a can of sparkling water on the coffee table. What we're doing feels remarkably easy. Like we're just hanging out. But that's the last thing I should be doing with her. She's Connie's friend first and foremost, not to mention my employee.

Fifteen years!

I'd suspected as much, but to have it confirmed is… good. Another reason for me to abandon this stupid attraction. So what if she's beautiful and lovely? *I'm not the man for her.*

"You're going to the wedding party this Friday," I say. It's a statement, not a question. Of course Connie will want her best friend there.

"Yes. Is that okay? I know you're going, and someone needs to watch the kids."

"I've already spoken to Katja. She'll spend the night." It's not part of her regular duties, but the kids have known her from the time they were both born, and she's amazing with them. I pay her triple on nights when she becomes my emergency babysitter.

If Katja wasn't already an integral part of our household when Victoria died, I don't know if we would have survived those early years. All three of us.

"Oh. Thank you," Isabel says warmly. "I'd love to go."

"Of course. Connie wants you there."

She makes a humming sound and silence falls between us once again. I lean back against the cushions and watch the screen. Two characters are talking rapidly, in too-long sentences with too-big words. I can't remember the last time I sat here and watched a show that wasn't animated, or had Sam or Willa by my side.

I should get up and leave.

But I don't. She doesn't either.

"Willa had a piano lesson today," Isabel says. "It went…"

That makes my lips twitch. "She's not very fond of her lessons."

"No, she really isn't."

"She's sticking with them, though," I say.

"Mm-hmm. I've tried to entice her with ballet, but she

doesn't seem to believe I'm a real deal." Isabel laughs softly. "I'll have to show her some recordings."

I roll my stiff neck. "You should. Watching you dance a few weeks ago was… You're talented." That's a wild understatement, and the compliment felt off rolling off my tongue.

What the hell am I doing here? With my half-finished whiskey and the small talk that doesn't feel small at all. It feels *comfortable*, and with each minute in her company, the disquiet I felt coming home melts away. It's replaced with a different kind of energy.

"Thank you," she says. "What's your hidden talent, then?"

She's smiling at me. It's a curious, slightly teasing smile. I focus on her eyes and not the shape of her legs in those short shorts. For a brief second, I want my answer to be something else. Something far dirtier than the man I've become. The father. The widower. Something that will shock those beautiful eyes into widening.

Why don't you let me show you?

Her smile falters and then dies on her lips with my prolonged silence. I'm staring. I know it, and I know the effect it can have. I've utilized it in plenty of corporate negotiations before.

"None of mine are hidden," I finally say. I knock back the rest of my drink and rise off the couch. The reprieve has been nice.

Too nice.

"You've been here for almost two weeks now," I say. "Anything you'd like to change?"

She sits up straighter on the couch. "No, things have been working out, I think. But if I ever need a night out—"

"Just ask," I say. "If I'm home in the evenings, your time is yours."

She nods. A black tendril of hair slips out from behind the hook of her ear. "Okay. Yeah. I think that's it. Oh! Can I organize things with the kids?"

I frown. "Organize?"

"Yeah. Like a picnic in the park, or going to a museum. If you're working late or traveling on a weekend?"

"Yes. Of course."

Her face lights up. "Awesome. I have some ideas."

I want to ask her what they are. I want to stay out here and listen to her detailing her plans. I want to ask her about her hip. The pain on her face from three weeks ago is etched into my memory. The tears glistening in her eyes, and how I could ensure they never spill again.

Instead, I extend my hand. "Well, your trial period is officially over."

She slides her palm against mine. It's warm, soft next to my skin. "Thank you. And you'll let me know if you ever need me to do anything else, right?"

"Yes," I say. "Good night, Isabel."

Her lips soften into a smile. "Goodnight, Alec."

I let her hand slip from mine and walk toward my bedroom. Her trial period might be over, but I feel like mine has just begun.

CHAPTER 9
ISABEL

"Look," Willa tells Katja. She holds up a piece of paper with a giant gold star on it. "I got this for my math homework."

Katja smiles wide. "Wow, will you look at that? Aren't you clever."

I frown, watching the exchange. I'd asked her after school how her math homework turned out, and the only word she had for me was *fine*.

Earning her trust is going to take forever, I think.

Beside me, Sam makes loud whooping sounds as he zips around the living room. We've tied a blanket around his neck as a cape, and he's pretending he's one of countless superheroes whizzing past.

The days here are long, and they're challenging in a very different way than dancing for hours on end. Back then, I would fall in bed, tired and boneless, and sleep soundly for eight or nine hours before doing it all over again. These days, I'm physically unspent but mentally drained.

I can't remember Sebastian and Elena ever being this exhausting. But then again, when I babysat them, I was only five years older, and they were my siblings.

This is very different.

"Willa," I say. "I have something to show you, if you'd like to see."

She looks over at me, eyes narrowing. "What?"

"It's a video recording of *Swan Lake*. The New York Ballet did a production three winters ago. Are you interested in watching?"

Her stare doesn't waver, but there isn't an immediate *no*.

"That sounds like fun," Katja says and rests her hand on Willa's shoulder. "How about we watch it tonight, after dinner? We can put it on the big TV."

"Maybe," Willa says. Her eyebrows lower. "Are you going with Dad to my aunt's party tonight?"

She already knows that I am.

But I nod. "Yes. We're both invited."

Not that we're going together. I don't know what time he'll get home from work today, so I already budgeted the cost of a taxi into my plans. He'd been busy the last two days, and the unexpected conversation we'd shared on the couch is… hmm. It's nothing but a memory.

And the longest conversation we'd ever had.

Katja gives me a smile. She's warmed up to me in the past couple of weeks, and I love her no-nonsense attitude and quirks. Apparently, she's great at reading dreams, and several times I've heard the kids ask her to interpret theirs. She doesn't strike me as very maternal—but she's a steady, comforting presence in the apartment, and it's clear that she cares for the kids. "Why don't you go get ready for the party?" she tells me.

"You're sure?"

"Yes, yes. Go."

I don't have more than thirty minutes to get ready before I need to leave, so I race through my preparations. My simple black dress will have to do, as well as the small gold hoops my parents got me for my twenty-fifth birthday.

I emerge from my room at the same time Alec exits out of his.

Oh. I hadn't heard him come home. He walks down the hallway toward me, rearranging the sleeves of the tux he's wearing. It stretches taut across his shoulders in a way that hints at tailoring, and his thick brown hair is swept back.

He looks distinguished. Handsome… and just a little bit dangerous, like this is the nighttime version of his businessman self. It's not a side of him I've seen before.

He glances up, and his steps falter. "Hey."

"Hi," I say.

His eyes darken as they scan me, and for a long moment, neither of us says anything.

I shift from one foot to another. "You're heading out?"

"Yes," he says, jaw tensing. "Mac's got the car downstairs. Are you ready to go?"

"Is it okay if I ride with you? I wasn't sure—"

"Of course," he says. "I was going to knock on your door."

"Oh."

He clears his throat. "Come on. Let's get going."

We ride the elevator in silence. I can smell his cologne, musk and smoke and it's painfully delicious. I remember finding little samples of men's cologne tucked among the pages of magazines as a kid. I used to put them under my pillow when I went to sleep because the scents were so good.

Silly memory. Silly thought.

He runs a hand over his jaw just as we reach the parking level. "Had a good day?"

"Yes. Willa had her piano lesson, and Sam and I worked on his project."

"For the show and tell?"

"Yes."

He holds the elevator door open for me as we walk out and head to the car. Mac greets us both, and then we're off, the quietness returning and filling the space between us inside the vehicle. It doesn't surprise me. He's always been the stoic kind.

The other night was the exception that proved the rule.

And God, did I blab about the *Gilmore Girls* as if he gave a damn about a TV show?

I fidget with my purse, my nerves rising. I've been to some of Connie's parties, but they've always been small get-togethers. A brunch with a few of her college friends, that sort of thing. A wedding party will be grand and will have people from a radically different world than the one I live in.

To me, Connie is just Connie... most of the time. My friend, who is just as ambitious when it comes to her career as I was about dancing, but just as down to hang out on Saturday afternoons.

Tonight, though, she's Constance Connovan. Alec's younger sister, heiress to one of the country's largest media and tech conglomerates, celebrating her marriage to the heir of another. I'm not used to seeing her in that role.

My heart races, like I'm minutes away from stepping out on the stage. Only, when I danced, the world turned silent. It was just me and the movements... My dance routines never required small talk. This party will.

"You okay?" Alec asks.

I smile at him. "Yes. Absolutely. How about you?"

He looks at me. "Fine. It'll be an... interesting evening."

"There will be plenty of Thompsons there, right?"

"Plenty indeed," he agrees. But his voice is merely dry, not pained. From what Connie told me, her new husband slowly won over her brothers in the weeks since their surprise wedding. "It'll be fine."

I nod. "Yeah. Totally."

It's not fine.

We arrive at the venue. Connie and Gabriel have rented a rooftop location, complete with a glass ceiling and a giant outdoor terrace, in central Midtown. The fall air is too cold for spending much time outdoors, but infrared heaters keep the terrace warm and well lit.

There are elegantly dressed people everywhere, none of whom I know.

Heads turn toward Alec when we walk in. I might not know anyone here, but it's clear they all know him. Whether personally or by reputation, I'm not sure.

And then, their gazes shift to me. Speculation is clear in many.

A dark-haired man approaches us. I've never met him, but I recognize him from the pictures. "Hey," he says to Alec with indifference that only a little brother can exhibit. Then, he turns to me with a smile. "You, I haven't met. I'm Nate."

"Isabel," I say and extend a hand.

His eyebrows rise. "Oh, you're Connie's friend?"

"Yes, that's right."

He glances at Alec before giving me another smile. "I've heard a lot about you. Come on, let's get you a drink."

It takes me a second to understand why he may have looked so excited as he walked over. Did he think I arrived as Alec's date?

Did the other guests who noticed us?

Nate starts heading toward the bar, and I glance back at Alec. His unreadable eyes are on me, and he gives a tiny nod. *Go.* So I do.

The bar is sleek and modern, all dark wood with a few silver accents. Just like the rest of the décor. A pulsing, melodic beat streams from the hidden speakers. It's a beautiful venue, filled with beautiful people.

Nate's charming and easy to talk to. It's clear that he's taken me under his wing, and I wonder if it's because Connie told him to do so. I can see her in the distance, but everyone at the party is eager to congratulate her, and I'm not about to interrupt her victory parade.

"So you're working for my brother," Nate says. "How did that happen?"

I give him a rueful smile and the entire story, albeit a condensed version, over a glass of champagne. My fingers feel tight around the delicate stem of the flute. For many years, I rarely drank. It was a liability, a detriment to my dancing. My physical health. Now, that's no longer a factor… but it still feels like I'm doing something I shouldn't.

Breaking the rules.

"My deepest condolences," Nate says when I'm done. "Not just for the hip injury, but also for having to put up with madness."

"Oh, I like my job. Sometimes it's challenging, but Willa and Samuel are fun. I enjoy spending time with them."

Nate's smile widens. "Yeah, my niece and nephew are great. My brother on the other hand… He's the one you have to put up with."

I look across the dance floor and the few couples swaying in tune. It doesn't take long to spot Alec. He's taller than most, and his profile cuts a sharp line in the distance. He's talking to a few other men in tuxes.

Even from afar, he looks tense.

I wonder if he ever relaxes. If anyone can ever persuade him to.

"He hasn't been so bad," I say. "At least… not yet."

Nate chuckles. "That's the right attitude. If he tries to boss you around, take it with a grain of salt, will you? He has the best of intentions but terrible bedside manners sometimes."

"Really?"

"Yeah. Connie speaks highly of you, and I'd hate for an employment-related misunderstanding to ruin your friendship." His eyes are kind, but there's clear calculation there. *Of course.* He's a Connovan, too.

While he's fun to talk to, it doesn't last long. Nate gets pulled away by other guests, and I'm left alone by the bar, hand around my glass and looking out at the crowd. Several couples have started to dance. Across the room, I spot Connie and Gabriel surrounded by a group of people.

This past spring, she was single. Now she's married and in love, busier at work than ever, and happy. While I'm... single as ever... and feeling rudderless.

I take a long sip of my drink. I haven't attended many parties, gone out, or done anything but focus on routines, stretching, sleep, and nutrition.

What do normal people do?

What should *I* do now?

"You look deep in thought," a voice says. It belongs to a man who came up to stand beside me. Tall, dark-blond, and with a smirk on his lips that suggests he sees amusement all around him. "Making guesses on how long the happy couple will last?"

My eyes widen. "Oh. Well... no. I think they have great odds."

He smiles. "You're a real friend, then. Connie's?"

"Yes."

"I'm Gabriel's friend." He extends a hand. "Evan."

"Isabel," I say, and we shake hands. "Are a lot of people making bets, then?"

"I've heard a few," he says. "You have to admit, the two of them getting married was one of the big surprises of the year. People are curious."

"Those same people probably don't know them all that well," I say.

He laughs. "True. It took less than ten minutes after meeting Connie for me to be certain that this is a real thing. Gabriel would rather chop off his arm than lose her."

That makes me smile. "I've gotten that impression, too. How do you know Gabriel?"

Turns out they've known each other for years, even though their friendship is now mainly long-distance. Evan is jokey, open, and warm. It doesn't take much time before I'm enjoying myself.

Maybe *this* is what normal people do. They go to parties. They drink one or two glasses of champagne, and they don't worry about having to get up at the crack of dawn to train.

They flirt. They talk. They make new friends and actually have time to spend with them.

"So," Evan says, leaning against the bar. "Do you have a date wandering around somewhere?"

A shiver runs down my back. I guess we *are* flirting. It's been a long time since I've done anything remotely like it. "No," I say. "Flying solo. How about you?"

Evan nods, his eyes crinkling with a smile. "I'm alone, too. Terribly, shamefully alone."

I chuckle. "Good thing—"

A shadow falls over us. Alec has joined us, his shoulders blocking out the light from the chandelier, and his eyes move from me to Evan. He gives Evan a brief nod before returning his attention to me.

Holding out his large hand, he says, "Dance with me."

And I slide my hand into his.

CHAPTER 10
ISABEL

Alec's hand grips mine tight, and I give Evan a small smile before I'm swept out to the dance floor. Warmth radiates from Alec's touch as his left hand lands on my waist. I don't think we've ever done more than shake hands before.

His voice is hoarse. "Enjoying yourself?"

"Yes, I am."

He seems tense, and while he leads me well, there's no fluidity. I glance up to see the sharp line of his jaw clenched tight.

Has something happened?

In tune with the music, we dance in silence for another few seconds.

"Are you?" I ask. "Enjoying yourself?"

He's quiet for a moment too long. "It's a well-planned event."

"That's not what I asked."

Alec glances down at me, and there's a flash of surprise in his eyes. "No," he admits. "I'm not enjoying myself."

"Why not?"

He spins me around slowly, and I wonder if it's to give

himself time to think. He pulls me closer, our bodies separated only by a few inches. "I haven't enjoyed parties in years," he finally answers.

"I haven't *been* to one in years."

"How come?"

I lift my free shoulder in a shrug. "Professional dancer."

"Ah. No time?"

"No time," I agree.

His hand tightens on my waist, and he tugs me half an inch closer. "I should have thought about that before I asked you to dance. You're a pro. I'm certainly not."

That makes me smile. "Your leading is excellent."

"And you're being kind. Again."

"I can be kind *and* honest," I say.

He sighs. "Those two things are rarely true at the same time."

I take a deep breath, and the scent of him washes over me again. Cologne, clean skin, and man. "Maybe not in a high-stakes corporate world."

"Not anywhere," he says. Our thighs brush, just once, as we take another dance step. There's so much of him. Always has been. He takes up more than his share of space.

"Maybe that's your experience," I say quietly.

He's quiet for a while, but then he nods, and his voice is warmer. "Are you free to party more now, then? Since you're not working every single night."

"I suppose I would have been, but I accepted a job that involves standby childcare."

His lips twitch. "Ah. Yes, so you did."

"Maybe when I'm done nannying," I say.

"You have a free day most weekends," he says. "That leaves ample time for... hobbies."

I chuckle. "Maybe I need to find some. There wasn't a lot of time for hobbies before, beyond reading."

He makes a thoughtful sound. "You've been training since you were... what was it? Eight?"

"Five," I say.

He makes a humming sound, and the silence between us stretches on. I look to the side, at the other dancers. A few are throwing curious glances our way. That makes my cheeks heat up. I wasn't even thinking about where we are. Maybe everyone is curious about who Alec is dancing with. He's been a widow for five years, and Connie mentioned that he doesn't date.

His voice is in my ear. "I haven't danced in a very long time."

"You haven't forgotten how," I say.

He gives a low half chuckle. *Amusement?* From Alec Connovan? "It certainly feels like I have," he mutters. "In more ways than one."

I look up at him. "How so?"

But he just shakes his head. "It's a good thing I have you to make me look good."

I smile. "Is that why you asked me to dance?"

Our eyes meet, and something flares in his gaze. I lean closer to him and feel the heat of his breath on my cheek. His hand is tight where it grips mine, enveloping my fingers completely. I've never had those hands of his on my body before.

For a moment, we just seem to freeze, looking at one another.

"Yes," he finally says. "That's why I asked you."

"Oh."

His eyes drop down to my lips, and a knot tightens in my stomach. "Alec," I say. "Thank—"

He snaps his gaze over my shoulder, and his frown gets replaced by a carefully neutral mask. It's the face of a man used to schooling his features. His voice turns resigned. "My sister is about to steal you away."

Connie arrives with the force of a whirlwind. She's grinning, happiness shining in her green eyes. Her auburn hair is up in a chignon, and the navy dress looks like it's painted on her curves.

"Isabel! I didn't see you arrive." She pulls me out of Alec's arms and into a hug. "How good of you to dance with my brother."

"I'm right here," Alec says dryly.

Connie gives him a crooked smile. "Yes, and I really appreciate you coming. I invited some of the Bransons, by the way. You could discuss the upcoming acquisition."

He raises an eyebrow. "You want me to work?"

"I want you to enjoy yourself," she says, "and I know that's your favorite activity. Now, come, Isabel. I want to introduce you to some people. Gabriel has *a ton* of hot cousins."

She tugs me away. Alec's eyes are narrowed on us, his mouth set in that faint frown again. I wonder what he's thinking. I've always wondered that...

But I'm no closer to knowing.

Connie does introduce me to people. *So many people.* I appreciate the effort, even if my head spins after the fourth introduction. She knows as well as I do that my friendship circle is small. Hers is, too. We've always been career-focused, and spending the weekends together during yoga or watching movies has been the core of our friendship. It never involved glitzy parties and glasses of champagne.

I'm on my fifth now. Or maybe sixth?

I don't know anymore. But I do know I'm enjoying myself. If this is what *normal* people do, it's all starting to make sense now. Maybe it's a good thing I fell in love with ballet so early in life or I wouldn't have been able to commit to it.

"You're beautiful," a man says. He's someone's cousin or maybe brother, and he's wearing a wide smile that seems more than a little alcohol-induced. "Anyone ever told you that?"

I laugh politely, taking a step back from him. "Once or twice."

"Well, let me be the third or fourth," he says.

Okay.

Maybe it's time for me to grab some air.

I excuse myself from the group and the flirty gentleman and look around for the terrace. There's one around here… there. A sign. I walk across the room as fast as I'm able in my kitten heels. I'm only used to sneakers and pointe shoes.

Cold air washes over me as I pull the door open. Night has fallen, but there's never true darkness in New York, and the city glitters around me. I step out on the terrace and breathe in deeply. The air smells like rain and fall.

Wrapping my arms around my chest, I breathe in again. And again. My head spins faintly, and then stronger, a sinking feeling swarms in my stomach.

I shouldn't have drunk as much as I did.

Not that there's a purpose for being restrained anymore. Not for my careful sleep schedule or my stretching regimen or my foam rolling. *I* don't have a purpose anymore.

I don't fit in here, either. Not in Connie's glittering world… and not anywhere else. The only world I've ever loved shut its door on me. Locked it.

Threw away the key.

"There you are! Thought I saw you slipping away."

Dread rises inside me, and I turn to see the too-complimentary man standing a few feet away. "I needed some fresh air."

"I get it," he says and takes a step closer. "Heard you're a dancer. That true, baby?"

My lip curls. Who uses "baby" with someone they've just met? My little sister would give him her middle finger right about now.

I try to channel some of her energy. "Sorry, but I'm not interested."

His eyebrows drop with irritation. "Interested in what? A little conversation? Don't be—"

The door opens behind him and Alec steps out. His face is set in lines of cold anger. They make him look older than he is, and scary in a way I've never seen.

He walks to my side. "She's fine," he barks, his voice arctic. Our shoulders brush. He's standing closer to me than a mere friend would.

The drunk charmer mutters something that sounds like an apology and turns on his heel. The terrace door shuts in his wake with a soft *snick*.

I release a breath I've been holding. "He was…"

"Yeah," Alec says. He's taken a step away from me now, but his eyes are locked on mine. "I saw him following you out. Are you okay?"

"Yes, thank you," I respond. "Maybe I was supposed to say *I can take care of myself* or whatever, but I really appreciated that."

His eyes warm, and, at his sides, he slowly unclenches his fists. "I get it. That guy was out of line."

I wrap my bare arms around myself. They're turning cold with the night air. "He called me 'baby.' Like, where do men get the confidence to do stuff like that?"

All warmth disappears from his gaze. "He said *what*?"

"He pulled the old 'heard you're a dancer' thing, too. Ugh." The number of times I've heard that from friends of friends, from my brother's buddies, from people in the area where I grew up. As if a dancer is synonymous with any number of sordid things.

Alec crosses his arms over his chest. There's a faint color along the ridge of his cheekbones, and I wonder if he's been drinking, too. I wonder if he ever lets himself drink too much —if he ever loses control.

"You've been turning lots of heads tonight," he mutters. "I'm sorry some of them don't know how to behave themselves."

I shake my head and walk over to the railing. It's hard to look at him at length when I'm feeling like this. Warm inside and cold outside; liquid heat in my stomach because of the champagne and a head that's lightly spinning, haziness clouding my thoughts.

He joins me, leaning against the railing. We watch the glittering lights of New York in silence.

A sadness rises within me. It's been there every single day these past weeks, since that fateful day in the ballet studio. *Heard you're a dancer.* Well, you heard wrong. Because I'm not anymore. And I likely never will be again.

That world is gone and done with.

The first tear falls silently, racing down my cheek like a thief in the night. It doesn't make a sound. But Alec notices, of course. He's always been too good at noticing things. He doesn't say anything for a while, but I feel his presence next to me. It's solid and steady.

"Hey," he says quietly. "I'll kick him out of the party for you. Would that make you feel better? He'll be gone immediately."

The offer makes me chuckle. "No, no. Thank you. But it's not that. It's… I'm thinking about ballet."

He hesitates for a few seconds, but then he puts a hand on my shoulder. "Tell me," he murmurs.

"Dancing was my dream. It was what I worked for. I wanted to be a prima ballerina so badly. I still do, and I know ballerinas have short careers, but I was hoping for *at least* five more years. I still… I don't… it's the only thing I've *ever* wanted." Another tear falls down my cheek. "I lost my apartment. I lost my chance to dance professionally. I lost everything. Including my dream."

His face is etched in tense lines like he doesn't like hearing this. Who can blame him? I'm a mess and can't seem to stop my emotions from welling, from spilling onto the surface, and I can only partly blame that on the alcohol.

He wipes a tear away with his thumb. "I'm sorry," he murmurs. "Don't cry, Isa."

The words make me cry harder. Maybe because it's the first time someone hasn't tried to offer solutions right away. My mother tried to solve it, Connie suggested other jobs, and my siblings told me how we could become a three-act stand-up comedy show. *Right.* As if it's just straight-forward and simple.

Tears streak unbridled down my face, and a broken sound escapes me.

Alec groans and pulls me against his chest. He smells even better up close, and I close my eyes, but it doesn't stop the tears from falling. One of his arms wraps around my shoulders and then the other joins, a steady band of muscle surrounding me.

Something comes to rest atop my head. His chin, perhaps. He brushes a hand over my hair, and it sends another shiver through me.

"I'm sorry," he says again. It's muffled against my crown, and God, he's holding me. Here, on a terrace, at his little sister's wedding party. "Fuck, I don't know what to say."

My tears subside as quickly as they came. For weeks now, my emotions have been erupting like a volcano, only to return to a simmer soon after. Sadness gives way to mortification. I take a step back and give him a weak smile. "It's okay. Sorry about that."

Alec shakes his head. There's a furrow between his brows and intensity in his eyes. He lifts his hand, like he's going to brush away my tears again, but it falls before reaching halfway to me.

"Don't apologize," he says instead.

I wipe my cheeks. "This wasn't how I expected the night to end."

"If Connie sees you, we'll tell her they're happy tears."

I force a smile. "A disproportionate response, don't you think?"

"You're very happy," he says. "Ecstatic, even. I can attest."

I catch sight of the wet splotch on his shirt. There's a streak of mascara across the front, and embarrassment burns through me. "Shit," I say. "I stained your shirt. I'm sorry. I'll—"

He waves it away. "Doesn't matter."

"I'm sorry."

"Don't think about it." He glances down at me and frowns. "You're cold."

"Oh." I do have goosebumps along my bare arms, but it's not so bad. But he's staring at my arms like they're offending him.

"Come on. Let's get inside." His hand hovers at the small of my back, just barely touching.

I take a few steps. One of them turns wobbly, and I chuckle in apology. "Sorry. I'm… I haven't really had this much to drink in years."

If ever.

His voice deepens. "Want us to go home?"

For a moment, I let those words spread through me. Let myself pretend that it means more than what it does. *Not my home, though.* And he's not mine in any kind of way.

"Yes," I say. "If you're ready to leave?"

He leans nearer, and his breath washes over my ear. "I've been ready since the moment we arrived."

We say goodbye to Connie, and call Mac to bring the car around. The ride down in an elevator is filled with a silence that feels companionable. I even brace against him to refasten the clasp on my shoe that's come undone, and he holds me with a steadiness that's tantalizingly reassuring.

Living with this man is going to make my daydreams *so* much worse.

"I think I might order pizza," I say in the car. I slump back against the seat and close my eyes, relishing the calm blackness and the cottony feel in my head. "That's something else I haven't had for a very long time."

A hand brushes over mine, and there's a chuckle. It's distinctly masculine. "I'll handle it," a baritone responds. I doze off, and it isn't until we're back outside the Upper East Side building that I'm nudged awake. Mac says goodnight, and Alec and I head upstairs.

My eyelids feel heavy.

But there's a wonderful scent filling the hallway on his floor. It smells like food. Cheese. *Bread.* Outside the front door of his apartment is a stack of pizza boxes.

"Alec…"

There's a smile in his voice. "I placed the order from the car."

"You got us *four* pizzas?"

"I didn't know which kind you liked."

"You could have asked me."

"You were sleeping," he says chidingly. But there's a playfulness to his timbre I haven't heard before.

I scoop up the warm boxes and follow him into the apartment. Katja is sitting on the couch. She and Alec speak in soft tones while I unbox the pizzas in the kitchen. Pepperoni. Margherita. Veggie. Meat lovers.

I wave goodbye to Katja and grab a slice. It's warm in my hand, the cheese gooey. Perfect ending to an interesting evening. Across the room, I see Alec heading down one of the corridors. The one that leads to his bedroom.

"Aren't you having any?" I call out.

He looks over his shoulder at me, and maybe it's the dimmed lighting or maybe the shadows, but I think he's smiling again. "Yes," he says. "I'll be right back."

My heart is racing as I take another bite of pizza. This whole night has been unexpected and strange, but I'm not quite sure if I'm ready for it to be finished, either.

I grab another slice and head for the large couch in the living room. Katja left the TV on, and I scroll through the streaming service's offerings, ignoring the hallway that leads to Alec's room.

I don't care, I repeat to myself. *It doesn't matter*

But he comes back. His ruined button-down is gone, along with my stain, and he's in a black T-shirt that leaves his muscled arms bare. I listen to him rummage around in the kitchen and decide on a show, almost at random. It's the last one I've watched.

He joins me a minute later with a large plate of pizza in one hand. "Watching that small-town show again?" he asks.

There's something deeply absurd about this. Sitting on Alec Connovan's couch after midnight, eating pizza, with *Gilmore Girls* playing in the background.

With Alec Connovan himself.

He can't possibly be enjoying himself. But I nod and glance at him. He's grabbed a slice of each. "There'll be tons of pizza left over."

"The kids will love it," he says and takes a bite. "So. Explain the premise of this show to me again."

My eyebrows shoot up. "Really?"

"Yeah."

"You can't possibly care."

"I don't," he says casually, but there's a trace of humor in the tone. "But I want to hear you describe it."

So I do. I eat my pizza and chug an entire bottle of water, and tell the billionaire I nanny for about the intricacies of Stars Hollow. Eventually, he leans against the couch cushions, resting his head on the back edge, more relaxed than I've ever seen him, and shaking it with a smile. "Do you wish your life was like that? In a small town where nothing bad could ever happen?"

"Sometimes," I admit. "Even though I'd probably get bored."

"I wouldn't last a day," he says.

I smile at him. "No fires to put out for the big bad CEO?"

His eyebrows rise. "The big bad CEO?"

"Yeah. I stand by that."

"Well," he says and runs a hand along his jaw. "I like putting out fires."

"Never seen you in a firefighter's uniform."

"I think Sam has one," Alec says. "Don't think it would fit me, though."

Absurd. The whole thing is absurd, but I can't help looking at him. Smiling. "Might be a bit tight across the shoulders," I say.

He nods. "Too short in the sleeves."

I curl my legs under my butt on the couch. He's not sitting very far away, and it's hard to forget how it felt to be held by him. His hand gliding over my hair. His arms around me.

"You don't have to do this, you know," I say.

"Do what?"

"Order pizza. Stay up with me. Watch this stupid show with me… just because I had an emotional breakdown at the party."

"Maybe I'm just in the mood for some terrible TV."

"Take that back."

The corners of lips lift. "No."

"I'm serious, Alec."

"What are you going to do about it? Smother me with a pizza slice? Kill me with a pillow?"

"Ballet is *very* similar to martial arts. I can kick you. Hard."

"I doubt the *similar* part in that sentence," he says. "But I'd rather not be kicked in my own home, so… the show is mediocre."

I pretend to wipe the sweat off my forehead. "Whew."

"I dodged a bullet, huh." He folds his hands over his chest and turns back to the show. "So, men say that to you a lot, then. Asking about your dancing."

"Um. Yeah, a fair bit. I mean, I don't really go out, and the majority of people I've spent time with these last few years have been dancers… But sometimes."

He looks at me for a long moment. There's something unreadable in his gaze, something I can't look away from. "I'm sorry that men come on to you like that," he finally says. "It must get tiring."

I shrug and feel my cheeks heating up. It doesn't happen *that* often. Not like what he seems to be implying. Sometimes, yeah… but does a weirdo in line at a coffee shop count? It's not like I've been dating a lot in the past few years. Dancing took precedence over a love life.

It took precedence over *having* a life.

Alec clears his throat. Puts the plate down and rises. With me curled up on the couch, he looks impossibly tall, and his neutral mask has slotted back in place. "Thanks for tonight," he says. "I'll let you relax in peace."

In peace?

I open my mouth to tell him that he's not bothering me, but he's already turned away, heading to his bedroom. This time, I don't stop him.

CHAPTER 11
ALEC

My fingers are clasped tight around the pen I'm holding. It's not necessary, but I need something to channel the frustration coursing through me.

Around the conference table, my executive team is bickering.

Oh, they'd call it something else, but that's what they're doing. The COO and the CFO have been trading barbs for the past thirty minutes, and it's about the acquisition we all know needs to happen. Everyone just seems to have different opinions as to *how*.

Differing opinions that have made this meeting run far longer than it was scheduled to. I've already texted Katja that I won't make it home for dinner with the kids. It feels like another strike, another black X instead of a checkmark on the record of my fatherhood. It joins a long list of other mistakes I've made.

I joined them for a school drop-off this morning, at least. Maybe that counts for something. Half a point on the scoreboard.

During the short car ride to school, Willa once again asked me for a pet, tried to get out of her piano practice that afternoon, *and* insisted we go to Disneyland. And considering she got a *no*, *no*, and a *maybe*, the tally on my scoreboard is probably wiped clean.

"Financially speaking," Tate says, "the next round of negotiations needs to include larger cost-saving efforts on their part. It won't make sense for us if it doesn't."

True.

Lauren sighs. "We're buying the company and expanding into the Midwest because of the profitability margins. They're high enough as is; if we pressure them too hard, they might pull out of the deal, and we lose it altogether."

Also true.

I rub my temples. I should be sharper than I am, but my patience is as thin as Sam's was this morning in traffic. Only my response can't be to start singing the tune to my favorite cartoon at the top of my lungs.

It's been three days since Connie and Gabriel's wedding party. Three days since Isabel cried, since we sat on the couch, since I was irrationally jealous and also angry at myself all at once. The men at that party wasted no time in introducing themselves to her. And why wouldn't they? She'd been... beautiful is too simple a word for how she looked. Even I can admit that, against my better judgment.

Long black hair, a black dress that hugged her slender form, and that preternatural grace she's always moved with. It had never struck me as clearly as it did then, seeing her in evening wear and makeup highlighting her features.

She looks Mediterranean. I think her parents are from Spain, but it's only a *guess*, because I can't remember what Connie's told me about Isabel. I should have asked more while I had the chance.

I could just ask Isabel now. But doing that risks opening a door to possibilities I should keep shut. Hadn't she told me men come on to her all the time? Hadn't I seen the very same thing happen not once, but twice?

Asking her to dance to get her away from Gabriel's friend had been petty. I'd known it and had done it anyway. But she didn't have to feel so good in my arms. I didn't expect that. Not on the dance floor, and not out on the terrace when the tears streamed down her cheeks and made her brown eyes glossy.

I've thought about her too much in the past few days. It's like a switch has been flipped, and my curiosity feels dangerous. I want to know more about her, and that's a bad idea if I've ever heard one.

I'd ended that night by being angry at myself for wanting her and fuming over not being able to suppress it. I always have a handle on myself. It's the one factor in life I can control, and I'd be damned if I let it slip around her. She is my employee. I might eat pizza with her, or comfort her when she cries, but I'll never ask her to dance again.

I'm not going to be one of the creeps who make her feel uncomfortable.

But burning beneath the resolve is the guilt. The condemning, nauseating, unrelenting guilt. I haven't wanted a woman in this way since my wife died. At first, the possibility had been remote, the odds slim. An issue to deal with in the future. But now that "future" is here, and my attraction is inappropriate in about fifteen different ways.

"Mr. Connovan," Lauren asks.

I slide my gaze over to hers. Fuck. I need to be here and I need to be attentive.

"Yes," I say.

"Should we postpone the next round of negotiations until we have a clearer picture of their financials?"

"No. I want this wrapped up as soon as possible. Tate, I appreciate your attention to detail with regard to the cost-saving measures, but if we don't buy this company, someone else will. And fast. I want the negotiations to continue this week. I want your team to keep pressuring them on financials, and, Lauren, I want you to push ahead with an aggressive offer. Make it clear that it's time-sensitive."

Both sides look unsatisfied. Well, tough luck. Compromise sucks. But I expect nothing but perfection from this team. I get up from the table and grab my phone and laptop. "Meeting adjourned."

The group breaks apart. They won't grumble in front of me, but the atmosphere in the room is thick with displeasure. I let it roll off my back and head to the elevators. I might not make dinner, but I'll be damn sure to make bedtime.

Mac is waiting for me in the car when I walk out of Contron. There are two cups of coffee in the center console, and it smells great in the car. The scent helps clear my head.

I grab one of them. "Katja?"

He nods and pulls the car out into traffic. "She suspected you would need something."

She suspected right. I glance at the other travel mug. He got one too, did he? It doesn't surprise me. They've known each other for years. Mac's been with me for almost as long as Katja, and both were by my side during the hard times after Victoria's death.

They'd been the scaffolding that held me up. I know that, and I make sure it's reflected in their Christmas bonuses.

When I make it home, it's not to the quiet apartment I'm expecting. Once the kids had dinner, it's usually their time to calm down before bed. They often watch TV in their pajamas.

Instead, I arrive home to chaos.

Loud pop music streams from the living room, and it doesn't sound like it's from a cartoon show. I can also hear jumping. Whoops. And Isabel's voice, encouraging more ruckus.

"That's it!"

I drop my briefcase in the hallway and walk into the living room. Stopping at the threshold, I take in the sight before me.

They all have their back to me. Isabel, Willa, and Sam. And

they are dancing like loons. Jumping, wiggling, shaking. Willa throws her hair back with a happy whoop, and Sam looks like he's concentrating hard on wiggling his hips.

Between them, Isabel is jumping from side to side, her dark hair swinging down her back.

"Should we try some salsa?" she asks and switches from jumping to dancing, using some surprisingly graceful steps.

I reach up and undo my tie. Bedtime is in thirty minutes. I'll never get them to sleep if they're like this. And yet… Sam trips into Isabel with a laugh. She straightens him effortlessly and twists around, a wide smile on her face.

It freezes in place when she sees me.

The kids notice. They turn, too. "Daddy!" Sam yells. "Dancing!"

"Yes, I can see that."

Willa performs a little pirouette, smiling from ear to ear. "Look!"

"I'm looking. You guys are doing great," I say.

Isabel runs a hand over her hair, smoothing it back. "We're having a post-dinner dance party."

"Right. Before bedtime?"

She nods. "I think that—"

Sam grabs her hand. "Do the spin! The spin!"

"Oh. I don't think…"

"Spin!"

Isabel looks at me a bit ruefully and takes a step back. "Okay."

Willa comes to stand next to me, and I put a hand on her shoulder. Her skin is warm, and her breath rapid. They're quite riled up.

"Look," she whispers. My daughter sounds awestruck, almost despite herself. She's not the only one. Isabel got Willa to dance with her? To play instead of sulk on her own?

Isabel starts to spin. It's similar to what I saw her doing at the ballet studio weeks ago, but less controlled. More carefree.

With one leg supporting her, she pulls up the other and spins. Around and around and around. From the sidelines, Sam cheers.

She might be in a pair of jeans and a T-shirt, but Isabel is every inch a ballerina come to life, here in my living room. Willa lets out a tiny sigh, and I bend down, not taking my eyes off Isabel.

"Maybe she could teach you some of that," I tell her. "If you ask nicely."

"Maybe," Willa breathes.

But then something happens. Isabel stumbles, and the leg that's supporting her suddenly gives out. It folds up beneath her, and she collapses gracefully to the floor in a heap of denim and dark hair.

Fuck.

Willa gasps beside me, and Sam yells out. "Isa!"

I'm by her side in the next second. "Isabel?" I ask, lightly touching her shoulder. My chest feels like it's turned to ice. Her hip. I should've remembered. I should have put a stop to the dance party the moment I arrived home.

"I'm fine," she whispers from beneath her hair. "Just give me a moment."

"Are you okay?" Sam asks beside me. His voice sounds shaky.

I feel it when Isabel pulls herself back together. She pushes her hair back and looks up at my son with an easy smile. "Yes. My hip just doesn't like it when I dance too much, that's all."

"I'm sorry," he whispers.

"Don't be," she says. "I wanted to dance. I love it!"

He looks at me with wide eyes, like he can't really believe it. *Right.* She's still crumpled on the floor, putting on a brave face for the sake of my kids, and I can't have that.

I slide my right arm behind her shoulders and the other beneath her knees. "This okay?"

She blinks. "Yeah. Where—"

"To bed." I lift her as gently as possible, but I hear a tiny sigh that escapes her. It sounded pained. I carry her out of the living room and down the hall that separates our rooms. She's warm in my arms. Her hair brushes over my forearm and she smells like floral shampoo.

"I'm okay," she says.

I kick open the door to her quarters. They're neat, her bed made, a light-blue sweater hanging over the back of the desk chair. "Do you ice it when it acts up?"

"Alec…"

"Do you?"

"Yes. Sometimes."

I set her down on the bed, and she lies back with a frown. "I'm fine. Really."

"Don't," I say. "I'll be back with an icepack. Stay here."

She sighs, but this time it's not with pain. It's with acceptance. "You're bossy."

"That's my job," I say, but my voice doesn't hold any humor. Seeing her crumble like a house of cards the first time was hard enough. Now it puts me in a mood that's far from gleeful.

When I get to the kitchen, I spy the kids sitting on the couch, side by side. Katja must have left after dinner. Someone, probably Willa, has turned on the TV, but they're oddly quiet.

"Isabel is fine," I say loudly and rummage through the freezer. There… a bag of frozen peas. I wrap it in a kitchen towel. "Why don't you guys put on some cartoons? I'll join you in a minute."

"Okay," Willa calls back. Her voice is unusually demure.

When I return to Isabel, she's still lying on her bed, her eyes closed. They open as I approach. "You found an icepack?"

"Frozen vegetables," I say and hand her the pack.

She takes it from me and places it on her hip, wincing

slightly. "Thank you," she says softly. "Damn. I didn't expect that to happen."

"Do you need a painkiller?"

"No. It'll pass." She leans back against the pillows. "I haven't been doing as much physio as I should. I was working so hard at it before, but after I got cut…"

"We have a gym," I say quietly. "With a sauna. You're welcome to use it whenever."

She looks up at me. "In the building?"

"In the penthouse. It's the door next to my bedroom, further down the corridor."

Her eyes widen. "Oh. Wow."

"I'm sorry we missed it on your tour of the place."

"No, no, that's… amazing. Thank you."

I nod. Look back down at her hip and the ice pack covering it. For a long moment, I can't think of anything to say to make this better. This should never have happened; I should have halted their dancing.

I clear my throat. "A dance party, huh?"

"Yeah," she says with a half smile. "I'm guessing you'd disapprove?"

"You're hurt. We can talk about it tomorrow."

She moves the ice pack around. "Your kids have a lot of energy. Especially on days when Sam didn't have his little league soccer practice and Willa didn't play tennis. She had a piano lesson that she hated, and he worked on his school project. If they didn't get some of that pent-up energy out, they would have struggled to fall asleep. Like they did the other week when you were traveling. Willa made me read every single book on her bookshelf out of pure frustration."

"You don't think dancing will make them hyper instead?"

"No," she says. "I think it makes them exhausted. Like little puppies that fall asleep midplay."

"Puppies," I repeat.

She shrugs. "Sorry. I know they're not animals, but my

parents had two litters while I was growing up, so it's… yeah. The analogy works."

"Don't worry, I'm not offended. They're definitely a bit feral." I look around her room. She's made it her own in small, imperceptible ways. There's a phone charging on the nightstand. A Kindle. The desk has a few notepads and a closed laptop.

And yet, something is missing. Something I can't quite put my finger on. "Is there anything else you need?"

"No. I'm fine. I'm sorry about that out there, you know. The kids. I'll make sure they know it wasn't anything they did."

"Don't apologize, it wasn't your fault, either. And I'll tell them," I say. Then I realize what it is. "You don't have a TV in here."

I'd never thought about that before. Never had a reason to be inside a nanny's room. I wasn't the one to set up or decorate it.

Isabel chuckles. "That's what you're thinking about? I can watch shows on my laptop."

"Or in the living room."

She shifts on the bed, her eyes turning curious. Has she always been this earnest? How had I not seen it before? "I'll keep doing that then," she says. "And you're sure you don't mind?"

It's an opportunity to draw a new line. To set some firmer boundaries. But I remember her soft voice and laughter from the other night on the couch, and I can't find the strength to draw it. "No," I say. "I don't mind."

A heaviness has settled in the air, and I can't look away from her gaze. Her hair is spread out around her on the pillow in a cloud of dark silk. The sight feels like a brand on my skin, a memory I know I'll never escape. A memory I shouldn't have. But now, it's there, and I imagine what she would look like splayed out on my bed.

If I could make her smile, and laugh as she lies beside me.

The soft creak of her bedroom door startles us both.

"Hi," a small voice says. "Isa? Are you okay?"

Isabel smiles at my son, standing in the doorway, holding a stuffed bunny under his right arm. "Yes. Come on in."

He rushes across the room, eyes locked on Isabel. "Are you sure?"

"Yes, I just need to rest for a little bit."

I catch sight of Willa standing at the threshold. Her bottom lip is between her teeth, and there's a conflicted look on her face. I wave her in. She walks across the space and lets me wrap my free arm around her.

Samuel sniffs. "It's my fault."

"It's not your fault," I tell him. "It was an accident."

"But if I hadn't asked Isabel to spin…"

"No, Sam," Isabel says. "I love to dance, and I danced with you guys because I wanted to. You didn't do anything wrong. Either of you."

Sam looks from her to me, his eyes wide. "Really?"

"Really," Isabel says.

"Really," I say.

Willa leans forward. "And maybe, when you're feeling better… you can teach us some new dance moves?" she asks. "But no spins."

Isabel's smile widens. "I'd love that."

CHAPTER 12
ISABEL

What drives a person to the edge of madness?

For a long time I thought I knew. It was a challenging choreography with only five days to learn it. It was eleven-hour practice days before the premiere. It was the feet that bled through my pointe shoes. It was the time two girls had cut all of my leotards when I got a lead role in our middle school production of *The Nutcracker*.

I know how to handle that kind of madness. The mental strength it takes to push through, to paste a serene expression on your face, and go out there and dance until your body aches.

So, I thought I understood what pressure feels like. But being a nanny to two kids is a whole different kind of craziness.

Sam's face is red with anger. He's furious, and it's all because Willa's been poking him with a pencil in the back of the car. Mac is shaking his head in the driver's seat, and I'm trying very, very hard to keep my voice calm.

The kids aren't. Sam is reaching over and hitting Willa anywhere he can get to in retaliation, and she's responding in kind. I've never seen them like this before. They rarely fight.

"Kids," I say. "Kids! Stop it. Right now."

They ignore me.

"Sam, stop that. Willa, I want you to apologize for—"

She lets out a shriek and aims a kick across the backseat. Surprisingly dexterous, considering both are belted into their booster seats.

"Enough!" Mac roars from behind the wheel. His baritone makes everyone in the car fall quiet, leaving the kids to watch him with wide eyes.

I sigh. Right. They won't listen to me, but they'll listen to the man they've known their entire lives. It shouldn't be a surprise. After all, I probably still feel temporary to them. He's permanent.

"No more of that," Mac continues. He looks over at me with a nod, and I give him a grateful smile. I don't know what I would do without him and Katja. The kids and I have grown closer over the past weeks, but it often feels like it's a "two steps forward, one step back" process.

Sam accepted me as a fun new playmate, and Willa... I *thought* we had found a truce. She no longer fights me at every turn, but her walls haven't dropped, either. I have a suspicion that she's been going easier on me than she has with other nannies and that I have my friendship with her aunt to thank for that.

"Willa," I say sharply, "put your pencil back in your backpack and apologize to Sam."

She rolls her eyes but mutters a half-hearted "sorry." Sam doesn't seem satisfied, but he unclenches his fists and looks demonstratively out of the window.

Well. It's a start.

I don't know why they're extra rowdy today. Willa had come out of school exploding with frantic energy, and it had quickly rubbed off on her younger brother. When I tried to ask her if anything had happened, she vehemently said no. *Of course not.*

Right.

The girl is a clamshell. A very smart, very spirited clamshell, and I haven't cracked her yet. Maybe that's the wrong approach. I need her to *want* to open up. Drop her walls.

Maybe she just needs to feel like she's allowed to.

As Mac pulls up outside the building, I glance at my watch. It's only 2:30 p.m. That means I have at least another three hours with them before Alec comes home. Three hours of trying to keep them from killing each other. Willa's tennis lesson was canceled this afternoon, and I received a text from Alec that told me she should use that hour to practice the piano instead.

No rest for the wicked. Or for the next generation of Connovan kids, apparently.

I suspect that Alec, Connie, and Nate were all raised in this exact way. Drivers. Nannies. Housekeepers. Language lessons, sports pursuits, the arts, and a few formal family dinners.

Maybe that sort of environment works for some. Maybe it worked for Alec. But *maybe* it doesn't work for his kids.

Katja has prepared a snack for them when we arrive home. I stand next to her, looking at the two kids devouring their perfectly made PB&Js.

"They're ravenous," she says.

"You can say that again," I reply and lower my voice to a whisper. "Is there anything new going on with Willa?"

Katja dries her hands and leans against the counter. "Not that I know of. But, sometimes, she doesn't tell anyone until she's ready. You know how kids can be."

I nod. "They were fighting in the car. Not listening to me, either. Mac had to step in."

Her eyebrows rise. "He did?"

"Yes. They listened to him." I give her a half smile. "Not

that it isn't surprising. He does not come across as someone you want to mess with."

The burly, tattooed, bearded driver is a testament to the strong and silent type. I often have thoughts that he is part driver and part bodyguard. Maybe Alec hired him because he needed a driver *and* someone to protect his kids.

Katja smiles. "No. Well, Mac looks like that. But he would never harm anyone."

"Of course, you two know one another pretty well, right?"

Her eyes flit from the kids to me. "A bit. We've both worked for Mr. Connovan for years. So, well enough, I suppose."

I think about what Connie has told me. About her brother… and her sister-in-law. Alec's wife passed away just a few months after I got to know Connie. It shocked her to the core. I can only imagine what it did to the rest of the family. "Did you both work here while Mrs. Connovan was alive?"

Katja nods and looks back at the kids. Sam has already finished his sandwich and is drinking juice from a cup, both of his hands securely fastened around the plastic.

"Yes," she says quietly. "Victoria interviewed me six months before Willa was born."

"Oh, wow. You've been with the family for a long time."

"I have. There's been a lot of changes since then. Mrs. Connovan, of course… and this apartment."

Now it's my turn to be surprised. "This isn't where they all lived … before?"

"No. They bought this place just a month before she passed. Mr. Connovan moved in with an infant and a three-year-old, and a cloud of grief." Katja looks over at me, and there's thoughtfulness in her gaze. "Maybe that was a good decision, though. Mac and I both thought so. A new place, and a new beginning."

The insight slots into my understanding of Alec, adding a puzzle piece to a picture that's still only partially complete.

He might be the least open person I've ever met. But it's not *just* him. The entire family seems to carry a weight that's not entirely their own. It's like they're all trying to shake off something that's dragging them down.

"Thanks for telling me that," I say to Katja. "It's good to understand them all better."

Her smile warms. "For what it's worth... I think you're the first nanny in a while who seems to really care. Anytime you have questions, I'm here."

"Thank you. I appreciate it." We exchange a final smile before I push off the counter and turn to the kids. "So," I say loudly. "Willa, do you want to practice the piano right away or after a little break?"

Her piercing eyes land on me. "Why do I need to do piano today?"

"Your dad wants you to, since tennis was canceled."

She slides off the chair and marches over to the grand piano. There's irritation in every line of her body. "Stupid instrument," she mutters. She sits down in front of it and ostentatiously opens the book of notes.

Maybe this is something that's worth mentioning to Alec. Willa could have hobbies she enjoys. But because her mood has been off since I got her from school, I'm not sure if the piano is simply collateral damage right now.

Sam grabs my hand with a sticky one of his own. "Come," he says, pulling me toward the playroom. His auburn hair is messy atop his head, and I notice that his glasses need to be cleaned again.

"What are we doing?" I ask him.

"I have an idea."

Ten minutes later, we've tied a blanket around his neck to create a makeshift cape again. He whizzes up and down the hallways shortly after, and his cape billows behind his little frame. I'm ninety-nine percent sure there's homework in his backpack, but I'll look at that later.

Sam grins as he swoops past me. "I'm flying!"

"I can see that," I say and pretend to flap my wings. "I'm a bird you're zooming past."

"A pigeon," he says.

I make pigeon noises and watch his eyes light up in delight. It's a priceless expression.

"What superpowers do you have?"

"All of them!" he says. "I'm superfast and superstrong. I can fly. And… and…"

"Read minds?" I ask. "Pass through walls?"

"Yes! Both."

I make a few more pigeon noises as he zips by me. "And where does the superhero live?"

Sam falters briefly before heading toward his father's bedroom. He pushes the door open. "On top of a skyscraper!"

He climbs onto the giant king-size bed at the center of Alec's room. I stall in the doorway. Maybe we shouldn't be in here. But I can't stop myself from looking in, and… it's a large room. The walls are painted soft gray, the floors are the same mahogany hardwood as the rest of the apartment. Thick curtains bookend a large window that overlooks Central Park and the buildings across it. An open door leads into a walk-in closet, and I spot neatly pressed shirts hanging in color-coordinated rows.

The bed has a dark-gray comforter. Large white pillows. Nightstand on either side but only one looks used. I see a book lying on it. A pair of reading glasses. A glass of water.

Sam jumps up and down on his dad's bed. "I'm flying," he says. "Look, look."

"I'm looking," I respond.

He jumps a few more times before flopping down on his back. The covers are mussed around him, and the cape forms a halo.

He turns to look out at the window. "I'm looking for bad guys," he declares. "They can't hide from me."

That makes me smile. "No, they can't. Do you see any?"

He makes a show of narrowing his eyes. "No. The city is safe. Today."

We continue playing superheroes for a while longer, chasing imaginary villains and saving the day. But it doesn't take long for Sam's energy to wane. He has the attention span of the five-year-old he is, and won't continue with a game a second longer after it stops being fun.

We move on to his other toys, and then homework, and by the time we've finished that, Willa's done practicing the piano. We're halfway through preparing for dinner when their father arrives home.

My stomach clenches at the sound of the front door opening. It's done that for the past several days. It's like my days both end and start when he arrives home.

The kids rush out to say hello. Well, Sam does. Willa follows suit with a faint frown on her face, the complete opposite of her usual sunny mood when Alec is around. She adores her father—that much has been obvious to me since the beginning.

There's a murmured conversation in the hallway. Kid voices, and Alec's deep, steady one in return. They eat shortly after, and from what I overhear, it's the usual mix of "kid talk." Alec listens to everything they say. He always does at the dinner table, giving them both space to talk about their days.

It all erupts after dinner. Alec's put Sam to bed, but when he goes into Willa's room, I can hear her annoyance all the way out in the living room where I'm clearing away Sam's toys. They all have to go back to the playroom at the end of the day.

"We never go to *anything*!" Willa says. "Everyone will be there. All of my friends!"

I pause, a stuffed dinosaur in hand. This sounds personal.

Alec's response is lost; all I can hear is a steady mumbling of his voice.

"No! It's... it's... they sent out invitations weeks ago!" Her raised voice quivers. I leave Sam's toys in the basket and walk quietly across the penthouse to my own quarters. I don't come out again until it's a bit past 9 p.m. Both kids must be asleep by now, and the apartment is quiet. Katja has long since left.

I don't know where Alec is.

I grab a cup of tea and curl up on the giant couch in the living room. Weeks of living here, and I still haven't seen anyone use it but me in the evenings. Alec never has guests over.

I know he doesn't date, but does that mean he's celibate?

I scroll through to find the *Gilmore Girls* and try not to let the notion bother me. He's been a widower for over five years. He's a grown man. Does he bring women here? That strikes me as unlike him...

But maybe some of his late nights aren't work events at all. Maybe he meets up with women in the city. I wonder what he'd be like, in those situations. If he smiles with the women he goes out with. Or at least the ones he's interested in sleeping with.

My thoughts leap from one thing to another, and I watch the TV with unseeing eyes. Somehow it's not hard to imagine what he might be like in bed. He's always been intense. A control freak, definitely. Highly competent. Intelligent. It's a dangerous combination.

What would he look like, if he was overcome with—

"Hey," he says. "Mind if I join you?"

I jump. Alec is standing beside the couch, his laptop in hand. He's changed out of his suit into a pair of black slacks and a T-shirt. It fits snugly over his shoulders.

"Yes. Sorry."

He frowns. "Didn't mean to scare you."

"No, no, I was lost in my thoughts." I smile at him. "Have a seat. If you don't mind me binge-watching *Gilmore Girls*."

"Still watching that show?"

"It has seven seasons."

"Oh." He sinks into the couch, propping his laptop up on his lap. His hair looks a bit mussed. Unusually so. Like he's been running his hand through it. To see him a little disheveled, even just his hair, feels thrilling.

I look at the TV screen and barely notice what's happening. I'm too focused on Alec, sitting only a few mere feet away.

He types something on the computer. Rory and Lorelai order food.

I glance at him from the corner of my eye. "Did you have a good day today?"

"Yeah. Got a lot done." But the answer doesn't sound complete. I look at the left-side corridor, toward the kids' bedrooms. I know both doors are firmly shut and they won't overhear.

"So, Willa wasn't herself this afternoon," I say carefully.

He sighs. "No, she wasn't."

"I tried to ask her why, but she wouldn't tell me. I'm not sure she enjoyed practicing piano today, either."

Alec leans his head back against the couch and looks at the TV. For a long moment, I don't think he's going to answer me. "Are they... wait, is that group of people recreating *The Last Supper*?"

"Yes," I say seriously. "They are. This is the quaint town of Stars Hollow. There *needs* to be a town event at all times."

"And what is this event?"

"A Festival of Living Art," I say. "I know. It's ridiculous and fantastic."

He shakes his head. "Do these people have nothing to do? No families, no jobs, no hobbies?"

"I think participating in community events *is* a hobby."

He stares at the screen as if it offends him. I can see the tense set of his jaw. But then he sighs and looks over at me. "Willa was angry at me. It wasn't anything you did, if you are concerned."

"Was it something at school? Because it started just today, and…"

"Yeah. There's a fundraising event tomorrow evening, for parents and kids to attend together. St. Regis puts on things like this all the time." His voice is dry, and his eyes look tired. "It wasn't like that back when I was a student there. These days, it's not enough to pay sky-high tuition. No, we're expected to participate in building and nurturing a community. I hope they never see this fucking show, or it would give them even more ideas."

I chuckle. I almost never hear him swear, and somehow it's even more effectual coming in his steady tenor. "What's the fundraising event?"

"It's a movie night under the stars. Apparently, they're transforming the schoolyard, there will be outdoor picnic areas and space heaters." He sighs. "Kids were talking about it today at school, about how their moms and their dads are going… Willa wants to go, too."

"Of course she does," I say softly. "Do you have the time?"

"We have investors flying in from Belgium tomorrow. I'm supposed to have dinner with them. It'll be an insult to reschedule, but I can do it."

"Send Connie instead, if she's free."

He runs a hand over his jaw, considering. Maybe I've overstepped by making a suggestion. But they're both Connovans, after all. And they both work for and represent Contron.

"I hadn't thought of that," he says after a while. "Yeah. Could work."

"What's the fundraiser for? At school?"

"I don't have a faintest idea," he says. "Endangered beetles in the Amazon. Orphaned pelicans in Florida. Something or other that St. Regis has decided is a *worthwhile* cause."

That makes me laugh. I hadn't expected a critique from him. "Yeah, that sounds like something a private school would deem worthy."

"Yes," he says. "Needs to be palatable and easy to explain to the kids, you know? God forbid it's an *actual* social cause here in the city."

I pull my legs up beneath me and turn to him. "I didn't expect you to... I don't know."

He raises an eyebrow. "I'm capable of criticizing my own. Very willing, too."

"Clearly." I pick at the edge of a throw pillow. "Is that why you avoid any school events?"

He glances briefly back at the laptop, but I don't think he's actually working anymore. "One of many reasons," he says, and his voice deepens. "There's a degree of... small talk that's necessary, and I don't feel up to it anymore. I just don't care where other people are planning to vacation."

I smile. "That doesn't surprise me."

There's faint humor in his hazel eyes. "No? I guess you can see right through me."

"A bit, maybe. But you're pretty opaque."

Alec doesn't look away. "Am I?"

"Yes. Seems like you don't really let anyone in, or show what you're thinking. Or feeling, for that matter." I shrug and feel suddenly embarrassed to have said all that. But it's easy to lose my composure around him. "I think maybe you prefer it that way, too."

He's quiet. The silence is filled by the rapid sparring of two characters on screen, but I can't make out a single word. He runs a hand along the sharp cut of his jaw. "Well," he says finally. "I think I do, too. Or at least I have for a long time."

Since your wife died.

I don't say it. It's not something we've ever spoken about.

I've cried in his arms at his sister's wedding party over my failed career, and my hip, but we can still move on like it never happened. However, something tells me he won't handle a question about his own past the same way.

"Doesn't it get lonely, sometimes?" I ask. My voice feels quiet in the large room. "To be a one-man fortress."

He smiles just a little, the corner of his lips tipping up. It softens the stern expression around his eyes. "A one-man fortress," he repeats. His hand rests next to mine on the back of the couch. "Maybe that's what I have to be."

"Maybe it feels like that," I say. "But I don't think so."

"No?"

"No." It's hard to look away from him when he's sitting this close. His presence is a physical thing, enveloping me entirely. "Maybe build a drawbridge over the moat. Let some family and friends in. I think there are times when everyone needs someone to lean on."

His eyes darken. "And you, Isabel? Who do you lean on?"

"Oh." I hesitate, feeling a flush creep up my neck. "My parents and my siblings. Connie. A few high school friends."

"You're close with your family," he says. It's not a question, it's a statement. "No partner?"

I shake my head. "Dancing for hours every day didn't leave much time for dating, at least not outside of the Company. Barely inside it too, to be fair. It was my entire life for so many years that... yeah. No partner."

"I can see that, about before. But now?"

"Now?" I ask. Nerves flutter in my stomach. "Well, I guess I'm open to it now. If the right person comes along."

"And what would the right person be like?" he asks. His eyes are intense, almost piercing. I'm not sure if the TV is even on anymore. The tea I brewed is forgotten in my cup, probably cold by now.

"I don't know. Funny. Intelligent. I think I want someone who's driven, because I... I was about to say that *I* am, but maybe the truth is that I *was*. He needs to be understanding. I hope to start dancing again, and he'd have to handle my crazy schedule."

Alec makes a humming sound. It sounds thoughtful, and I'm scared of what he might say next.

"What about you?" I ask.

He looks away. Eyes lock on the windows behind me, and something around them hardens. I can see him restacking brick after brick of the fortress wall. Even as his hand still rests right next to mine, on the back of the couch. I look at that instead of watching him visibly closing himself off.

I've always had a thing for men's hands, and his… tanned and agile, with neatly trimmed nails. They look manly. Capable and strong. A bit weathered. Large.

He doesn't answer my question. I can feel him working up to it, the air between us turning tense. If it was charged before, it feels electric now.

I put my hand on his.

He flinches slightly at the contact but doesn't pull away.

"I'm sorry," I say quickly. "I shouldn't have asked that. I know that… Well, I'm sorry."

He doesn't answer me. He turns his hand over instead, his long fingers wrapping around mine. Electricity shoots through me as we touch, and I can't look away from our intertwined hands.

"It's fine. I just don't really think about it," he says.

"That's understandable," I whisper. Heat radiates from his skin into mine.

His voice is self-deprecating. "Is it? Maybe."

"Everything in due time."

"Yeah," he says, and we sit there, our hands together, the silence between us charged. It feels like something passes between us. A secret I can't decipher, a hint at something to come. I don't know what it is, but I taste it all the same.

His eyes flicker down to my lips, and darken. I have the

wild thought that he's thinking about kissing me. But then, he lets go of my hand. The moment disappears, floats away, and I'm left rooted to the ground.

"Good idea about tomorrow," he says. His voice sounds gruff. "I'll ask Connie if she can attend instead of me."

I clear my throat. "Great! You could go to the movie night with Willa, and I'll stay home with Sam."

His eyes slide back to mine. "Oh, no. You're coming, too."

"I am?"

"Yes," he says. "I'm happy to watch movies with my kids, but I don't want to suffer through a single conversation with the other parents."

My voice comes out teasing. "Am I your chaperone, too, then?"

"Oh, Isabel," he says. "You're my saving grace."

CHAPTER 13
ALEC

The St. Regis schoolyard has been entirely transformed. Even I can give them that. String lights swing between buildings, illuminating the grassy lawn, and a giant screen has been positioned against the side of the sports hall. All over the grass, little seating areas are set up. Blankets and pillows form makeshift sofas, one for each family.

The scent of popcorn hangs heavy in the air. It's a beautiful October night, clear and cool, with a gentle breeze blowing through the schoolyard. Heaters are evenly spaced to keep the surroundings from being too cold.

"Okay," Isabel breathes by my side. "This is magical."

The kids seem to think so, too. Willa gazes up at me with a look that is equal parts triumph and happiness. *Look, Dad? I told you it would be awesome!*

Something clenches painfully tight in my chest at seeing her expression. Yes, she had. Maybe I should have listened the first time.

I lose control of the kids almost instantly. So many of their friends are here, although more of Willa's than Sam's, and I watch as they dart off in the directions of their classmates.

Sam ends up right next to the popcorn machine. I don't think that was accidental, knowing my son.

Isabel lingers beside me. Her hair is long and loose over her shoulders, a flowing black curtain, and she's in casual clothes. A denim jacket and a pair of pants. She looks young and comfortable. At ease. Calm.

Everything I feel the opposite of.

"Now, should I stay by your side or with your kids?" she asks. There's a gentle teasing note in her voice. "Who needs chaperoning the most?"

I look at her and not at the other parents mingling around the lawn. I've already noticed some of the curious looks directed my way. These events are a common occurrence, but my attendance is not.

"Me," I say. "Let's grab one of the spots?"

She smiles. "Yeah. There's a good one off to the side there."

We put our stuff, including the bag with kids' extra jackets, next to an empty picnic setup. The area doesn't look like a site for a school-based fundraiser. It looks rather like an expensive restaurant with a modern approach to seating.

More people are watching me. I can feel their stares, and what's worse, I notice Isabel picking up on it, too. Of course, she would. She notices everything, and there's no reason this would be an exception. But she doesn't say anything about it.

Sam comes bouncing back to us. He's holding a giant bucket of popcorn, smelling like butter and salt and everything good in the world.

"Look what I got!" he says and smiles widely. The little gap next to his front tooth winks with its absence. His first baby tooth, gone. He's growing up fast.

I ruffle his hair. "You got popcorn for all of us?"

He looks down at the bucket. *I wasn't planning on sharing* is clear enough to read, and it makes me smile. "We can always get more if it runs out," I tell him. "Did you see your sister?"

"No," he says and flops down next to Isabel. He hesitates only a moment before he offers her the bucket. "Do you want some?"

She smiles at him. "Thank you very much, Sammy. I think I'll have some."

Sammy. That's what Victoria called him when he was born. I did too, for a time. I don't know why I stopped.

Isabel looks at me. Her eyes are large and dark, framed by impossibly long lashes. "Do you want to have a seat?"

I clear my throat. "Not yet. I'll get Willa and grab us something to drink first."

I find my daughter engrossed in a deep discussion with another girl her age. They both have their hair in similar ponytails and, every now and then, they'll turn and look at something in the distance.

Ah. There are temporary tattoos at this school event. I'm not surprised. I already know she'll come back with butterflies up her arm.

She lights up when she sees me. "Daddy, come. They're doing face painting and tattoos. Can I go with Dora to get one?"

"Yes," I say. "If you come back right after. The movie will start soon."

She nods and grabs Dora's hand. "Let's go."

I'm left next to a woman who must be Dora's mother. Her hair is in a delicate updo, and I recognize the pattern on her shoulder bag that flaunts the expensive price tag. She looks like a classic St. Regis mom. My own mother had looked much like that, only in another decade.

"They're so adorable at that age," she says and smiles at me. "I'm Francis."

"Alec," I say. We shake hands.

She smiles like she already knew that. Maybe she did. "It's nice to see that you're here with Willa. It's been a while since I've seen you around at these things."

Okay, so she definitely knows who I am. I rack my brain to figure out if I recognize the face, but I can't place it. "Yes," I say. "Work has been busy."

She nods knowingly. "Of course, how couldn't it be? I read about the recent acquisition of that tech start-up, by the way, in the Business Digest. Contron seems to be doing great this year."

My eyebrows lift. "Yes, it is."

"I work in investing. Well, my husband and I both do. Marvin Sullivan? Maybe you know him."

"The name doesn't ring a bell, I'm afraid."

Her smile doesn't falter. "Oh well, I'd love to introduce you at some point. We like to host—our dinner parties are legendary! I always say, *Marvin, let's not go overboard this time*, but then we're standing there with six dozen oysters and a too-large guest list." She laughs and puts a hand on my arm. "Really, you should come to one. We only invite interesting people, so there's always someone to talk to."

I glance over at Willa. She's still getting her face painted. "I appreciate the invitation," I say. "I'll keep it in mind."

Francis's hand drops, but her smile remains in perfect place. We're joined by two other women, slinking effortlessly on either side of Francis. The hair on both is carefully groomed and their smiles even more so.

"Alec," the blonde one says warmly. "I didn't know you'd be here!"

Fuck. Am I expected to know these women, too?

"It was a last-minute decision," I say, glancing over at Willa again. How long does it take?

"Well, we're all glad you came," the other one says. "It's nice to see fathers getting involved in their children's activities."

"It definitely is," the blonde one retorts with another smile in my direction. "Lord knows my ex-husband can't be bothered."

Francis nudges the blonde woman softly. "This is Evelyn. She often comes to my dinner parties, actually."

"Oh yes, I do!" she says. Her eyes glitter. "Are you coming to the next one?"

Jesus.

"Most likely—"

Not.

But I don't get the final word out, because another person comes up close beside me. Isabel. Her dark hair brushes against my arm.

"Hi," she says. Her voice is clear and soft, a sharp contrast to the sultry tones of the women in front of me. "The movie is about to start."

"Oh, well, in that case, you'll have to excuse me, ladies. I need to get my daughter and some drinks."

"Of course, we'll let you go," Francis says. But then, she does the complete opposite. Her eyes land on Isabel instead. "I'm sorry, I don't think we've been introduced. I'm Francis."

"Isabel. It's a pleasure to meet you all," she says.

Evelyn—was that her name?—looks at me. Her voice is still warm. "Alec, I didn't know you were bringing someone."

No, and why the hell would you? Before today, I've never spoken to you in my life. Unless I chatted with her at the last parent-teacher conference? I have no memory of the small talk I endured then, only of the information that actually pertained to my kids.

Isabel stiffens beside me, and the words the blonde spoke finally break through my brain fog. *Date.* They think Isabel is my date. The realization is like cold water dumped over my head.

"Isabel is my children's new nanny," I say. "She's doing an excellent job, and they wanted her to join us tonight."

The women all exchange polite smiles. But there's a tension in the air that wasn't there a few seconds ago, and it feels thick enough to cut with a knife.

Isabel shifts from one foot to the other. They're looking at her like... oh. *Fuck.* Now they think I'm sleeping with the nanny. Most of the parents at these events employ babysitters and nannies, but they don't go to events with them.

"Have a nice night," I tell the women. Isabel and I get Willa in silence, and she chats happily as we grab a few sodas. A rainbow decorates the left side of her face, spanning toward her forehead, and she looks so happy about it that it's worth the cajoling I'll need to do later to get her to wash it off.

We head back to our spot. Willa plops next to her brother, who has his head buried in the popcorn bucket. Isabel follows suit next to them, folding down with all the grace of a professional ballerina.

Looking at her, I just know that those women were thinking only one thing, and it had been clear in their eyes as they moved from Isabel to me. And I hate that there's a kernel of truth in their assumptions.

Hate myself for being so cliché.

Even if it's hard to admit it to myself. Because yeah, I'd accepted her beauty. I'd admitted to myself that she's interesting and kind. Our interactions over the years, brief and far in between as they were, had always been charged with enigmatic energy. Feeling her dark eyes resting on me. Evaluating. *Seeing.* Even when it was for just five minutes in Connie's apartment.

It had been a reluctant but clear truth in my mind that, had things been different, in another universe, without my marriage and our age difference... I would have asked her out.

But the fact that she's now living in my apartment, and that I want... fuck, the things *I want* are depraved. Unseemly. She'd quit on the spot if she knew what my mind had conjured up in the last few days. What I'd been close to doing the other night, on that couch, with her TV show on in the background.

"Daddy," Sam says. He looks up at me with a little frown. "Sit down."

"Right." I sink between him and Willa and try to make myself comfortable against the pillows. I grab the heavy blanket and drape it over us. From her spot next to Sam, Isabel helps. Soon, the four of us are covered, legs all smooshed closely together.

More families settle around us, getting comfortable, chatting softly.

Willa and Sam are munching on popcorn.

I glance over at Isabel. "Hey."

She shakes her head. Her eyes are a bit too cheery. "Don't worry about it."

"I shouldn't have…"

"You told them the truth," she says. "Whatever they might think, we both know it's not the case."

My stomach feels like a lead stone. "We do," I say. *But my fantasies say otherwise.* Fantasies I should not be having. Of her, and her hair spread out on the bed beside me, feeling like silk in my hands. Of holding Isabel tightly against me, not a single stitch of fabric in our way.

Her smile is warm before she looks over at the screen.

I don't deserve any of those smiles.

The movie starts to play. It's animated, something I vaguely remember hearing about a few years ago. I wrap my arm around Willa and she rests her head against my shoulder.

"This was a good idea, honey," I murmur in her ear.

She sighs and snuggles closer. On my other side, Sam is munching away, his eyes glued to the screen. I do a double-take when I see that his free hand is resting on top of the blanket, and it's clutching Isabel's.

Oh.

That's a good sign. My children are getting along with a nanny. *Finally.* But the selfish, depraved part of me that had imagined Isabel and me together has an entirely different response. *Why* this *particular nanny?*

It would be easier if she wasn't getting along with my kids. Then, I could—

I shut the thought down. It's not as easy as it should be, but I manage. I have plenty of experience with it. Emotions get in the way. I've always known that. *Seen it,* even, first hand. My father was a mess after Mom passed. But he pulled himself together, and he did it for the good of both Contron and our family.

I have to continue doing the same.

My kids last through about a third of the movie before their attention wanes. For Willa, it's the beckoning eyes of Dora. She disappears toward someone else's pillows, murmuring beneath the string lights and having a thumbs war with her best friend. Sam continues to struggle valiantly, switching spots to sit next to me, but he only makes it until the middle of the movie before his heavy eyelids win the war. He falls asleep.

Leaving the two of us sitting next to one another in the near dark.

"I understand what you meant," she says in a hushed tone. "About wanting a chaperone."

I glance at her. The flickering lights warm her olive skin, and the shadows make her brown eyes look even darker. "They were unusually ferocious tonight."

"Everyone looked at you when we arrived."

I sigh. "Yes."

"Is that because everyone is familiar with Contron and they know what you do?"

"I suspect so. One of the women invited me to her dinner parties. Three times in total, I think."

Isabel chuckles lightly. "Wow. That's persistence."

I run my hand over the back of my neck. People have acted this way around me for almost a decade, but it got worse after I took over as CEO of one of the country's largest companies. "Yeah."

"Is that why you avoid these kinds of events?"

"Partly, yes."

Mainly.

"I think one of them was coming on to you, too," she says. Her voice is light. A bit teasing. "At a school event for your kids? I didn't know that was a good flirting scene."

I meet her gaze. "She was not."

"She was," Isabel says. "I could see it all the way from over here. Did I interrupt?"

"No. I wasn't interested." I grab the empty popcorn bucket from where it's lying in Sam's lap and tuck it off to the side.

Isabel makes a thoughtful sound and settles further back against the pillows. Her leg brushes against mine beneath the thick fabric of the comforter. It's an accidental touch.

But it puts me further on edge.

"So," she says. Her voice is quieter, a bit conspiratorial. Almost a whisper to not bother the others. "Did you find out what cause we're fundraising for here tonight?"

"Not a clue," I say. The tickets for this thing had been astronomical in price, like everything typically is at St. Regis. "Penguins lacking ice? Wigs for balding dogs?"

She leans in closer, and I catch her scent again. That warm floral fragrance which clings to her hair. I wonder if it clings to her skin, too.

"You're such a philanthropist."

"One tries," I murmur. On the screen, two animated characters are fighting over something, standing precariously on the edge of a crumbling bridge.

I can empathize.

Her hand tightens around the edge of the blanket, and I glance down at the fingers. She has short nails and a tiny golden ring on her pinky.

Questions form in my mind. I dismiss them, one after the other. I shouldn't be interested.

The other mothers are already thinking you're fucking your nanny, I think bitterly. I don't particularly care what they think of me. Except, the world I move in is tiny, socially speaking. It hadn't mattered to me in a long while. Nothing has, unless they're named Willa, Sam, or Contron.

But I don't want them to think that of Isabel.

Something brushes against my calf, and then it stays there. Her foot? Her leg? I cross my arms over my chest and stretch out my legs. Moving them a bit to the left.

Our legs touch. All the way from the hip down to the calf, under the secrecy of the thick blanket.

Beside me, Isabel doesn't react. Her eyes are glued to the screen like she's never been more invested in a children's movie. But she doesn't pull her leg away, either.

"It's a bit different from your show," I say quietly.

She chuckles. "Just a tad, yeah."

"What else do you do?" I hear myself asking. Curiosity has claimed me, and I can't seem to escape. "When you're not working."

She sweeps her hair to the side and starts to slowly braid it. I watch the movement out of the corner of my eye. "I haven't had the time to cultivate a lot of hobbies," she murmurs. "Dancing took up everything for so many years. I do yoga, I like watching TV, and I really like to read."

"You do? What?"

Isabel shrugs. "They're not books you'd like."

"And what do you know about that?" I ask. It's meant to be joking, but it comes out a bit gruff. Something about her seeing how the other parents reacted to me tonight has set me off. I don't want her to see me any differently.

Her slim leg pressed against mine might have something to do with it, too.

She nudges me with her shoulder. "I *know* this. Trust me."

"I'm imagining the worst now. What can it be? Horror? Or kinky stuff, like those smut books?" I ask.

Isabel doesn't respond.

My brain short-circuits, replaying what I've just said to Connie's best friend, my employed nanny.

"Kinda like that, yeah," she whispers. "And maybe don't say the word *kink* at a school event, Alec."

Energy races down my spine at her voice whispering my name and "kink" in the same sentence. We're silent for almost a minute while I find my bearings.

"Can you please say something?" she finally murmurs. On the blanket, I can see her hand tightening. There are goose bumps along the exposed skin of her wrist.

This time of year, even with the space heaters and the thick layers everyone is wearing, the air isn't exactly warm. Maybe that's why they are there. And maybe that's why I want to shrug out of my own too-warm coat and wrap it around her.

But I know that would only pour fuel on the fire I accidentally started with the nosey mothers.

"Alec," she mutters.

I lean my shoulder against hers, and this time I keep it there. "Sounds like a great *hobby*," I say. "You'll have to give me some book recommendations."

Her silence is so loud it makes me smile in the darkness.

Yeah, I think. *I'm screwed.*

CHAPTER 14
ISABEL

I sigh and put my Kindle down, and look at the clock. It's almost ten thirty, and he still hasn't arrived home. I can't even pretend anymore that I'm not waiting for him.

That's what I've been doing for the past hour, but my excuse is wearing thin, even on myself. Throughout the day, the busyness that was a constant companion in my life since I started dancing professionally kept me on my toes. Before I picked up the kids, I had gone out for a run and then an hour-long yoga and stretching session. Then it was the usual hustle and bustle at home. And after Sam and Willa fell asleep, I did my laundry, watched two episodes of *Gilmore Girls*, and read ten chapters of a new romance book on my e-reader.

But I haven't been able to focus on the story.

It's by an author I love, and I can tell the characters are great. The tropes are exactly what I like. But I can't focus beyond the deafening silence of the apartment.

Being attracted to Alec Connovan had always been inconvenient. It was harmless when he was just Connie's older brother and permanently out of reach. Someone I bumped into no more than twice a year.

But it's much harder now that I'm living under his roof

and he's my boss. Still permanently out of reach, but so close that I can almost touch him, and that's worse.

So what if he's handsome, and closed off, and radiates power in every room he enters? Women have resisted men like him before. Crossing that boundary isn't a good idea for about a hundred different reasons, and he's given me no indication that he's interested in anyone romantically. The complete opposite, actually.

Maybe I'm doomed to suffer through this stupid little crush, but I'm hardly the only woman who's been attracted to a man like him. The books in my Kindle prove that.

Only, things tend to work out in the heroine's favor, and she gets her Happy Ever After, alongside a healthy dose of repeat orgasms and dirty talk. Somehow, I doubt that Alec would ever talk dirty.

But it's amusing to imagine it. His dark, steady voice, saying the kind of things I sometimes read about... *no*. My life is in shambles already. The last thing I need is to add an ill-advised come-on to Alec, lose this job, and ruin my friendship with Connie.

And if he's lonely too, he doesn't seem to be bothered by it. The man is an island, and all that. *I bet he has it tattooed on his ankle,* I think wryly.

I lean back on the couch and close my eyes. The soft chatter on the TV in the background is my only companion, like it so often is when the kids are asleep. Being a nanny to families like this doesn't seem to come with a lot of unrestricted time. Alec attempts to limit late nights and out-of-town trips, but they're still a weekly occurrence.

There's a click in the door, and all my thoughts grind to a halt. I run a hand through my hair and listen to the sounds of Alec in the entryway, shrugging off a jacket and putting something down on the hardwood floor.

A few seconds later he walks into the living room. He

looks tired, and his hair is darker than usual. He must have gotten caught in the rain that's now coming down outside.

He stops. Glances at me.

"Hi," I say. A bit awkwardly, and a bit hesitant.

He nods hello and reaches up to undo his tie. "Hey. I didn't think you'd still be up."

"I shouldn't be," I say. That's the truth. What I say next isn't. "But I got to the really good part."

His gaze flickers from me to the TV and then back again. "Right," he says. He drapes his tie over the back of an armchair and gets working on his sleeves, rolling them up with methodical precision. "And what idiotic town event are they having tonight?"

"None, actually," I say. "She's going off to college. The daughter. Rory."

He nods and walks across the open-concept room to the kitchen area. I hear as he grabs something to drink. There's restlessness in him that I recognize from a few weeks ago when he'd returned just like this. Only the hour is later now, and the weather is moodier, and he feels raw somehow. Less in control.

He sinks onto the couch next to me with a heavy sigh. Close, too. Our thighs almost touch. There's a glass of ice water in his right hand.

I watch as he runs his free hand over his face. "Long night?" I ask.

"Yes," he says. "The worst. We had suppliers in town from Japan for a new deal we're brokering. Would give us access to the Japanese market in a way we haven't had before. After an all-day meeting, we went out to dinner."

"Oh. How do these kind of dinners usually go?"

"Well," he says and kicks his long legs out, "it starts at a private booth in a Michelin-stared restaurant. We quibble over the check, but naturally, Contron picks it up. The wine flows. The talk isn't quite as smooth, but it's getting there.

Everyone gets to know one another. Testing the waters, basically."

"You were just on a date, then," I say.

He huffs out a chuckle. "Yeah. And at the end of dinner, the Japanese investor said it was their turn to choose the next place to go. So, we went to a rooftop sake bar."

"Oh no," I murmur.

"Yeah." He takes a long pull of his iced water. "And I was ready to head home after dinner."

"Did you seal the deal, at least?" I ask. "Think you're getting a second date?"

He lifts an eyebrow. "If I want it, I always get a second date."

Oh. Something tightens in the pit of my stomach.

"Aren't you awfully confident?" I ask.

"Just realistic," he says. His thick hair is starting to dry. It's usually neatly brushed back, but now it's turning just a bit unruly.

"The annoying part is that you're probably right," I say. "I noticed how all the parents looked at you the other night. *All* of them, and it wasn't just the single women who were interested."

He breathes out a sigh. "Right. Didn't want you to notice that."

"No?" I pull my legs up beneath me and turn to face him on the couch, my arm draping along the back. "And why not?"

He takes another long drink of his water, and I'm not certain if he'll answer me. While some walls might be down tonight, I doubt all of them are.

"You've never looked at me like that," he says. "Didn't want you to start."

I smile. "Well, I don't throw a lot of dinner parties," I say. "You're safe from me. I won't use you for clout or social climbing.

"You're not going to ask me to invest in your start-up, either, are you?"

I cross my heart. "Promise."

"Good." He drapes his arm along the back of the couch, too, and it comes to rest next to mine. Our forearms brush. His eyes, usually hazel, look dark in the dim lighting. "I'm sorry about those women. The assumptions they were making were clear on their faces."

I shrug. "It's okay."

"No," he says, and his voice is unexpectedly hard. "It really isn't."

"I don't run in those circles," I say. "It doesn't matter what they might think of me."

"It matters to me," he mutters.

I dig my teeth into my lower lip. "Are you concerned they'll think less of you because of it? I don't know, I would think the relationships between... that... well, that it's not that uncommon. In your world. In the St. Regis world, I mean."

My cheeks blaze at my stumbling words. I'd just implied that it was common for men in his social circle to sleep with nannies who work for them. That it would be common if *he* did it.

"That's not it. It's just..." Alec trails off, his voice turning hoarse. "I don't want anyone to think that I'm using you. That I'm taking advantage of you."

"They won't," I say. "I bet, next week, they won't even remember meeting me."

His eyebrow rises. "Not so sure about that."

Silence falls between us, and he glances back toward the screen.

I've never seen him watch TV in here, not unless he was with kids or joined me. I make my voice light. "How do you relax?"

"I'm relaxing right now," he says.

"I mean, you asked me about my hobbies the other night. So far, the only things I've seen you do is work and parenting, and neither of those qualify."

"I use the gym."

"In the mornings?" I ask.

He dips his chin in a nod. Somehow, we are closer to one another than when he first sat down, and my bent knee brushes against his leg.

"Doesn't count, either," I say. "That's... no. Doesn't qualify."

"Didn't know I'd be interrogated when I got home."

"Wishing you stayed at the sake bar?"

"No," he says. "Not even a little bit."

My breath hitches. "I get that. There's only so much sake a man can have."

"And I've already had too much," he says darkly.

"Maybe you can sleep in tomorrow."

A spark lights up his eyes. "Isabel," he says. "You know as well as I do that's never going to happen. Did you ever sleep in when you danced ballet?"

"No," I whisper. We're similar that way, despite all the ways that we're different. The dedication to the dream comes above everything else.

"Life of a perfectionist," he says. His fingers brush against my shoulder, a barely-there touch. "Always striving for something just out of reach."

"Never quite satisfied with what you have."

"No," he says. "So tell me, Isabel. How do I relax?"

My body feels strung taut. He's so close, the top two buttons undone on his white shirt, and there's a faint shadow of stubble along his jaw. I lean in closer without meaning to. He smells like rain and cologne and a slight trace of alcohol. Something else, too. A hint of cigar smoke.

His hand brushes my shoulder again.

I kiss him. It's a quick brush of my lips against his, with

my heart pounding in my ears. The world feels like it's crashing down around me.

He sits still as a statue.

I draw back and feel the apology hovering on the tip of my tongue. *Shit.*

But Alec looks at me with eyes that burn the *sorry* right out of me. He closes the distance between us, kissing me with so much force it takes my breath away. His lips are warm and strong, slanting over mine. I can't think over the roar in my ears. Can't feel anything but the sensations he evokes.

I put a hand on his cheek and kiss him back. His skin is warm and slightly rough. Heat courses through me with every kiss, pulsing through my veins like lava. He deepens the kiss and brushes my lower lip with his tongue.

I've never been kissed like this.

It's all-consuming, all-encompassing, pervasive like he would rather die than stop kissing me. There's thoroughness in each kiss. He's not rushing. We're not rushing. I slide my hand into his hair, my fingers gripping the thick strands.

He groans, low in the back of his throat, and his hand lands on my knee. I wonder dimly if I can climb onto his lap. If that's allowed. He seems to think it is because his free hand finds the curve of my waist. It's large and strong and tugging me forward, and he just keeps kissing me, switching between deep, slow pulls and soft brushes.

I shift forward on the couch and he catches me, pulling me firmly against him. One of my legs ends up across his lap, and I can't think, can't breathe, can't focus. There's only him.

He runs a hand over the length of my hair. "Isabel," he mutters. His voice is low and hoarse. "Tell me to stop."

I brush my lips against his. "Why?"

"What are we doing?" he asks. It's less of a question and more of a groaning admonition, but I answer him anyway.

"I don't know," I whisper.

His hand slides to my neck, and it stops there. Curving

around to my nape. He pulls back and rests his head against the back of the couch. He's breathing fast, and his eyes are nearly black.

"No," he mutters. "No, we're not doing this."

I brush my thumb over my lip. *Why?* But I can see the beginnings of a shutdown in him, the walls beckoning. The rejection stings. "Okay," I whisper.

He closes his eyes. Takes a deep breath. And then he's pushing my leg off his lap and pulling out of my arms.

"Alec?" I call to him as he starts to move away from the couch.

He stops a few feet away. His shoulders rise and fall visibly with his breathing.

It takes him a moment to speak, and when he does, his voice is that of Alec Connovan, my boss, and the CEO of Contron. It's not the Alec of the nighttime couch.

"I'm sorry for that," he says. "It was a mistake, and I assure you it won't happen again."

"Okay," I whisper. The world is still faintly spinning around me, and my lips still feel swollen from his kisses. But his words chafe as much as his tone.

He pauses for another second, as if he might say another word, but then he thinks better of it. He disappears down the hallway leading to his bedroom. In the silence that follows, I hear the characters on TV laugh.

It sounds mocking.

CHAPTER 15
ISABEL

The temperature in the Connovan penthouse turns arctic for the next few days. I'm not sure anyone but Alec and I notice the lack of warmth, but between us, it's palpable.

He's his usual self with Willa and Sam in the evenings—at dinner and when he puts them to bed. And I have my free time. But there are no more evenings on the couch and no conversations apart from discussing the logistics. *I packed Willa's bag for tennis tomorrow. Here's a slip from Sam's teacher, it requires your signature. Willa complained about a tummy ache yesterday.*

We work well together. He's direct and to the point, but I'm used to that. It's not like any of my dance instructors or company directors coddled me before. If anything, Alec might be the most lenient boss I've ever had.

I'm not sure most other people would agree, though. He doesn't do small talk with Katja or Mac. He doesn't give his smiles and approvals readily. But he is consistent, and if you do what he asks of you, easy to get along with.

It's almost ten on a Thursday morning, and the day is mine entirely until it's time to pick up the kids. Many of my days are like this, and it's an unexpected span of freedom. For so long, each of my hours was earmarked, my food controlled, and I trained until my body ached every night. And now, I'm staring at Central Park outside the window, on a weekday, with nothing to do.

My phone chimes again. It's done that consistently over the past few days, my family group chat and the chat with my siblings, both equally active.

Dad loves sending memes to the family. He discovered them a few years ago and now forwards about five too many every week. I think he gets most of them from the guys at his office, and more than a few times, the memes are wildly outdated.

Use this for your routine, he'll write, adding five exclamation points. He rarely specifies who he talks to, but he doesn't really need to, either, when it's only my little sister who has a routine anymore. She's a budding stand-up comedian, premiering a new comedy set on Friday night next week. I'm going, and so is my brother. Sebastian won't ask as many questions as my mother and father would... which is why I've been avoiding visiting my parents. They ask out of love, but I dread the inquisition anyway.

Because it's not like I know the answers.

Will I go back to dancing? What is this nannying job? You're not planning on making this a career? What about going to university—you were always bright in school! Tell me more about this hotshot you're nannying for. He hasn't tried anything, has he? Are you paid all right? How terrible are the kids?

Well, I know the answers to some of those. He hasn't tried anything. I was the one who tried, and he was the one who shut it down.

Humiliation had kept me awake during the nights since. I half expected a phone call from him or a formal email. *This isn't working out.*

You're fired.

It's not that I doubted his attraction. He'd kissed me back. My cheeks heat at the memory of the intensity, of the way he kissed me like he wanted to savor and swallow me whole. But he had been pretty clear in other conversations that he wasn't looking to date. Wasn't open to anything romantic.

Grabbing my yoga mat, I unroll it onto the living room floor. October sunlight filters in through the giant windows and makes the polished hardwood floors gleam. If there's one thing that's always been able to center me, it's exercise. I should have at least an hour before Katja arrives and starts her daily rounds of meal prepping, laundry, and cleaning.

I start the yoga routine that Connie and I follow every Saturday, but it doesn't take long until I'm pushing the limits. Holding poses longer than we usually do, until the muscles in my arms and stomach are shaking. It feels good. Familiar. At least this part of my body works, and it knows the movements intimately. The ache of my muscles, the soreness after prolonged stretch have been my companions for as long as I remember.

I could become a yoga instructor. The thought is bitter. There's nothing wrong with that, but God, going from the thrill of performing on stage every night to telling a room full of people to breathe deeply feels tragic.

My phone chimes again. I should have put it on silent. Elena and Sebastian have been painfully active in our group chat since I got cut from the Company. It's like they need to check on me all the time. But asking *how are you feeling today?* gets old rather quickly, so they have been rephrasing it by sending pics out of school yearbooks and family albums, or weird photos of things that happen in their lives. An oddly shaped bagel. A funny sign on the subway. *Engage,* every message begs me. *Laugh.*

Be happy.

None of us knows how to adjust, I think. They were newborns when I started dancing ballet. They've never known a world where being a prima ballerina wasn't my ultimate goal, either.

I sink into a three-legged downward dog, kicking my left leg up as high as it can go. It feels good. Like I'm a spring, gathering energy, coiled to strike.

I breathe deeply. In through the nose, out through the mouth.

One day at a time.

That's all I need to focus on.

One day at a time, and maybe to *not* kiss my employer again.

There's a sound to my right, and then an indrawn breath. I look over my shoulder and catch sight of someone standing in the living room.

I lose the pose immediately. My leg drops to the floor and, feeling panic in each cell of my body, I push up to stand.

It's Alec. He's in a suit, hair impeccable, and he's staring at me with borderline anger in his expression.

Shit.

I'm not wearing a stitch of makeup, my hair is in a messy ponytail, and I'm in my skimpiest of workout clothes. A sports bra and shorts that are more like hot pants. I've spent many times in outfits similar to this one while stretching and training during the warm summer days, especially when the room felt more like a sauna than a studio.

But I'm not in a studio. I'm in his living room.

His eyes rake over my body before rising to meet mine. There's a furrow between his brows, drawn low over his darkened gaze.

"Sorry, I didn't know you'd be coming home," I say.

"Me neither." His voice is hoarse. "Needed something from the home office."

I find the band of my sports bra and tug it down, as if the fabric could suddenly cover more of me. "Oh. I could have taken it to Contron for you."

He shakes his head slowly. "You have the middays off."

"That's okay."

"No," he says. His jaw is tense, and his shoulders look like they're following suit. "It's important to respect your working hours."

I nod mutely. *Our working relationship* is what he's really saying. But he doesn't leave, and we stand there and stare at one another.

His eyes drop down again, like he can't help himself. "Yoga. Is that what you're doing?"

"Yes," I say.

He glances down at the mat beneath my feet. "Does that help your hip?"

"It doesn't hurt it, at least."

"When was your last checkup?"

I cross my arms over my chest. It won't hide the skin that's on display, but it feels like protection. "What do you mean?"

Alec frowns. He does that a lot, I've realized. His face is set in stern lines that make him look older than his forty.

"Isabel," he says gruffly. "Are you telling me you haven't been to a doctor or a physiotherapist for your hip?"

I shrug. "I don't have access to the Company's medical staff anymore, no. My last appointment was a week before I got cut."

He closes his eyes. "Shit."

"It's fine. I was examined a lot before I left, and I know what to do."

"Still, you should be getting proper medical attention," he says. "You're my employee. You have healthcare. I can get someone here tomorrow."

I raise my eyebrows. "Someone?"

"I'll find an expert in hip tears," he says, almost in warning. "Or send me a few names to choose between if you want to make the selection yourself. But I won't have an employee of mine suffering."

"I'm hardly suffering," I protest.

"The collapse the other week proved—"

"I was doing consecutive fouettés without being properly warmed up," I snap. But then I take a deep breath and force the irrational anger out. It's not his fault that my hip has betrayed me. "But I appreciate it. I'll… send you some names."

He nods. Runs a hand over the back of his neck. "If you need more, or time to train, to potentially make it back into dancing—"

But I'm already shaking my head. Can't have that discussion, not right now, and not with him. The road to recovery is impossibly long, and the world of ballet companies moves fast. You're only as good as your last performance, and there's always someone waiting to take your place.

"Thanks. I appreciate that," I say. "Maybe in a few weeks. I just need… I don't know. But I'll send you the names of a few physicians who specialize in treating dancers."

He nods again. Glances down at my body for a split second before looking away, his eyes landing on the TV. His shoulders square. "Look," he says. "I've been meaning to apologize for the other night."

I'm already shaking my head. "Alec—"

"I shouldn't have sat down next to you that evening. The night had been long enough, and I acted unprofessionally. I hope that you'll consider continuing working here."

"Of course. Please don't apologize," I say. Mortification is creeping up my neck like a heated blanket.

His eyes snap back to mine. "Don't apologize?"

"No, please, it's fine. Truly. I wasn't unwilling."

The word stretches out in the space between us, becoming larger than the three little syllables themselves.

He's gone very still. "Really," he says.

I take a step closer to him. "Really. And to be fair, I was the one who kissed you, so I should be the one to apologize.

You hinted that you weren't in a headspace for... for... for dating, I suppose, but I guess that means all kinds of relationships."

He chuckles. Even if it's a dry sound, he sounds genuinely amused. "Isabel, I think it was pretty clear I was the driving force."

"Oh," I say. *Oh.*

A smile curves the corner of his lips. It makes him look real again, like the same man who hugged me on the balcony when I cried.

"Sorry for occupying your living room," I say.

He shakes his head. "Don't apologize."

"I won't if you won't," I say. "For the other night."

He reaches out and sweeps a strand of my hair back. I hold my breath as he tucks it behind my ear.

"Deal," he says quietly, his fingers lingering along my cheek.

It happens more naturally this time, two people falling into one another. I don't know if it's me or if it's him who moves first. My heart pounds wildly in my chest as he lowers his head, and it's so sweet, the moment right before.

And then he's kissing me.

It's slow, thorough, and just as all-consuming as the other night. He tastes faintly like freshly brewed coffee, and I lean into him, my hands coming to rest on his chest. The fabric of his suit jacket feels rich and thick. I grip his lapels, tugging him closer.

He deepens the kiss and slides his hands down, wrapping them around my bare waist. The skin-on-skin contact sends heat racing through me.

Alec draws me flush against his body. I'm a bit sweaty from my workout, but that thought disappears in the next instance. It's drowned out by the sensations of his lips on mine, his hands gripping me tight.

I push my hand inside the collar of his shirt. The skin of

his neck is warm and my fingers snake their way in, curving over his collarbone.

His hands move too, thumbs sliding forward until he's almost encircling my waist and pressing down gently a few inches above my hipbones. I'm on my tiptoes, and I never want to leave the circle of his arms.

Alec's mouth travels down my cheek, my neck, his lips brushing against the sensitive skin there. He hasn't shaved today and the feeling of stubble over my skin makes me shiver.

"I need a shower," I murmur. With his head bent, I feel his hair tickling my skin, and I thread my free hand through his strands.

He kisses my collarbone. "No," he says gruffly, "you don't."

I've never felt this kind of heat this fast before. It builds inside me, between my legs, making my heartbeat race, and my breathing rapid. I want to kiss him again. I want to feel his skin, I want his shirt *off*, and I want to lie on the couch with his weight on top of me.

He tips my head back and kisses a slow, heated trail back to my lips. Pressed against him as I am, I feel an unmistakable ridge against my stomach.

He's hard.

My eyes close on instinct, and I pull him back toward my lips. He groans, and his hands glide down, over the curve of my ass, and settle beneath it with a firm grip.

Is he going to lift me?

I lock my hands behind his neck and crane into his touch.

The sound of someone whistling cuts through the fog of desire that blankets us both. Alec releases me instantly, his hands gone in the next moment, and takes a step away.

He's breathing so hard I can see his chest rise and fall with every intake, and his eyes are nearly black. "Fuck," he mutters.

He retreats after a beat, walking toward the home office with long strides.

Katja strolls into the living room a few seconds later. She's carrying a large grocery bag and whistling to herself. There's a little bakery bag in her free hand, and a delighted glint in her eyes.

She startles when she sees me. "Isabel! Didn't know you'd be home. Oh, are you working out?"

I run a hand over my lips. "Yes."

"Well, don't let me bother you," she says. "I'll enjoy my cupcake on the patio before I start work."

I watch her leave the living room and wonder what the hell just happened.

CHAPTER 16
ALEC

On Saturday morning, I wake up to the nearly complete darkness in my bedroom. A quick glance at the clock tells me the score. It's not even six thirty, yet. After years of following the same schedule, my body refuses to treat the weekends any differently from the rest of the week.

Right now, it's also refusing to let me fall back asleep. Beneath the comforter, I'm hard. Achingly so. Even the friction of my boxer's elastic makes me hiss.

My sex drive has been at a steady simmer over the last few years. Something I can easily take care of myself, twice a week or so, and move on with my life. A need, just like food and sleep and showering. One I've rarely given a thought to.

But now it's a burning desire that scalds the blood inside my veins. It's not simmering. It's not under control.

And it's not something I can ignore.

I stare up at the ceiling and try to ignore the painful erection resting against my stomach. It's frustrating, my body betraying me like this.

In a pre-Isabel world, I would have taken care of it in the normal fashion. Locked the bathroom door, stroked in the shower, and ten minutes later, I would have carried on with my day. But nothing is normal anymore, and I know that the instant I grip my cock, images of her will explode before my eyes.

I'm not supposed to think about her like that, for more reasons than I can list.

Though I *should* probably list them. It would do me and my erection some good. Some count sheep, I count the reasons why I'm an immoral asshole…

It's incredibly easy to picture her. The slender curve of her neck, the warm smile, and the strength of her body, an instrument and a home she takes care of so well. She'd been almost naked the other day. Long, strong legs, a flat stomach, and muscled arms. She's like the first letter of her name. An *I*, with a hint of delicate curves over her waist and hips.

Her skin had been warm to the touch from her workout, and soft, and I wanted to tear the teensy fabric clean off her.

My cock throbs, and I curse, reaching down beneath the covers. It's hot and hard in my grip, and a shiver passes through me at my tight squeeze.

Kissing her was so damn sweet. Like eating a decadent dessert, and never wanting to stop. She responded so beautifully. Both times, she gripped me back, leaning into me. I didn't know I was missing that. Being someone's pillar. Feeling a woman holding on to me for support.

Guilt dances alongside my desire. I haven't wanted anyone like this since… I can't finish the thought. Can't be thinking of *her* right now. Not while Isabel has me tied up in knots, or the shame will drag me under.

The need coursing through my system makes it easy to push away the guilt. To shove it into a drawer that I know will haunt me later. So I stroke myself tightly and let the fantasies flood as if I'd not tried to erect a wall.

Isabel, with her hair down and her top undone, showing a hint of bra. It's white in my mind. She is glancing at me with that shy warmth as she unbuttons her shirt the rest of the way and drops it to the ground.

Fuck, she looks delicious. Her tits are small and perfectly formed, and I shouldn't have noticed but I have, I have. I tighten my fingers around my base to stave off a too-early release.

Alec, she sighs in my fantasy, and then she's pressing her naked body against mine, and her arms twine around my neck.

The fantasy shifts, keeping pace with the increased speed of my hand. Need races down my spine, pulsing in my thighs at the image in my mind. Isabel laid out beneath me. Her dark eyes are pleasure-drunk, and her hair is silk on my pillow. Her legs spread wide to welcome me inside, like she truly wants me. I buck into my hand and wish it was her I'm fucking, her heat instead of my right hand, her breathy moans in my ear.

I imagine she'd be natural, no artifice, just the truth in her responses, and I'd love to evoke every single one. Looking up at me, she's lithe and so painfully pretty, and whispering my name. Her legs are wrapped around my waist, and her heat feels so good, so deliciously good. My balls tighten and my heels dig into the mattress, and then I'm coming.

Inside of her. But, in reality, it's in my hand and on my stomach, and in the silence that follows, I hear my heartbeat pounding in my ears. The fantasy slips away along with the last vestiges of pleasure.

And the guilt bursts free out of that drawer. I shouldn't have done that. Shouldn't have thought that. It's only going to make the inconvenient attraction that much worse… and I haven't fantasized like that about a woman in years. Beat off to pictures of her in my mind. I came, because of her.

And yet it's the best orgasm I've had in weeks. And judging from the way my thoughts are spinning, it won't be the last time she's my cock's muse.

I run my clean hand over my face. Shit.

Kissing her twice had been... regret is the appropriate emotion, and yet, it's hard to feel it when the kisses are that sweet. Maybe that only makes me worse.

She's Connie's best friend.

She's fifteen years younger.

She needs a job and a place to live.

She's already complained about guys coming on to her. And I'm her employer. And so far outside the lines I've set and maintained for most of my life.

And... my wife has only been dead for five years.

Nausea makes my stomach roll.

What are you doing, I ask myself bitterly. Isabel doesn't want you. Not really, even if she had made it beautifully clear the other day that she liked the kisses. That made my ego swell to the point that I had to kiss her again, right there, in the bright daylight of my own living room. It had been sheer luck that stopped us before Katja arrived.

I pull back the covers and head to the bathroom. Getting into the shower, I turn the water temperature to cold, and colder, until the icy stream stings against my skin. It washes away the remnants of my orgasm and the lingering heat.

And it feels exactly what I deserve.

The kids will be awake soon. Saturday's are our days, without Katja and without work, unless I'm traveling for business. Between Contron and my kids, it's not like I have anything to offer Isabel. The thick rod between my legs might think differently, but it's wrong. I'm not going to start an affair with my kids's nanny.

She deserves infinitely better than that.

And it wouldn't be right for me to cross that boundary.

Thirty minutes later, I'm clean and in the kitchen. I'm halfway through making the pancake batter when the first kid wanders in. It's Sam, his eyes blinking rapidly and his superhero pajamas slightly askew.

"Dad?"

"I'm here." I leave the bowl on the counter and pick him up. It won't be long now until that becomes an impossibility. He smells like sleep and kid, and I walk us back to his bedroom. "Your glasses, buddy. That's why you can't see clearly."

"Oh." He rests his head against my shoulder as I gather the discarded frames from his nightstand. The optometrist mentioned Sam will likely grow out of needing glasses, but only if he's diligent about wearing them.

"Can I watch TV?" he asks.

"Sure. Pancakes will be ready soon," I say and halt by the couch. I raise an eyebrow. "Want to go flying?"

The smile lights up his whole face. "Yes!"

I toss him onto the couch, and he shrieks in delight, bouncing on the cushions. *Again, again,* and I do it two more times before turning on the TV and returning to the bowl of batter.

That's the sort of thing Victoria would have disliked. I've stopped feeling bothered, but in the first few years of being a single father, I heard the ghostly traces of her voice every time around the kids. *Don't do that. Do it like this. You can't let her get away with it. Alec, don't hold him so high.*

I don't hear the admonitions anymore.

During some of the hardest moments, when both kids were small and crying at the same time, I would hear her berating me, and it would piss me off. *If you wanted to be a mother so badly, you shouldn't have died and left me to do this by myself.*

Later, when the kids were calm and peace once more restored, those thoughts always made me feel guilty. She didn't choose to leave their lives. Or mine. But when you're sleep-deprived and toeing on the edge of sanity, fairness feels like a very foreign concept.

I watch the top of Sam's head as I whisk the batter. He's

humming along with the intro song of his favorite show about crime-fighting dogs. I should have more weekends like this. Weekends with my kids. But the demands of Contron and my family feel like a never-ending civil war.

Willa wakes up soon after. She gives me a hug, and I kiss the top of her hair. "Blueberry pancakes?" she asks.

"You bet." They're one of the few things I know how to make by heart. We've had them as a weekend treat for years, whenever I'm home.

She looks so happy that my heart constricts in my chest. "Are you working today?"

"No," I say. "Not even for a minute."

Her smile widens. "Can we go to the park?"

"We sure can. Whatever you two want."

I watch her skip over to the couch, a feeling of guilt souring my mood. It never seems to go away. I want Willa and Sam to know that when I'm working, I'm doing it for them, but that concept is hard to translate for kids. I want to be here for them… *and* I want them to have a family legacy when they're older. The way Nate, Connie, and I do.

I start frying pancakes and listen to the kids on the couch, the low drone of the TV, and the absence of squabbling. Good.

I'm flipping a pancake when she speaks. The sound of her soft voice has the opposite effect on me, striking like a lightning bolt down my spine.

"You're cooking?" There's a hint of surprise in her tone.

"Yes," I say. She's standing by the kitchen island, dressed in workout clothes and some kind of teddy jacket. Her face is clean of makeup and ponytail in her hair. Beautiful. "Does that come as a surprise?"

"I don't want to offend you, but… yes. Kind of."

I look down at the pancake I'm flipping. This is enough. This is the boundary I need to tread. Friendly, companionable, *professional* conversation.

"You know, there are a lot of talents I haven't shown you," I say.

Fuck.

Didn't take long to step over that line.

She chuckles, and the sound makes the transgression worth it. "That sounds interesting, and a little ominous. Contron doesn't secretly assassinate its business rivals or anything, does it? You're not trained in Krav Maga?"

"I could tell you, but then I'll have to kill you."

She leans against the counter with a little smile. "So, that's a yes. You know, Connie has always been pretty tight-lipped about what you guys *really* do at work, but I already suspected it was something illegal."

I shake my head. "Oh no, we never do anything *actually* illegal. Gray areas, Isabel. That's where most of the money is made."

Her eyebrows lift. "You know what, I don't even think you're joking."

I'm not.

But she doesn't come from this world. Hers has been one of rigorous training and discipline, too, but in an entirely different field.

Her eyes, flaring and just a little bit cautious, lock with mine. Why wouldn't she be wary? At any moment, I might start apologizing again. Or kissing her again. *Or both.*

God, do I want to do the latter. Now that I've tasted her, it's all I want to do. The need I slaked earlier this morning is already rearing its head again. How had I thought hiring her wouldn't be a problem? That it wouldn't be a mistake?

"Good morning," I say.

Her lips part on a soft exhale. "Good morning. Are we… everything's okay, right?"

"Yes. Absolutely."

She digs her teeth into her lower lip. "Good. Because I was thinking that—"

Sam's loud shriek cuts her sentence off. He comes racing into the kitchen with a blanket in hand. "Isa!" he says. "Cape, cape, help me with the cape."

She ruffles his hair and takes the blanket from him. I watch as she ties it around his neck, loose enough that he can easily slip it off his head himself.

"There," she says. "Who are you fighting today?"

"Willa," he declares.

I point the spatula in his direction. "No, you're not. She's not one of the bad guys. Why don't you go get her instead, because the pancakes are almost done. That's a superhero task."

He blitzes off, and I start plating. "Do you want some?" I ask Isabel.

"Are you sure? I don't want to bother you guys. I'm actually heading out in a while to meet Connie."

"Connie?" Willa asks, marching into the kitchen. She looks at Isabel with no trace of the rancor she'd shown in the beginning. "You're meeting with my aunt?"

"Yes, we're going to an early yoga class in an hour."

"Oh. Is that like ballet?"

"A little bit, but it's none of the dancing and all of the stretching."

Willa jumps up onto a chair and grabs a fork. She digs into her pancakes while I get Sam settled. They're both munching away, but Sam is looking at Isabel while he eats.

"We're going to the park today," he tells her. "Wanna come?"

Isabel's eyes flick to mine for a second before returning to his. "Today is your day with your dad."

"You can ask Aunt Connie to come along," Willa says. She nods like that's settled. "We can all be at the park together."

"Maybe, yeah. I'll ask her," Isabel says.

I push a plate of pancakes across the counter to her, and she accepts it with a small smile.

"Only if you want some," I say quietly.

"Thanks," she murmurs. She grabs her plate and comes to join us at the table. She starts cutting into her stack. I dig into my own and try to ignore the way our thighs brush briefly beneath the table.

Sam is looking at her with appraising eyes. "Do you have a brother?" he asks. It's one of his many beautiful non sequiturs.

Isabel smiles. "Yes. One younger brother and one sister. They're twins, actually."

Willa nearly drops her fork. "*Twins?*"

"Yeah."

"Do they look the same?"

"Well, no, not really. They're not identical twins. They're fraternal, a girl and a boy," Isabel says.

"Is it nice to have a sister? I've always wanted a sister," Willa says. She's chatting happily, talking with Isabel without an ounce of animosity. "I've asked Dad for one before but he said no."

"You've also asked me for a pet just as often," I tell her. It doesn't seem like a particularly deep want either. Sometimes it's a cat, sometimes a dog, and on a few occasions a guinea pig. I can't think of anything I want to cohabit with *less* than a guinea pig.

"Yes, and you always say no," she says.

Isabel hides her smile behind her hand. "Well, I'm sure your dad knows best. At least most of the time."

"Yes, and you need a mommy to get a sister," Willa says sagely. She digs into her pancake with her fork. "And we don't have a mommy anymore."

The statement is matter-of-fact. It's not pained, sad, or bothered. She and Sam are rarely troubled about Victoria, accepting her absence as a fact of life. They have questions. Concerns, sometimes, about what to tell their friends if they get asked. I've tried my best to navigate it all.

But while Willa and Sam continue eating with the same happy air, Isabel and I have gone still.

"No, I'm sorry about that," Isabel says with a glance at me.

"Thank you," Sam says. His mouth is full of food, and he clearly has no idea what he's thanking her for. It breaks the tension, and I chuckle. Isabel joins in, and then Willa, and then Sam himself, even though he definitely doesn't know why.

God, this is what I do it all for. For them. I'm all they have, and I can't afford to let my focus slip. Can't afford to add any more guilt to a plate that's already heaping.

But Isabel puts her hand on my shoulder after breakfast, and the thoughts of restraint immediately vanish. "Is it okay if Connie and I drop by the park later? I don't want to intrude."

I find myself shaking my head. "No, please do, if you want."

It'll be good for the kids to see their aunt, I think.

As if that's the only reason I agreed.

CHAPTER 17
ISABEL

I glance one final time in the mirror. Tight black jeans, waist-high. Brown leather boots with short heels. A beige oversized coat that I bought at a vintage store for far below its actual value. I've even applied makeup, and the dark eyeshadow makes my brown eyes look bigger than usual.

I look good. Different. It's been a while since I dressed up like this, with the exception of Connie's wedding party. *A night on the town.* I've let my hair out and it hangs loose down my back.

Casual enough for a comedy club. Dressed up enough for a night out.

Grabbing my bag, I leave my room. There are familiar, soft sounds in the living room. The TV is on, and Sam is laughing. Willa saying something I can't hear. And then, Alec's voice.

Steady. Authoritative. "No, that's Willa's. You chose this bedtime show, Sam. Don't you want to watch it?"

The tap of my heeled shoes against the hardwood floors announces my arrival. Three heads turn around. Willa's eyes widen, Sam smiles, and Alec...

Well, his eyebrows lift. "You're going out?"

I nod. It's my night off, with Alec staying in town all weekend, no work scheduled.

"Where are you going?" Willa's voice is happy, her face beaming. "Do you have a boyfriend?"

That makes me chuckle. "No, I don't. I'm going to my sister's stand-up show."

"Stand-up," Sam repeats. He sits back with a frown similar to the one his father is sporting, but his is one of confusion.

"It's like a comedy show. Like being on stage and telling a bunch of jokes," I explain.

Alec pushes off the couch. "How are you getting there?"

"I'm taking the subway."

"You should have told me. Mac could have driven you."

"Mac works for you," I tell him. "Not for me."

His frown deepens. "Where is the comedy club?"

"The Village."

"What?"

"It's not far," I say. I'm a born and bred New Yorker, the same as him. But I'd bet everything I own that I've ridden the subway infinitely more times than him.

"Tell me you're taking a taxi home," he says. His voice is hushed, but there's a clear demand in it.

I want to roll my eyes. "Maybe. Depends on how late it'll run."

"You're taking a taxi," he says. "I'll reimburse you."

"Is this you talking as my employer?" My voice is just shy of mocking on that last word.

His jaw tenses, and there's a fire flashing in his eyes. Maybe I haven't spoken back to him like this before. But it's been a week since we kissed, since he broke it off and disappeared into his home office, and I'm tired of feeling on edge all the time. Waiting for him to come home, hiding my excitement when he enters a room. It's worn me down.

"Yes," he says testily. "It is."

"Okay then. I'll take a taxi."

He doesn't breathe a sigh of relief. He doesn't breathe at all. Just glances down at my lips with an angry sort of stare, and I know how he's feeling, because I'm feeling it, too.

I leave with quick steps, and the front door shuts behind me with a heavy click.

The subway journey *is* long. The weather when I emerge on the other end isn't great either, dark clouds roll in overhead, and I'm glad I've brought an umbrella. One of my mother's many rules that I rebelled against as a kid. Now I never leave the house without one.

Funny, how we become just like our parents, even when we try our hardest not to.

Elena is nowhere to be found when I arrive at the half-crowded comedy club. It has a neon martini glass sign outside the door and a two-for-one special on Bloody Marys, which has to be the world's least popular cocktail.

"Think they ordered too much celery?" Sebastian asks. He was already here when I arrived, my cute little brother, who isn't so little anymore. His hair is long enough to hang over his eyes, and I brush it away while he chuckles.

"Maybe," I say. "I'm all for saving money, but we're not getting that two-for-one."

He'd grabbed us a table close to the stage. I get us beers, weaving around a group of rowdy college kids goading their friend to take the stage during the open mic portion.

"Where's Ellie?" I ask.

Seb nods toward the restrooms. "Getting ready."

"Nerves?"

"Pretty high," he says and runs a hand through his hair. He's added a new silver ring to the collection on his fingers. "But she'll kill it."

I nod and look around at the crowd. More people have filled the space in just the fifteen minutes I've been here. "Might be a full house tonight."

"Yes, but don't mention that to her," Seb says with a grin. "So your rich asshole boss gave you tonight off?"

"What? He's not an asshole. And I have plenty of evenings off."

Seb rolls his eyes. "Not the vibe you've been giving off in your texts. Seems like he keeps you pretty busy. How awful are the kids? Tell me," he says with obvious relish. "How spoiled are they?"

I open my mouth to reply, but he keeps going. "On a scale of one to ten, where one is Oliver Twist and ten is screaming that their morning lobster is overcooked."

I chuckle. "There's no lobster. And I am kept busy, but they're not particularly spoiled kids. My boss just works a lot."

"Okay, okay. So he's just a simple man of the people. Just one of us, except with a chauffeur and a penthouse apartment." Seb holds up his beer glass with his pinky out. "Maybe he's pro-tax-the-rich, in that rhetorical way plenty of rich people are, where it's actually just a defense mechanism to stave off the 'eat the rich' protests?"

I shake my head. "Are you writing Ellie's material again?"

"Of course not. But I could do stand-up too, right?"

"You'd be great," I say.

My sister joins us, and thankfully the discussion about Alec drops. I understand my brother's joke. We're from an entirely different world than the Connovans. Same city. Different universes. A few years ago, I would have been making similar jokes.

Ellie flops onto the vacant chair. Her bob-cut black hair is a bit teased, just shy of frizzy in a cool way. She's wearing her septum ring and a T-shirt with an old-school pop band printed across it. I think she's wearing it ironically, but it's not always easy to tell with Elena.

"I'm so glad you're here," she tells me with pure sincerity

and grabs Seb's half-drunk beer. She drains it while he looks on in affronted horror.

"Elena," he whines, sounding like he's been gravely injured.

"I need it more than you," she says. She leans back in her chair and looks at me. She has my dad's eyes, almond-shaped and more green than brown. "How did you *do* this? Every night for years?"

"Performing?"

"Yes," she says. "I know my set inside and out, and I still feel like I'm gonna throw up."

I smile at her. "You do it anyway... you live with the feeling because there's nothing else you'd rather do than perform. Even if it means getting stage-fright."

"You're crazy."

"We've always known that, though," Seb says with a crooked smile. "The only person I know whose parents tried to get her to sleep in when you insisted on seven in the morning workouts."

"On Saturdays," Ellie says. "God, you make it easy to hate you."

That makes me laugh. I've missed hanging out with them both, and the gentle—and sometimes not so gentle—ribbing they always know how to deliver. "You're going to do great," I say. "And if you don't... you'll survive that, too. It's okay to fail sometimes."

"You do hear the irony, right?" Ellie asks, her smile widening. In moments like this, she and Seb look so similar, even though they're different in almost every other way. "You have never been okay with failure."

I raise my glass. "Maybe I'm okay with learning."

"Maybe you're okay with giving advice you can't follow," she says, but she touches Seb's empty beer glass to mine. There's only a soft bite to her words, and if anyone knows me, it's the two of them. They've seen the sweat, blood, and tears I poured into ballet.

The sheer number of performances they've sat through. I owe Elena a lifetime supply of butt-in-the-seats if she continues pursuing her dream of comedy.

She goes on after the open mic session. Seb moves his chair closer to mine and we watch with bated breath as Elena comes out on stage.

She looks effortlessly cool, my baby sister. Baggy cargo pants and a tight T-shirt, a nod to the androgynous fashion of the nineties that's so popular now. She's never followed the norm. Gone against everything our parents once planned for us when we were three little children, blank pages ready to be filled. Our father doesn't understand her passion for comedy rather than college, but not once has Elena let that faze her.

Beside me, Sebastian leans in closer. "Ten bucks she brings the house down."

"Twenty bucks she brings down the entire block," I say.

She does.

She's disarmingly funny, in the way that creeps up on you. Sarcastic, and a bit dry and earnest, and she charms the motley crew of people in the club. She jokes about herself, about dating as a queer young woman in New York, and about the norms she loves to challenge. By the end, she gets a roaring applause and wolf whistles from someone in the back.

"I wish Mom and Dad could see this," I whisper to Seb. They're mildly supportive, but it's in a questioning, *Are you really sure?* kind of way. I'm convinced they both think it's a phase.

"Elena probably doesn't," he murmurs back, "considering that joke about vibrators."

I chuckle. "Good point."

I stay longer than I would've in the past. Both my siblings seem delighted when I drink my third beer.

"Who are you," Seb asks at one point, his eyes alight with humor, "and what have you done with our big sister?"

I feel warm and happy, and I've missed them. Missed *us* hanging out together. As adults. When did they become these people? Still young adults, but grown. Not teenagers anymore.

I've always known I missed out on things while in pursuit of my own dream. The price had felt worth it to me, week after week, year after year. But maybe I've never realized just how steep it was.

"She's on sabbatical," I say, and hold up my beer glass in a toast. "Let's see if she ever returns."

It's late when we leave the comedy club. I grab a taxi, just as Alec instructed me to. *Ordered.* He is so bossy. I'd always known that, and not just from Connie's descriptions. Every interaction with him I've ever had, made that perfectly clear. It wafted off him, the scent of power and control. I wonder how many employees are directly under him.

Of which I'm one.

The city passes by outside the car's window, a blur of lights, partygoers, and closed shops. Heading back toward the Upper East Side, the area of New York that has, somehow, in some way, become my home.

The cab is obscenely expensive, and I unfurl my umbrella from the safety of the car. The clouds that had threatened earlier with their shuttering darkness have erupted now, and they're drenching New York in rain.

Alec's building is dark. It's past midnight, and the night concierge is the only one around. I ride up the gold-wrought elevator to the penthouse.

My siblings would never understand, I think. His world. How it works, *why* it works. That the kids aren't spoiled. Maybe materially, but not with time and attention. Alec. They'd never understand Alec or what makes him work the way he does. Act the way he does.

Maybe I don't either. But maybe I want to.

I open the front door to the Connovan penthouse as quietly as I can. The foyer is dark and quiet, and I walk on the balls of my feet to keep my heels from making sharp sounds against the hardwood.

I tiptoe through the living room, turning into my hallway.

"Made it home at last," a voice says.

It startles me. My heels drop back onto the floor with a *thud*, and I turn to face Alec. He rises from the couch. His hands are in the pockets of his navy slacks, and a gray T-shirt stretches across his broad chest.

And he looks angry.

CHAPTER 18
ISABEL

ut the anger on his face doesn't stop his eyes from running up and down my body, too long for it to be only in concern. There's a tenseness in his form. Behind him, a glass of amber-colored drink stands on the coffee table.

The TV isn't on.

"Didn't know I had a curfew," I say. Liquid courage burns in my veins, along with the irritation of last week. Wanting someone who wants you back *sometimes* is the definition of frustrating.

He blows out a breath. "You don't."

"And yet you're awake," I say. "Have you been waiting for me?"

He doesn't answer right away, and a thrill races through me. He has. He really, really has. "Wanted to make sure you got home safe," he says.

"I've lived in New York my whole life. Same as you."

He frowns. "Then you know that things can turn wrong on a dime."

"You could have texted me," I say. "If you were worried."

His eyes narrow, and I know he won't say it. Won't admit

to it. Maybe texting would have been too much capitulation—to his feelings, to his concern. I can see the war reflected in his eyes.

"You took a cab?" he asks.

"Yes. I took a cab." I shrug out of my coat and throw it over the back of an armchair. Then I meet his gaze with my own.

We're standing there, in his living room, in silence. Two people who are well aware of the tension that dances between them, but who won't act on it.

"Isabel," he mutters. "Stop looking at me like that."

"Like what?"

"Like you want me, too. Like you're okay with this."

"What if I do, and I am?" I ask. My heart is galloping. *Want me too*, he said.

Alec shakes his head, slowly, but his eyes don't waver. "You shouldn't be."

"Don't tell me what I should feel."

His eyes spark. "Not even when it's in your best interests?"

"No," I say. Those three beers coupled with a pounding heart make me brave. "Not even then. Alec… Why are you still up?"

"You know why," he says.

My stomach tenses. *Yes, I do.*

"Maybe I just want to hear you say it."

There are a few sweet, tense seconds where the silence between us thickens. When I don't know what he will do or say, if I have pushed it too far, or not far enough.

Alec's hands tighten into fists at his sides, and his shoulders rise and fall as if he's fighting an inner battle. But in the next second, he's closing the distance between us.

He slides his hand beneath my jaw, and gently tips my head up. "I care more than I should."

The words feel like a caress.

"What are you going to do about it?" I whisper.

He shakes his head, a slow, small movement that's weighted with frustration. He lowers his head, his mouth ghosting over mine.

"I don't know, Isabel." He groans, and it sounds like it's pulled out of his soul. "I don't fucking know."

The kiss is slow, at first. It tastes like the burn of alcohol, and I lean into the length of his body. I want to learn it properly. Feel it pressed to mine, against me. On top of me.

"Sweetheart," he mutters against my lips. The word sends a shiver of warmth down my spine. "Tell me to stop."

I slide my hand into his hair. "No."

He groans and kisses down my jaw, my neck, his hand tilting my head for better access. His lips on my delicate skin, and his other hand gliding down to my waist.

The kiss scalds.

I melt into his arms, loving the feel of them around me. His body is intoxicating. Tall and strong, but it's a strength that comes from a life lived, from experiences, from the hurts and the victories, rather than the sculpted muscles of dancers I've known in my past.

And then it's over, as abruptly as it began. Alec takes a step back and stares at me like I'm his worst nightmare come to life.

"No," he says, shaking his head. "No. I can't do this to you."

He turns and walks away. But not toward his bedroom. No, he walks to the patio door and wrenches it open. The rain pelts against the terrace, the heavens letting loose, but he steps out into the storm.

"Alec," I say. "Alec!"

He stops in the middle of the patio. Eyes closed, water sluicing down his face.

"What the hell are you thinking?"

But there's no response. The city glitters around him, and,

in the distance, I can hear the sound of a wailing siren. I walk outside, into the rain, and grip his arm.

He looks down at me, his eyes widening. Like he can't believe I followed him out here. My lips still burn from his kiss, and I'm angry, frustrated, and tipsy.

I can't do this to *you,* he'd said. Don't *I* get a say?

"What if I told you to stop holding back." My hand on his wrist tightens. "To stop denying what you want."

His eyes look almost black. "You don't want me to do that."

"Don't tell me what I want," I say. "Because I want you."

Alec's jaw clenches, like that wasn't what he wanted to hear. But then, his brows lower and his chin drops. "You're sure."

A statement. Not a question.

But I nod anyway.

The rain rushing down his face makes him look like a stranger. Someone I know, and yet someone entirely new. Maybe it's another facet of the real him. The man who isn't perfectly in control.

The man who burns inside.

He tugs open the patio door, pulling us both back inside. "You're cold," he mutters and wraps his arms around my waist. They slide down to my thighs, and he lifts me. Carries me across the living room and into his bedroom, the place I've been to only with his children.

He pushes the door shut. Locks it with his free hand, and that sound, the promise of privacy, moves through me like a warm caress.

He kisses me. Warm, steady, determined kisses, until I no longer feel the dampness of my clothes or the hair clinging to my skin.

But he can. His fingers glide over my hair, and he pulls back with a frown. "You're wet."

That makes me chuckle. "Yes. *Someone* decided to go out into the rain."

He carries me to his large bathroom and sets me down on the marble counter. A second later he's pushing a towel into my hands. But he's also kissing me, his lips on mine, like he can't stop now that he's started. The kiss is slow, too. Deliciously slow. It's hard to think about anything else.

The towel falls to the floor.

He makes a tutting sound. "Dry yourself, sweetheart."

"I like being wet," I murmur.

There's a brief pause, and then I feel his smile against my cheek. His hands dig into my hips. "Maybe I should check," he says.

His hand slides over my thigh, up to the zipper of my high-waisted jeans. The sound of it being tugged down echoes through the bathroom. In the next breath, I feel his fingers, brushing against the skin of my lower stomach.

His mouth is by my ear. "Talk to me."

I wrap my hands around his neck and lift myself off the counter. My own voice is a whisper. "Pull down my jeans?"

Alec groans against my neck. His hands grip the waistband, and he tugs, wrenching the denims down to my knees. They lock me in place, and him between my legs, his hand stroking over the cotton of my panties.

His forehead rests against mine, and I'm not sure which one of us is breathing heaviest. He's looking down at me.

At his hand *on* me.

His lips brush over mine, and then his fingers find the edge of my panties. He pulls them aside with wan fingers, and I gasp at the first stroke of skin on skin.

He groans. "Fuck. You *are* wet."

"Told you," I purr.

"Mm-hmm." He looks down, at his fingers moving over my sensitive skin. "Isabel... let me taste you."

My breaths are coming fast. I don't know what to say, or how to respond. *Yes.* But I also want him to keep doing this while holding on to me. It's not like guys going down on me did a ton in the past, and this, him holding me like this… it's amazing.

"Sweetheart, I *need* to go down on you," he says. There's agony laced through his words. His fingers stroke, up and down, and they make it hard to think straight. My nerve endings feel exposed.

"Okay," I whisper.

Alec doesn't dive straight in. He doesn't even acknowledge my answer for a long few seconds, his fingers keep moving, familiarizing with the shape of me.

I haven't been touched in so long.

He kisses me and then mutters against my lips. "Thank God."

His fingers do nothing but tease. Touch. Stroke. No circling and no entering, and maybe that's good, maybe that's foreplay, even if my body feels ready for more. Much faster than I expected I would.

He kisses my collarbone. My chest. He drops to his knees, right there on the bathroom floor, and then he just stops moving altogether. His eyes are locked on the spot between my legs, my panties still pulled to the side.

I feel bare.

"You're perfect," he says. His voice is husky, and the hands brushing up my thighs, spreading me wider against the cage of my jeans, are rough. "So perfect, it hurts to look at. I've been in pain since you moved in, but I wouldn't stop this ache for anything."

I can't breathe.

I bury my hand in his hair and let the words wash over me, through me, doing the same things as his touch.

He kisses the inside of my knee before gripping the fabric of my panties. "Lift yourself again."

I do and, a few seconds later, I'm completely bare. Well,

I'm still wearing my top, my boots, my jeans… even if the latter are down around my calves now.

Alec presses a hand to my lower stomach and leans in. The first touch of his lips against my heated skin makes me sigh. *Oh.* He's teasing, and insistent, and uses his lips the same way he'd used his fingers. To familiarize himself with me.

I look down at his thick hair, strong forehead, closed eyes… his head between my thighs. The image sends another pulse of need through me.

I can't believe Alec is doing this. I can't believe it's him I'm hearing, his groans against my pussy.

"You're perfect," he mutters. His tongue joins the action, and I lean back against the mirror, trying to relax. *Holy shit.* It feels so different than it has before. He's hot and relentless against my clit, and in between licks, he does these little sucking motions like he wants me in his mouth. "So fucking perfect. Always knew you'd be."

I close my eyes and surrender to the sizzling pleasure coursing through my body.

"You've been thinking about this?" I ask. It comes out breathy.

His left hand presses on my lower stomach, forcing me to lean back and give him better access. "Yes," he says. He locks his lips around my clit and oh. *Wow.* This is good, it's good, maybe even good enough that I can come if he keeps doing this, and that makes me feel out of control.

It also makes me feel powerful.

"Isa," he says, using the nickname I've always been called by my family. The one Sam recently started using. But Alec's voice is husky, his warm breath ghosting over my swollen flesh. "Tell me what you like."

"Um, this."

His fingers caress up my inner thigh, and his mouth speeds up. A groan escapes him. "Finger inside at the same time?" he asks, and something about his deep, familiar voice asking me, makes a fierce blush break out on my cheeks.

I've had sex before. Of course I have. Even *consistently*. Although, that was only for the six months I had a boyfriend in my early twenties.

But we never talked during sex like this. Never gave words to actions, never articulated our desires. It was all about interpreting signals and hinting at what felt good, pleasing and performing, and it was nice, very nice, but *this* doesn't feel nice at all. *This* feels so much more than nice.

Alec looks up at me. His eyes are dark, and there's fire burning in them. "Sweetheart, tell me what you need to come. Tell me what you like."

I'm breathing fast and shallow. "What you're doing," I whisper. "If you're not getting tired."

His lips tip into a smile. "Tired? I'm not that old, and even if I were, this pussy would raise me from the dead. I'll do what I've been doing, but you tell me if what you want changes."

"Mm-hmm. Yes," I say. It's uncomfortable, sitting here with the lights on and my legs spread, and him kneeling right between them while having a *conversation*. Even if hearing him say those words makes the muscles in my stomach clench.

Alec kisses my upper thigh. Returns to the spot between my legs, and this time, it's with the intensity he applies to everything in his life. I grip his hair again and focus on breathing, because he knows what he's doing, and he's flicking his tongue, and his large hands are spread over my hips, thumbs pushing against the top of my slit.

It's too much. Energy courses beneath my skin, and it needs to release somehow, or I'll explode, or maybe that's exactly what I need. My fingers tighten in his hair. I'm about to push him away because it's too much when the orgasm barrels through me.

It robs me of my breath. My thighs tighten around his face, and he licks me through it, finishing with a few soft kisses. I slump back against the mirror.

"I didn't know that could happen," I murmur.

He grins. I wonder if that's the first grin I've ever seen on him, and that smile makes him look gloriously alive. "I did."

He kisses my inner thigh again, and I grip his shoulders, trying to pull him up to me. He stands, but it isn't to kiss me. No, he helps me off the counter and runs his palms down my arms.

My heart is still beating at lightspeed. It's not fair that he's fully dressed. I want more. I want it so badly. And it's so close, he's so close. I want to feel his bare skin on me, and more of his kisses.

My hands grip the fabric of his shirt. He lets me pull him down for a kiss. One turns into two, and two into seven, until we're making out in the bathroom. He's hard against me, and my whole body zeroes in on that bulge, and the possibility of *more.*

But he doesn't do anything more. Just keeps kissing me, his hands on my waist and ass, groaning every now and then.

"Alec," I finally say.

He rests his forehead against mine. His skin is flushed. "Yes."

I squirm against him. "I'm ready for more."

"More what?"

His eyes hold a hint of amusement, and I narrow my own at him. "Don't you want to sleep with me?" I ask.

Alec's half-huffed chuckle is hoarse. He pulls my hand tight between our bodies, right against the hard length of his cock. Even trapped behind the fly of his slacks, it's impressive.

"Pretty obvious what I want," he says gravelly. "I've wanted you for much longer than I should've, and the things I've imagined… Isa, I need to have you. I think I might die if I don't. But I won't until you can tell me the same thing without blushing."

My mouth drops open. "What?"

"I want you to tell me what you like." He leans in, his mouth by my ear. "How you want me to touch you. The way you like to be fucked. I need your words, sweetheart, and I haven't heard them tonight."

"That's not fair," I say. My voice is high with shock.

He chuckles and slides a finger down my cheek. "Maybe not. But I'm not fair, and I've never claimed to be. What I am, is thorough."

"You're backing out again."

His hand around my wrist tightens, pulling my palm flat against his erection, like it's proof. "No," he says. "I'm giving you a task. Next time, I want you to show me how you like to be touched."

My eyes widen. "What?"

He tugs my hand up, dragging it over his chest before he lays it flat against his neck. There's a wicked smile dancing at the corner of his lips. "You've said that twice already. We're not doing this until you can talk to me about sex."

"I can talk about sex."

"Can you?" He lowers his head, his lips brushing over mine. "What positions do you like? What makes you come the hardest?"

I stare at his eyes, so close they're almost blurry, and my mind blanks. Positions. With him. It sends a shiver down my back, and an answer leaps to my tongue, but it's a mortifying one. I don't usually come during sex. It's before, or maybe after, and *sometimes* during. Rarely.

He kisses me. It derails my thinking further, and I wrap my arms around his neck. But he lifts his head far too soon.

I hate that he's right.

He releases me and I sway lightly on my feet. Alec pulls up my jeans, and there's gentleness in his hands that's at odds with the tense lines on his face. Through the fabric of his pants, I can still make him out. He looks huge and straining.

"What about you?" I ask.

He raises an eyebrow. "What about me...?"

There's a clear taunt in the question. Like he knows I won't use the words, won't rephrase the question. Won't be able to go there.

I meet his gaze with my own and ignore the nerves swirling in my stomach. "What about your orgasm?"

He runs a hand along his jaw, and his gaze narrows. "I'll do what I've been doing every night since you moved in."

"Oh," I breathe. The desire to see it sweeps through me and I try to picture it, but I can't. Alec Connovan losing control.

Alec Connovan pleasuring himself.

He looks at me like he can see that desire and more, but he's true to his word. Until I say it out loud, he won't go there. It's a line I never expected him to draw. So far I've never needed to be too much of an "active" participant. Sex was something I did *and* something that happened to me, and I was fine with that. I could just go with the flow.

But just a taste of being with Alec, and I know I want more than that.

"Go," he says and nods toward the locked door of his bedroom. "Or I'll be tempted to break my own rules."

I back up toward the door. He looks tortured, standing in the doorway to his en suite. His eyes locked on mine, and his hands clenched at his sides.

"Think of me," I say.

He reaches down, gripping himself over his slacks. The sight makes my heart constrict.

"I always do," he says.

CHAPTER 19
ISABEL

I'm next to Willa in the grand auditorium at St. Regis. She's standing closer to me than she usually does, looking adorable with her hair twisted into braids. I'd done it up for her just half an hour ago in the girls' changing room.

On stage, a child is playing a pretty decent rendition of Beethoven's "Für Elise." Much better than anything I'm capable of.

"Has he texted you?" she demands.

I look at my phone again, but there's no new text from Alec. "No. He must still be struck in traffic."

Her eyebrows are drawn down low, and there's such an adult expression of disappointment on her face. But also a shard of something else in her eyes. She's sad.

My heart breaks.

"I know he really wants to be here," I say. "Do you want me to ask the director if we can switch the order? So you play last?"

She shakes her head. "We're going by grades. I can't switch."

"Oh."

Her arms cross over her chest, and for a horrible second, I see her lower lip start to quiver. We're only minutes away from her onstage performance.

"He has to be here," she mutters.

I have a terrible suspicion that she won't go on stage unless he is. Shit.

I crouch down next to her. "Hey," I say. "I'll record the whole thing, you know that, right? If your dad doesn't make it, he'll still see it all later. We can watch it on the TV with you, and Sammy, and Katja. We can even invite Mac. Pop some popcorn."

Her eyes light up for a moment before they narrow. "It's because of you," she says. There's sharp anger in her voice. "It's *your* fault that he isn't here!"

I sigh. "I'm sorry, but it's not. It's traffic."

And it's his *fault,* I think. She's angry, but she's not the only one. He should have been here by now. I had triple-checked that the times for the piano recital were communicated to his assistant. Willa talked about it all week.

He knew.

Yet he still isn't here.

Willa turns away from me with her arms still crossed, and I want to hug her. She looks so small in her pretty dress and braided hair, and her furious expression.

I understand her.

So while she might not want to hear from me, I have to say it anyway. "Good luck," I say. "You go out there, and you just focus on the piano. Not the crowd. Just do your best and let the music take you away."

Maybe it's not the advice you give a kid, but it's what worked for me night after night after night for years. Focus on the music and on the steps.

Nothing else mattered.

Willa doesn't reply. Seconds later, her name is called, and she walks out on stage with her little head held high. I'm so used to just seeing her next to Sam, as the big sister, that I've forgotten how young she really is.

I hurry back to the seats in the front row reserved for the parents of the performers. There's an empty chair beside mine. I've draped my jacket over the back, saving it for him.

I text him again. **First row to the right. Willa's performance is starting now. Get here.**

Then I hit record and watch Willa.

He arrives halfway through.

I'm aware of it, even though I don't turn my head to look in his direction. A thick thigh presses against mine, and I catch the scent of him, of the coffee and rain that clings to his wool coat.

Willa is sitting ramrod straight on the piano bench, halfway through her concerto. She's playing well. There are a few minor stumbles, but I only pick up on them because I've been listening while she practiced. I doubt the rest of the attendants notice.

Alec's holding a bouquet of roses.

A bit of my anger drains away.

It's obvious when Willa spots her dad in the audience. She peeks at me in the front row and then right at him, and her face lights up. A big smile spreads across her lips.

In my peripheral vision, I see Alec nod at her.

God, these kids want their father's approval so badly. It's never been clearer to me than right now.

And it's never made me angrier that he doesn't see it.

After the show, Willa comes bouncing down the stairs to Alec. "You came!"

"I did. I'm very sorry I was late, honey." He puts an arm around her and hands her the roses. "Flowers for you."

She looks up at him. "Really?"

"Yes. A time-honored tradition," he says. "I bet Isabel got loads after performances, too."

She glances at me, a quick look before refocusing on her dad. "What did you think?"

"You played really well. Your practicing has clearly paid off," he says.

The compliment washes over her, and all the traces of her previous annoyance are gone. She looks radiant.

But I'm still fuming when we arrive home. The anger has warped into something sharper. My family was at every single one of my performances before they became so commonplace that it made attendance impossible. All four of them, Mom, Dad, Elena, and Seb. There wasn't money for flowers all the time, but my mom would always bring my favorite chocolate. But Alec couldn't make it to his daughter's recital without being late.

Katja cooked Willa's favorite dinner. And once the kids are fed and bathed, Alec puts them to bed. It's usually a good night when he's home in time to do it. Sam is first, and Willa's later. Thirty minutes of reading a story, and then lights out.

Unless he's gone, which he is fairly often, out to dinners with investors or to company events.

The apartment is quiet as I wait for him to finish with the kids. I make myself a cup of tea and sit by the large kitchen counter, sipping the too-hot liquid. Frustration makes it hard to relax. He's a good dad, but I feel like there are things he doesn't notice. Opportunities he doesn't take.

I hear his footsteps before I see him, walking in from the kids' hallway. He stops when he spots me.

"Hey," he says.

I put down my mug. "Hi."

"Had a good day?"

"Yes," I say and take a deep breath. "But the piano recital was challenging."

His eyebrows lower. "How so?"

"Willa was really upset that you weren't there on time."

"She was?"

"Yes," I say. Upset might even be an understatement, and as I think back on her sad expression, my voice hardens. "No nanny in the world is going to be a stand-in for a parent."

His own expression harshens, all openness swept away. "I know that."

"Then you should start acting like it."

"I work," he says. "And I do it *for* them."

"Yeah, but they don't know that, and they won't remember that. What they will remember is your absence." I cross my arms over my chest. "But I can understand that part. What I don't understand is the lack of... Look, why does Willa have to play the piano?"

"What?"

"Why the piano?" I ask. "She doesn't like her lessons."

"I'm aware." His voice lowers, and I know I'm on shaky territory. "But she will enjoy it later on. Learning a skill isn't always fun. You probably know that better than me."

"I do, but I *wanted* to learn ballet. Does she want to learn the piano?"

"She will. I played the piano for fourteen years growing up," he says. "I know it's not always fun."

My eyebrows rise. "You did? Does Willa know that?"

"She knows I used to play."

"Then *you* teach her. At least practice with her every now and then! Make her understand why it's fun and why it matters. She wants your attention and your time *so badly*, and most of all she wants your approval."

Alec's eyes narrow. "My approval," he repeats.

"Yes. You mean well," I say. "I know that, I've *seen* that, but they don't need Contron to go from the forty-eighth biggest company in the country to the forty-fifth or something. They need to make core memories with you instead."

"Fifty-third," he mutters. But he runs a hand over his nape, face still set in hard lines.

"I don't mean to overstep, and truthfully, I already have…

but I've heard from Connie about how you guys were raised. I know it wasn't always hands-on, at least not after your mother died. I don't think you should do what your dad did."

He just stares at me.

I stare back, and I know I'm about to get fired. What happened between us the other night will never happen again. And maybe that's why I'm so frustrated, because he drew the boundary and gave me a task I don't know if I can rise to.

I lean against the counter. "That's it. That's all I wanted to say, and... I get that it might have been hard to hear."

Understatement.

He runs a hand over his jaw. It's clenched tight. "Well, you obviously don't have a problem communicating clearly with me when you're angry."

My eyebrows rise. "*That's* what you're thinking about right now?"

He crosses his arms over his chest. "It's easier to focus on than the comments about me being a bad father."

"That's not what I said."

"Yes," he mutters. "It was. Look, I already know that I'm not enough. That I can't be everywhere, do everything, and make everyone happy. That's not as big a revelation as you seem to think it is."

"That's not what I meant." I shake my head, struggling to find the right words. A way to express it. "They need you *present*, too. Emotionally present. Willa needs you to validate her—"

"You've been with us for a little over a month," he says. His voice is sharp, his face drawn. "I've known them their entire lives."

"That's why she doesn't like nannies!" I say. "Because she thinks we take you away from her."

"That's ridiculous."

"It's kid logic," I say. "And you have *kids*, so their logic matters."

He glares at me. I stare back at him, and the air between us draws tight. I don't know what to say. What to add. And it doesn't seem like he knows, either.

But then something softens around his eyes, and he looks tired rather than angry. "Seems like I can never feel enough of it," he says.

"Enough of what?"

"The guilt." He runs a hand over his face, and his voice turns dry. "I can't have this conversation right now. Not while I'm fighting—"

A door creaks open. Light patter of little feet out into the kitchen, and we both turn to Sam arriving at the threshold. He's in his superhero pajamas.

He blinks at the light. "Daddy?"

Alec's face goes blank, returns to the stoic expression I'm used to seeing. "I'm here," he says and bends to pick up his youngest child. "What happened?"

Sam rests his head against Alec's shoulder with the droopy flop that only kids are capable of. "Can I sleep in your bed tonight?"

"Yes. Come, let's go."

They retreat down the hall without another word. I'm not even sure Sam saw me, and Alec doesn't turn around.

It takes a long time for my heartbeat to calm down.

CHAPTER 20
ISABEL

Working out usually saves me. It gets the body moving in a way that quiets the mind, and makes my overthinking halt. But it's not happening today.

I lie on my back, doing a hip bridge, and stare up at the recessed ceiling lights. Alec's home gym is…

Impressive is an understatement.

Each piece of equipment here is state-of-the-art. The selection of weights impeccable. The air conditioning is unrivaled.

I should have used it before.

The physiotherapist, the one Alec had insisted on, had laid out a rehabilitation program for me to strengthen the muscles around my hip. *No intense movements. No ballet.*

Five to six months.

Not surprising. I'd known it for weeks already, for months, so hearing the proclamation out loud didn't hurt as much this time because what I'd feared to lose had already happened.

I miss the scent of pine resin and the dusty dance studios. I miss the sound of applause and the orchestra. The coordinated movements on the stage, like flowing water, rippling and crashing. I miss the adrenaline after a finished performance, when all the dancers collapse into the dressing rooms, panting and giddy with another night done.

I miss feeling like I'm good at what I do.

I miss the high of pushing myself to do better.

Five to six months. Maybe I *could* come back. Not the New York Ballet Company. That dream feels too dangerous to hope for. But maybe to another company. Maybe… there's still hope. A faint, thin thread of it, but it's there. I can't do *this* job forever. And judging by what happened last night, I might not be doing it much longer at all.

Sleeping had been hard. I replayed my own words and heard how harsh they sounded, and still… the larger part of me didn't regret them. I understand that he's in a tough position. That the company is important to him. But that doesn't mean he can't acknowledge his kids' feelings more often.

And to be fair, the wealth Alec and Connie have… he doesn't *have* to work. I understand the compulsion, but it's not a necessity. And his kids will know that soon enough, too.

I don't know the last time someone spoke up around him. Told him something that wasn't positive, or encroaching on the carefully maintained walls he had erected around his life.

I have a sinking suspicion that it's not something he tolerates.

I shift onto my side and start the leg raises, using a resistance band. The movement is as familiar as breathing. I had an old teacher who would make us do these until we collapsed, our muscles quivering. The first person who stopped was always punished.

That teacher wasn't particularly well-liked.

If I were to teach… how would I do it? Because Alec was right. Learning a skill isn't always fun, but that's not why we do it. If the only thing we chase in life is brief dopamine hits, we'll never achieve anything worthwhile. But there has to be a middle ground somewhere.

The door to the gym opens.

I startle, my leg lowering. It's Alec.

He's in his workout shorts and a T-shirt. There's a towel slung over his shoulder and an earbud in his left ear. There's so much of him I've never seen before. Strong, thick forearms and biceps. Long legs and muscular calves.

His expression tightens when he sees me. He takes out his earbud. "Hey."

I sit up. "Hi."

"Okay if I join?"

"Yeah, of course. It's your gym," I say.

He nods. Looks like he's about to say something else, but heads to the treadmill instead. Turns it on. It puts him right across from me, and I don't know what to do with my hands or my feet. I try to lie back and focus on the exercise I'm doing, but it's hard to think of anything but Alec in the room.

He starts walking at a brisk pace.

I technically have more reps and three more exercises left to complete, but any tranquility from my workout is gone in an instant. I grab my water bottle and take a long sip instead.

The bare skin of my arms and legs tingles. Is he watching me? I don't dare look over to see if it's true.

"You recorded yesterday," he says. "Willa's performance."

I nod, then look at him anyway. "Yes. I'll send it to you later today."

He is watching me. "I was late because of traffic."

"Yeah. I understand," I say.

"But that's not an excuse. It's New York. There's always traffic, and I should have factored that in."

My eyes widen. "Yes, that… yeah."

"What you said, about Willa seeking my… approval. You really meant that?"

I nod again. "God, yes. She loves you very much. Idolizes you, really."

He looks like he doesn't know what to do with that. But he

doesn't look away from me either, and there's a small crack in the composed facade.

"You don't need to make big changes," I say. "You're a great dad. But... maybe a few more core memories. Practice piano with her sometimes. Let her watch *you* play. Take a trip to Disneyland, tell them you're proud of them and that you love them. Do a few things like that... and they'll be golden. You have great kids."

He looks away, out the window of his apartment. At the city that is just starting to wake. "Yeah. They sure are."

I clear my throat. "Maybe I should apologize for telling you all of that last night, though? I know it wasn't my place. Didn't mean to imply that you're a bad dad. You're not."

There's a beep as he turns off the treadmill. "Never apologize."

"Never?"

He comes to stand at the edge of my workout mat and holds out a hand. I grab it, letting him pull me to my feet.

He doesn't let go of me once I'm standing. "Never," he repeats. "I liked you expressing your opinions."

"Do you usually like it when employees do that?" I ask. His hand is warm around mine.

A smile plays at the corner of his lips, and he tips my head back. "When they're useful opinions."

"I can stop," I say.

"I don't want you to. No one has spoken back to me like that in years. Keep speaking your mind. Tell me when I'm wrong, and shout at me if I mess up. I can take it," Alec says. "You're my equal."

"I'm your kids' nanny and your employee," I say. "Equal isn't even *close*."

"Fuck that. That's just a job. That belongs to the world out there." He nods to the gym door, shut behind us. "It holds no weight here, not between us, and not if we're going to do this."

"If we're going to do this," I repeat softly. "You mean…?"

"Yes, that's what I mean. I need you to talk to me freely if we're going to sleep together. *When* we sleep together."

Speaking the words, here in the bright light of day, with New York City outside the window and the ceiling light on… sends a flush to my cheeks.

"Why are you so insistent on that?" I ask. "It's never been a problem for me before."

His eyes narrow. "To communicate with the man you're sleeping with? Or to proceed with no communication at all?"

"The latter. I know what I want," I say and rise onto my tiptoes. "I can *show* you."

Alec's eyes dip down to my lips, and then further down to my workout tank top and shorts. The air between us thickens.

"Can you," he murmurs. It's less a question and more of a statement.

"Was the only reason you stopped the other night because you thought I wouldn't be able to tell you what I like?"

"Yes," he says. But then he leans closer, his breath ghosting over mine. "And I didn't have any condoms."

Oh.

A strange sort of relief rushes over me. He doesn't sleep with women regularly then, if he doesn't keep condoms on hand.

I brush my lips over his, just barely, and revel in him turning to stone. "Do you have some now?"

He kisses me. It's a slow promise of what's to come, and soothing after last night's argument. "Yes," he says. "I had to ask Mac to idle outside a convenience store. He probably thought I'd lost my mind."

I chuckle and grip his bare arms. The muscles beneath my fingers are solid, the skin warm to the touch. He's so different from anyone I've ever been with. So much *more* somehow, in every way. Taller, broader, older, stronger, more competent. I have a feeling he doesn't forget anything, and that whatever I might say, he will hear. Not just listen to.

I trust him, I realize.

"Isabel," he mutters. He glides his hands down the sides of my body, fingers just barely touching the outer curves of my tits and waist. They land on my hips and pull me closer. "What do you want to do next?"

I wet my lips. "Right now?"

There's a smile in his voice. "Well, I only have minutes until I need to wake the kids up, so no. But between us. When do you want me? And how?"

The questions, asked in his deep, hoarse voice, make my head spin. Somehow, I thought he'd take charge. I *wanted* him to. Wanted to fall into his arms and let him sweep me away.

But I don't say that. It feels…

Well.

Vulnerable, I suppose. To say those kinds of things out loud.

"Still shy?" His hand slides down my thigh, grabbing the back of my knee. He pulls it up and wraps it around his hip. "Maybe you can read some of those books of yours. Get some inspiration. Use their language."

That makes my cheeks heat even further. *If he only knew.*

But the way he looks at me makes me think he does.

"What do you want to do next?" I murmur.

He shakes his head, but there's a slow smile spreading over his lips. It makes everything inside of me tighten. "Sweetheart, every filthy thing there is. I want to make you come against my tongue again. I want to spend a night seeing how many condoms we can go through. I want you naked, pleasure-drunk, and tired in my bed." He kisses me again, and it's slow and deep. "But most of all, I want to learn every single way to give you an orgasm, so I can do it over and over again."

It's hard to breathe. Harder still to speak.

"That sounds good." I lock my hands around his neck and kiss him. It's starting to feel familiar, the strength of him moving against me and the rhythm of our kisses. It's easy to lose myself in it all, in him, in the warmth.

My head starts to spin when he slides his tongue over my lower lip. *I can* show *you*, I think and wiggle my hand into the narrow space between our bodies. My heart is pounding out of my chest, but I do it anyway. I run my fingers over his length, trapped behind the fabric of his workout shorts.

He's already half-hard.

Alec drops his forehead to mine with a groan. "Shit," he says.

I stroke him again and feel his cock pulse beneath my fingers. He really does seem big, and apprehension mingles with excitement.

"Fuck. Stop, sweetheart. We don't have the time." But he groans again when I grip him over his shorts, and doesn't make a move to stop me. "I hate that I have plans tonight."

"You're big," I say.

He swallows. "Never compared it to anyone else's. Fuck, Isa, I can't take it. Not when I can't take my time with you." He steps back, a pained expression on his face, and rearranges himself.

That makes me smile. "Payback," I say. "If you're giving me 'a task,' the least I can do is make you hurt a little in return."

He runs a hand over his neck. Something about the gesture makes him look younger. More alive, somehow, and I wish we didn't have work to do today. I wish I could do what he's asking, and show him what I want.

And maybe… maybe I can.

Because *he's* working. But I have hours of free time before I need to pick up the kids, and I've never been one to skimp on an assignment. I'm an overachiever.

"Trust me, I am in pain," he says. "But I'm used to it by now."

CHAPTER 21
ALEC

The music is loud but bearable. The noise from the wall-mounted TV is another matter. There's a deafening roar as England scores, and, despite myself, I can't look away.

"Guys," Connie says. My sister's voice is annoyed. "Why did we have to meet *here*?"

"The game," Nate says. My younger brother is back from London for a few days, and Connie had let it slip that they were meeting up for dinner.

I invited myself along.

She was surprised when I said it. She'd hidden it fast, but I saw the flash of it nevertheless. I haven't been around much for the last few years. Can't remember the last time we did this, met up just the three of us.

Seems like I should be better in all kinds of ways, lately.

"Since when are you a soccer fan?" Connie asks.

"Since I moved to England."

"Living over there has completely warped your senses," I say.

"Enhanced," he says. "Perfected. And I work with Brits,

you know. Every single day in our London office. It's a good strategy to care about their interests."

I shake my head at him. He just grins back, the picture of nonchalance. He's always been that way. Everything just runs off him, like water off the back of a duck. As kids, we were always joined at the hip. Only two years apart, we'd competed about everything. Competed and fought and argued until we got old enough to leave all that behind and start working together instead.

"I'm going to have to recall you soon," I tell him, "or we'll lose you to the dark side entirely. Your home is New York."

"Yes, sir," he says.

Connie's eyes narrow. "You're not seriously thinking of staying over there, are you?"

"Con," he says, "you know I don't think further than two months in advance."

That makes me scoff. "You're the head of our European strategy, so you better."

They both chuckle at that. I grab another sip of my beer and watch their ease with one another. It's been a while since we all laughed together. For years, our interactions have been about work. Logistics. Dad. Holidays and expansion plans.

"Are you seeing anyone over there?" Connie asks.

"Again, you know me," Nate says easily.

"So that's a yes."

I clear my throat. "I think that's actually a no. Isn't it, Nate?"

His gaze darts to me for a second before he shrugs. "You keep me busy with work," he says and deflects to Connie. "So, where's your traitorous husband tonight?"

Connie rolls her eyes. "You know, because it's you, I can handle that comment. I know you don't really mean it. He's in Boston for a conference."

"Taking notes for both companies?" Nate asks.

"No." She turns to me across the table and her smile sobers. "You know we don't discuss business at home."

"I know," I say. But I can't help my frown. Is she saying she couldn't have handled that comment from *me*?

"He's not that bad, you know," Nate tells me. "When you get to know him. I *almost* think he's good enough for Con."

"Almost," I repeat. "I didn't know you two hung out."

"Not really," Nate says with another shrug. "I was actually surprised that *you* joined us tonight."

"Yeah. Not every day my brother's home from London," I say and twist my beer bottle around. It's cold from the frothy liquid and somewhere in the sports bar another cheer rises up.

I don't know when I was in a bar like this last. There had been times in college. The first few years back in the city after college, when I was just a junior marketing executive at Contron. My first year with Victoria.

Somewhere down the road, evenings like this had been filtered out, lost to memories of youth and free time. Being here means not working *or* being with my kids. It's hard to justify that price.

"How's Dad?" Nate asks.

Both of them look at me like I hold all the answers to that question. In a way, I suppose I always have. Dad calls me several times a week with opinions, thoughts, and advice on Contron. Things he's read in the papers or heard on the golf course. Ways to intercept and interfere.

I clear my throat. "Good. I think he's in Palm Beach this week. Told him you were back in New York for the weekend. He wanted to join, but…"

"But he didn't," Nate says with an easy smile. "Probably didn't want to miss his tee time."

"He's talking about starting a new company."

"What?" Connie asks. "He is?"

"Yeah. Something about golf caddies… I don't think it'll

go anywhere," I say with a wave of my hand. "It's a hobby project to fill his days."

"He might need that, so he stops bothering you," she says.

"Yeah. When was the last time you spoke with him?" I ask.

She cocks her head. "I think... three weeks ago now, give or take. Right before the wedding party that he didn't bother attending."

"I'm sorry he did that," I say.

Connie shakes her head. "Don't. He's his own person," she says. "Eventually, he'll realize that me marrying a Thompson doesn't mean I'm a traitor to our business... or he won't. And that'll have to be okay."

Nate nods into his beer like they've had this conversation before.

I frown at her. "He'll accept it."

"Will he?" she asks dryly. "Maybe, but if he's expecting me to come crawling with an apology, I won't. I'll never apologize for falling in love with Gabriel."

That's exactly what he's hoping for. I stare at her, my baby sister. She's always been so young. Born when I was already eleven, when my voice was breaking and my body shooting up in height. She'd been tiny in my arms when Mom let me hold her the first time.

She's not little anymore, not with that statement.

"You shouldn't," I say. "You're doing a great job at the Foundation, by the way. Maybe I haven't said that."

She blinks at me. "Thank you. I'm enjoying the work."

"It shows."

Silence descends on our table, a bit stilted, and a bit awkward. I take a long pull of my beer and look back at the TV screen. She is my baby sister... and yet, Isabel is even younger than her. Only a few years, but still.

Fifteen years.

Another wave of guilt washes over me. I shouldn't want

Isabel the way I do. Even if she's a fully grown woman, even if I've never known her as anything but. Even if it doesn't feel wrong when she's in my arms.

I doubt others will see it that way.

Connie definitely wouldn't. The guilt intensifies, knowing she sent Isabel in my direction with a belief that she can trust me with her friend. To give Isabel a job and a place to stay.

Not to argue with her. Not to kiss her. And definitely not to sleep with her.

"So who are you meeting after?" Connie asks Nate.

He grins. "Are you implying I double-booked tonight? I would never."

"Except that you have. Right? You're only in town for a few days."

"Yeah. I'm meeting Dean later."

Connie frowns. I get her reaction. Nate's college buddy isn't someone I've particularly liked, at least not in our few interactions. He's brash in a way that grates.

Nate chuckles. "Yeah, I know. But he's better."

"He met someone, didn't he?" Connie asks. "Maybe she's helping him learn to tone it down a bit."

Nate looks down into his glass and shrugs a bit too casually. "Harper. She's coming tonight, too."

"Poor girl," my sister says and nudges Nate. "I mean, I get that Dean is a catch and all, but I would've needed to knock him down a few pegs if I were her."

Nate gives her a crooked smile. It doesn't look like it reaches his eyes. "Yeah. She's... great."

"That kinda reminds me... I've been thinking lately," Connie says, "how was Dad before Mom died? Did she change him?"

I look back at her. Nate is looking at her, too, but she just gazes serenely back at us. "Come on, guys," she says. "It's not that weird of a question. I've asked about *her* a ton, but I realized, I've never asked about him. I've only known him as a widower."

Nate runs a hand through his hair. "Well, he was… at work all the time. Contron was in a big expansion phase at the time. It was gaining ground in the Canadian—"

"Not the company. Dad. How was he at home, with you two?"

The question stings. It shouldn't, but it does, on the heels of what Isabel had told me yesterday.

Nate looks at me. I look back at him. It's not a time we've spoken about a lot, either. And it was almost three decades ago.

"Mom was the one who was present," I say quietly. "She went to every game, every school event. Dad came sometimes."

Nate nods, but he looks thoughtful. "Dad was more fun, though. He was definitely not such a hardass when Mom was around. We used to go on trips as a family. It was different, yeah. He was different. I don't know if he's ever truly gotten over her death."

Another silence. This time, it feels oppressive, and both of them glance away from me. For fuck's sake, I'm not…

I don't know what I am.

I'm not still grieving Victoria's passing. I don't think. Who knows what that even means? She left a hole in our lives and blew up everything I had expected my future to be. It's unfair beyond belief that she never got older than thirty-four, that she never got to see Willa play piano at a recital… that she remains frozen in time, with her children still babies, and her husband working too much… fuck.

I take another sip of my beer. All this time, I've never once considered that my siblings may think I'm irrevocably lost in grief. But now, it's stuck in my mind. One more thing to worry about.

A roar of excitement sweeps through the pub, and it

drowns out our own awkward silence in a heartbeat. On the screen, the score reads 2-2, and only a few minutes left till the end of the match.

"Look at that," Nate says. His voice is filled with awe. "Maxwell leaving it all out there before retirement."

I watch the English footballer race across the field. He's easy to spot because the camera makes it impossible not to. The man is a worldwide legend. I've seen more of his half-naked body plastered on the Times Square billboards than I've ever wanted to.

"The British press keeps wondering if he'll get to play in the World Cup next summer," Nate says. "With his history of injuries."

"Yeah, you've definitely been gone too long," Connie says.

Nate just shakes his head, and despite Connie's comment, she's watching the TV, too. I take the opportunity to look down at my phone. Two messages from my assistant, a message from Mac confirming the pickup time later... and a text from Isabel.

We've texted before. About the kids, logistics. But this is nothing so mundane.

> Isabel: I know what I want now. I left my Kindle on your bedside table. The first five books have highlighted parts in them... if you want to check them out.

My brain short-circuits, and then I have to put my phone away. Her Kindle is waiting for me on my nightstand. I've never been more interested to read anything in my entire goddamned life. To see what Isabel reads, late at night and in the comfort of her bed, where she can reach down and—

Fuck. Painful thought. *Wrong* thought.

Connie excuses herself to go to the bathroom, and I force my focus back to Nate. He's smiling into his beer.

"Looks like you got bad news," he says. "Or… surprising news?"

"All good," I say.

"Right." He glances over at where Connie has disappeared. "So, Isabel. How are things going, working with Con's best friend?"

The fucker. "It's going fine."

"Just fine, or better than fine?"

"Just fine," I say.

He leans back in the booth and stretches his legs out under the table. "She's really beautiful, isn't she? I didn't realize until I met her at Connie and Gabriel's wedding party."

I narrow my eyes at him. "I hadn't noticed."

"No? Well, I'm sure you won't mind if I ask her out," Nate says.

My hand tightens around the beer. It's irrational, the anger, but it rises to the surface anyway. And it's tinged with an emotion I haven't felt in years.

Jealousy.

Of Nate. Who's charming and funny, and doesn't have two kids to take care of and a company to run. Isabel could do worse… like me. And that's not a happy thought.

Nate chuckles. "Yeah. That's what I thought."

"You live in London," I say. "It wouldn't be practical."

"Mm-hmm. Smart," he says with a nod. "Look, just be open and honest with her, okay?"

I cross my arms over my chest. "About what?"

But Nate doesn't waver. "About what you can offer her, and what you can't. Have you even been with anyone since Vicky died?"

I don't answer him. This convo is the last thing I wanted out of tonight, the absolute last fucking thing, so I glance over my shoulder. But Connie's still in the bathroom.

Nate's staring me down like he expects my response. I stare back at him, daring him to cave. But he doesn't. Seems like both of my siblings are determined to be rebellious tonight.

"Yes," I finally admit. Twice. Both had been quick, rushed meetings in hotel rooms. Women I knew tangentially, women who wanted the same thing that I did. But even so, I'd regretted both times.

"Good," he says. "That's great. Just treat her right. She's Connie's best friend."

"I *know* that."

He holds up his hands. "And treat yourself right, too, okay?"

"What does that mean?"

"Just… It's been five years. It's okay," he says with a shrug. "To move on."

I don't have a single thing to say to that.

Move on? Is that what he thinks I'm doing with Isabel? It's another one of those nebulous terms, like *still grieving* and *treat her right*. I don't know how to do any of those things, or even if I'm doing them right now. The empty platitudes people have offered me over the past few years have never made much sense to me.

Being honest about what I can offer Isabel means shutting down whatever we're doing right now, before I hurt her, and before I get her hopes up. I doubt she has any at the moment, not beyond the physical, and that feels like a blessing.

I run my hand over the back of my neck and feel like the asshole I am. Because I want her too, more than I've wanted anyone in years, and far more than I know how to handle. Making her come the other night in my bathroom, her thighs around my head, and the taste of her on my tongue, has only enflamed that need.

I shouldn't have done that.

I can't be responsible for her and Connie's friendship blowing up, or for her losing her job. It's very possible that she may want to quit after she realizes just how little I can offer anyone. Even someone as beautiful and kind as her.

Maybe that's what hurts the most. I know, that if I was ten years younger, without responsibilities and obligations, it would have been *easy* to be the right man for her. I would have enjoyed that.

But I'm not that man.

It's not my job to guide her as she discovers her own pleasure or help her verbalize her needs, and it's sure as hell not my right to take my own pleasure. It's someone else's. Someone better, and more suited for her. I hate the thought of that bastard, but it's true. The guilt eases down my throat at the decision. Settles a little bit. I'm still an asshole. But one who won't act on his desires.

Connie returns a few moments later. She sits down next to Nate with a sigh and complains about the long lines for the women's restrooms. I nod along and drain the rest of my beer, listening to the easy conversation between them.

When I arrive home late at night to the quiet apartment, both of my kids soundly asleep, I find Isabel's Kindle lying in wait for me on my bedside table.

And I put it directly into my drawer—powered off and unread.

CHAPTER 22
ISABEL

The morning after I left my tablet at Alec's bedside, I'm a nervous wreck. I don't know why talking about sex is so much harder than *doing* it, or where my shyness about it lies. I'm not shy in my head. But the idea of speaking the words out loud…

It's a Saturday, and I'm only scheduled to work half a day. Alec has a meeting of some kind, though I don't know the specifics. Maybe that's for the best. I answer texts while I get ready after my shower. Connie wants to meet up for drinks tonight. It's not as easy anymore, seeing her, when we're not living in the same building. I miss it.

I miss the camaraderie with my ballet troupe, too. Even if it was often superficial, and sometimes catty. But there's a bond forged over hurt feet, sweaty brows, and difficult performances.

I text Connie back to say that I'm in. She's been busier since she married Gabriel. That makes sense, too, but it does mean less time for us.

And maybe that's good right now. I have no idea what she would think about Alec and me.

If she knew…

But she doesn't, and I just need to make sure we keep it that way. At least I can count on Alec to never tell a soul. I've never met anyone else who keeps his personal life so close to the vest.

I leave my part of the penthouse and walk down the hallway. The scent of pancakes hangs heavy in the air, wafting from the kitchen. I follow the aroma and the high-pitched sounds of the kids' voices.

They're standing on either side of Alec as he works his magic with pancakes by the stove.

I pause at the threshold, watching him. He's in dark jeans and a gray T-shirt, his hair still damp after a shower. And he's teaching Willa how to flip them, his hand around her much smaller one.

"That's it. And slide it under... yeah. Perfect."

She beams. Sam squeals.

It's the second time now that I've observed it. This little ritual when he has a weekend day off. All of the other food is cooked by Katja, prepped meal-ready and neatly stacked in the larger-than-life fridge... but not this.

I didn't see him involve the kids in the actual making of the pancakes last time.

"Good morning!" Sam says loudly. He looks at me over his shoulder, and there's a smudge of flour on his chubby left cheek. His glasses have a smattering of batter on them.

I smile at him. "Good morning, guys. Are you making pancakes?"

"Yes," Willa says. She looks up at Alec. "When are they done?"

"When they're golden brown." He takes back the spatula and gazes at me. Did he read the Kindle last night?

But Alec's face doesn't give away any clues. "Good morning."

"Hello," I say.

Willa tugs on his sleeve. "Isn't it burning?"

He looks back down and shakes his head. "No, it's all right. Here, try flipping it again. After breakfast, I was thinking we could do something fun. What are you up for?"

Sam's busy reaching for the syrup, and I scoop it away, out of his sticky-fingered reach. "I thought you were working today."

"I made some changes to my schedule." He glances at me briefly before pouring another round of batter. "Someone told me about the importance of making memories."

"Oh."

"I was thinking I'd take the kids out for a picnic," he says. "It's early November, but we can just bundle up in our jackets. We can bring a soccer ball, pack some sandwiches, and find a good spot in Central Park. Looks like it'll be a sunny day."

"We can buy ice cream after," Willa says. Her statement makes me smile. She rarely phrases things as questions, because she's learned that statements have a higher likelihood of getting a yes. She's a Connovan through and through, and she's only eight.

"It could be freezing outside, and you'd still want ice cream," Alec tells her.

She nods in agreement. "Yes."

He chuckles and flips another pancake onto the plate. "All right, sounds like a plan. The park it is."

I watch as he continues to cook, his movements practiced and efficient. It's clear that he's done this before. That he enjoys it.

He insists I join them for breakfast, and when Sam tugs on my hand to make me come along to the park, I do that, too. Alec and I pack food for all of us in silence, broken only by kids' excited chatter.

"Sure this is okay?" he asks me quietly. "If you have other plans…"

"I don't, not until tonight. I'm meeting Connie for a drink."

His eyebrows rise, but he just nods. "All right. Good."

The mention of his sister amplifies the silence between us. I wonder if he's thinking the same thing I am. What would she think if she knew?

The air outside is chilly. Fall has painted Central Park in a beautiful kaleidoscope of bright colors, and fallen leaves are crisp under our feet. Sam holds Alec's hand while Willa skips ahead. She's so different from the little girl I met when I first started, especially with her father or her friends around. Since she's forgotten or abandoned her task of testing me. I hope we're past that stage now, but every time I think we are, she reminds me that her walls haven't entirely dropped.

I steal a glance at Alec as we walk. His brown hair has dried naturally, and a lock has fallen over his forehead. He looks serious, focused on the kids, but when he glances back at me, all I can see is the secret that's taut between us.

My stomach feels tight with anticipation.

Did he read it? What did he think? I didn't put the worst of the worst in there, but some of the scenes were graphic. Detailed. The language wouldn't shock a romance reader, but he isn't one. Maybe he's disgusted. Outraged.

Turned off.

Sam picks a spot we should stop at for our picnic and sits down before Alec and I can get the blanket unfolded. He lies among the leaves and starts making a "snow" angel, and it stops us all in our tracks.

"Your imagination is something else," I tell him with a smile. "Want to help us with the blanket?"

"Yes." He sits up, with a leaf sticking to his hair. "Where did you live before you came to live with us?"

That keeps the smile on my face. He's the king of non sequiturs, in the way small kids so often are. "I lived a few blocks away, at the Greystone Building. The same place your Aunt Connie used to live in."

"Oh." He lies back down and ignores us setting up the picnic entirely, unlike Willa, who helps unpack the water bottles and the coffee thermos. "Ben lives across the river."

"He does?" I ask. I don't have a clue who that is. "Which river?"

Sam's quiet for a long moment. "The watery one."

That makes me chuckle. Alec huffs too, an amused sound, and sits down next to me on the blanket. "It's a friend from his kindergarten class who moved to Brooklyn. That's the East River, buddy."

Sam repeats the word slowly, still lying on the dying grass instead of the blanket. My parents would have made a fuss over that when we were kids. Somehow I love that Alec doesn't care. He cares about plenty of things, like piano lessons and proper etiquette, but the kids' stained clothing isn't one of them.

Here, in the brisk air of Central Park, in dark jeans and a navy jacket, he looks different. Much more approachable, and handsome in a way that's unfamiliar to me. It's mostly been suits and tuxes, or just dress shirts and slacks. Now, he's "off-duty" and is simply a dad, and the hottest one in the park by miles.

He leans back on the blanket, propping himself on his elbows next to me, and watches Willa and Sam play soccer. I observe his profile, and the five o'clock shadow that darkens his jaw.

"This was a good idea," I say.

He nods, still looking straight ahead. "Yeah. I'm just sorry it took you getting upset for me to have it."

"That's okay. You guys see Central Park every day from the living room windows. I imagine it's hard to notice what's so close sometimes."

That makes his lips curl, but it doesn't look like a happy

smile. "Yeah. Hard to see, indeed. Isabel… I didn't read what you left for me last night."

"Oh."

He turns and looks at me, and I recognize the conflict in his hazel eyes. He's, somehow, again the man I've met through Connie and saw over the years, determined and in control, but he's *also* the man I've grown to care for. The man who struggles with needing something he thinks he shouldn't.

"This thing between us isn't fair to you, and I can't… We can't let it happen again. I'm sorry."

I nod, slowly. He's retreating. *Again.* The wash of rejection floods me, but I keep the disappointment off my face. *He wants me,* I think. But he won't let himself have anything that he wants.

"You're not ready for any kind of relationship," I say.

He's quiet, but then he nods. "Right. You're Connie's friend, and I don't want to interfere with that, or with your job. The way I've been acting has already been inappropriate enough."

"Maybe it's only inappropriate if it's unwanted," I say with a shrug that looks far more nonchalant than I feel. "But it's up to you."

Silence falls between us, and we watch the kids race around. They're playing unusually well with one another, and it's a beautiful day, the sounds of children, dogs barking, and birds singing filling the park. But the chill in the air is a reminder of the changing season and the turn soon to come.

It already feels colder between us.

I can hear the seconds ticking away and wish we could still talk openly. Communicate the way he said he wanted us to. But I guess that only mattered regarding one kind of intimacy.

But then his hand brushes mine on the blanket, his fingers

glide over my own. "It's not that I don't want to," he says. "You know that."

My breathing speeds up, and I focus on the kids instead. Watching the ball as it rolls over leaves-covered grass. "I know that. I just wish it would be enough."

His hand lingers on top of mine. "It is."

"It's clearly not," I whisper. "You said you felt a lot of guilt, the other day. Is this... do you feel it because of me, too?"

"Isabel," he mutters. "I feel so guilty it's eating—"

The ball comes rolling straight at us. Alec reacts immediately, sticking his leg out and averting the crash into the picnic basket. Willa comes barrelling after it and asks her dad to join them. And that's that, that's the whole conversation. Sam and I explore the surrounding area, and the day reverts to the kids, as it should, on their day off.

Later that afternoon, I feel numb as I'm getting ready for my drink date with Connie. And I feel irritated and want to vent to her, tell her about the man currently giving me whiplash, the man I've wanted for so long but who, even when he wants me back, won't choose to have me. And *I can't.*

I can't talk to my siblings about it, either. They wouldn't understand, and maybe they'd judge me, and I'm stuck carrying my frustration in my head for the rest of the night.

I walk by the living room on my way out to the front door. Alec is sitting on the couch, a kid on either side of him. The little munchkins are quiet and intent on the children's show playing on TV, unusually beat from the long day, and don't look up at me.

Alec does. His eyes narrow as they run over me, as if I'm dressed in something far more salacious than a black dress, coat, and boots.

"I called Mac," he says. "He's downstairs, and on standby for later."

"You shouldn't have done that," I say.

He shakes his head. "I should have done it last time, too."

"Have any of the other nannies been offered car service?" I ask. There's an edge to my voice.

He frowns, and the non-answer is answer enough. *He wants me*, I think again. *Just not enough.*

"Have fun tonight," he says.

"You too."

Mac is indeed waiting for me in the garage. He's leaning against the Bentley with headphones on. There's a serene expression on his face, and when he sees me, he smiles.

Seems like he has no issue working a Saturday evening, at least. But I still feel bad.

"I'm sorry, I didn't know Alec called you."

He shakes his head and pulls us out into traffic. "More than happy to help," he says. He fiddles with the radio a bit and seems to read my mood, because he leaves it on an upbeat pop station and doesn't say another word.

Connie is already at the bar when I arrive. It's good to see her. Her auburn hair is smooth around her face, and the wrap dress she's wearing hugs her curves. She looks fierce and familiar, and it feels good to hear her talk, to listen to her stories about her new life. The last few months she's become fiercer still, standing up to her family, and embracing marriage to Gabriel.

They compliment each other very well. Two people who have the right combination of similarities and differences.

It feels like a distant dream, to find that myself someday.

She asks about her niece and nephew, but only briefly about Alec, and I've never been more grateful for that. I don't know if I could keep the frustration out of my voice if I had to talk about him.

Your brother's great, except he's got the strongest self-control of anyone I've ever met, and I'm a professional ballerina.

A part of me aches for what he might be feeling. The

mention of his guilt... I can't imagine being in his position. But that doesn't make being in mine any easier.

Connie wants to focus on me instead, and that's almost worse. I don't have solid career plans, but I lay out the options I have, and she analyzes them with as much care as I suspect she brings to her job. We leave the bar shortly after eleven. Neither of us is a night owl, and she hugs me goodbye outside the establishment's front door.

"You'll solve this," she tells me. "I know you will, even if the future will look a bit different from the one you wanted."

I hug her back. Maybe she's right. There is a solution out there... I just have to reach the stage of acceptance.

Mac drives me home and I return to a dark apartment. Alec's not sitting on the couch like the last time I was out, and he's not in the kitchen. And why would he be? He made his stance clear.

We can't go there again.

I close the door to the large room and the en suite that's become my home. Removing my makeup takes no time at all, and then I crawl into bed, luxuriating in the softness of the mattress. And cursing Alec. He hasn't read my Kindle, but he still *has* it, and now I can't get any reading done before falling asleep.

I'm lying on my back, considering marching over to his room and getting it back myself, when there's a knock on my bedroom door.

CHAPTER 23
ISABEL

Two sharp knocks, and then silence. I swing my legs out of bed and walk to the door with a pounding heartbeat. It can only be one person.

I open the door.

It's him.

He's standing at the threshold in nothing but a pair of gray pajama bottoms. They hang low on his hips, and the rest of him is on full display. The broad shoulders and chest, the smattering of brown hair, the flat stomach with well-defined abs, and the happy trail disappearing into his pants. Seeing everything up close, the strength of a body honed by decades of consistent workouts… and it's him. It's Alec.

Standing shirtless outside my door.

"Can I come in?" he asks. His voice is low, a bit hoarse, and his hair looks mussed. Like he's been running his hand through it.

He's holding my Kindle in his right hand.

My heart stops in my chest, but I nod and step back to let him in.

He stops in the middle of my room. His eyes land on my unmade bed, and then on me, and the oversized T-shirt I'm wearing. I'm suddenly very conscious that a pair of simple black cotton panties is the only thing I have on underneath and my otherwise bare legs.

I cross my arms over my shirt. "Alec?"

He shakes his head slowly, a pained expression on his face. "I tried. I... fuck it. I read what you left for me," he says. "It was... very enlightening."

He's read it all.

I can't believe I showed him. The books I'd chosen... they're all some of my favorites, but they're not anything that could be considered tame. A non-romance reader would call it straight-up porn.

But he said he wouldn't read it.

He'd drawn a line in the sand.

"I don't understand you," I say. "You said you wouldn't look at it. You were the one who said we couldn't do this!"

"We shouldn't," he says. His face looks strained. "I shouldn't... but I can't stop thinking about you. Every minute since we talked, I've hated that I put a stop to things. You're stuck in my head, sweetheart, and I can't get you out. It's only gotten worse after being with you the other night. After reading this. Fuck, I've been replaying the sounds of you coming, and wanting nothing but to hear them again." He closes the distance between us and cups my face. It's a tender movement, at odds with the frustration etched on his features. "I shouldn't be doing this. But fuck it, I can't seem to stay away."

"Do you mean it this time?" I whisper.

He lowers his head to mine. His kiss takes my breath away. It's not like the slow ones he's so good at, the ones that raise my heart rate with each press of his lips. This is a firestorm from the first touch.

He slides his hands down my back with a groan, pulling me flush against his body. I've never had this much of him to explore before. My fingers trace along his shoulders and over his back. His skin is warm and firm to the touch, and I can't get enough of running my hands all over him.

Alec kisses down my cheek and to my neck, his left hand winding itself into the length of my hair. "You drive me insane," he mutters.

I grip his upper arms. "So do you. Telling me to learn what I like, and to figure out how to tell you, and then you shut the whole thing down?"

He gives a hoarse chuckle that tickles the skin over my collarbone. "I was trying my best to not give into temptation. But I'm just a man, and I can't fight it anymore."

He kisses me again, his tongue brushing against mine, and sensations overwhelm me. There's so much of him, so much skin against mine, so I lock my arms around his neck.

"What did you think?" I whisper.

His hands slide down again, but this time, they reach the hem of my T-shirt where it ends below my ass. His fingers caress my thighs.

"Think about what?"

"The… things you read."

I feel his smile against my temple. "Enlightening."

"You already said that."

"Mm-hmm. Right. Well, it made me rock-hard."

I exhale. "Really?"

"Yeah." His hand slips beneath my T-shirt and travels up, over my ass and my back. Electricity buzzes over my skin. "The scenes themselves were out of this world. But knowing you use them to make yourself come?"

"I never said that," I say, but I'm smiling.

He kisses me, and beneath my shirt, his hands are slowly skimming up my ribs. "But it's true."

"Yeah," I breathe. His fingers brush the underside of my breasts, and then higher, over my nipples. Sensations ripple over my skin at the touch.

He groans, and then his hands are gone from my body.

They're gripping the hem of the T-shirt instead. He pulls it up, and I raise my arms. Slipping it off, he tosses the tee away, leaving me in nothing but a pair of panties.

Dark eyes rake over me. The intensity he's always had is back, only it's all turned on me.

His hands grip my hips, and he looks and looks and looks.

It makes me shrug. "They're just boobs."

And tiny ones at that. I've always been small-chested, an A most days and a B on the best of them. It had been an asset in ballet, and for that, I'd been grateful. But it's never been a body part I love.

Alec leans down and wraps his arms around my waist, and his mouth captures my left nipple. I close my eyes. *Oh.* He uses his teeth, and his stubble scrapes over my skin. I've always liked this but didn't know it could feel this good.

"There's nothing just about them," he mutters. "You have perfect tits." He lifts his head and gives the other nipple the same attention. One of his hands slides to grip my ass cheek, and all of it fits in his large palm.

He kisses down my ribs, to my stomach, and falls to his knees on the plush rug in my room. His lips reach the waistband of my panties, and he starts to pull it down my hips, an inch at a time, kissing the exposed skin as he does.

Watching him do this is its own kind of thrill. His broad shoulders, the strong arms braced on my hips, and the brown head of hair.

"I've been dying to taste you again," he murmurs, kissing the inside of my thigh. He finally tugs my panties down all the way, and they drop to the floor, around my ankles. "That's it, there it is."

He locks an arm around my thighs to keep me steady and uses the other to help spread me apart for his tongue.

The first touch against my clit makes me sigh in relief. God, I'd thought about this since the other night, and wanted it again, and thought it wouldn't happen. There's something about his clear need to do this that washes away my self-consciousness and embarrassment.

My fingers tighten in his hair. "Alec," I whisper. "I want to do this to you, too. I want us to... oh. *Oh.*"

He slides a finger inside me at the same time as sucking on my clit, and I can't focus anymore. All I know is that I want more this time. *More.* I can hear my heart pounding in my ears, and my hips move against him of their own accord.

I don't know how long he works me, but it's till I'm at the very edge. I tug on his shoulders. "Alec. I want you."

He looks up at me with eyes that are near-black. All pupils, and all desire. "I can do this all night."

I shake my head. "This is me telling you what I want. That's what you wanted, right? Well, I want you."

A smile ghosts over his lips. "You want me to do what?"

"Fuck me," I whisper.

He slides another finger inside of me. "You're ready for me, too, aren't you."

"Yes," I breathe.

"So wet and so pretty." He kisses my clit a final time, making me shiver, before he rises. I step out of my panties and reach for his bottoms, wanting to tug them down and off.

He lets me this time.

I pull on the elastic to get it over his erection, and his cock bounces free. I was right. He is big, and he's so hard, and I *have* to touch him.

He hisses at the contact. "Careful, sweetheart."

The skin is hot beneath my palm, and I stroke him clumsily, carefully, but he doesn't seem to mind. His chest rises and falls with heavy breathing, and I want to make him feel just as out of control as he's been doing to me.

He's longer than average, and definitely thicker.

Alec just breathes heavily and watches me stroke his cock. But when I brush over the swollen head, his trance breaks. He shakes his head. "No. You can play around with me later. But not now."

"Did you bring…?"

A smile flashes across his lips. "Yes. But what's the word?"

"Condoms."

"That's it," he says. He kicks his pants off entirely and digs through the pocket to pull out a single wrapper. The gold foil reflects the light of my bedside lamp.

He tears it open and rolls the condom on with those large hands of his, the ones I've admired for years. Long-fingered and broad-backed, and so masculine. Seeing him grip himself is a sight I'll never forget.

He looks at my body, and his jaw tenses. "Sweetheart, you have to be in control of this, because I can't. I have no control left in me."

"Good." I run my nails over his chest, and he hisses out a breath. "I don't want you in control."

He closes his eyes for a second, and when he opens them again, they're blazing. He moves to my bed and lies down on his back. His cock juts out, tilted north. It looks obscenely large against his stomach. "Come here," he says and reaches for me. "You're on top."

I climb onto the bed next to him. "Okay. I'm not good at—"

"You'll be fucking amazing, and I need to be inside you," he says. "But this will let you control the entry."

I straddle his hips. He looks massive on my bed, lying with his head on the pillow I sleep on every night. The tendons in his neck protrude, and there's a deep groove between his eyebrows, like he's aching.

I grip him, holding him straight, and try to notch him at my entrance. He grips my hips and watches me, watches *us*, as I finally slide the broad head of him inside.

I exhale shakily at the feeling. Yeah, he really is thick, and it's been over a year since I had sex.

"That's it," he mutters. His fingertips dig into my flesh, helping to slow my descent. I lower another two inches, and the stretch turns delicious. "You feel so good."

He groans when I sink all the way to the hilt. The feeling of fullness is overwhelming. I don't know how I'm going to move.

Alec's face is still etched with pleasure-pain, and I can't look away from him, from the expression on his face and his body beneath mine.

"How does that feel?" he asks. His right hand moves to where we're joined, and he starts rubbing circles around my clit.

My breathing quickens. "You're big, you know."

"Hmm." There's a flash of humor in his eyes that tells me he *does* know. "That's why I wanted you to pace yourself."

I brace my hands on his chest and try rolling my hips. Lifting them up and down or shifting them forward, and the pleasure starts to build from the friction.

His finger is still rubbing my clit, as the other hand reaches up to tweak my nipple. The combination has sensations washing over me, heightening them all, until I'm back at the edge. Feeling as I did in his bathroom when he went down on me.

"That's it," he mutters. His voice is raspy and deep, and I close my eyes, focusing on it and the feelings. "You look so good, sweetheart. So good at riding me. And fuck you're so pretty. Too pretty, it hurts to look at you, but I can't look away. That's it, Isa… that's it. You feel so good, *too* good. I need to feel it when you come around me."

I do.

The orgasm sweeps over me and through me, my hips stuttering in their movements, my hands on his chest turning into claws. My body is in tremors. It's just like earlier in the week, but stronger.

I didn't think it could be.

Alec's hands stroke up my back. He's still rock hard inside me, but the hand smoothing over my skin is soft.

"Well done," he murmurs. "You're so pretty when you come for me."

The praise sends warmth through my system. I kiss his chest and slowly straighten out, still straddling him. "I didn't think I could do that."

"You can do anything," he says. But the pleasure-pain on his face has heightened, and he looks tenser than I've ever seen him. Tendons stick out in his neck.

He's right at the edge himself.

I run my nails down his chest again, and he shudders. "Turn me over," I say.

His hands tighten their grips on my hips. "It'll be hard," he warns.

"I'm tougher than I look."

Alec flips us over. He stays inside me the whole time, and as soon as I'm on my back, he starts to move. Hard. Fast. He gets deeper like this, so deep, thrusting rapidly.

I wrap my legs around him. He groans, gripping my thigh and pulling it even tighter around his waist. Brown hair hangs over his forehead as he stares at my body, at the way he's moving inside me, and his eyes are dark with lust.

I've never seen a hotter sight.

My hands rake over his back, and he leans down onto his forearms, our chests pressing together. He's heavy and warm, and I love it.

I can't think around the hard tempo he's set.

The sound of his loud groans vibrates through his chest and into my body. Alec thrusts one more time, and then he comes, his hips sharp against mine.

He collapses on top of me and remains still, his weight crushing me into the mattress in the best possible way. We're both breathing fast. I run my hands over his back, my fingers kneading into the muscles of his shoulders.

We lay there for a few long moments.

He pushes up with a low moan and reaches down, grabbing the condom at his base before pulling out. It makes me wince a little. He notices, and gives me a wry smile.

I smile back at him and turn onto my stomach, watching him tie off the condom and throw it into the trash in my bathroom. I feel boneless and light with pleasure, and a bit drunk on emotions, and I really don't want him to leave right away.

Alec grabs a glass of water from my kitchenette. He drains it before getting a refill and heading back to me. "Here," he says and hands me the glass.

I drink, and he sits down next to me on the bed. He reaches for me immediately, his right hand smoothing over my stomach, my hipbone, and down to my legs. He spreads them a little and traces the redness on the inside of my thighs.

He frowns. "I was rough."

"I liked it."

"Mm-hmm. I've craved you for so long," he says. It comes out as a matter-of-fact, but it makes warmth spread through my chest. He's still frowning as he traces the inside of my other thigh, pushing the two apart wider. The intensity of his scrutiny between my legs makes me a bit self-conscious. "Hopefully you won't be too sore."

That makes me chuckle.

He looks up, eyebrows raised. "What?"

"I've been sore most days of my life. I used to stretch and dance for a *living*. I'll be perfectly fine."

His expressions turns into anger. "Fuck. Your hip. I shouldn't have wrapped your legs around me."

"First of all, I did that, and it was perfectly fine. As long as you don't want me to do twelve consecutive fouettés in bed, we're good."

His hand switches to my hip, smoothing over the skin. His expression turns thoughtful and a little closed off, and I don't want that. I don't want him to retreat.

I don't want him to regret this, and I don't want him to feel guilty.

"What are you thinking?" I whisper.

His index finger traces along one of my ribs. "That you're just as beautiful as I imagined, and feel even better than I hoped," he says.

"You sound like that's a problem."

"It is," he says. But there's a tilt to his lips. "Because I'm not going to be satisfied with just once, sweetheart. Figuring out what turns you on is my new favorite thing."

I pull him down and he lets me, stretching out beside me on my bed. I kiss him, and he kisses me back, the slow, skilled, leisurely tempo taking over again.

Alec runs his large hand down my chest, his fingers skimming between my breasts and then dipping into the centerline that runs down my stomach. "Tell me," he says, and his voice is the raspy one I love the most. "What things from those books do you want to do in real life?"

I chuckle. "Alec."

"Tell me," he repeats. His hand caresses my left hipbone. "If it's too hard to say, I'll give you options from what I read. Dirty talk?"

I turn my head into his shoulder. "Yes. I... yes. I'd like that a lot."

"Mmm. Praise, maybe." His hand brushes down to my thigh, fingers sweeping. "I'll keep telling you how good you feel. Look. Taste."

I close my eyes. "Yeah. That sort of thing. If it's real, of course."

He chuckles. It's a husky sound, and my eyes fly open again. I have to look at him when he laughs like that. It warms his entire face. "Sweetheart, talking dirty to you will be the easiest thing I'll ever do."

"Oh." I run my fingers along his jaw. His five o'clock shadow is heavier tonight. "I could do the same, you know."

"Mmm. Tell me I'm your good girl?"

My eyes widen, and then I chuckle. "Yes, if that's what turns you on."

"I think I'll call you that instead, if you like. Lord knows it's the truth. You're so good, it's painful." He drops his mouth to my neck, kissing across the sensitive skin. "Sex in public?" he asks. "That was in one of the scenes you highlighted. I would be game, but I have too much on the line for that."

"Oh. No... that's fine. It's not my jam, either."

He pauses. "Then, what was it about that scene in particular that you liked?"

"Um. The quickie? I liked how the hero just kinda... went for it. Because he was so turned on." My voice is coming out thin. This is so embarrassing to say out loud, to describe why I liked it so much.

But he just hums. "Interesting."

"What about it?"

"I didn't think women liked quickies, generally speaking."

"Yeah, maybe most don't. I'm not sure I do either, but that's not really the key thing there."

"What's the fantasy, then?"

"That you're... well, just too turned on. Like, you can barely control it, you just need me too much. I know that might not be very realistic."

He raises an eyebrow. "Sweetheart, I *am* so turned on by you that I *can't* control it. I wouldn't be in my hired nanny's bed if I wasn't."

That makes me smile. "Oh? I've been driving you wild?"

"Let's just say I haven't needed any help to come up with the fantasies I've had about you." His hand traces circles on my leg. "Show me."

I turn my face to his. His eyes are so close, hazel and warm, and his skin is flushed with pleasure. I must look the same. "Show you what?"

"How you make yourself come using those books you read."

I dig my teeth into my lower lip. "Okay."

"Yeah?"

"Mm-hmm." I'm a bit surprised by my own eagerness. I reach down and take his hand off where it's resting on my hipbone. I place it between my legs and guide his fingers to my clit. "I always start here."

He lifts himself onto an elbow, watching our hands move. "On your back, like this?"

"Usually, yeah. But, sometimes, on my stomach."

"Mm-hmm. What motions do your fingers... ah." He watches intently, his fingers finding their groove next to mine. "Don't stop."

Pleasure is rising through me again. I didn't think it was possible, but it is.

I draw my hand back. "I want you to do it."

He's there in an instant, replacing my touch with his own, but repeating the same pattern. It feels so much more pleasurable when it's him. He slides his free arm beneath me, and I turn against his shoulder, focusing on nothing but the electricity spreading through me. He smells good. Like man and sex and soap.

"Alec," I say.

I don't know what I want to say. The feelings I've always had for him are lurking right beneath the surface, so close now that he's here, holding me, *touching me,* and I feel high on the sensations.

"Yes?"

"Don't pull away again," I whisper.

His fingers speed up, moving like my own but better, and I bend my knees to give him greater access.

"I won't be able to," he says. "Who would make you come so prettily?"

That makes me sigh softly. "Exactly."

"Can you come for me again, like a good girl?" he asks.

I close my eyes against his shoulder, my breathing increasing with the praise. Hearing him say those things in his deep voice, with his hand between my legs… giving him my Kindle had been a great idea.

"Yes," I whisper, and the sensations sweep me away.

CHAPTER 24
ALEC

Work has a way of expanding past its initial limits. Every meeting, email, and phone call is a potential threat. Some days, I feel like I spend most of my time ensuring they don't take over. Like I'm a watchman rather than a CEO, putting out embers before they ever flare into fires.

But there's one distraction I've been unwilling to avoid.

The texts.

I'm preparing for my meeting with the board this afternoon when my phone pings with another message.

> Isabel: The physiotherapist just left. Thank you again for arranging weekly sessions, Alec. I really appreciate it.

> Alec: Of course. What's the verdict?

> Isabel: Unchanged, unfortunately.

I put my phone away and look back at the agenda. My COO will be chairing most of this meeting, and the CFO will update us on the quarterly numbers. The acquisitions team will be there, too, going over the new additions we've added to Contron over the past year, and Connie will report on the Foundation's work...

I reach for my phone again.

> Alec: What are you doing today?

She has at least three more hours before she needs to pick up the kids, and I realize I've never asked about that before. Does she hang out with friends most days? Spend time with her family? Read those books of hers?

> Isabel: I'm going for a run in the park now, and then I'll probably read for a bit. I've already prepared a treasure hunt at home for Sam and Willa.

> Alec: A treasure hunt?

> Isabel: They often have a lot of energy after dinner. Don't worry, they'll both get their homework done.

Right. That is important, but... so is play. I know that. But I've never put a lot of work into ensuring it happens. It has always struck me as something that kids just *do*. It's the parents' job to encourage the things they don't. Homework. Piano. Sports. Languages. *Discipline.*

It's how I was raised.

Still, there's no denying the effect Isabel's activities have had. Her little dance parties tucker Sam out like nothing else, and even Willa started to ask for them, with a caveat that Isabel is not allowed to spin.

I add some notes to the meeting agenda, filling out points that were underdeveloped. Shoot an email to my COO that we need to address the rumors of a workers strike within the renewables industry and how it will affect us.

And then my own discipline cracks again.

> Alec: I'm looking forward to that. What did you hide as the treasure?

> Isabel: I think I'll let that be a surprise to you, too.

> Alec: Hiding things from your employer?

> Isabel: Only things he doesn't need to know.

I stare at her name on my phone, at the six letters, and feel a tugging in my chest. I knocked on her door last night, after getting home late, and found her waiting for me.

She's too sweet for this world. Far too sweet for me.

> Alec: What book are you reading now? Another one of those sex novels?

I know she'll protest. I'm expecting it before she even responds, but it still makes me huff a chuckle when it arrives.

> Isabel: They're ROMANCES that happen to have spicy scenes. And the answer's yes. I was going to tell you where I left the hero and heroine, but now I won't.

Ha.

> Alec: Let me guess. They're trading sexy texts, and the hero just finished telling the heroine what he will do to her when he gets home from work.

There's silence on the other end, and that sudden pause makes me smile. *Yeah.* The hero can do that, for sure. I have more than a few fantasies about Isabel. Lately, they've been occupying valuable real estate in my mind, leaving me distracted, on edge, and horny.

A sharp sound emits from my speaker, and then my assistant's voice cuts through the room. *"David Connovan here to see you."*

I run a hand over my face. *Of course.* Someone in the company, most likely Lauren, must have tipped him off about the board meeting.

"Send him in," I say.

The solid wood door to my office opens, and Dad strides into the space that used to be his. His thick gray hair is brushed back, and his hands are locked behind his back.

I rise. "Dad. To what do I owe this pleasure?"

He strolls past the bookcases in my office, pausing at times to inspect a book or a knick-knack on one of the shelves. His attention lingers on the image of his grandchildren I've placed there.

"Thought I'd attend the board meeting," he says. "As a silent partner, of course. I won't interfere with your leadership."

Right.

But just him being there would. Interfere with how comfortable everyone around the table is, for one. Muddle the hierarchy when it's actually crystal clear.

He's Contron's former boss. Not its current one.

Dad raises an eyebrow. "Something wrong with that?"

"No," I say.

He sits down on the chair across from my desk. He's shorter than me by two inches, and stockier in build now, but other than that, we're very similar.

People love to comment on it.

"I think Mark is considering retiring from the board."

Oh, fuck.

"He hasn't made any formal decisions," I say.

Dad runs a hand over the edge of the desk. "I think I should step back in. Retiring from the board was the wrong decision, and there's still expertise I can share."

Not being on the board doesn't seem to stop you from doing that anyway, I think. I already know that Lauren still reports to him. Now he's had an informal conversation with Mark, too?

I don't want him back on the board. If he was thinking about what's best for Contron and not with his own ego, he'd realize that, too.

Dad built Contron from a national brand to an international corporate superpower. A conglomerate with more legs than a spider. He made it what it is today. But that doesn't mean it was a company without faults when I joined the executive team.

Under my stewardship, we've taken *wiser* risks, rather than clinging to the ones that made David Connovan feel good. We've gotten leaner and faster, streamlined management, and hired top-notch outside counsel. We're not in the growth phase anymore. We're thriving at the maintenance stage.

I also got rid of most of Dad's "yes men." He'd noticed, even if he only slyly commented on his former favorites being demoted, retired, or replaced.

"So?" he asks. "Will you make the announcement?"

He stares me down in the way that is so uniquely his. *Cave,* that look says. And for many years of my adolescence, I had. Every single time.

Why didn't you get an A? Practice the piano. You'll work here over the summer.

But he has no foothold left in Contron, apart from his shares.

"That wouldn't be wise," I say. "It would be better for you to focus on your retirement. You just bought the Aspen lodge, didn't you?"

He frowns. "You don't think it's a good idea."

"No, I don't."

"Promise me you'll reconsider it," he demands. "Mark won't retire for a few months, yet. I'll make the rounds, hear what the others think. I have no doubt that they'll accept my candidacy."

My hand fists on my desk. "I'll consider it," I say.

He crosses his arms over his chest. "Good. Now, for family matters. Thanksgiving is only a few weeks away. Are you planning on hosting, or shall I?"

"Whatever you'd prefer," I tell him.

"Mine, then." He looks past me to the wide windows. "Will you invite Connie and her husband?"

I want to shake my head at his pettiness. "I think that's up to you, if you're hosting."

"Mm-hmm. But you'll mention it to her."

"Yes, I can do that."

"Good. And give me an update on her."

"She'll be at the board meeting," I say.

He doesn't reply, just gives me an annoyed glance. I'm not playing ball today. I know it's pissing him off, too, but I can't find a single part of me that cares. Not disappointing him had been mine, Connie's, and Nate's main purpose our entire lives. But *he* stepped away, retired. He's the one who made that decision, and I wish he'd give up this attitude, too. But I bet that's the one thing he'll take with him all the way to the grave.

"She's great," I say. "Happier than I've ever seen her, and she's doing fantastic work with the Foundation. It's a great outreach resource for Contron, and it's raising our charitable profile."

He makes a humming noise in the back of his throat. "Good. That's good."

"You should call her and chat, or take her out to dinner."

Dad's eyebrows lower. "She's the one who married a Thompson without telling us."

"You're the one who still hasn't congratulated your daughter," I shoot back.

He harrumphs. Rises from his chair with a low groan. "You're in a mood today," he says.

"Am I?" I ask pleasantly. "Hadn't noticed."

He leaves, no doubt to chat with the executives still here from his time. I rub a hand down my face and think of what Connie had asked about Dad. How he was different before Mom died. Where he is now.

Would Willa or Sam be sitting in this chair thirty years from now? And would I be pestering them in the same way? The thought isn't a pleasant one. It lodges in my mind like a thorn, and I reach for my phone to drown out the pinprick of pain.

She's texted back.

> Isabel: Yes, that's where I left off. Think you can stand-in for the hero?

Gladly. Even if standing in for him is all I'm going to be able to do. Because I'm not a hero in a romance novel, and certainly not hers. Nobody would craft their dream man with this much fucking baggage.

> Alec: Tonight, I want you to tell me why that sex scene on a boat that you highlighted turned you on so much, and I want you to do it while you're riding my face.

I hit send, and imagine her receiving it. Reading it. There's a shyness in her that's adorable, but it's only about the verbalization of her wants and needs. I know her imagination is wild. The scenes in the books she highlighted for me told me more than enough.

Public sex. A quickie at a party, hard against the cabinet. Going down on a woman at the kitchen island. Rough sex, smooth sex, massage sex. And everywhere, dirty talk-filled the pages, with the heroes declaring how much they needed to fuck.

I didn't know women wanted that, but Isabel has taught me in no uncertain terms that she likes it. Wants it. Wants to be wanted, and Lord knows I do. It's the easiest part of my day, being with her. It shouldn't be. But it is. I've never been this preoccupied with a woman before. The comparison with Victoria stings, and brings back the guilt I'm doing my best to suppress. I can't hold all the thoughts in my head at once.

Of where this might go; of the things Isabel will want that I can't give. Of Connie finding out. I banish it all, together with the guilt, push it down and try to focus only on the present.

And as long as I can give her pleasure, as long as she wants this, it'll have to be enough.

———

The treasure hunt is a success. Isabel stands to the side and declares in her calm, kind voice whether we're "warm" or "cold" in our search.

Eventually, Willa's the one who cracks the clues. The treasure was hidden by the fireplace, stashed behind the decorative logs. She and Sam dig it out while Isabel and I cheer them on.

Two small bags of candy, one for each.

Isabel gives me a small smile. "Sorry, I hadn't planned on you joining, or I would have hidden three."

"I have my own sweets," I say. It comes out a bit hoarse, and she glances away. But not before I saw in her eyes that she took my meaning.

Fuck. I can't say things like that.

I turn to my kids instead. "Hey, why don't I grab you each

a bowl, and you can eat your bounty while watching some cartoons before bed?"

The kids don't need to be told twice. The normal evening chaos ensues, and I have to wrestle them into bed following their excitement. But it's worth it, seeing the happiness on their faces. A family game and candy, on a normal Tuesday... I think Sam's mind might be blown.

It takes longer than usual for Willa to settle down. I read her favorite book, and she follows along on the page, her eyelids growing heavier.

"I think," she finally whispers, "that she's not that bad."

I stroke my daughter's hair. "Isabel?"

"Mm-hmm. Maybe," she adds in a mumble, ever reticent with her praise, and I smile down at her. She reminds me so much of myself. Some days so like Victoria in appearance, but in other ways, very similar to me. I hadn't been the easiest for babysitters and nannies to deal with, either. I remember correcting them when I didn't think they were good enough for Connie.

Willa's breathing evens out, her face relaxing with sleep. I listen to her soft breaths for a minute longer before closing the book and heading out into the living room.

Isabel is curled up on the couch, the TV on low. Her legs are long, even when folded, and are clad in black leggings. The sweater she's wearing dwarfs her frame. Her black hair is braided and hangs down over her shoulder.

Her eyes meet mine.

"Hey," I say.

She smiles, a warm one that feels reserved only for me. "Hi."

"I'm ready for my treasure hunt."

CHAPTER 25
ALEC

Isabel's eyes widen, and then she chuckles. I could listen to that sound all day. "You are?"

I sit down next to her and wrap an arm around her shoulders. My free hand lands on her thigh, and the tension inside me immediately starts to drain out. Touching her is becoming a drug.

"Yes. Your idea today was brilliant."

"I thought you'd be annoyed."

"No. Why?"

"Sugar on a Tuesday, waste of valuable time…" She lowers her voice, makes it mockingly deep. "They should be building skills for the future, Isabel."

I pinch her thigh. "Is that supposed to be me?"

She chuckles. "Yes. Maybe I should have been scowling to really nail it."

"I don't scowl."

"Sure," she says, a smile dancing in her eyes. "You're the picture of happiness and ease at all times."

"Okay, that's enough. Come here." I grip her waist and tug her on top of me, so she straddles me.

She wraps her hands around my neck. "Is this my punishment?"

"Yes. Forced to entertain me," I say. "You want me to be the picture of ease?"

Her eyebrows rise. "Oh, it's like that, is it?"

"Sure is." I settle my hands on the indent above her hips. Her waist is firm beneath my hands, as toned as the rest of her. "You're happy today."

A smile plays over her lips. "I got a really interesting phone call this afternoon."

"Oh?"

"The ballet choreographer wants to meet with me for a drink next Tuesday."

My hands tighten. "They do?"

"Yes. He is a master, brilliant at what he does. It's his production we'd been dancing... *I'd* been dancing in before I had to leave." She smiles with excitement. "I've never had a one-on-one with him like this before."

"I see."

"I don't know what he wants," she says. "He knows about my injury, of course, and he was probably the one who recommended I be cut in the first place. But he might have a new production coming up. You know, when I'm healed."

I slide my thumb under the hem of her sweater, stroking over the warm skin of her stomach. "Mac will drive you both ways."

She grins. "You know, I always knew you were bossy."

"I am. And I'm glad you're excited." My free hand tugs at her braid, pulling off the hairband. I undo the thick tendrils and let her locks fall around her shoulders, thick, glossy, black strands.

She twists her fingers beneath the collar of my shirt, resting against my skin. "Are you my hairstylist now?"

"Mm-hmm." I spread the hair out over her sweater, brushing it down over her tits. It's beautiful. She's always been too beautiful, and too distracting, from the first time Connie introduced us years ago.

I pull her forward, drawing her head to mine. We touch at every point. "I shouldn't text you during the day," I say. "Distract you during your free time."

She smiles. "My boss is very demanding."

"Yes, he is." I run my fingers down her back until I find the hem of her sweater. My hand slides up beneath it. "He's been thinking about you all day, thanks to those little texts."

"Has he?" She rolls her hips, a smooth movement that grinds against my groin. A flush spreads up her cheeks, darkening them. "You made me think about you, too, with that description."

"Oh yeah?"

"Mm-hmm. And I'm thinking I might pay you back for that tomorrow."

I feather my lips over hers, intending to tease, but she tastes too good. I deepen the kiss and tug her down more firmly against my lap.

"How?" I ask.

She threads her hand into my hair. "I think that'll be a surprise."

"You'll get me hard at work if you stick to that."

She leans back, her eyes sparkling. "Think I could do that?"

"Easily." I run my hand around her hips, letting my thumbs glide down to the fabric-covered V between her legs. It's been twenty-four hours since I touched her like this last, and it feels like twenty-four hours too many. "I'm hard all the time these days."

Her eyes light up. "Really?"

"Yes. It's been a long time for me, sweetheart."

She stiffens in my arms, but her hand continues to drag through my hair. There's hesitancy in her voice. "Has it been since…?"

I sigh. "No. I've had… encounters since."

"Oh. Many?"

"Two," I say. This isn't the conversation I thought we'd have.

It's not one I *want* to have, either, and it's not a topic I'm proud of. But she just rakes her nails deliciously against my scalp, and there's only curiosity on her face.

"Tell me about them," she says.

"The first was a one-night stand at a conference, and the second was a woman I knew from high school. She was back in town for a week." I shake my head. They had been misguided attempts at a connection, a release of sexual need, and a test of the waters. To see if moving on was possible. "You can't honestly care about this."

Her eyebrows rise. "Of course I do. Was it hard?"

I know what she's asking. But it's not what I want to answer, because the guilt drawer is still locked, so I tug her closer instead. "Yes, very," I say. "Abstinence definitely makes some things grow harder."

But it had only taken the edge off a need I kept under lock for years, tempered and satisfied in the usual solo way.

Somehow Isabel had found the key, and now all I can think about is having her.

She rolls her eyes. "So you're a deprived man, is that what you're saying?"

"Incredibly." I kiss her again and grip her ass in my hands, encouraging her to keep grinding against me. "I've never needed anyone this much."

Her nimble fingers undo the top button of my shirt, and then another, so she can slip her hand inside. Her touch spreads warmth through me. I tip her head back, kissing her neck, when a sour thought strikes me.

"What about you?"

"Huh?"

"When did you have sex last."

"I think it was last night."

I chuckle against her collarbone. "Smart-ass. Come on, tell me."

"A… year ago. Maybe a bit more."

Despite it all, the answer pleases me on a deep level. If it had only been three months ago, there might still be someone in the picture. Another dancer, an old friend, someone sending her messages at night. I'm not sure I would have been able to handle the jealousy then. I'm already certain she's destined for someone her own age, but I don't want to know a thing about that man.

She reaches between our bodies and slides her hand over the hard length she's grinding down on. I hiss out a breath at the tight grip. The fabric of my pants is rough, and the friction only makes me harden more.

"Morning, day, and night," I tell her. "You don't know how crazy you've driven me."

She's breathing hard against my ear, and her hand strokes me over the fabric. "Really?"

"I've jerked off more since you moved in than in the last few years."

"Where?"

I lean my head against the couch and watch her lust-filled eyes. I could watch her forever when she's like this. Fully in her body, and flushed with a fever she can't slake alone.

"The shower every morning. The bed every night."

She blinks. "The shower?"

"Yes."

"I want to see."

I lift an eyebrow. "You want me to grab a shower now?"

She digs her teeth into her lower lip, like she's suddenly realized that she made a demand. *Come on, baby,* I think. I want her to verbalize it.

"Yes. Now," she says.

I pull her along into my bedroom and shut the door firmly

behind us. On second thought, I lock it, too. I'd rather one of the kids find it latched and knock or yell at me than walk in on something they definitely shouldn't see.

She's watching me, leaning against the vanity in my en suite, her brown eyes wide. *Praise,* I think. She's always responded so beautifully to that, and she wanted me to talk dirty.

It feels like another challenge. To give her the best orgasms she's ever had, and to fulfill every fantasy she's only read about. This won't last. I know it with bone-deep certainty, the way nothing good in life ever lasts, but damn it if I can't give her the best sex of her life in the meantime.

I want to ruin her for all future men.

I want to be the one she thinks about when she touches herself, while she fucks her boring future husband, and when she tells her girlfriends about the hottest fling of her life.

I start to unbutton my shirt. Undo the belt buckle. "Every morning," I tell her, "I'd wake up hard and thinking about you. It would drive me insane. I knew it was wrong. Knew I shouldn't think about you that way."

Stepping out of my clothes, I walk into the shower. Turn on the warm water. It cascades from above in a gentle spray. I've left the glass door open, and she leans against it, watching me.

"Why," she breathes. Her eyes are on my body, and I let her look. I run a hand down my stomach and along my cock.

"Why I shouldn't think about you?"

"Mm-hmm."

I grip myself and groan at the pressure. It's been twenty-four hours of anticipation, of wanting to be right back here, with her. I pump in a long slow stroke, squeezing right at my head.

"Because you're good, and you're so young. Nobody would understand," I say.

She stares at me, breathing heavily. "Our age difference isn't that big."

"Big enough," I say. Fifteen years isn't nothing. "Too big for the people in our lives not to question it. My sister asked me to help you, and you came to me for a job. You're my employee. Still, there I was," I say, stroking myself from base to head, "coming to thoughts of you every morning."

Her breath catches. "Here, in this shower."

I brace one hand against the tile wall. "Yes. Here in this shower."

She looks down at my cock, and at my hand pumping it in a steady tempo. Fire licks down my spine. The way she's watching me is enough to bring me close to the brink.

All the mornings I stood here, I never once thought she'd join me.

Isabel fingers the hem of her sweater. "And you thought about me."

"Yes." I widen my stance and quicken the strokes, making sure to curve my palm over the head. "I tried to stop. Couldn't. Just saw your body, your hair, your smile, and all the ways I wanted to fuck you. Make you come. After I saw you do yoga in those tight little workout clothes… Fucking hell, Isa. I wanted to tear them off you."

She pulls the sweater over her head and drops it to the stone tiles below. She's wearing a soft-looking cotton bra, lilac against her skin. Her nipples strain against the thin fabric.

I drink in the sight of the long, slim lines of her body.

"Is this what you would think of?" she asks. "How I'd look naked?"

"Yes."

She hooks her thumbs in the waistband of her leggings and tugs them down her gorgeous legs, kicking them off, but leaving her panties on.

"And after we'd kissed, after I went down on you…" I

shake my head. "I replayed it in here. Over and over again. Now take the rest of your clothes off, sweetheart."

She reaches for her bra but pauses with a smile. "Is that an order, boss?"

"Yes."

Isabel tugs the bralette off, and it joins the rest of her clothes on the floor. I groan. She has the best tits. Small, just barely a cup to hold, firm, with taut nipples. They're like the rest of her. Perfect.

She plays with the elastic of her panties. "Let's see... did you ever fantasize about me joining you in the shower?"

My voice is hoarse. "Yes."

She tugs the panties down and steps out of them, and I growl at the sight of her pussy. I grab the base of my cock tightly to stifle the release. "Fuck, you're pretty."

Isabel steps under the stream with me. It dampens her hair and sends droplets over her bare shoulders. I let go of my cock and move my hand to my balls, rolling them.

"If I'd have joined you," she says and runs a hand down my chest, "I would have gladly taken over the morning duties."

Her hand replaces mine. It's smaller, and the grip is less firm, but it feels much better. I groan and rest both of my arms against the wall. It cages her in and lets the water break upon my back, away from her face.

"Just like that," I mutter. "Just a little tighter, sweetheart."

She adjusts and speeds up, and then she's pressing tiny kisses to my jawline, to my neck, her naked body wet and right in front of me. I can't tear my eyes away from her. Can't stop myself from cupping her tits and tweaking her nipples.

"Did you come in the shower?" she asks.

"Yes." I slide my hand between her legs and stroke her silky skin. I nudge her entrance. "I'd think of coming inside you, of filling you up right here."

Her breath whooshes out of her on a soft exhale. One of her hands keeps stroking my cock and the other is rubbing my balls, pressing up at the base of my shaft. "You thought about coming inside me."

"Isa, I've thought about it a million times." I rest my forehead against hers and close my eyes. Fuck, her hands on me feel too good. "It's all I've thought about. My hand on my cock, thinking about your mouth, your tits, your pussy."

Somehow her grip gets tighter, better, hotter. "Come for me now, then," she murmurs against my cheek. "Come all over my stomach."

Shit. I feel painfully hard, and something has to give, and something *does* give. I throb in her hand, and then I'm coming. My release pulses out of me and over her stomach and chest, while she continues to stroke me through it all. I groan against her temple and let the fire roar through me.

It feels like I just lost ten years of my life.

"And here I was planning on giving you a blow job," she murmurs. "Shame you didn't last longer."

I glide my hands down to cup her firm ass, giving one cheek a soft smack. "There's always later," I say. "How old do you think I am?"

She giggles and leans back in my arms. A few drops reach her and mist the crown of her head with warm beads of spray. She looks lovely, with her dark hair plastered around her head, and her lithe body in my arms. Her cheeks bloom in a rose hue, and her skin looks dewy.

Too good for me, I think again. I spin her around, pulling her back against my chest, and turn us to face the spray of water. She giggles again when I grab some soap and start washing us both, taking extra care over her breasts and stomach, rinsing all of my remnants away.

"I wanted you, too," she murmurs, leaning her head back against my shoulder. "For months, before this."

I close my eyes against the softly spoken admission. My plan was to ruin her for all future partners, to be the best sex she's ever had, even if I can't be the man for her.

I never anticipated that she'd ruin me too.

CHAPTER 26
ISABEL

I'm nervous before Antoine arrives, sitting at a table in a downtown restaurant. Candlelight sconces illuminate the room, dancing over the faces of other guests and the servers weaving between the tables like they know each placement by heart.

He is a legend in the ballet world, and the New York Ballet Company has employed him for two consecutive seasons. This is his last one, with the final show in December, and then he's off elsewhere. From what I've heard, it's back to his native Paris.

Maybe he needs dancers for the next show he's choreographing.

Antoine arrives ten minutes late. Cigarette smoke clings to the collar of his leather jacket, but he smells like mints, too.

"Isabel," he says in a soft French accent. It's worn down by so many years working abroad, a barely noticeable lilt. "Thank you for taking the time to meet with me."

I sink back down on my chair with a smile. "I was happy to get your call. How are things at the Company?"

He shrugs. Smiles a bit. "The way they always are. Irina is complaining more than usual, and two male chorus dancers have pulled their hamstrings. We're teetering on the verge of collapse, but you know how that is."

That sounds about right. I ask him about his next show in Paris and he's more than happy to regale me. It's a ballet interpretation of a Puccini opera, and he details the choreography he's working on. It's fascinating. I haven't heard him talk about his process quite so much before. Haven't spoken to him like this at all, never one-on-one, and not over wine.

Something also feels so *right* to hear about this world again. To talk about ballet, to even *think* about it again. It's like I've carried an entire lexicon in my head that I haven't been able to use for the past couple of months.

We follow the first glass of wine with another, and then another, and he still hasn't asked about my hip. But he does ask about my current work.

"I'm nannying now," I say with a wry smile. "It's very fulfilling, and it pays the bills while my hip is healing. I think it'll be back to normal in a few months."

His eyebrows rise. "Ah shit, that's right. It's better now, then?"

"Yes, much better," I say. "I'm working on exercises to keep limber while it heals."

Antoine nods, humming. "Good, good. You were a beautiful dancer."

That warms. "Thank you."

"Stunning fouettés. Very useful in the chorus." His eyes turn teasing, and just a bit… flirtatious. "Tell me, are you single?"

I blink at him. "Um, yes."

He reaches out over the table and puts his hand on mine, playing idly with my fingers. "Aren't we all in this business," he says with a crooked smile. "No relationships, no love, just work and pain. We're all lonely, but that's ballet for you."

I feel frozen with shock.

Companies can become incestuous over a single weekend.

Male and female dancers switching bedfellows the way we switch dancing partners is common enough. But artistic directors sleeping with ballerinas is another thing entirely. It happens. Just not as often... but I've heard of his reputation.

"Isabel..." he says and taps his fingers against the back of my hand. "You were beautiful to watch in practice. I think I watched you more than I should have."

Oh.

No.

There's something painful in my chest, as the last hopes I'd carried around crack. "I've heard about your... reputation," I say. "It doesn't seem like you're very lonely."

His teeth flash in a smile. "There are different kinds of loneliness. Sure, I've been known to have fun with the ballerinas, but not at the company I'm running."

That's a lie, I think.

His eyes soften. "Now that I'm leaving New York... I want to remember my time here. Make the most of what's left. Don't you want that, too?"

It takes me a few seconds to fully digest what he's saying. To make it make sense in my head, and I can't quite, and it hurts.

"I thought you were going to talk about dancing," I say. My voice comes out a bit stiff. I look at his hand lying over mine, and it looks all wrong. It's not the right hand, not the hand or the touch I've spent years longing for. The hands that have become so familiar to me now.

He chuckles. "Dancing? Ah, if I had a spot for you? Oh, Isabel, never say never," he says. "We'll share a good time together, you will heal, and uh... we'll see. Maybe, yes?"

I pull my hand back. Disappointment races through me, and it feels like a weight on my chest, slowly crushing me down to earth. I want it to open up beneath me and swallow me whole. Take me far away.

"Thanks for the wine," I say. "It's time for me to head out."

He leans back in the chair and makes a chiding sound with his tongue. "You're leaving already? Something I said? Come on, have another glass. You can drink now—you're not dancing anymore!"

I wonder if that was his thinking. If he's done this with other ballerinas who've left the company, if there's a whole roster of them, and if he dangles the promise of a new job before them all.

I feel too hot, and I need the cool of November air. I need to get out.

"Thank you," I say. "Goodbye."

I hurry out of the restaurant with my coat thrown over my arm. *Don't cry,* I think. Get away from here. My eyes sting, but I force back the tears and keep walking. I can't wait at the front entrance of the restaurant.

Not if Antoine will leave soon, too.

I text Mac with numb fingers. *Waiting outside the fast-food place on the corner.*

He's there three minutes later. I sigh in relief at the familiar black town car. Mac opens the door for me with a smile, and I sink into the plush leather seats, hidden behind the tinted windows. Odd how it's starting to feel like a second home. There's an iPad tucked into the seatback pocket, the one we use on longer trips with the kids, and a small backpack with after-school snacks I keep stocked here.

Mac pulls us out into traffic. I focus on breathing, but it hurts. My chest feels too tight. Like I can't take a full breath and get enough oxygen.

He looks at me in the rearview mirror. "Are you all right, Isabel?"

"Yes," I say. But I'm shaking my head, staring at the intricate stitching on the back of a leather seat in front of me. "No. That didn't go as I'd hoped."

Mac's voice deepens. "Did someone hurt you?"

"Well, yes, but not physically. I…. God, I feel so stupid." A tear slips down my cheek. "So stupid."

"There are tissues in the center console," he says. The car subtly increases speed, heading back toward the Upper East Side. "And if you ever want to talk, I'm a pretty good listener."

The drive is short. I'm more composed when we say goodbye, but not by much. It's only 10 p.m. The kids are long since asleep… but Alec won't be.

I don't know if I want him to see me like this.

I unlock the front door as quietly as I can. The apartment, with its soft recessed lighting in the entryway and the wide doorway into the living room and kitchen, welcomes me in. I have to walk through it all to get to my room.

There are muffled voices on the TV; it sounds like the news. Quiet clicking of a keyboard. He's working from the couch.

I take a deep breath and walk through the living room.

Alec sees me. "Hey," he says. But then his face darkens. "Isabel?"

"I'm okay, really."

He puts the laptop away and rises in a single smooth movement. "What happened?"

I shake my head, and the tears start to flow. I can't seem to stop them this time. "I'm just such an idiot."

"No, you're not." He wraps an arm around my waist and uses his free hand to brush along my cheek. His voice hardens. "What happened? Who hurt you?"

"Myself, and my stupid hopes."

His eyebrows furrow, and concern flashes through his eyes. "Not possible."

I rest my head against his shoulder and let the tears stream unabashed. Why had I thought this meeting would result in my return to ballet? The hopes feel so foolish now, and so naive, in retrospect.

There might not be a way back for me at all.

Alec strokes his hands over my back, holding me tight against him. "Sweetheart," he mutters. "Come. Let me… here."

He leads me to my bedroom and closes the door behind us. I head for my bed, and he follows, stretching out beside me. I shift over into his arms, and the tears keep falling. I can't seem to make them stop.

It feels like another death of my career. Maybe that's a hyperbolic feeling, but it's what I'm thinking now.

The door has closed. The path is blocked.

Isabel Morales the ballerina. It's an identity that will slowly be worn away, like the tag on a well-used piece of clothing. It'll fade, and, gradually, I'll get a new one. Isabel Morales, the nanny. The yoga instructor. The college student.

But right now, I'm just Isabel, and I'm lost.

Alec's hand drifts over my hair. His chest is firm beneath my cheek, rising and falling with steady breaths.

"Tell me," he says.

I close my eyes. "He didn't want me to dance for him again, not in New York or Paris."

"Then what did he want?" Alec's voice grows rough as he asks me.

"He just wanted to sleep with me."

His body beneath mine stiffens, and his voice turns sharp with anger. "He wanted *what*?"

"Yeah." I chuckle, but it's entirely humorless. "I didn't… I couldn't even imagine that's why he'd called. I thought he remembered my dancing. That he wanted to check on my hip. But I'm just another girl he tried to get into bed."

Alec mutters something against my temple, and his arms close tight around me. "I'm so sorry."

"I won't dance again," I say. The words send a fresh wave

of sadness crashing over me, and I bury my head against his neck. It's the second time I've cried in Alec's arms over this. Two more than I'd ever planned on.

The first time had been very different from this. It was all immediate sadness, the loss of my everyday profession. This feels more like the loss of an identity.

The realization that there truly isn't a way back to the stage.

"Have you considered other options?"

"Yes," I murmur. "But every single one feels like defeat."

"Other professional ballerinas must have changed careers," he says. He reaches down and grabs my knee, pulling my leg over his body until I'm half-draped over him. "What have they gone on to do?"

That question makes my tears slow. "Their lives are pretty varied. If they were fairly famous, some have become… experts in the field. But most… I don't know."

"Can you contact one of them? Ask for advice?"

I blink against his shirt. "Yes. I suppose."

"Good," he murmurs. His right hand drifts over my head, my hair, down my back. "And while you're at it, give me the contact details for this choreographer."

"Why?"

"Because I want to make sure he never works again."

I chuckle weakly against his neck, but he doesn't laugh. I take a deep breath, and then another. Let the last of the tears ebb.

I push up onto my elbow and look into Alec's eyes. They're steady, concerned, and just a bit enraged.

I run my free hand along his jaw. "How did you handle it?"

"Handle what?" he asks.

"You lost the future you had planned for, the future you thought you'd have. Your… identity as a husband. How did it not tear you apart?"

He swipes his thumb over my cheek, catching the tear. Tucks my hair behind my ear. "It did tear me apart," he says quietly.

"Oh."

"But I *had* an identity, sweetheart. I had two others. I was a new father and a Connovan. It kept me going. You have other identities, too."

"They're feeling really weak at the moment."

"Of course they are. But you'll find them. You're a sister and a daughter. You're a friend. You're a hard worker. You're kind." He says the last word like it pains him, his thumb smoothing over my lower lip. "You'll land on your feet. People always do, even if it hurts like hell to get there."

I take a shaky breath. "You did."

"Did I?" he asks. But there's a trace of wry humor in his voice. "Yes, I suppose I did. We all did."

"I can't imagine how hard that must have been. Two kids, and all on your own."

He looks at the curve of my ear, his fingers brushing over the shell. "Sam was only six months old when she passed, and I became the CEO a year after that."

"I can't believe you juggled it both. I can't believe you still do."

"Well, I don't do it very well, according to you," he says with a lift of his lips. There's no accusation in his voice. Just calm acceptance.

I shake my head. "No, no, you do. It's impressive. *You're* impressive."

"I have help. Including you, and you're the impressive one. The kids haven't broken you yet. I'm the one who's in awe."

I trace my fingers over his face. Along his temple, along the dark eyebrows. Down to the five o'clock shadow that makes him look older, and rougher somehow. I love it when he doesn't shave. "You didn't smile the first few years I knew you," I murmur.

His eyebrows lower. "I didn't?"

I shake my head. "It's still rare today. But in the beginning... I got the feeling that you were carrying a lot inside. Holding it all in."

Alec releases a long breath and closes his eyes. And I realize with horror what I've just said. There are several things he's made clear from the start. We don't talk about his dead wife; we don't talk about his grief; and he's not in the market for a relationship.

But then he opens his eyes again. "I think you do, too," he says.

"Maybe that's why I recognized it in you."

He sweeps his thumb over my other cheek, wiping away the last remnants of my tears. The tip of it lands on my lips, moving in slow circles. "Do you want space tonight?"

I shake my head. "No. Don't leave."

"I won't." He pulls my head down and brushes his lips over mine. It's a gentle kiss at first, but it quickly deepens. I want to drown myself in these emotions and leave the others behind, at least for now.

I unbutton his shirt and slide my fingers over his chest. I love raking my nails over this skin. It always makes him groan, and he does it now, too. It's one of my favorite sounds.

His hand tunnels into my hair, and the other moves over my thigh, hitching it more firmly over his hips.

But then he lifts his lips from mine. "I'm sorry. You're sad."

"I want you," I murmur. My free hand finds the belt on his pants and plays with the buckle.

He exhales hoarsely. "Yeah?"

"Yeah."

He turns us over, cradling me in his arms. "Well then," he

says and bends to kiss me again. "Let me make you feel better."

He takes off my clothes, one item at a time, until I'm stretched naked beneath him. Alec drops kisses over my skin with a dedication I'm becoming used to. He never does anything halfway. He pushes my legs apart and kisses my inner thighs, his fingers stroking along my slit.

I close my eyes and relax into the feelings. He likes to do this. He's told me, and judging by the way he groans when he licks me, that's still true. He kisses me with open-mouthed gentleness.

"So pretty," he murmurs.

My breathing speeds up with every lavish touch of his tongue. He dedicates himself to it like there's no time limit, no goal to reach, just this act to enjoy, and I sink deeper into the comfort of the bed. Waves of pleasure rise through me, each one stronger than the next.

He slides a finger inside me, curling it, and the additional pressure makes me sigh. I push my hand into his hair and tightly grip the short strands.

I didn't think I could come tonight. I just wanted him to chase out the sad feeling with these warm ones he evokes, and to feel his skin against mine. But an orgasm is growing deep inside me all the same.

I shift to his shoulders, tugging on them. "I want you."

He looks up at me with hazy eyes. I can feel him assessing me, watching my face for signs of lingering sorrow.

My grip on his shoulder tightens. "Now, Alec."

His lips curve into a crooked smile, and he pushes up to his knees. He undoes the buckle of his belt.

"All right, sweetheart," he says. "Shall we practice a bit, too?"

"Practice what?"

He pulls down his zipper. "What is it you want?"

I want to roll my eyes at the question. But his hand is

hovering at his pants, thumbs hooked into the waistband, and he's going to make me say it.

"I want you to fuck me," I plead on a soft exhale.

A shiver runs through him, and he glides his other hand along my inner thighs, still spread before him. "With what?" he asks, and tugs his pants down. He's hard and still as large, jutting straight out.

"Just come here," I say, and grip his cock tightly. I tug him forward, and Alec falls over me, bracing on an elbow beside my head.

He groans at my harsh strokes. "Damn, sweetheart."

He uses his knee to spread my legs wider apart and lines himself at my entrance. As he pushes in, my back arches at the sweet pressure. God, he's thick.

"That's it," he murmurs against my lips. "That's my girl."

My eyes flutter closed at the praise, and another rush of warmth races through me. He starts to roll his hips, and I grip his shoulders, my face pressed against the smooth skin there. He's slower and more precise than usual, each plunge deep and measured.

I let my legs fall open and tilt my hips up to meet his thrusts. He's warm and heavy against me, and I love his hooded eyes and heavy breathing.

He grips my calf and pulls it up, and up, and up until he's nearly split me in half. I hook my arm around the back of my knee to keep the leg raised. He's avoided my hurt hip, and I love him for it.

His thrusts stutter. "Shit, you're flexible."

"Professional hazard."

Another shudder goes through him and his movements shift, becoming faster, harder. He looks down at where he's entering me, and with the new angle, it's easier to see.

"You take me so good, Isa," he mutters. "Look at that. Look how well I fit inside you."

With this positioning, he hits against my clit with every

stroke, and it pushes me right to the brink. He watches me as my body tightens in anticipation. His right hand cups my face, and his hips speed up.

I come, breaking apart around him and beneath him, tremors racing down my limbs. Alec buries his face against my neck. "Fuck," he groans. His hips jerk, and then he's coming too, his back tense beneath my hands, and his hips pushing deeper. I feel him pulse inside me, and then he relaxes, muscles turning loose under my touch.

I lower my leg and lock it around his waist instead. I try to pull him down, to have him rest all of his weight on me, but he resists.

"You won't crush me," I murmur.

He gives in, and I'm pressed deliciously into the mattress. I close my eyes and breathe in the scent of him, of his warm neck and the hair tickling my cheek. He's so large, I'm covered entirely by him.

His lips move over my ear, my neck. "That wasn't one of your highlighted fantasies," he murmurs against my shoulder. "Vanilla missionary sex."

Yes it was, I think. *It just wasn't on my Kindle.*

Alec pushes up onto an elbow. His skin is flushed, and the tension that I'm so used to seeing mar his forehead is wiped clean.

His eyes suddenly narrow. "Shit. Condom."

"I'm on birth control." I run a hand through his thick hair.

"You are?"

I nod, raking my fingers across his scalp. "Yes. Being a ballerina and getting your period every month isn't super helpful. I've skipped my periods for years."

"Oh." He frowns. "Is that safe?"

"Yes, I think so. It's common, at least." His concern makes me smile. Somehow my wellbeing is always his first thought, whenever I do anything. *Let Mac drive you. Is your hip okay? Are you safe?*

He rolls us onto our sides, keeping his hips locked to mine, and still buried inside me. "I can't believe I forgot."

"Swept up in the moment."

"Yeah," he says. But he's frowning, like he can't recall the last time that happened.

"What if I told you that was part of the fantasies?"

His eyebrows drop lower, and a languid, macho smile spreads across his lips. "Interesting."

"That's all you have to say?"

"For now." He kisses me again and slowly pulls out of me with a twist of his hips. I lie on my back and watch him head to my bathroom. The water turns on a second later, and soon he returns, a washcloth in hand.

He's matter-of-fact about it, pushing my legs apart. His gaze lingers on the warmth leaking out of me. "I get it," he says. There's a hoarseness to his voice. "That part of the fantasy... I definitely get."

He's gentle as he wipes me clean, and then he tosses the cloth aside. He remains sitting on the edge of my bed with his hand in mine.

I want to ask him to stay.

I don't know if he will.

He never has before.

There are kids in the other room, kids that sometimes wake up and knock on his bedroom door in the middle of the night. It's also a boundary. Another layer between us that we've used, one that keeps things neat and orderly. That keeps this from being a romantic relationship. And we've discarded one layer tonight already.

I wrap both of my hands around his familiar one. "Stay with me a while longer."

He looks down at our hands, resting together on the cover of my bed. For a drawn-out moment, I don't think he'll answer.

But then he nods. "Get into bed."

I climb beneath the covers, into the familiar softness of my bed. He slides in after me with a quiet sigh. He pulls me against him, tucking my head beneath his chin, and wraps an arm around me.

I close my eyes against his shoulder as his hand draws soothing circles along my body. Tomorrow, I know the sadness will return. The questions about what I'd learned tonight will flood me. The fear over my future.

But right now I feel nothing but an overwhelming exhaustion.

His mouth is warm over my temple. "Be good for me one final time," he murmurs, "and fall asleep."

That makes me smile against his skin. *Always bossy.* But it doesn't take me long to do what he'd asked and drift away in his arms.

CHAPTER 27
ISABEL

He's gone when I wake up. The comforter is tangled around me, like I've been turning and twisting in my sleep, and my head feels heavy. He'd stayed long enough, though. He'd been here when I fell asleep.

The events of last night return in a painful realization. Antoine. The drinks. The proposition. I turn over and bury my face in the pillow.

Gone.

That life is gone.

I failed at the dream I've always had.

For so many years, the prevailing wisdom was always *just work harder*. And I've just worked harder so many times. Earlier mornings, longer training sessions, rigorous stretching hours. But I've seen this injury take out dancers before. There's no *just work harder* with recovery or healing.

You have other identities, Alec had said.

Well, I don't know if I want to make "nanny" a full-time one. The kids are lovely. I'm enjoying myself, working here, living here… more than I suspected I would. But it's hard to imagine myself doing it all over again for a different family when this runs its course.

I knew retirement was coming. It's always coming for a professional dancer, and it never comes when they're ready.

I just never thought it would be at twenty-five.

Dragging myself out of bed, I head into the shower. Alec has already roused the kids, and the warm scent of breakfast wafts from the kitchen. I start packing their backpacks and listen to Sam recounting the dream he had.

The rest of the morning goes by in the same domestic chaos: packing homework and lunch boxes, herding stray hats and shoes, and an endless chatter in the car to St. Regis's. Mac and I drop them off, both waving, and watch them race up the steps of the school.

We get back in the car in companionable silence. He pulls the Bentley out into morning traffic, heading back to the apartment. I look out the window at the now familiar stoops. We drive this way every morning. Brick houses, tree-lined streets.

"You know, I wasn't always a driver," Mac says.

I look at him in surprise. But he's staring at the road, shoulders relaxed.

"Oh? What did you do before?"

"I served time, actually." He says this casually and merges into the right lane with a glance over his shoulder. "Got twelve years, served eight for good behavior."

My mind has gone entirely blank. I don't know what to say, how to respond to any of it.

"I'm sorry," I say.

That makes him chuckle warmly. "Don't be. It taught me a lot. Want to know what I did to serve time? Most people do. It's their first question."

I swallow. "Yeah. If you want to tell me."

"I'm not from New York," he says. "No, I'm from Boston. My dad worked with cars. Ran his own car shop. I loved it. Every moment I wasn't in school, and there were plenty, I was in that shop. Tinkering with the engines and polishing the hoods. Dropped out of high school the minute I thought I'd learned everything I would ever need to know, which goes to show how mature I was at sixteen. My neighborhood was rough. Dad was pretty absent, and he wasn't that good to begin with. But cars..." He shakes his head, reverence in his voice. "I loved them as much then as I do now. I planned to take over the auto shop. Thought I deserved it.

"But," he continues and looks at me in the rearview mirror, "I wanted to live the high life first. Drive the fastest cars, the sexiest cars. Race them. Doing that quickly gets you into bad company. I wanted it all, though. Didn't take long until I started committing grand theft auto with a few buddies. Boosted cars, raced them, then flipped them for profit. Porsches, Bugattis... it ran like a fine-tuned machine."

"I didn't know any of this," I say carefully. "How old were you when...?"

"When I got caught? Twenty-seven. My girlfriend at the time was pregnant, and I wanted to make just a bit more money for us. But shit went sideways." He shakes his head, and his tone turns somber with regret. "There wasn't supposed to have been a security guard there, but there was. Things got violent. He survived, but only barely. I was terrified. Of what would happen and of what we'd done. The cops knocked on my door three days later.

"I pleaded guilty. Served my time... got out. It took years of work just to get to meet my son. He was eleven the first time I got to see him." Mac's voice inflects with pride. "He's twenty-two now, living down in DC with his mom and going to community college. I go to see him every break I have."

"What's his name?" I ask.

"Jeremiah. Sarah named him all on her own, but I think she did a pretty good job."

"I'm glad you got a second chance," I say.

"So am I." He taps his fingers on the steering wheel. "And

you know what? I still work with cars. This might not be the fastest car in the city, or the flashiest, but it's elegant. A real classic beauty. And I might not own it, but I don't need to. I get to drive it every single day and keep her polished to the nines." He glances up at me through the rearview mirror, and his eyes crinkle with a smile. "I get to be a part of those kids' lives and drive them safely to and from school. It might not be the high life I once thought so important, but it's a much better one."

I blink at the sudden moisture in my eyes. "I'm sorry you had to go through all that."

He looks back at the road and shakes his head. "Don't be. I deserved to serve time, and I needed it to knock my head straight. My point is just... well, I'm not that great at words. But I think maybe you got it?"

I smile at him. "Yes, I did. Thank you for sharing this with me."

He'd been there yesterday, driving me home after I walked out on Antoine. He knows about my failing dancing career. And maybe, just maybe... Alec said something on their trip this morning.

Things don't have to end up the way you planned for them to be wonderful.

And that's something I can work with.

When I arrive back home, I do my usual off-duty routine in the home gym. Working out, stretching the muscles around my hip. Then I take a long shower and spend thirty minutes looking at dance teaching positions in New York. The idea of becoming a ballet instructor chafes a little. I hadn't expected it to, but it does.

Many of the ballet teachers I've had were... harsh. It's a

world I'm used to and learned to adapt in. But I'm not sure I want to be the one to mete harshness out in turn.

I answer texts I've been avoiding. *Yes, Mom, I'll come to family dinner on Sunday. It's my day off.* I sent Connie a funny picture a few days ago, and she finally responded, sending me one of her own. It's of her sitting at her desk, half covering a yawning mouth. *Having a husband is tiring me out,* she wrote beneath it.

I'm making lunch when I catch a sight of the thick leather wallet lying on the stand in the hallway. Alec's. He must have forgotten it. This has never happened before, and I pull up my phone to text him.

But a thought starts to form. One that's brazen and risky, and everything I'm usually not. However, I'm not who I usually am right now, anyway.

So I write something different.

> Isabel: Looks like you forgot your wallet at home. Do you want a visit at your office?

> Alec: Yeah, I know. Annoying. And… yes. If you have the time.

> Isabel: I have the time. Do you?

> Alec: No, but I will make it.

I dig my teeth into my lower lip and look down at those six little words. Warmth spreads through my chest and pools in my stomach.

> Isabel: Remember that one highlighted scene on my Kindle?

> Alec: It's burned into my brain. And the answer is yes.

> Isabel: Really?

> Alec: Yes. Get over here.

I grin and hurry to my bedroom. It takes me ten minutes of whirling through my clothes before I settle on a dress that ends halfway down my thighs, no stockings, and throw a long coat over it. I fluff up my usually flat hair and stare at myself in the mirror. My eyes look wide, my cheeks flushed, and I look just a bit crazed.

Good, because I feel it.

I grab Alec's wallet and my bag, and wave bye to Katja. She's just arrived and is doing her usual meal prep. Breakfast for everyone for the next day, lunch packs, and dinner.

"He's usually not forgetful," she says with a cluck of her tongue. "Is Mac driving you?"

"Yes," I say.

Katja opens the fridge and grabs a wrapped sandwich and a cool soda. "Here," she says and pushes the items into my hands. "Could you bring him his lunch?"

"You make him lunch?"

There's a tinge of pink on her cheeks. "Some days," she says. "Okay, now go."

Mac drives me to the Contron skyscraper in Midtown. My heart is pounding when I enter the giant lobby, just as it had done weeks and weeks ago for my very first interview.

I stop at the reception. She gives me a sharp look.

"And who are you?"

"I work for Alec Connovan," I say. "Here to see him."

Her eyes narrow, but she clicks away at her computer. It only takes a few seconds. "Name?"

"Isabel Morales."

"Great, we have your name on file. Here's your key card. It's valid for the entire day and will take you straight to his floor in the elevator. Please return the card to me on your way out." Her red lips tip into a professional smile. "Enjoy your day, Ms. Morales."

The elevator takes me up a dazzling number of levels to the top floor where Alec's office is. I remember it from last time, the white corridor, the glass partition walls, and the framed photographs on the walls. I walk through the space like I belong here, my heart is beating now at a staccato in my chest.

His assistant nods at me and presses a button on his desk, speaking into a mic. *Ms. Morales here to see you.* A second later, the giant wooden door to Alec's office swings open, revealing the bright space and the man inside.

I walk in. If people are watching me do so, I ignore them. Nothing else exists but Alec, sitting behind his giant glass desk with the skyline of Manhattan behind him.

The door shuts closed behind me.

"Hello," I say.

A smile tips his lips. "Hi."

"I have your wallet."

"Thank you." He pushes back from his desk but remains seated, his arms draped along the armrests. Silence stretches out between us, and he lifts an eyebrow in question.

And?

Right. The scene I'd made him read had me initiating it. The heroine arriving at the hero's office, forcing him to take a break…

I drop my bag and shrug out of my coat. Nerves suddenly make my throat tight. "So this is where you work."

"Yes," he says. His deep voice is amused. "I'm not usually visited by beautiful young women, though."

I slide a palm down my dress to smooth it. "That's good to hear."

"Mm-hmm. You look pretty."

The compliment sends warmth through my chest, and it's *him.* For all of the impressiveness of this office and the pressed suit he's in, it's Alec.

I walk around his desk. "Have you been working very hard?"

"Always." His legs are spread, head back, watching me intently. "But I could use a break."

I step between his legs and run my hand through his hair, feeling the soft strands slip between my fingers. It still feels unreal that I'm allowed to touch him like this, when he's always seemed so untouchable. That he's now mine in this way.

Alec grips my hips. "This dress is…"

"Good?"

"Mm-hmm. Understatement."

I lean down to kiss him. He tastes like warm coffee and determination, and he pulls me closer with a groan. I let him tug me forward, but I don't sit down on his lap.

I sink between his legs instead.

His eyes darken. "Isabel…"

I stroke my hands up his thighs. This feels insane. Something someone else would do, but it's me here, on this carpeted floor, and with Alec Connovan looking at me. His forehead is furrowed again, like he can't really believe I'm here. That we're doing this.

I untuck his shirt and start working on his belt buckle.

Alec's voice is low. "I can't believe you're here."

"Never done this in here before?"

"Hell no," he mutters. I pull down his zipper and reach in to grab his cock. He groans at the contact. He's already half-hard, and grows thicker in my hand as I stroke.

I take him into my mouth, and I'm rewarded by the hoarse sigh from the man above me. Alec's hand slides into my hair. "Unreal," he mumbles. "Oh… fuck. Yes."

I haven't sucked his cock before, and I've been wanting to. I didn't think the first time would be in his office. It heightens the sensations, knowing all of his employees are right outside that door, and that this building is his kingdom. He tastes good, salty, and I love the husky sounds of his breathing.

My heart is beating fast, like I've been through a workout session, and I think about the scene in that book. I can't believe I'm living that kind of life. It sends a thrill through me.

I tighten my lips around him and take him as deep as I can until he hits the back of my throat. And then I do it again, and again, making his fingers tighten on my hair.

"It's so good. Fuck. I can't… I'm trying to remember what you liked about the scene, but I can't think."

That makes me giggle. It sends vibrations around his cock, and he groans again.

His other hand smooths my hair back. "That's it," he mutters. "Do that again for me. Laugh like that."

I do, and he hisses out another breath. Nothing has ever sounded better. I do it again, bobbing my head, and his breathing speeds up. His fingers threaded in my hair don't apply pressure, just a steady weight, following along with my movements.

His left hand brushes over my cheek. "This view," he rasps. "I could watch you with my cock in your mouth forever."

Oh.

The words spread heat through me, and I speed up my movements, flicking my tongue over his broad head. Alec groans again. I look up to see him drop his head against the back of the chair, eyes hooded and locked on me.

"That's my girl," he mumbles, his thumb caressing my temple. "Can you take all of me?"

I take him as deep as I can, deeper than before, and he groans again. It makes me feel ten feet tall. That I'm the one doing this to him, at his desk, in his office, inside the building of the company where he's the CEO. That he's coming undone, and it's all because of me.

I sheath my teeth and seal my lips tighter around his cock.

"Fuck. Too good," he says through gritted teeth. "I'm too close. Sweetheart, I need to fuck you."

I keep going, but he won't let me.

"Isa. I want you on my desk."

I look up at him, my movements halting. He brushes my hair back. "This view," he says hoarsely. "I'll never forget it. Now get up, baby. That's it."

I release him with a soft pop, and he pulls me into standing. His hands grab the hem of my dress, and he tugs it up, past my thighs and hips. It bunches into a tight mess around my waist.

Alec's fingers skim over the lacy thong that covers almost nothing. It's the first time he's seen me wear anything like this, anything that's not my usual cotton. "You wore these for me."

"Yes, I did."

He rests his forehead against my lower stomach, his nose grazing the tiny triangle over my core. He takes a deep breath, and the hands on my thighs tighten.

"Sweetheart, one of your fantasies was a quickie. You wanted me to fuck you fast."

"Yes," I breathe.

He tugs my thong down and bares me to his view. He kisses sensitive skin a few times before rising from his chair.

His hand cups between my legs, fingers curving, testing. "You're wet," he mutters. Then, his right arm sweeps over his desk, pushing papers out of the way and his laptop to the side. A pencil holder is knocked over, but he doesn't seem to notice, turning me toward the desk.

"Bend over, Isa. Right here."

I lean over the glass desktop and stick my ass out as high as I can. I hear my pulse in my ear and feel it thundering in my chest. I'm exposed. Behind me are endless concrete towers, windows upon windows, too far to see closely but still *there*. And so is Alec. Standing at my back, his hand spreads me apart, and then he's pushing in.

I grip the edge of the desk and try to muffle my moan. I'm getting more used to his girth, but I'm also less prepared than usual, and the burn is delicious. His hands land in an iron grip around my hips. He fucks me fast, and hard, and I love the sounds he makes. The grunts and groans and the harsh breathing.

I feel like I'm coming undone at the seams.

"You feel so unreal. Gripping me so good." He bottoms out and stays there for a moment, rolling his hips, and the pressure makes me mewl. My clit is hitting the edge of the desk with each of his pumps. Adrenaline, nerves, pleasure, it all combines into piercing ecstasy.

I bite my lower lip to keep from moaning when I come. The orgasm is unexpected, but it barrels through me regardless, strengthened by the illicitness of what we're doing, the location, and his steady deep thrusts.

Alec's close. I can hear it in the shallowness of his breaths, his lack of dirty talk, and the sharpness of his hips. His breathing snags, and then he's coming, too, and with a low groan that sounds like his soul is being ripped out of his body. He pulses inside me, and I *feel* it, feel it in a way I never could before with the condoms.

When we've both caught our breathing, he tugs me onto his lap, still buried deep inside me. I lean back against his chest and feel boneless.

His hands roam over my bare thighs, my lower stomach, every part of me that's exposed. "That," he murmurs against my cheek, "was fucking unreal. I can't believe you came here."

"I can't believe I came, either."

"I can," he says. His hand plays between my legs, touching my sensitive clit, and I push him away. His chuckle turns into a laugh. "God. Now I know what I'm missing every other workday."

"I can come back. Do this again."

"Mm-hmm. I wouldn't get any work done, but somehow, I don't think I'd mind." He runs a hand through his hair and sighs softly. "I feel amazing."

That makes me giggle again. "That was my goal."

"I don't… Isabel, never stop being my nanny."

I wrap an arm around his neck. "Oh? Is this officially included in my duties, then?"

His teeth dig into the side of my neck, and I swat at his hair. "Yes. I'll add it into your contract. Keep your boss thoroughly drained at all times."

"Drained, huh?"

"Drained dry," he says.

I play idly with his hair, and find that I'm smiling for no particular reason. I didn't know it could be like this. So… easy, somehow, to be intimate with someone. To say openly what I want and have it reciprocated.

There's a loud ping from his half-open laptop. It sounds like a calendar reminder. Alec doesn't even lift his head, buried against my throat. His arms are still wrapped tightly around me and his breathing is deep.

"I'm keeping you from work," I say. "What did you reschedule, anyway?"

"A meeting with the mayor of New York."

"No way?"

"No," he says, and there's a smile in his voice. "A meeting with my marketing team. I only pushed it an hour, though, so I need to be there in fifteen."

"What do you *actually* do for work?"

He chuckles again. Has he ever done that so much before? The warmth in my chest swells again. "Sweetheart, I'll tell you as much as you want tonight, after the kids are asleep. But I think it'll only put you to sleep."

"No, I'm interested."

"I'm more interested in hearing about you and your dancing career," he says. "I have questions. Sweetheart... did you see that you have Sunday night off?"

"Yes, I did."

"So do I," he says. "I've asked Katja to stay and watch the kids. Have dinner with me."

"Just the two of us?" I ask. The question feels intimate, and it hangs in the air, the words *two of us* growing until I think I've misspoken. We've never talked about an *us*. Never spoken about more than just sex and pleasure and stolen moments like this.

But he nods. "Yes, just us two."

"Okay," I murmur.

"Good." His hands stroke up my bare thighs one final time before he sighs. "I was half-hard the moment you walked into my office, suspecting what you had planned."

"You were?" I whisper.

"Mm-hmm. Just like you were wet as soon as I touched you." He turns my head and presses his lips to mine. For a long moment, we just kiss, his hand sliding over my legs while he remains buried inside me. "You're making me feel twenty years younger, like a teenager again, with how much I need you and how often I want to come."

"You're still young," I say.

He raises an eyebrow, and there's a self-deprecating glint in his eyes. "No, I'm not, sweetheart. Not the way you are. Now let's move. I have an en suite."

I get cleaned up and pull my thong back in place as he looks on, leaning against the doorframe of his bathroom. I tug my dress down and brush my hair into some semblance of order.

He watches me with eyes that still hold a trace of desire, and are much softer than when I first entered his office.

I trail my hand along his suit-covered chest. "I hope I'm the first woman you've ever fucked on your desk."

He turns to follow me, his hands in his pockets. "You are the first," he says. "I'll never be able to look at that desk the same way again."

I pull on my coat. "Well… mission accomplished."

He smiles at me.

I smile back at him.

There's another ping from his calendar, and I laugh. "Okay, okay. You're a very busy man. I'll leave."

"I wish I wasn't," he says. "Round two doesn't sound so bad."

"Tonight," I say.

He nods and reaches down, adjusting himself through his pants with a wry smile.

That makes me chuckle, and I hoist my bag up on my shoulder. "Okay. Bye."

"Bye," he says.

"Go conquer the world."

"Already conquered," he says.

It's such a cocky thing to say that I roll my eyes. He looks like a conquerer, too, standing there with his watchful eyes and in his pristine suit, with a messed-up desk and the New York City skyline behind him.

"Rule it well, then," I say.

"I always do."

I shake my head at him, and his lips tip up, and I finally reach the door. I don't want to go. But I do, and the door swings open on electronic hinges to reveal the bright space of the outer office.

Alec's assistant looks up at me. "Have a great day," he tells me in a tone that is so professional it makes me certain he suspects *something*. I round the corner, heading down the hallway away from the CEO's office and toward the other executive suites.

"Oh!" A woman stops a few feet away. Auburn-haired, familiar, and smiling. "Isabel? What are you doing here?"

"Hi!" Connie and I hug, and my cheeks burn. Maybe the hug was a wrong move? Maybe I smell like cologne and sex now?

But she just steps back, a smile still gracing her face. "What are you doing here?"

"I had to drop something off. Alec forgot his wallet at home this morning."

She shakes her head. "Really? He made you do that?"

"Oh, I was happy to. It's fun to see Contron," I say like an idiot. It feels like what Alec and I just did is written all over my face, stamped on my forehead, hovering in the air between us.

But Connie just laughs. "Really? Well, I can give you a tour any day. You should have told me, we could have had lunch."

"I'm sorry, I thought you'd be busy," I say. It's a total lie. I hadn't even thought about it, and guilt washes over me.

She sighs. "You're probably right. I'm working on our latest investment right now, and there's so much paperwork to get through and to understand. Hey, it's actually great that you're here. Are you free on Sunday? Gabriel and I are throwing a party."

"On a Sunday?"

"Yeah. Remember how he used to have those poker nights? Well, we're doing it again. Trying to merge our groups of friends." She reaches out, puts a hand on my shoulder. "There'll be a ton of new people there. Hot guys, too. You should come."

I find myself nodding. "That sounds amazing. I'll be there."

She beams, smiling brightly. "Great! I was actually just heading to Alec's to tell him that he has to come, too. I think he'll have a harder time refusing me if I ask him in person and not through an email."

I chuckle. "Yeah, I see that."

"He needs to get out more," she says. "See you Sunday?"

"Yes, that sounds great. Can't wait."

She gives me a goodbye hug before disappearing down the corridor in the direction of her brother's office, and his large, now-cluttered desk.

And my guilt grows.

CHAPTER 28
ALEC

It's a warm November day, unusual for the season, and we all choose to walk home from Willa's tennis game. She struts happily in front of me with her ponytail swinging, as always tired from her practice but happy in spirit. I should make it a point to show up to her practices more often. She'd been great on the court. Played her heart out, the same way she does everything, putting in her whole soul.

Sam's hand is in mine. Unusual, because he dislikes being shackled to my side, preferring to run and touch and inspect everything a New York sidewalk has to offer. He's chatting happily to Isabel. They're coming up with absurd superhero powers. I don't know who started, but it's clear this is a running topic between the two of them.

Her voice is calm and interested, responding to everything he says, even as crazy as some of his comments are. It's nice to listen to.

More than nice.

I had planned to spend tomorrow night with just her, maybe take her out to a restaurant, selfish as that would have been. But then Connie had walked into my office and guilt-tripped me into coming to her party. It's shameful to admit, even only to myself, that her mentioning Isabel's attendance had tipped the scales.

My little sister has an entire life now that I know practically nothing about. A husband, a new apartment, and work that is increasingly separate from mine. The last few months have shown me that I've been failing at being a big brother, too. Seems like I'm falling short in all of my roles.

Son, father, brother, CEO... the only role I feel confident in is *lover*. Making Isabel come, giving her pleasure, and playing around with her fantasies. Maybe adding a dinner to the mix was a bad idea. But starting this with her in the first place was a tremendously bad fucking idea, and I've already made it.

And I can't find it in myself to regret it. I don't think I ever will.

Even if I'm only a passing stop, destined to be nothing but a fun memory before she dances onward and upward in life. Away from me and this nanny position, out of my arms and into someone else's. A man her own age. A man without two kids. One who isn't a widower or a CEO, who has the time to take her out to dinner every night, and make love to her in a bed they share.

"The power to have endless bowls of cereals," Isabel tells Sam. "No matter how much you eat, it's always full."

He makes a low *oohing* sound. "The power to... blow bubbles!"

"Oh yes, that's a good one. You'd distract bad guys with that, for sure," she says. "Willa, do you have a weird superpower idea?"

My daughter turns, walking backward and looking at us with bright eyes. "Hmm. Maybe... the power to grow grass."

"Grass?"

"Mm-hmm. Like really tall grass."

That makes me chuckle. "The bad guys will definitely be confused if you throw around lawns right and left."

Willa smiles at me. "Daddy, what's yours?"

The ability to stop time, I think, looking at her. Feeling Sam's small hand in mine and Isabel's calm presence. Before they grow up... and before Isabel leaves.

"Sneezing super hard," I say. "It'll knock the bad guys right out."

Both Sam and Willa laugh. They're easily entertained, and I glance to the side, watching Isabel.

"That was inspiring," she says.

"Thank you."

"You should write a children's book about him," she teases.

I shake my head. "I think I like your superpower with the cereal more. Far more useful."

Her smile widens, and I feel my own tug on my lips, and it's ridiculous, what we're doing. Talking about. Flirting in front of the kids. But I can't find it in myself to stop this, either. Not to shamelessly enjoy her company every chance I get.

Willa skips a little. "Isabel," she says. She has the voice of *a-big-question-is-coming,* and I hear the amusement in Isabel's responding *yes.* Whatever comes next will be good. I'm betting it's something about what snack she'll get at pickup tomorrow.

"Do you want your own kids?" Willa asks.

Well.

That wasn't what I was expecting at all.

Isabel cocks her head. "Yes, I think so. I'm pretty sure I want children one day. But that's still years away," she says.

"Mm-hmm. I want three kids," Willa says. "All girls. What do you want?"

Isabel chuckles. "Two, I think."

"Boy or girl?"

"Either, or both. I don't have a preference," Isabel says. "Sounds like you've thought about this a lot. What are you going to name your daughters?"

With the authority of someone who considers this an ironclad plan, Willa lists names that I recognize from some of the cartoons she likes to watch. At my side, Sam disagrees vehemently with the idea of three girls.

Of course Isabel wants kids. *Two.* It's not a surprise, but it still feels like one. Another nail in the coffin of whatever it is we're doing. She'll be a fantastic mother one day. It's easy to picture it, and the image sets off an ache in my chest. That's still years away, she'd said. When she's settled and ready.

And it's unlikely I can give her any of that. I barely have enough time as it is, and the thought gives rise to fresh guilt inside me about the possibility of more between us. Of making her mine in every way that counts. Of being someone's husband again.

Of having someone to lose again.

And why would she choose me? The fifteen-year difference might feel like nothing now, but if kids are years away for her, I might be in my late forties by that time. It's impossible.

But I *can* be the man who makes her come, for as long as she'll let me.

They talk about names, comparing lists, Willa serious but happy, and Isabel engaged and amused. I try to focus on the conversation. The hand in mine. Sam's voice, trying to interject with better names, like the names of superheroes he likes.

I clear my throat. "Who will you marry, honey?"

Willa frowns. Clearly her thought process hadn't extended that far. "He'll be a prince," she decides. "So, I'll be a princess. And my daughters, too."

Isabel laughs. "Really? That's amazing."

"Who will you marry?" Willa asks.

"Oh, I don't know who. I'm not sure if I've met him yet," Isabel says lightly. "But I don't think he'll be a prince. Those are reserved for you. But the most important thing is that he'll be good."

"Good," I repeat quietly.

She glances at me, a small smile on her lips. "Yeah. I think I'd like that. Caring, protective… and making time for what's truly important in life."

It sounds like the opposite of me, then. She's made a point of telling me to do more of the latter. Whoever it is… he better treat her right. Hold her when she's crying and encourage her dreams.

He better know what a treasure she is.

"I think," Willa says loudly, "that it's better to marry a prince."

I run a hand over my jaw. "Yeah, maybe that's the key."

We make it back to the apartment, and to Katja waiting with dinner. She's a steady presence in our home, and this time it's no different. The kids flock to her immediately, and she lets them both have a tiny snack before they rush to wash their hands.

Isabel and Katja chat quietly. I take a seat at the table and feel a hundred years old. She wants a good man. Two kids. A home of her own, probably. A new job and a life that's filled with times at that home and adventures outside of it. A stable family life. And someone to spoil with her smiles and kindness she dispenses so liberally.

She's only twenty-five, so there's no rush for any of it. She can easily wait another decade before settling down.

I run a hand over my face. The picture she'd painted is easy to imagine, and my mind fills in the blanks of what a life with her would be like.

It's hard not to want it.

Dinner is the usual chaos. Food is eaten, even if some of it has to be coaxed. Bath time and bedtime, and I stay extra long beside Sam after he's fallen asleep, watching his chest rise and fall steadily beneath his star-spangled cover.

Could I have more kids?

Do I *want* more kids?

The thought lingers for longer than it should before I shake it loose. It's an absurd question, and I know exactly why it had risen to the surface.

No, I can't have any of that. Can't go down that path again, even if it's with her. The hurt was far too great the first time. I don't think I can survive it a second time... not if there's a risk of the same outcome.

Loving and losing Isabel would kill me.

I pause in the hallway, lean against the wall, and take in the view. She's changed into a pair of leggings and an oversized sweater again. She's sitting cross-legged in the middle of the giant couch, and the TV is on, the volume low. Her hair is unbound, long and black down her shoulders, reaching almost to her waist. No makeup on. I've learned to tell the difference now. She's achingly beautiful both ways, but I think I like this the most. When she looks soft and relaxed and at home, here with me.

She catches sight of me, and a sweet smile spreads across her face. "Hey."

"Hi."

"Are you going to stand there and watch or join me?"

"I haven't decided, yet."

She rolls her eyes. "Well, I know what I want."

"Mm-hmm. And what's that?"

Her smile glows. "You, sitting here next to me. I know how much you love watching *Gilmore Girls* with me."

I cross the distance to her. The couch is soft beneath me, but she's softer still, leaning against my side. "This damn show," I murmur.

"I thought I'd lost my mind when you first asked about it."

"Yeah?"

"Mm-hmm. Here was Connie's sullen brother, asking *me* about my favorite dramedy."

"Dramedy?"

"Drama and comedy put together. Tell me," she says, her hand on my knee, "when you used to join me here in the evenings, with your laptop…"

I raise an eyebrow. "Was I only looking to spend time with you?"

"Yeah. Were you?"

"Well, let's just put it this way," I say. "I don't find the fictional town's antics *that* interesting."

She giggles and shifts closer, and I wrap my arm around her. It feels so right to hold her like this. To have her pressed against my side and feel her chest expanding with every breath. I want to keep her tucked here forever.

She watches her show, and I can't help but think thoughts I shouldn't. The what-ifs. The whens. Her future, and where it might lead her.

I kiss her temple. "I saw your face today."

"You did?"

"Mm-hmm. When you watched the street dancers, during our walk home."

She smiles a little. "Yeah. It just looked like they were having so much fun. It reminded me… well, of myself years ago. I haven't danced like that since I was a teenager. Ballet isn't really about freedom of expression. It's rigorous, and disciplined, and those street dancers were the exact opposite."

"You could do that," I say.

She chuckles, and I tighten my grip around her waist. Something about today makes me think I won't be able to touch her this freely forever.

"Maybe, but I wouldn't know where to start," she says. "It's a thought, though."

I pull her legs over mine and settle back against the couch. My thumb strokes small circles over her outer thigh. On the screen, two young women look like they're fighting, one blonde and one brunette. I didn't catch about what.

We're almost at the end of the episode when Isabel speaks again. "Alec…"

"Yes?"

"There's something on your mind."

I look down at her, at her kind brown eyes filled with questions. They're the color of chocolate. "Tell me," she murmurs.

I look back at my hand on her legging-clad thigh. "You want kids in the distant future," I say.

She's quiet for a moment, but then she nods. "Yeah, I think I do."

I keep circling my thumb, watching the movement. "I've been thinking about the man who can give that to you. The good man you mentioned before."

"Oh."

"I've been thinking about him, and hating his guts," I say bitterly. Her eyes widen, but I can't seem to stop. "That's not the right thing to say, but it's the truth. That's who I've been thinking about. How you'll look at him, the way you'd… fuck. How you'll tell him all your fantasies as you've told me, and how he'll get all of you, your present *and* your future. How you'll bear his kids and be a wonderful mother, and this will be nothing but a memory to you. And how it'll be *his* bed you sleep in every night."

"Alec," she whispers.

"I know," I say roughly. "It's irrational. But that's what I've become, apparently, since the day you stepped into my apartment and flipped my mind inside out."

"*Alec*," she says again, and I hate that I love the sound of my name on her lips that much. That I've come to crave it, her voice whispering it in my ear or moaning against my chest. "I was talking about *you*."

My eyes narrow. "What?"

"The good man who's caring and protective?" She digs

her teeth into her lower lip, and there's a shy glint in her eyes. "I was talking about you. You are that good man."

Oh.

Oh… and oh *fuck*.

I close my eyes and take a deep breath, pushing down the joy at her words. The way they make my chest swell. "That's so much worse."

There's complete silence from the woman in my arms, and I realize what I just said. I shake my head and meet her confused gaze with my own. "Sweetheart, I'm *not* that man. I'm barely enough the way I am now, torn in every direction."

"That's not true."

"It is," I mutter. I know that far too well. The call I received that day flashes through my mind; the news of Victoria's sudden aneurysm. The missed warnings and the accusation from her mother. *If you hadn't worked so much, you would have seen the signs.* And the shattering emptiness afterward, the bleak apartment, and her voice gone forever.

I couldn't handle it if… I can't.

Never again.

"Sweetheart…" I continue and slide my hand over her cheek. There's quiet devastation in her eyes, and I hate it, too. I hate that I've put it there. "I'm fifteen years too old for you. I've got kids, a job that keeps me too busy, and nothing else to offer. You've got *everything* in front of you. An entire beautiful future."

"So do you," she says. There's a furrow between her brows, the stubborn refusal that I've come to learn is one of her defining traits. It's restrained, but it's there, her spine made of steel.

"No, I don't. You just said you want kids. I've already had mine. I've done all the things you still want to experience."

Her mouth opens, but no sound comes out.

There's no protest against that undeniable fact.

"I shouldn't have touched you that first time." I trace

down her slim neck, over her warm smooth skin that I've come to adore. "But I'm a selfish man, a greedy one, and I did. You'll probably hate me for it by the end, but so help me, I can't find it in myself to be sorry."

Her lips tip down into a frown. "So, what does this mean?"

"It means the same thing it's always meant."

"Just sex?" she whispers.

The words sound like defeat. I hear it, too, and I *feel* it. I want to be more than just the man who gives her orgasms. More than the man she may recall sometimes, long after she leaves me, more than a memory or a party anecdote.

More than a cliché. *The boss and the nanny.*

"Just sex," I agree.

Because I know I can't be that man for her, no matter how much I want to.

CHAPTER 29
ISABEL

Mac weaves through the streets of New York toward the huge condo Gabriel and Connie share. He drives as calmly as always, but the ride feels bumpy regardless, and it's all due to the man sitting next to me.

Alec is looking out his window, and I'm looking out of mine.

He's in a tailored suit. It's far from the first time I've seen him in one, but it is the first time I felt an itch to run my fingers over his chest and into his hair, to muss up the pristine neatness.

I don't do any of those things.

After our conversation last night, I'd gone to bed alone. It had felt like the right move at the time, but I'd ended up lying in the bed that's become mine, staring up at the ceiling and replaying his words in my head.

He doesn't want *more*. Not the more that I want, that I've always wanted with him, the pipe dream I nurtured for years. I've never even told him that. How my heart would speed up every time he entered a room. How I'd linger around Connie if she mentioned her brother would swing by, just to get five minutes in the same space with him.

These last couple of months, I felt like we'd really gotten somewhere. He'd started to open up, to smile, to let me in... but he won't. Here but no further.

Just sex.

I stare at the buildings outside as we pass by them in the car. The people on the street, more diverse here than anywhere else in the world. I've never taken that for granted about New York, despite being raised here. Every nationality is represented. Tourists from every corner of the world. Expats and diplomats and business delegates. Art, culture, languages, and... endless possibilities. Endless open doors.

I used to relish that. Now I feel like the only two doors I've wanted to walk through are closed.

Ballet.

Alec.

He'd been silent today too, focusing on the kids with the same intensity as I did. The words last night had broken the easy companionship between us, the security I've always felt around him.

Mac makes a turn and I recognize the long street of highrises. We're close.

"Hey," Alec says. His fingers brush mine, resting on the empty middle seat between us.

I look down. At his large, broad hand resting over mine, the back of it lightly tanned. His hands are familiar to me now. Still just as masculine and attractive.

"I've always liked your hands," I whisper.

His fingers curve over mine, hiding my hand from view. His lips part like he has more to say. But nothing comes out, and he looks down at our hands, too. His grip tightens.

Maybe that's all there is to say.

Mac stops the car in front of a condo, and we get out. The

November air is appropriately chilly now, but it feels good. Better than the tense heat in that car.

"Enjoy the night," Mac tells us.

I smile at him. "Thank you. You, too."

I haven't forgotten what he told me, or why he did. I wonder if Alec knows about Mac's past. Glancing sideways at him, I know the time to ask might have passed. *Just sex.* Maybe I won't lie in his arms on the couch anymore, lazily watching *Gilmore Girls* and talking about nothing at all.

Connie and Gabriel's apartment has been completely transformed. The large open-space living room, with its two story windows and giant bookcases, is hard to recognize. Now it's a poker palace. Two large tables, covered in green felt cloth and attended by hired croupiers, have been set up in the center. The place is brimming with people. I can see at least twenty at first glance, and that's not accounting for those outside the opened door to the terrace.

Alec sighs by my side. "This is…"

"Yeah," I say. "They've gone all out. Wow."

The large kitchen island is laden with appetizers, beautifully plated and displayed in a way that can only be arranged by an expensive caterer. I stop at the sight of a fancy ice sculpture.

"No way," I mutter. I've known Connie for years. I know her well. But I've only been tangentially aware of this side of her, the Connovan side, the one with priceless heirlooms around the apartment as if those are nothing at all, the one who attends elaborate parties and flies in private jets and spends money like it's a never-ending resource.

For all of them, for Gabriel and Connie and Alec, that's reality.

Alec stays by my side. He feels stiff, and reluctant, and I understand why. He doesn't go to these kinds of events unless he absolutely has to.

Connie spots us from across the room. Her smile is

beaming as she heads our way. "You made it, both of you." She pulls me into a hug. "I'm so glad you're here. There are a ton of people I want you to meet."

"There are?"

"Oh yes." She turns to her brother and hugs him, too. He wraps an arm around her with a frown. "I'm also glad you're here. I stocked the scotch you like."

"Macallan?"

"Yes."

"Thank you," he says, but his frown remains intact. I can almost hear what he's thinking, and the instinct to reach out and grab his hand is strong.

She just wants you to return to the world of the living, I want to say. *To talk to people and actually enjoy yourself.*

But I don't. Connie sweeps me away instead, away from her tall and silent big brother. She introduces me to a group of her friends, all dressed in finery with drinks in their hands. I recognize a few as those from her college days, but most are new, friends of Gabriel. Connie tells everyone I'm one of her best friends.

It makes me feel nice, what she's trying to do.

We grab a refill from the bar after a particularly long conversation with one of the groups.

"Okay," I whisper to her, "this merging of friends project seems to be going well."

Her eyes sparkle. "You think?"

"Yes."

"Thank God. Gabriel always used to host these poker nights, and I thought we'd continue the tradition together."

"Just elevate it a bit?" I nod toward the kitchen. "An ice sculpture?"

"Okay, that was my idea," she admits. "I wanted a bit of decadence."

That makes me smile. Connie would never half-ass something. I'm not sure she knows how. "Well, there's plenty of it here. But this is a great idea. People look like they're getting along."

"They do, don't they? I figured, our families will never be comfortable being in the same room... so we better ensure at least all of our friends are."

I put a hand on her shoulder and make my voice mock-serious. "Just so you're aware, I hold no institutional grudges against Gabriel or his friends."

She laughs. "I know you don't. You're my most uncomplicated friend, and I love you for it."

"Only for that?"

"No, you're also my yoga accountability partner."

"Right, right." I clink my glass to hers and ignore the pang of guilt in my stomach. *My most uncomplicated friend.*

If only.

I lean against the kitchen counter and look out at the party. Her husband Gabriel is sitting at one of the poker tables. He's grinning, holding a couple of cards close to his chest.

"Gabriel is playing?"

"Yup. We made a bet tonight, and he's very motivated to win."

"A bet?"

"Yes." She smiles at me and shrugs a little, and I realize what she means.

"Oh. *A bet.*"

"Yeah, exactly. I won't be too unhappy if he wins, either, let's just put it that way."

I nudge her shoulder with mine. "I'm not saying I'm jealous, but I'm also not *not* saying it."

"I know what you mean. But you have more free time now, right? To date? Compared to when you were at the ballet company."

"Yeah, some. But I don't even know where to start. The dating apps feel kind of depressing."

"I'll set you up with someone," Connie says. Her eyes

sparkle with a sudden mission. "There're definitely people here who are interested."

"As long as they're not like that guy at your wedding party—"

"Oh, no, he's not coming back. It was a friend of a friend of a friend." She shakes her head firmly. "Not everyone can handle open bars, especially not assholes. Okay. Let's see who I can introduce you to…"

We both scan the room. My eyes drift to the man they always gravitate to, finding him easily. He's not at the poker tables or the bar. He's standing by the large built-ins, gripping a glass of scotch and talking to someone.

I lean to the side to see who it is… A brunette. I can't make out anything more.

He nods once, eyes steady on the woman.

"Who's that?" I ask.

"Hmm? Oh, the woman Alec's talking to? She's one of Gabriel's cousins. A pretty good sign, actually, that they're talking." She leans forward, like she might get a better look. "And… it doesn't seem like it's a fight. Huh. Maybe there's hope for our families being in the same room after all."

"I'm sure there is." I glance at Connie out of the corner of my eye. What I'm about to ask is… but she knows him in a way I don't.

And I'm desperate for the answers to the puzzle that is her brother.

"You don't think Alec has thought about dating again?" I ask.

She takes a long sip of her drink. "No," she finally says. "I wish he would. I don't know anything about his romantic life. Not that I knew much about it before, either… I mean, he and Victoria met when I was only fifteen, I think. They were together for almost a decade, and I get it, but… it's been five years." She shrugs and looks at me. "Unless you've noticed anything? You're the one living in the same apartment as him."

"Separate wings, though."

"Yeah. I've seen those nanny rooms. Pretty good, right?"

"Absolutely, I have no complaints. And no. I haven't seen or heard about any... dates." It feels like a lie, even though it's not.

Just sex.

I clear my throat. "How did he and Victoria meet, anyway?"

"I'm not sure, really. I think it was through mutual friends." She sighs. "I think finding love again would really do him good, though. Did you ever meet him before Vicky died?"

"No, I didn't." Her passing happened right as I became friends with Connie. I remember it vividly. Having brunch, one of our first times hanging out together, and then seeing her face as she got the news.

"Right. Well, he was still *Alec*. His sullen, orderly, overbearing self. The perfect son and big brother. Nate and I have never been able to live up to his example." Her voice softens, and then she sighs again. "But that was taken to an extreme after she died. I'm really glad I got him to come here, actually."

"Yeah?"

"Oh yes. I thought he was going to say no when I went to talk to him, but he was surprisingly quick to accept. Even came out of his office to talk to me." She chuckles. "Never seen him do that before."

I keep my eyes on the poker tables in front, and the croupiers dealing out new cards. "That's great," I say. I'm sure it had nothing to do with the pens and papers scattered all over the floor or the scent of sex in the air.

She nudges my shoulder again. "And I think it had something to do with you."

My heart stops. "You think?"

"Yeah. I told him you were coming, so Mac would be driving anyway, and he'd have someone else here he knew to talk to." She smiles wide. "Thanks for being so good to my niece and nephew, *and* to my brother. I know he's not easy to put up with."

I nod woodenly. "Yeah. My pleasure."

She threads her arm with mine. "Now, let's go mingle. I've thought of at least three guys here I want to introduce you to. One is super hot but kinda hard to talk to, but the other two are the perfect balance of attractive and interesting."

"You, a married woman?" I say in pretend outrage.

She pulls me along. "A girl can still look. Besides, Gabriel was the one who suggested I introduce you to Todd. Let's go."

I drain the last of my drink on the way and grab a new one. Something with a sprig of rosemary in a frosted glass, courtesy of the bartender Gabriel and Connie have hired for the night. It's strong.

Todd is indeed nice. He's about my height, with curly brown hair and warm eyes. I chatted with him for a bit when I realize that Connie has quietly disappeared, slipping away into the crowd. I spot her sitting next to Gabriel by the poker table. He has his hand on her knee and is whispering something in her ear.

A pang goes through me. That's what I want. It hits me with painful clarity that this party could be so different from what it is. That could be me and Alec, but he's made it clear it won't be.

That it never will be.

"So where do you work?" Todd asks.

I handle the question as well as I can, and he responds the way everyone does. Eyebrows raised at the mention of *professional ballerina*, and then an understanding smile when I mention *hip injury* and *early retirement*.

He's easy to talk to. Nice, too. Judging from the way he's watching me, and me alone, he's interested.

I drain my second drink too.

It feels like I'm flirting, and it feels wrong. But it's not like I'm taken. On the contrary, I've never been less attached than I am right now. To a job, a city, to a man. *Just sex,* he'd said. And if Alec isn't going to be with me, then I shouldn't keep nurturing my little crush on him, either.

Even if it doesn't feel so little anymore.

Across the room, I notice Connie watching us. She gives me a happy little smile. *Great job,* it says.

She's already helped me with a job after the ballet company dropped me, and now this party, introducing me to everyone under the sun. She means well, and I'm so grateful she's in my life.

But I'm also tired of being the one in need of people's help.

I used to be a woman with a mission, every day. Wake up at dawn, dance till my feet hurt, perform every single evening. I was driven. Now, I've just driven off a cliff.

Todd puts a hand on my arm. "Looks like you could use another drink."

I look at my empty one for a long second, but then I smile up at him. "You know what? That's a great idea. Have you seen the terrace, by the way?"

He brightens. "No, I haven't. Want to show me around?"

"My pleasure," I say.

I'm hyperaware of him next to me as we walk through the party. Emerge on the terrace. As we talk, in full view of all the partygoers inside, and when he notices I'm cold... I even let him drape his jacket over my shoulders.

I feel numb.

Listening to what he says, engaging in the conversation, even smiling, but inside I don't feel anything at all. There's a shocking absence of it, of all the emotions I've been battling since my conversation with Alec last night.

We've been speaking for almost twenty minutes when I excuse myself to use the restroom. "I'll be right back," I tell Todd.

He smiles at me. It's an uncomplicated smile, an *I'll be waiting* smile, and I want so badly to want someone like him. Someone who isn't complex and brooding and afraid of commitment.

Someone who wants me too.

I weave my way through the partygoers, reaching the hallway that leads to a guest bathroom.

Alec grabs my hand.

He pulls me into the darkened corridor, his eyebrows furrowed and eyes narrowed. "You're flirting with someone now?"

"Well, it's not like you're receptive to flirting," I shoot back. "You made that clear."

He frowns. "That's not what I said."

"Yes, that's exactly what you said."

"I said I can't give you what you want. Not that I don't want you." He fingers the lapels of Todd's suit jacket thrown over my shoulders. His frown turns into a sneer. "You knew I was watching."

"No, I didn't. Because you haven't been paying attention to me all night."

His hand tightens over mine, and he tugs me down the corridor, pushing open the first door he finds. It's to an office, dark and tidy. He shuts the door behind us.

"I've *only* been paying attention to you." His hands grip the jacket and push it off me, letting it fall to the floor. "Come here."

He kisses me. His lips are hard against mine, determined, and I soften under the onslaught. It's like a drug, touching him, kissing him. Feeling his arms around me.

I wish I didn't crave it the way I do.

"If you're sleeping with me," he mutters, his hands sliding down to grip my ass, "you're not sleeping with anyone else."

"That goes for you, too," I say. He smells good, like cologne and warm skin.

He chuckles against my temple. "I can't even think about anyone else. There's only you. There's only *been* you for a long time. Even before you became my nanny."

I lean back. "Before?"

His gaze drops down to my lips, and his thumb traces along my jaw. "Yes. I tried not to notice it, to notice you... but of course I did. So pretty. It was hard not to think about you."

I feel like I can't breathe.

"And so nice," he mutters.

"Nice?"

"Mm-hmm." His eyes grow hooded, and he pulls me closer. "Genuinely nice. *Good.* Sweet and determined, and I wanted you even then, but knew I had no right to have you."

"You have every right," I whisper.

His lips hover over mine. "Don't wear another man's jacket again."

"Then let me wear yours in public," I whisper back.

Alec groans, and his hands tighten around my body. "You know why I can't do that."

"No," I say against his lips. "I *don't*. If you want me... make me yours."

He kisses me again, strong, bruising brushes of his lips against mine. His hands slide down under my ass and he lifts me. I wrap my legs around his waist, locking my feet together at the small of his back.

Every kiss says the same thing. *You are mine.* He supports me easily, groaning when I grip his hair tight.

"I can't think when you're around," he mutters. He kisses my neck, down to the slim strap of my little red dress. "It's fucking infuriating."

"What do you think it's been like for me?" I murmur.

There's not enough air between us, and still far too much. I push my hand inside the tight collar of his shirt, trying to reach his skin. Anything to touch and to get closer.

He tugs the strap of my dress down, kissing my collarbone. His lips burn. "I need you all the time," he admits. "I hate you a bit for that, sweetheart. For making me need someone again."

I run my hand through his hair. "I know. I feel it, too."

"Don't flirt with other men," he admonishes.

"Then don't tell me this is just sex."

His lips brush mine. "It's not just sex," he says. "And so help me, I don't want it to be. I do want to make you mine."

I kiss him, and he groans against my lips, his hands tugging at my dress. I help him, ruching the fabric up to my waist. He rests me against the edge of a desk and kisses me so deeply, I can't catch a breath.

"Then do it," I say, reaching for his belt buckle. "I don't care if the odds are against us. I just want you."

His breathing is hard, and he shifts to stroke between my legs, over the thin fabric of my panties. "You're wet."

"Yeah."

"Fuck. Here, let me—"

The door opens, and a bright light shines into the darkened space.

In the doorway, the illuminated shape of a familiar person.

"Isabel?" Connie asks cheerfully.

Then she freezes, seeing Alec and me together.

CHAPTER 30
ALEC

I block Isabel from my sister's view. Isabel is still fully dressed, but it's instinctual, something I can't resist.

"Alec?" Connie asks. My name sounds faint on her lips, and then she backs out of her own home study, and the door slams shut in her wake.

"Shit," Isabel says. She pushes me away and jumps off the desk, pulling her dress down over her hips. "Shit, I can't believe that just… Oh my God."

"It'll be fine," I say. But my voice sounds hollow.

Isabel runs a hand over her face. "This wasn't how she was supposed to find out. I can't… I need to talk to her."

"Let me do it," I say.

She shakes her head. "No, I'm the one who needs to… shit. What if she'll hate me?"

I frown. "Of course she won't."

"She very well might, because I've been pretending like nothing's been going on, and because *she* is the one who set me up for this job…"

"Hey, I'll do it. Let me talk to her. Do you want to go home?"

Her eyes linger on mine for a long moment, but then she shakes her head. "No, I need to do it. We'll go together."

"All right. Let's go."

I sound a lot calmer than I feel. We walk back out and into a party that looks no different than when we left it. People are still laughing, and playing, and chatting, as if a bomb hasn't just gone off.

Gabriel is leaning against the kitchen counter. I take one look at his eyes and know Connie's already told him. My stomach sinks.

His gaze is inscrutable, moving from Isabel at my side to me.

"Where is she?" I ask.

"I'm not sure she wants to talk to you right now," he tells me. His voice gentles when he turns to Isabel. "She's in the bedroom upstairs."

"Thanks," Isabel whispers. She disappears, weaving through party guests to the staircase that leads to the upper floor.

I watch her disappear. "So Connie doesn't want to hear what I have to say."

"Not right now," Gabriel says. "Your sister's best friend? Your hired nanny?"

I cross my arms. "Like you're the expert on convenient attraction?"

"Touché," he says. Then he sighs, and the usual smirk turns into something hesitant. "Look, you once told me that... well. Be careful, but not too careful."

"What's that supposed to mean?" My question comes out harsher than I intended. For all his "Thompsonness," Gabriel has been nothing but a good husband to Connie these past few months, and I need to trust her judgment.

"Look, the two of you? Didn't see that coming. But I suspect you didn't see me and Connie happening, either." He shrugs. "You're pretty similar to your sister, and I know her well, so I feel like this applies to you, too. Don't overthink it."

I narrow my eyes at him. "Right. Thanks."

"It'll make sense to you eventually. Now, do you want to drown your sorrows in another glass of scotch, or escape with your tail between your legs? Because I suspect the girls' conversation will take a while." He sweeps an arm out, indicating the party around us. "This isn't a bad place to wait."

It's not. They've gone out of their way, and it shows. The mix of people is pretty damn great too. No one has come up and tried to pitch to me an event or hint at business deals. This has surpassed my work parties and fundraisers at my kids' school by a mile.

But I can't stay here. If Connie doesn't want to face me… so be it.

"Tell Isabel I took a cab home, and Mac is waiting for her," I say to Gabriel.

He nods. "All right. Will do."

"Thanks for the invite tonight."

"You're welcome anytime," he says.

Nodding at him, too, I don't really know what to say to that, but… all right. I suppose there's truth to that. We're family now, after all, even if he's the last person I ever expected to be my brother-in-law. I can only imagine he feels the same.

"Good luck at the poker tables," I say.

His grin turns crooked, and a bit sly. "Thanks."

I leave the raucousness behind, and the sudden quiet of the elevator is jarring. In my mind, I can see Connie silhouetted in the open doorway and hear Isabel's panicked gasp. *Shit… Oh my God.*

Yeah.

This was the last thing I wanted or needed.

Maybe it's a good thing that Connie didn't talk to me, because I wouldn't have the faintest idea of what to say to her.

I run a hand over the back of my neck and consider walking instead of cabbing it. It won't be quick, but I don't need swiftness tonight. The kids are on sleepovers. Neither Isabel nor Connie want me near. The office is closed. It feels odd, to not be needed.

I start walking, surrounded by the magic of the city, and try not to think at all. If I do, I know I'll just feel regret.

Isabel doesn't come to my bedroom at night.

I hear her when she returns, but the click of the front door and the careful steps across the hardwood floor are so muted that it's clear she's trying to sneak in. I don't go to her room, either. I do check my phone, scroll through our messages, but there are no new ones from her.

I type one out. *How did it go?* But the memory of my behavior earlier stops me from sending it. I'd lost my fucking mind in that hallway. Something about seeing her talking, enjoying herself, wearing that guy's Italian-cut suit jacket over her slim shoulders…

I toss in bed. Infuriating. That's what it had been. And not because she can't do whatever she wants, but because I don't have the right to do the same with her in public. Because we're a secret, and damn it, I *wanted* us to remain a secret. So, why does that fact still make me see red?

I haven't felt jealousy in a very long time.

She's brought it out in me on several occasions. It's a bitter feeling, like ash on your tongue, and disappointment flaring in your stomach. Maybe it feels more intense with her because I don't really have her.

I close my eyes. Force the thoughts away. Others rise to the surface instead, like my mind can't handle the vacuum, and each of them is more impossible than the last.

Isabel living here. Sleeping beside me every night. Me helping her with her career, listening to her recount her days, making her laugh. She's amazing when she laughs. I love the way her mind works.

What would it be like, to marry again? To be *her* husband?

I shove my phone face down on the nightstand and turn onto my back. That's not a thought I can entertain. I know that. She wants kids. She wants me to be present, to be close. I can't make her a stepmom at twenty-five. Her friends, her family... everyone will see nothing but a cliché. The nanny and the boss. Eventually, she might, too. She might also want more than that. To strike out on her own and build her own life, instead of just slotting into mine.

And I couldn't handle it if she left me.

But that doesn't mean I can't imagine the future if the obstacles didn't exist. If she was truly mine.

I reach down and grab a hold of my cock. It thickens quickly in my grip. Behind my closed lids, I imagine Isabel in a wedding dress. Peeling it off her and hearing her laugh when I'm stunned by the lacy underwear she'd worn for the occasion. On her finger, a wedding band and a diamond engagement. She'd protested against the large stone but secretly loves it. She giggles when I tug down the cups of her bra, calling me eager, gripping my hair when I suck on her nipples.

In my fantasy, there's no guilt, no one looking down on us for being together, only pure joy on her face. She's looking at me like I can give her everything she's ever wanted. She's calling me her husband. And when I imagine it's her left hand around my cock instead of my own, I pretend to feel her wedding band against my sensitive skin.

I orgasm to the vision of coming inside of her in our bridal suite. Isabel whispering my name, her back arching beneath me, and her beautiful body on display in the brilliant sunlight. It's not a stolen moment in my bedroom at night. It's slow, and luxurious, and ours. It's the start of something.

And when I finally fall asleep, it's with a dream that all of it could be a reality.

I'm in a terrible mood the next morning. The kids must notice it, too, because Sam acts up during breakfast and has a small meltdown at having to wear his rainboots. *It's the weather* doesn't have much sway over a five-year-old.

Isabel and Mac take the kids to school, and I grab a cab to the office for an early meeting. It's with a firm in Europe that Nate's trying to acquire, and with the time difference, it's harder to get the meetings scheduled.

Things move smoothly. As smoothly as they can, at any rate, until there's a buzz at my desk from my assistant.

"Constance is here to see you."

Ah.

We don't have a meeting scheduled, and there's only one reason she's here.

"Send her in," I say.

The door swings open, and my sister walks in. Her auburn hair, the detail that makes her look so much like our mother, is pulled back into a sleek ponytail. Her face is set in tense lines.

"Connie," I say.

"Alec," she counters. She sits down on the chair across from my desk and crosses her legs, like she's preparing for a battle.

"I'm sorry you found out like that," I say.

Her eyes narrow into slits. "Sorry because you wanted to be the one to share the news? Or sorry because no one was ever supposed to know?"

Okay. So it's going to be one of these conversations.

Conflict with Connie has always been rare. It wasn't until earlier this year that she started to show me the fire I've seen her display elsewhere.

I tap my fingers on the desk. "What did Isabel say to that?"

"No," she says, and her voice hardens. "I'm asking you."

"And I'm not going to answer that question."

"You're not allowed to go into CEO mode here. This isn't a business negotiation."

"Isn't that what you're doing with me?" I ask her. "You're doing well, by the way."

She shakes her head. "Look, I'm the one who recommended her to you. I'm the one who insisted on it, and I did it because I knew, or thought I knew, that you'd be a great employer. Tough, yeah. But not one who would take advantage of her."

"I'm not taking advantage of her."

"Yeah, she said the exact same thing," Connie says.

"What more did she say?"

But Connie just crosses her arms over her chest. "You can't fire her if it becomes too inconvenient for you."

I narrow my eyes at her. "I'd never do that."

"Okay. Good. She told me it wasn't serious between you two."

"She did," I say slowly. "Right. Good."

"I honestly don't know if that makes it less or more weird for me," Connie says. She sighs, and there's a world of emotions in that sound. "God. I just don't want you to hurt her, Alec. She doesn't need that right now."

"I have no intention of hurting her."

"Guys say that all the time, and then do the exact opposite," she says. "What are your intentions? If it's not serious?"

"It's complicated," I say.

"Complicated because you're her boss, and you don't want to mix business and pleasure?"

"Yes," I say curtly. "Among other things."

There are about twenty other reasons, one of which is sitting right in front of me.

Connie sighs. "I know you haven't been particularly open to anything since Victoria… and I know we've never spoken about this. But don't you think she'd want you to move on?"

I grind my teeth together. This is the last thing I want to talk about. It'd be easier if she yelled at me instead.

"Most likely," I say.

Thinking about Victoria isn't something I try to do most days. Not now, not with Isabel. It's too complicated to hold it all in my head, and to reconcile the man I was with her with the man I currently am.

My sister's voice is firm, but I can hear the vulnerability in her tone. "It's fine if you want to move on. Have some fun. I would be your biggest supporter in that case. But did it have to be with my *best friend*? I trusted you with her! She needs this job and somewhere to stay while healing."

This is much better.

"I know. Never meant for it to hurt you," I say. The words are hard to say. They shouldn't be, but they are. We don't often talk like this. But disappointing my little sister is something I've done a lot lately.

"It's just so… weird," she says. She rises from the chair and glances at her watch. "I have the meeting with the marketing team. And to be honest… I don't know what else to say. Just don't hurt her, Alec. Be very clear about what you want."

"Because that's so fucking easy?" I ask dryly.

Connie's eyes widen. She's quiet for a moment, but then she shakes her head. "No. It's not. But do it for her sake. She's already looking at other jobs, and when this ends, just make sure she comes out on top."

I knew she'd been thinking about what career paths to pursue in the future, but actively applying for jobs?

That's news to me.

"What else did she say?" I ask Connie again. If it sounds like I'm begging, I'm too far gone to care.

"Talk to her instead," Connie says.

She disappears out of my office, and the door slams shut, leaving me in a deafening silence that is nowhere near serene.

I bury my head in my hands.

Fuck.

I need to talk to Isabel. But tonight is Contron's annual gala, always held a week preceding Thanksgiving, and I have to be in attendance. The speech is already prepared, the stage is set. Dad will be there too, and I know he'll ask me about the board position again. Connie and Gabriel will be there.

But Isabel won't.

And for the first time, I really wish I could bring her as my date.

CHAPTER 31
ISABEL

Willa and Sam are my saviors. Focusing on their infectious energy gives me no time at all to think about my own life, about their father, or their aunt. After school, Willa has tennis practice, Sam plays soccer. Afterward, we collapse on the thick plush carpet in the living room. Neither of them wants to do homework, so I decide we'll get it done lying down today instead. Picnic-style.

They both find this inordinately funny. Although the position isn't *great* for Willa's handwriting, we make it through their homework quickly enough. Sam's is always a blast. He's in kindergarten, so his tasks are things like identifying items at home in each primary color or counting the number of steps between the rooms.

Alec is out all night.

I knew he would be attending a gala tonight. Saw it on the schedule that's mounted on the fridge, the one Katja, the kids, and I use as a bible to orient our lives around. It means we haven't spoken, not properly, not since Connie found out at the party.

The talk with her scared me. It scared me because we've never had that kind of conflict before, not between the two of us, and this isn't something that's easily smoothed over. Not something that we can shrug our shoulders at and move on from in a heartbeat. She was clearly freaked out by what she'd seen. *I never thought... you don't feel taken advantage of? I don't want you to be in a position where you're afraid of saying no.*

That analysis felt as far from Alec's and my dynamic as one could get.

I'd told her we weren't serious. Tried to downplay it all, even if the truth had hovered on my lips. *I think I'm in love with him, but I'm fairly sure that he doesn't feel the same way.*

He's jealous. He's protective. He's kind and interested and attracted, yes, but that doesn't mean love. And he's made it clear every step of the way that he can't see himself having more kids.

I think what he really means is *marriage*. A real relationship, one where there's a risk of being hurt just as much as there's potential for healing.

I read to Sam at bedtime. He falls asleep before I'm even on the third page, exhausted as he always is on the days he has soccer. He looks sweet, long lashes over flushed cheeks, and his chest rising with quick breaths. I kiss his forehead and pull the door closed behind me.

Willa is already reading when I walk into her bedroom.

"Hey," I say quietly. "Want me to read?"

It's usually fifty-fifty whether she'll let me help her fall asleep on the evenings her dad is gone. Lately, though, the answer has more often been *yes* than *no*.

She puts her book aside and nods.

I sit down on the chair near her bed. She turns over, brushing her bangs out of her eyes. "Page six."

"Okay, I'll continue from there."

I read in a hushed voice, and she looks at the text with me, her eyes moving. She's learning so quickly. It's amazing how kids absorb the information at every turn, with their minds like sponges.

I'm on the last page when she speaks again.

"I'm sorry," she says.

"For what?"

"For being rude. When you first got here."

I smile at her. "Oh honey, that's okay. I imagine it was hard having nannies come in and out of your life. But I appreciate your apology."

She nods. Sighs a little. "I don't like nannies. But I like you."

"Thank you." I settle back on the chair and fight the urge to reach out, to stroke her hair. It's so rare that she's this sweet and open with me, and it feels like a gift. "Why don't you like nannies?"

She looks at the edge of her comforter, fingers playing with the fabric. "If we didn't have a nanny, Dad would be home with us." she says. "He wouldn't be able to work."

Ah. My heart breaks a little, hearing the conviction in her voice. I shift closer. "Honey, your dad wants to be with you. Both you and Sam. He'd be here all the time if he could. He just has a lot of other people depending on him, and he likes helping them, too."

"Mm-hmm. I know."

"Have you ever told him this?"

She shakes her head.

"I think he'd be happy to hear how you feel."

"Yeah." Her fingers weave into the fringes of her blanket. "And if my mom wasn't dead, she'd be here too. Dad is alone. I know he has to work."

"Yes, that's true too," I say carefully. "Do you miss her?"

Willa glances over at me quickly before looking up at the ceiling. "Yes. Sometimes I remember her. Sometimes I think… maybe I don't?"

It's posed as a question, a bit quick and quiet. "That makes sense to me," I say. "You were so little when she died. Younger than Sam is now."

"Yeah."

"You don't have to remember. Your dad remembers for both you and your brother, and he'll tell you everything you want to know."

She turns to look at me. "Is your mom alive?"

"Yes, she is. She lives here in New York."

"Must be nice," Willa says. "Does she braid your hair?"

That makes me smile. "Not anymore, but she did when I was your age."

"Katja braids my hair sometimes. If I ask nicely," she murmurs. She yawns, so wide that I can see the beginnings of a new tooth in the gap where her baby one used to be. "And you."

I stroke her hair. "Whenever you want."

"Mm-hmm. Keep reading," she mumbles.

I open to the last page of the book. Willa's breathing has evened out before I reach *The End*. I stay with her for a while, making sure she's well and truly asleep before tiptoeing toward the door.

I can't help but smile as I glance around the room on my way out. It's so Willa. A mixture of purples and beiges, plush carpeting, and a large bookcase filled with toys. I leave her door ajar, just like I did with Sam's.

Her whispered confession is touching. For an eight-year-old, nannies really only have one purpose, and it's to let her dad walk away. But he's already made more of an effort to be with his kids. More weekends with zero work, more evenings at home. Practicing piano with Willa.

I sit cross-legged on the couch, within earshot of the kids' bedrooms in case they need anything, and stare at the message on my phone. I've had it drafted for days. The only thing left is to hit send.

Three ballerinas had left the Company in the past two years. I want to ask if they'd be interested in grabbing a coffee with me.

I stare at the message for another few minutes before I decide I can't be a coward anymore. My future may not look like what I had planned, but that doesn't mean it can't still be great. And the only one who can make that happen is me. For so long, I was working toward someone else's image of perfection. Someone else's choreography, and someone else's vision. I loved it. At the time.

But it's time for me to try something else.

I hit send.

I'm still on my phone, compiling a list of dance studios in New York, when the front door opens. Alec walks in. He looks tired, his hair is mussed, and his suit is a bit rumpled at the collar.

"There you are," he says.

I put my phone down. "Hey. How did it go?"

He tugs at his tie and crosses the distance between us. "Kids asleep?"

"Yeah. Willa was sweet. She apologized for how she acted in the beginning."

He sinks onto the couch. "Really?"

"Yeah." I give him a half smile. We haven't had time to speak, not really, since Connie and Gabriel's party. "Hey."

"Hi," he murmurs. He takes my hand in one of his, and his thumb rubs circles along the back. "How was your conversation with her?"

"Connie?"

"Yes."

"It was hard. Really freaking hard."

His eyebrows pull down low. "Was she angry?"

"Yeah, but I don't think it was at me specifically. More at the situation. That we hadn't told her... that it was such a surprise."

"She was angry at me," he says dryly.

I look up at him. "Really?"

"Yeah. Came into my office earlier today to tell me I'm not

allowed to hurt you. It wasn't a very productive conversation."

"I'm sorry about that," I whisper.

He sighs. "Don't be. It's not your fault. Nothing about this is."

I shift closer, our legs resting against one another. "You look tired."

"It's been a long day." His eyes are heavy on mine. "She told me that you said this isn't serious."

My heartbeat speeds up. "Yeah. I said that."

"Is that how you feel?"

I close my eyes. "Alec," I murmur, "that's what *you've* told me. I can't keep trying to play catch-up."

His thumb strokes up along my cheek, tipping my head back. The tension between us grows with every second that ticks by.

"I haven't been fair to you there either," he finally says. There's frustration in his voice. "I've tried over and over again to stop thinking about us, and *I can't*. It's fucking impossible. So, you'll have to be the one who walks away, because I can't do it. Not even when it's in your best interest."

"My best interest?" I say. "Being with you *is* in my best interest."

He shoots me a dark look. "Isabel."

"Why wouldn't it be?"

"Isabel," he repeats, like my name pains him. "Because you're meant for greater things. For men your own age, for trips across the world, for new job opportunities. I want you in my bed, but I know you don't belong there. There are a thousand reasons why. A thousand and one. Because I doubt your parents will approve of a man my age. Because I have two kids, and you're too young to be a stepmother. I'm torn over time as it is and there's never enough of it to do things right. And I'm shit at this… relationships, feelings, connection.

"But I've also never felt like this before, and that's why I can't walk away. God help me, *I want us.* But *wanting* doesn't mean I'm going to be perfect at this. At us. And I can't bear it if I'm less than what you deserve."

I shake my head. "But I don't want perfect. I've spent twenty *years* trying to attain it, and I'm done with that. I want a happy medium."

He runs a hand over his face. "A happy medium."

"Yes. Do *you* want perfect? Is that what this is about? Because if you're comparing me and what we might have to what you had before, I can't... I can't live up to that."

His eyes flare. "What do you mean?"

"Your wife. Your marriage." I wrap my arms around my chest and power through the rest of it. "I can only be who I am. If you're thinking that I'm not mature enough, or that I'm not... some powerful businesswoman or a high—"

"Isabel," he says. "I don't compare you to Victoria."

"You don't?"

"No. I've tried... fuck. She is my past, always will be, but she has nothing to do with what's between us now. I can't believe you'd think that."

"I don't know *what* to think," I say. "You never talk about her, or your marriage, or anything related to it. All you've mentioned is your grief. Connie has mentioned it, too. How different you were before she died."

His hands slide down my shoulders, gripping my arms. "Sweetheart," he says. "That's not why I don't talk about her."

"Then why is it? What makes you think that you won't be what I want in my future?" I lock my hands around his neck and feel the steady drumming of his pulse, a beat beneath his warm skin. "Talk to me. That's all I want, Alec. Just talk to me."

His hands land around my waist, and he pulls me closer until I'm seated on his lap. It feels right, being this close to him again. We've always communicated best when we're touching.

"I don't talk about her," he finally says, "because I don't know how."

"What do you mean?"

"Where would I begin?" he says. "Why would you want to hear about her? How would it not upset the kids if I mention her all the time?"

I run my hands over his shoulders. "Your mom died when you were a kid. Right?"

His eyes narrow in confusion. "Yes. I was thirteen."

"Did your dad speak about her afterward?"

Alec's eyes darken. "Not really. He was devastated and disappeared into Contron. It swallowed him whole, or he swallowed it, I'm not quite sure."

"So that's what you've learned. You don't talk about people who die, and you focus on work."

He frowns, his eyes narrowing further. "I don't know where to start. How would talking about Vicky with you just not complicate things? You're… Isabel, you're the first truly *good* thing I've had in my life for years, other than my kids. Being with you is everything. These stolen moments we have, together on this couch, or you in my bed… they make my day."

"They do?"

"By a mile," he says. "So if you want… I'll talk about it. About my marriage."

I smile at him. "Will you tell me about her? You don't have to recount the end. But maybe, the beginning? How did you two meet?"

He's quiet for a beat. "Through a mutual friend. It was a dinner party, and she was there."

A stab of jealousy pulses through me, but it's there and gone again. It's not fair of me to feel like that. He's had a life before me, just like I have. I've had boyfriends. Shared firsts with others.

I curl my fingers around the lapels of his suit jacket. "How long did you date before getting married?"

"Three years, give or take a few months. I proposed over a candlelit dinner. She'd hinted that it was what she wanted." He shakes his head, his eyebrows lowering. "Do you really want to hear this?"

"Yes. It's your history."

"I would hate to hear about your past boyfriends. Wouldn't have any right to. But I would." He leans his head against the back of the couch. "We wanted similar things. She was ready to be a mom. Excited, actually. She was funny and supportive, and she really loved socializing. She was the one who kept up with all of our social engagements. Dinner parties and events and movie nights."

"Fundraisers at St. Regis," I say.

His lips curve. "Exactly. She would have organized that fundraiser movie night."

"Where did she work?"

"She'd studied marketing, but she didn't work after getting pregnant with Willa. Sam came along only three years after Willa, so there was never any talk of Victoria going back to work."

"Do you miss her?" I ask.

He looks away from me, toward the rooms of his children. The doors are still slightly ajar, but the bedrooms are far enough away that the kids shouldn't overhear our quiet conversation.

"I miss her on behalf of my kids," he says. "They're denied the very same thing I lost. I never wanted that for them, and now it's their life."

"I'm sorry," I whisper.

His thumbs sweep in low circles over my hips, absently, and I'm not sure he knows he's doing it. "For my own sake…

of course. In the first years. There was a very clear hole in the center of our family, in this damn penthouse that she helped pick out, and I tried to patch it the best I could."

"You've done great. Katja, Mac? The routines you've built?" I think of the schedule on the fridge, the dinners he tries to never miss, and the bedtime stories he reads. "You've done it."

"Maybe. I tried," he says. He leans forward, resting his forehead against mine. "You said that you've tried to be perfect for twenty years?"

"Yeah," I murmur.

"Well, I've done it for twice that long," he says. "And the last few years, I've been failing in every possible way. I suspect I'll fail with you, sweetheart, and that pains me more than I can say. But I'll handle it. Because stopping *this...*" He kisses me, his lips brushing over mine in the faintest of touches. "It would kill me. You've become my happiness, Isabel."

I slide my hands up to his neck. "Then don't stop."

"Don't leave," he murmurs against my lips. His voice sounds hoarse. "Promise me you won't without talking to me."

"I promise," I whisper.

He stands with me in his arms, and I lock my legs behind his back. He carries me down the hall in the opposite direction of his bedroom. I help him push open the door to my suite.

"Stay," he says, and kisses my shirt off me. Running his hands up my body in a slow, reverent caress.

I shiver at the need in his touch and can only answer one thing. "I will."

CHAPTER 32
ALEC

It's late.

Late, and she's not home. I shouldn't worry, but I do anyway, sitting in bed with my laptop open, doing some work. The kids have long since fallen asleep, and the apartment is quiet, the lights are out. My door is ajar. I want to be able to hear when she gets back.

Her sister had another comedy show tonight. Isabel had been excited to go, getting ready while I lay on her bed and tormented her with questions about the latest read on her Kindle.

Do you really have a fantasy where you're tied up? Not specifically, but I like the dominance aspect of it. *Have you ever wanted to try role play?* I think it could be fun.

Every answer she'd given, she'd been blushing. Smiling. Giving me responses that increased my understanding of her, and made me unable to take my eyes off her. Off her smile and her infectious joy.

It's Mac's weekend off, so she'd taken a taxi. She'll grab one home, too. Still, by now it's nearly midnight, and she hasn't texted or called.

I shut down the laptop and rub my eyes. A part of me

wanted to go with her. Grab a beer or two and sit in the corner of the comedy club with my arm around her, watching Isabel cheer on her sister. To feel her lean into me, laugh together. Whisper things in her ear. To simply be with her in a place where we could just be *us,* a couple out on a town.

It struck me as unbelievably fun… and just plain unbelievable. I didn't even suggest it to her. Couldn't imagine her agreeing. I didn't have another babysitter, either.

And won't that always be the case? I'll never be able to do those things with her unless I find an alternate babysitter. Never going to be free to date her in that fun, uncomplicated way.

My phone rings.

I grab it immediately. I don't recognize the number, but after a second, I hit the green button anyway.

"Hello."

"Alec? Hi. It's Isabel." Her voice is rushed, and there's bustle behind her, like she's on a very busy street.

"Isa? Where are you?"

"I'm with my sister. We were just robbed."

"*What?*"

"I'm calling from a passerby's phone. Can you order us a rideshare? I… I don't know where we should go. Can—"

"Come home," I say. "Your sister, too, or I can drive her to her place."

"They took everything. Our phones, keys, wallets…"

"She'll sleep here." I'm already getting out of bed, and I grab a pair of slacks I'd left thrown over the dresser. "I'm putting you on speaker. Tell me the address. Are you safe now?"

She rattles off the location, and I jot it down on my phone. They're by some fast-food restaurant a few blocks away from where it had happened. But from her voice, she's calm and in control… probably in shock.

I don't blame her.

The need to grab the car keys and go get her myself is overwhelming. It's nearly strong enough for me to say *fuck it*, the kids are asleep and will be all night. But I can't take that risk. I need to call Katja.

"I'll come get you. Stay inside, in the fast-food joint."

"What about the kids?"

"I'll solve it."

"Okay. I think I have to go now."

"I'm coming," I tell her. "Don't worry."

She sighs softly. "I'm not anymore."

We hang up, and I immediately call Katja. I put the phone on speaker and pull on a sweater while the ringing echoes through the room. She answers on the fourth ring, and I explain the situation as succinctly as I can.

My housekeeper sounds horrified. "What? Go get her!"

"That's my plan. Can you come over? If one of the kids—"

"Yes, yes, of course. Putting on my shoes now."

I'm forever grateful she lives two buildings away. Buying that condo four years ago had been worth every single penny I'd spent. With the highly reduced rent I'd offered her, it allows Katja to be close by in case of emergencies.

She shows up a few minutes later and we meet at the door. I already have my car keys in hand. Mac might drive my car most days, but that doesn't mean I've forgotten how. It's waiting for me in the building's quiet garage, pristine in the parking spot closest to the door. I'm pulling out thirty seconds later.

She was robbed.

At knifepoint? *Gunpoint?* The roar in my head is loud enough to drown out the sounds of traffic around me. I drive on autopilot, toward the bridge and out to Brooklyn. How was she robbed? *Robbed.*

I never want to let her out of my sight again.

It's far too long before I finally pull up at the busy intersection. The neon sign of a burger place and people lingering outside, smoking, talking, laughing. It's a weekend night in a hip area of Brooklyn. The city is alive.

I idle by the curb and roll down my window. It only takes a second before I see her, pushing open the front door of the restaurant. A short-haired woman, in an oversized jacket and boots, follows her.

Isabel's face softens when she sees me.

I get out, and I'm by her side in seconds, my hand on her waist. "Are you okay?"

"Yes, I'm fine. We're fine. Just shaken up."

"What happened?"

"We'll tell you in the car. Let's go," she says. She turns to her sister, and my hand falls from Isabel's waist. Right. "This is my little sister, Elena. Elena, this is Alec Connovan."

Her little sister is clearly cut from the same cloth. Similar genes, just rearranged in a different way. An inch shorter, slightly wider shoulders, but with the same black, glossy hair. Hers is shoulder-length, and dances over a well-worn leather jacket. She has a septum ring and bright eyes.

"Hello," she says. "You're our shine in knighting armor."

"Knight in shining armor," Isabel corrects.

"Right. It's been a long night," Elena says. "Made even longer by the drunk college students inside that place. Thanks for letting me crash at your place."

"Of course." I open the back door for them, and Elena climbs in first. Isabel's eyes linger on mine for a moment more before she follows her sister.

It's hard to focus on anything besides my anger. How could this have happened? Who did this to them? I settle my hands on the steering wheel and grip it too hard.

Isabel sighs in the backseat. I look into the rearview mirror and see her resting her head against the seat, her eyes half-closed. "I can't wait to get home," she says.

I look back at the road. "What happened?"

"We were walking towards the subway stop, and... it just happened. It was so quick."

"Three guys came up to us," Elena says. "They asked us for wallets and keys."

"They had a knife," Isabel adds.

"They had *what*?"

"They flashed it at us. I'm not sure they would have actually used it or anything. They were just teenagers." She shakes her head, and I look back at her through the mirror. "It was unsettling."

"Unsettling? It was scary AF," Elena says. "My first response was to laugh, but they were dead serious about it all. My keys were in my wallet. Tucked neatly into the coin pocket so I wouldn't lose them. I can't believe this happened. I think I'm still in shock."

"Yeah, me too," Isabel says. "At least you killed your set."

Elena chuckles. "Thanks. You know, as awful as this experience has been, I will definitely add it to my next routine."

"I can't wait to be able to laugh about it," Isabel says.

Despite their attempt at easy normalcy, their voices sound strained. Hearing that unease makes my blood boil.

"Did you get a good look at them?" I ask.

"It was pretty dark," Isabel says. "But Elena and I have spoken about it, and we'll go to the police station tomorrow."

"Mac will drive you," I say. "He'll drive you everywhere from here on out, *especially* if you're going out at night."

There's silence in the backseat.

"That's a kind offer," Isabel finally says.

A kind offer?

I want to swaddle her up in bubble wrap and never let her out of my sight again. Mac driving her around isn't kind. It's for my own goddamned sanity.

I reach into my pocket for the phone and hand it back to them without taking my eyes off the road. "See if you can call your banks. Cancel all your cards."

"Shit, you're right," Elena says. "Well, if they wanted money, they chose the wrong person to rob. My checking account was already in the red."

Isabel chuckles, but it sounds weak. "Yeah."

Fuck that. I'll ask her what money they stole, and I'll pay it all back. To both of them. Those motherfuckers won't leave a lasting mark.

I listen to them, first Isabel and then Elena, call emergency hotlines for banks and credit cards. They're done by the time I pull into my building's underground garage.

Elena jumps out before I can open her door, and Isabel follows right after. The need to pull her into my arms feels overwhelming. An itch inside my chest, and only feeling her against me will soothe it.

I lock it down and force it away. Her sister doesn't know.

We ride the elevator up to the penthouse. Isabel talks softly to Elena, about the guest room, and how she can't wait to have a shower and something cold to drink, and the kindness of the chatter makes my anger sharpen.

How could someone rob these two?

When we arrive back home, Katja hugs Isabel tight. She asks if the girls are okay and how they're feeling.

I lean against the kitchen island with my arms crossed tight over my chest. Listening to all of it, I can feel my jaw grow tenser by the minute.

Katja and Isabel throw me a wary look before talking about logistics. Guest rooms and food and the kids.

Elena comes to stand closer to me. Her gaze wanders around the living room, stopping at the bar cart, the grand piano, the large TV.

"Wow. You do pretty well for yourself," she tells me.

I slide my gaze to hers. "I manage."

"I can see why my sister likes living here. Damn. Is that a fireplace?"

"Yes."

"Okay, my joke just got a hundred times better. Robbed by New York lowlights, only to be picked up another kind of robber. A New York billionaire." She smiles. "That's a joke, by the way. This is me testing the waters. To see if you're okay with a bit of sarcasm?"

I blink at her. "Yeah. That was a great joke."

"See, now I can't tell if you're serious or not."

"He's serious," Isabel says, coming up to her sister's side. "I just don't think he's in the same adrenaline-filled, giggly mood we're in. Come on, let me show you my room."

They disappear down the hall. I say goodnight to Katja, who gives me a grim smile. "Mac will hate that he wasn't there."

"It's his weekend off."

"Still. He'll hate it."

I roll my neck. "He would have been great in that situation."

Katja nods. Lingers for another moment before she leaves too, heading back home for the night.

I release the breath I'd been holding. I once again find myself alone. The apartment is quiet, but it's not empty now. And it's not serene.

Someone pulled a knife on her.

On Isabel.

There's a sour taste in my mouth, something foul and bitter, and I can't seem to wash it away. Not even with the glass of scotch that I drain. So I pour myself another and sink onto the couch in the living room.

I need to hold her. To hear her tell me she's okay.

It's almost an hour before her footsteps echo down the hall. I've come to recognize them, the way she sounds walking barefoot over the hardwood floor. Near-silent.

"Hey," she says quietly. She's changed into her sweatpants and a tank top, and her hair twisted into a wet braid. No bra, no makeup.

I put my glass down. It's now my third.

"Your sister?"

"Asleep."

I reach for her, and she softens in my arms. I wrap them tight around her waist and breathe in the scent of her shampoo. The hair beneath my chin is damp, but her skin is warm.

I close my eyes and just hold her.

She kisses my neck. "That was scary."

"Fucking terrifying," I mutter.

"Thanks for picking us up."

I stroke a hand along her back, over her hips. Feeling her safe and sound. "Mm-hmm."

She leans back in my embrace. "You've been tense since you came to get us." Her brown eyes are creased with concern. I hate seeing that. She shouldn't be worried about me, not after what she's been through.

"You were robbed," I say. "At knifepoint."

She nods. "Yeah. I really appreciate that Elena can spend the night here. Her roommates are asleep by now. We tried calling one of them after I hung up with you, but no one picked up."

"Of course," I say. Having Isabel in my arms helps, but it's not enough. Knowing she'll never disappear might be.

Her hand traces my jawline. "What are you thinking?" she whispers.

"What do you mean?"

"You're shutting down again," she says. "I can see it. Tell me what you're thinking."

"You're the one who was in danger."

"Yes. But I still want to hear what you're thinking."

I close my eyes and breathe in through my nose. "I'm thinking that I should have driven you there and back myself."

"Alec," she whispers. "You have the kids."

I shake my head slowly. "I know, and I always will. But that doesn't change a thing. I should've been there."

"You can't be everywhere."

"I need to be. I *have* to be."

Her hand settles on my cheek. "Why?"

My hands turn to fists, resting against her lower back. "Because I can't have anything happen to you."

Her lips part on a surprised exhale. "I see," she murmurs. "Caring about someone is… terrifying. I get it."

"Terrifying is an understatement."

"You're angry?"

"I'm fucking furious," I say. "The guys who did this… I want to wring their necks. Lock them away and throw away the key."

"You don't mean that," she whispers.

I release her, and she sinks down on the couch beside me. I'm feeling too much too fast, and I don't know why. Don't know why it feels hard to breathe.

"Yes, I do."

"Why?" she asks. Sitting there, just watching me and looking so painfully *good* and sweet. Like she wants to understand. The idea of someone hurting her, of her being gone, makes my throat close up.

I push off the couch. Walk around the coffee table, and then back, my movements frantic.

"Alec," she says softly. "What are you feeling?"

"She just *died*!" I say. The words explode in the quiet room.

Her eyes widen. "Oh."

"One hour she was alive and well, and the next, she was gone." I snap my fingers. The sound echoes in the space between us. "No warnings, no goodbyes. I barely handled it the first time. I won't survive it again. Never again."

"Alec…"

I shake my head. "I won't. Those guys… I want to kill them."

"No, you don't," she says. "You won't say the same thing tomorrow."

I run a hand through my hair. "I'm not so sure about that. You feel like a part of me, one I never knew I needed. An infinitely better part, and I can't lose you. The idea of never hearing you laugh again or seeing you smile or feeling…" I shake my head, trying and failing to clear it. The anger is still palpable. "I can't handle it."

She steps closer. "Alec," she whispers again. "It's scary, caring for someone new."

I don't say anything. I don't think I can.

She wraps her arms around my waist and presses herself close, her graceful body melting into mine. I feel the hardness of her nipples through her thin camisole. Smell the floral scent of her soap and shampoo. Feel the warmth of her skin.

I close my eyes and run my hands over her head, her shoulders, down to the small of her back. It's bigger than I knew it was. This. Her. Us. Bigger than I feel comfortable with.

"You knew my number by heart?" I ask.

"I memorized it when I started working for you," she says. "It's in the nanny contract you had me sign, to make sure I could always contact you on behalf of the kids."

"Oh. That's good. Smart."

She smiles against my shoulder. "Yeah. I take it you weren't even aware of that."

"I read it, but that was years ago. Come here. I need you," I say against her hair. "More than I've ever needed anyone. But…"

"I get it." Her cheek is pressed against my shoulder, her voice a soft mumble. "It means you could end up hurt again. Just like I might."

Slipping a hand beneath her tank top, my palm flattens against the smooth skin of her back. "Yes."

"That risk is the price we pay for caring about someone," she says. "Are you willing to pay it?"

I just hold her for a few long moments. Then, I tip her head back and touch my lips to hers. The need to be close to her that has been scorching beneath my skin flares to life, to feel her and know she's safe and sound.

I don't know, I want to say.

But my hands and my lips say something else. *I don't know if I have a choice anymore.*

She twines her arms around my neck. "Take me to your bed," she whispers.

I lift her, and she clings to me on the way to my room. And once we're beneath the sheets, she presses her naked body so tight against mine that I feel the beating of her heart.

I don't know if I can handle the pain of losing her.

But I can't let her go, either.

CHAPTER 33
ISABEL

"You didn't sleep in your own room last night, and I saw how he touched you yesterday." My sister crosses her arms over her chest. "Tell me the truth. What's going on here?"

I roll my eyes at her. "Elena."

"Isabel," she says. She's sitting cross-legged on my bed, still wearing the oversized shirt I lent her as pj's . "You were always a terrible liar."

"I'm not lying about anything."

"You're avoiding answering, and that's practically the same thing," she says. "So… he's pretty rich, huh?"

"Yes," I say. There's no point denying that, not when she's slept the night in the penthouse. But it still feels uncomfortable to admit. Elena is part of my family, my home life. Not of my ballet, Constance Connovan-as-a-best-friend life.

It's two worlds meeting.

"And not rich like the Cohens down the block from Mom and Dad rich. No, like *Bill Gates* rich. Doorman and housekeeper and private plane rich."

"He doesn't have a private plane," I say. But then I frown. "At least, I don't think so."

"Isabel." She shakes her head, and her eyes are sparkling. "I can't believe you're having an affair with this man. *You!*"

"We're not having an affair. That implies we're doing something... wrong."

"Okay, so you're hooking up with him," she says. "Right? Because the way he looked at you last night... he looked destroyed when he came out of that car. Like he expected to find you dead on the sidewalk or something."

I dig my teeth into my lower lip. I'd seen that look, too. "Yeah, we're in a relationship. Kinda. I think."

Both her dark eyebrows rise. "A *relationship*?"

"Yeah, something like that. It's still really early. And he's..." I trail off, shaking my head. I don't think he's still hurting from his wife's death, but last night had made it clearer than ever what scars it had left. Scars that affect his decision-making to this very day.

Yesterday was also the closest he's ever come to saying that he cares for me. But he had showed it, with every look and every touch of his hands, and that means more than mere words.

I press my hands to my cheeks. "He's pretty hard to read."

Elena's eyes widen. "You really like him."

"Yeah," I murmur. "I really do."

"Wow. Damn." She shakes her head slowly, lips turning down. "Are you sure that's wise? I mean, you do what you want, but this guy... he's so much older than you. He's like, middle-aged."

"He's forty," I say. Turning forty-one in just a few days, actually. I'd seen it on the schedule. Katja said he never wants his birthday to be a big deal, but that the kids love surprising him in the morning. He begrudgingly agrees to celebrate every year to make them happy.

"Yeah. Like I said. Middle-aged."

"He was thirty-nine last year. Would it have sounded better if he had thirty in his age number?"

"Yes," she says without hesitation. "But that would still be old. He's... Your birthday is in December. So he's..."

"Fifteen," I say dryly.

Her face lights up. "Right. Thanks. Fifteen years older. Isabel!"

"Elena!"

"Mom and Dad will *freak*."

I sink down on the desk chair. Her words cause a knot of worry in my stomach. "You think?"

"Of course. You coming home with an old, rich Upper East Sider who already has two kids and a housekeeper?" She puts her hands together in a praying gesture. *"Buena suerte."*

I cover my head with my hands. "No, they're not allowed to freak out. Or he'll freak out even more."

"He's freaking out? He was the picture of angry competence last night." She drops her voice into a mock baritone. "Here's my phone. Cancel all your cards."

"Yeah, he does that sometimes. But I'm pretty sure the whole age gap thing bothers him a lot, more than he's letting on. And his wife died really suddenly. I can't imagine how hard that must have been."

"Oh. How?"

"Aneurysm," I say. "Their youngest was just a baby, only a few months old when it happened."

"Shit. I can see how that would be traumatic." She cracks her knuckles, frowning in thought. "But he's not using you or anything? 'Cause I can't have that."

"No, of course not."

"Good. And you're sure?"

"I'm sure."

"Good," she says again. "Because I know that some of your ballet teachers treated you and the other dancers awfully. I don't want you to have normalized that shit and expect it in your relationships now, or something twisted like that."

I blink at her. "Elena, I haven't. Not at all."

She holds her hands up. "Okay. It was up to me to ask, you know. As a sister and your only family member in on this secret affair. I'd feel honored that you told me if it wasn't for the fact that I guessed." She frowns. "You know, I can *almost* see it. He's sort of hot, in a very straight, very old kind of way. Like that strong silent type of masculinity."

I groan. "He's not *old*."

"Sure."

Her comment about our parents lodges in my mind like a thorn, and I can't quite get it out. "I wish I could be more like you," I say.

She's quiet for a moment. "What do you mean?" she asks in a voice that holds none of her usual bravado.

"You've always been so brave," I say. "Like, you don't care about what anyone thinks or says about you. From your piercing that Mom cried all night about, to dropping out of college, and now pursuing stand-up. You get up on that stage every time and you kill it. I wish I could have some of that right now."

Elena just looks at me. Then she laughs a little and looks down at her hands on her lap. "That's not at all how I see it."

"It's not? You've always been so fearless."

"You're the one who paved the way," she says. "Seb and I had a big sister who pushed herself every single day to be the best she could be. We saw you up and stretching before breakfast, or running on the weekends and practicing choreo. I sat in the audience when I was twelve and saw you perform absolute perfection in front of thousands of people." She half laughs. "You've been the fearless one. I've just tried to follow suit. Well, I knew I could never be as hardworking or as graceful as you are, so I went a different route. Seb and I were always going to be less successful than you, in comparison. Why even try to please people, then?"

I'm up and out of my chair before she finishes her last

sentence, sitting down next to her on the bed. "You're not going to be less successful than me. That's crazy."

She shrugs a bit, and smiles. "You're the family's crowning achievement. All of us, cousins, aunts, uncles, grandparents, always talk so fondly of you."

"I'm sorry," I say. "I never realized how that would impact you, or Seb. Recently, I've discovered that I did that a lot. Gave everything to dancing and nothing to life outside of it."

"Don't say sorry. You were a great role model."

"God, I didn't even think about being a role model. I was just a teenager with a single-minded goal." I lie back on my bed with a sigh.

Elena flops next to me, both of us staring up at the ceiling.

"Maybe," she says, "you need to get used to doing things that won't get you a standing ovation. Stop performing, and start living."

I focus on the overhead lights. "That sounded poetic."

"I did a semester of English Literature before I dropped out," she says. "Some of it stuck."

I chuckle. Turn to look at her, so familiar and somehow all grown up. "You're telling me to ignore what people think?"

"Yes," she says immediately. "Even me. What I said earlier about Alec being old? So what if I think that? What do *you* think?"

I smile. "Mom and Dad will really freak, if this becomes a serious relationship."

"They will," she says matter-of-factly. "At least at first. But then, I'm sure it'll end up being another thing you over-achieve in. Seb and I might just date around, or find normal partners, but not Isabel. You just *had* to land a billionaire."

I chuckle. "That's never been why I like him."

"I know," she says. "It's not your style. But you simply can't help outperforming the rest of us, anyway. Don't worry." Her hand grips mine over the bedcover. "I love you, even if you're annoyingly perfect."

I grip her hand back. "I love you, too, and you're perfect just the way you are."

We go to the police station later that day. The kids come along. They'd been told what happened, but both Sam and Willa continued to ask me about it over and over again. They got a censored version. Nobody mentioned anything about a knife, and Alec made it clear that things like that only happened very, very late at night when small children were already asleep.

It's a Sunday, and the sun is shining beautifully on the fallen leaves. Thanksgiving is this Thursday, and New York is already in the grips of that chill, the one that signals winter's fast approach.

I've always loved this season.

Elena gets along great with the kids. They take to her immediately, asking questions about her and me and our siblinghood. *What's it like to have a sister?* That one's from Willa. Sam wonders about her septum piercing, and squeals in delight when she spins it around dramatically for him.

Alec is a steady presence beside me the entire time. He helps us every step of the way, and ends the day by ordering a car to take Elena home.

"Let Isabel or me know directly how much money they took from you," he tells her when they say goodbye. "I'll solve it."

She just shakes her head, but she's smiling. "Okay, you really are rich."

"I really am," he deadpans. "I also want to help Isabel, and that includes her family. I'm sorry this happened to you."

"I appreciate it," she says. Then she turns to me with a wink. "Okay. I'm starting to get it."

I shake my head at her. "Get in the car."

"Yes, ma'am."

She climbs in and waves at us through the window. Her

ride pulls away, leaving us all on the sidewalk outside the building I've come to think of as home.

"She's so cool," Willa announces.

"I'm hungry," Sam says.

"Your sister knows?" Alec asks.

I turn to all of them, standing next to each other, two short and one very tall. I clasp my hands together. "Let's go inside. Should we have another indoor picnic? Sam, I think there's food left over from last night's dinner."

The kids run ahead of us into the lobby. Alec walks next to me, the back of his hand brushing mine.

"Yeah, she figured it out, and I didn't want to lie to her," I say.

"I get it. Now both of our sisters know."

"We're even." I nudge his hand with mine.

He nudges it back. "I'm glad she took it better than Con."

"Yeah, she was amused. She pointed out what our family would think, though."

"What your family would think?" Alec's voice darkens.

"Don't worry, I'm not assuming anything. I know we're a long way from introducing one another to our families. If we ever get to that point," I say. I nudge him again and watch the kids as they wait for the elevator. "That's not me exerting pressure or anything. I know you're not ready to be in a relationship."

He turns to me, a frown marring his face. "What *would* your family think about us?"

I wet my lips. "They'd be surprised. I've only brought home one boyfriend before. I do think they'll have questions. About how we started… dating."

"Hmm. Any reservations?"

"They'd think you're a catch," I say. That much I know is true, unequivocally. Even if they might have something to say at first about the age difference between us.

He snorts. "Right. Maybe on the surface. You're the one who'd be sacrificing by being with me."

That makes me pause. Sacrificing? Does he really feel that way?

But then the elevator doors open, and he walks through them, joining his kids. I follow and vow to ask him more about it later.

CHAPTER 34
ALEC

It's hard to shake off the mugging. The fear lingered the day after, and the one after that. For several nights straight I'd held her as she fell asleep, in her queen-size bed, on the other side of the apartment. Her naked body half-draped in my arms was worth lying awake for. Hearing her soft breathing, knowing she's safe and sound, and mine. At least for the time being. Until I looked at my watch and knew it neared the time my kids sometimes woke up and looked for me, and I had to disentangle my body from hers.

It's getting harder and harder to do.

When I get home from work that Tuesday, it's to the now-familiar sounds of laughter in the apartment. Another dance party, most likely. I undo my tie and walk into the living room to find them, Willa, Sam and Isabel, dancing to the sounds of an upbeat salsa song.

Isabel is holding Willa's hand and twirling her around. They're both smiling. It's a beautiful sight.

Sam sees me first, racing toward me on quick legs. I lift him high. "Whatcha doing?"

"Dancing!" he says. "Isabel got a job!"

I turn to her. She's stopped dancing at Sam's words, her happy smiling dimming.

"You have?" I ask.

Isabel nods. Willa's hand slips out of hers, and my daughter dances toward the piano. "I waited to practice until you got home," she says. "Can you help me today, too?"

"Yes, of course, honey," I say. But my voice comes out strained. "Let me just talk to Isabel first about this job."

"It's not really what it sounds like," Isabel says quickly. "Why don't you guys go see if Katja needs help with dinner in the kitchen?"

Sam wriggles in my arms, and I let him down. He joins his sister, running to the large kitchen island where Katja is chopping vegetables.

I nod toward Isabel's room down the hall. She passes me gracefully and walks quickly down the corridor. I follow her, shoving my hands in my pockets. Of course she's gotten another job. It shouldn't surprise me. A nannying position here was always a lull in her journey and not a destination. A pit stop to refuel and rehab.

She walks into her room and I push the door half-shut behind me. It's funny how familiar this room is to me now when I'd only been in here twice before Isabel moved in. Now, I know the bed behind her as well as my own.

She digs her teeth into her lower lip. "It's a job *idea*. I met up with Diane today. She's a ballerina who retired nine months ago. We had coffee and started talking and…" She smiles. "I think we could start a dance studio together."

"A dance studio," I repeat.

"Yes. A place that embraces dance for fun, and for exercise, and not for perfection. It would be for every age group." Her eyes shine with excitement. "We spoke about it for hours, until I was almost late to pick up the kids from school. I haven't felt this energized about dance in quite some time."

Her exuberance makes me glad. "That's great, sweetheart."

"There's a long way to go still. But we have some leads about other dancers who quit... who might want to teach a few classes." Her smile turns crooked. "It's not performing in front of an audience. But it's dance, and it's joy... and those two weren't connected for me for years. I'm kinda looking forward to experiencing that again."

"You'll be exquisite," I say.

She raises her eyebrows. "You're biased."

"I'm always an excellent judge of business ideas."

"Right." She rolls her eyes and steps closer, reaching out a hand. I grip it and pull her against me. "This doesn't mean you need to find a new nanny, you know."

I settle my hands on the small of her back. It's become my favorite place in the world to rest my hands, along the smooth curve of her spine.

No, she's not quitting today. But that doesn't mean she'll be with us forever.

"Not yet," I say.

She runs light fingers along my jaw. Her brown eyes are warm, so warm, the color looks almost liquid. "Just because I might have a different job," she says softly, "doesn't mean we have to stop seeing one another."

No, it doesn't. I'll be here for as long as she wants me. Stolen nights in hotels when I have a babysitter. Dinners, if she'll let me take her out on the few nights I might be free. I want to send her flowers when her studio opens and the lavish gifts she'll never buy herself. Drape her in diamonds and cushion her in luxury. Keep finding new ways to make her come.

But the fear won't leave me. That when she's out of this apartment, when she starts to rebuild a life for herself, she'll want more than that. A boyfriend her own age. A man without kids, a man who wants *more* kids, and a man who won't one day be fifty when she is gloriously thirty-five.

"No, it doesn't," I say.

Her eyebrows drop down, turning her warm eyes troubled. "Alec?"

I kiss her instead, pulling her slim body against mine. She tastes good, and fresh, and familiar. The thought of one day losing this makes my head hurt, even as I'm kissing her, and even as she's melting in my arms.

This, kissing her like this, is more than enough. It has to be.

She wraps her arms around my neck, and I groan against her lips. I love it when she does that. Like she wants to hold on to me forever.

There's a small gasp across the room.

I release Isabel. Her hands slide down to my chest, and we both turn.

Willa is standing in the doorway. Sam is right next to her, peeking out around her arm. Both of their eyes are large.

Katja rounds the corner and comes to a halt behind them. "Kids, there's no going— *oh!*"

All three of them stare at Isabel and me.

Her hands drop from my chest, and she takes a step back.

"Daddy," Willa says. "Why are you kissing Isabel?"

My mind goes blank. It has disintegrated entirely, and I can only stare at my children with a sinking feeling in my gut. They're the most important thing in my life. I've never introduced them to a woman. Never even raised an idea of me and another woman, other than their mother.

"Come on, kids," Katja says. She has a no-nonsense tone in her voice, and I have no idea what she's thinking of me at this very moment. "Let's leave the grown-ups to finish their conversation."

"But they weren't talking!" Sam protests.

I run a hand over my face. "It's fine. Thank you, but come on in, kids. Let's talk about it."

Beside me, Isabel shifts from one foot to the other. "I'm sorry," she whispers.

The apology makes my stomach sink even further. "Don't," I tell her. She's done nothing wrong.

Sam walks into the room as if he's here all the time. Willa follows at a distance, her eyes moving between me and Isabel like she's trying to put a puzzle together.

I have no idea what their reaction will be.

I sit down on the edge of Isabel's bed. "Okay," I say. "What are your questions?"

Sam climbs up on the bed next to me. Willa drifts toward Isabel instead, who's taken a seat on her desk chair.

My daughter rocks from side to side. "Does this mean you're going to marry my dad?" she asks Isabel.

Isabel glances at me quickly before looking back at my daughter. "Uh, no. It doesn't mean that."

"So you won't marry him?" Willa probes. Her voice has a trace of disappointment in it.

I clear my throat. "Isabel and I like each other a great deal. But it doesn't mean that we know what will happen in the future."

Willa doesn't look impressed with my words.

"Will you be our new mom?" Sam asks.

Oh, wow. Isabel eyes widen and she looks at me. My stomach twists again. This is too much. This is exactly what I didn't want to saddle her with, the sort of expectations that might drive a twenty-five-year-old woman with the entire world at her feet away.

"Don't be stupid," Willa says. "We have a mom. She's just dead."

"It's not a stupid question," I tell Sam. He glances away from his sister to look up at me, his eyes wide and trusting. "But Willa is right. Regardless if I get married again or not, your mom will always remain your mom. She'd be here with you if she could."

He nods. Kicks his legs out.

Willa is frowning, though. "Do you still love mommy?" she asks me.

Jesus.

I brace my arms against my knees and look at my daughter. "Of course. I'll always love your mom. She was wonderful, and she gave me the two of you."

Willa nods. "Okay. But can you love two people at once?"

I glance from her to Isabel. Love? We've never had a discussion like this.

Isabel looks away from my gaze immediately. She puts a hand on Willa's arm instead, and her voice is soft but firm. "It is absolutely possible to care about more than one person at a time," she says. "I care about *both* you and Sam, just like you love both your dad and your brother."

Willa nods. Cocks her head and looks at Isabel. "So you're Daddy's girlfriend?"

Isabel looks over at me. There's uncertainty on her face. "Um…"

Shit.

I can't ask her to decide on the spot if she wants to be my girlfriend or not. It's not something we've spoken about, labeling this, going public. The whole thing started as physical. Reading her Kindle. Making her come. Fulfilling fantasies. Two adults alone at night, seeking comfort in one another.

It's bloomed into something much, much more, but we've never had *the talk*. I don't know if it would be right of me to have it, either.

"It's almost dinner," I say instead. "I promise I'll speak to both of you about this some more later, before bedtime. But why don't you go wash your hands now, and then help Katja set the table?"

Willa nods. Sam follows her, almost reluctantly, shooting a look back at me. "I like her," he tells me.

I give him a crooked smile. "Of course you do."

He's my kid. He's got great taste.

The kids disappear out the door. Isabel rises to follow them, and there's a fierce color on her cheeks. She's embarrassed.

"Sweetheart," I say.

She gives me a smile over her shoulder. It looks strained. "I should go help with setting the table."

"I'm sorry they all found out that way," I say.

She shakes her head, her eyes unusually bright. "No, it was bound to happen eventually. We can talk about it later."

She disappears out the door, leaving me alone in her room. I sigh and push off her bed. Fuck. What woman wouldn't be overwhelmed by those questions? There's nothing casual about being in a relationship with me. If we do this, it will become *something* right away.

And that means I'll also have something to lose.

CHAPTER 35
ISABEL

The next day is fully packed. I'd seen it on the schedule, and prepared for it, and even been excited about it a few weeks ago. Now I'm struggling to muster the same level of exuberance.

He didn't want to state if I was his girlfriend or not.

The calm, rational part of me says that's perfectly reasonable. We haven't had the conversation, yet. Haven't defined the relationship, and certainly not made anything official, yet. But that doesn't appease the part that feels hurt.

And I'm so tired of feeling hurt.

I throw myself into preparations instead. It's the day before Thanksgiving, and it's Alec's birthday. He's forty-one today.

"It's ready," Sam says. He's pulled a chair into the kitchen, and he's standing on it next to where I'm making blueberry pancakes. Willa is on my other side, delicately arranging blueberries on a plate next to the stove. There's a half-opened box of candles lying close by. We'd gotten up ridiculously early before school to make all this happen.

"This looks nice," she murmurs, and adds another blueberry to a ring she's creating along the outer edge of the plate.

"Do you think your dad will want some coffee with his breakfast?" I ask.

Willa looks up at me, wrinkling her nose. "Orange juice, I think."

"Okay, let's pour him a glass…" I find a huge tray, and we arrange the food together. Sam plucks a flower from the fresh bouquet Katja always keeps on the entryway table and tries to stick it into the glass of orange juice. We settle on placing it on top of the napkin instead.

Willa pops a few candles into the stack of pancakes, and I light them, with the two kids watching on in rapt attention. Sam does little excited claps. His glasses are askew, and I right them before squatting in front of him and his big sister.

"Okay. What's the plan?"

"I open the door," Sam says right away.

"And we sing," Willa says. Her eyes are glowing. "I start, and you join in. Right?"

I'm going to miss them so much when I'm not their nanny anymore. "That's right. Let's go. And let's be really quiet."

"That's our superpower," Sam whispers. He crouches down theatrically and sets off from the kitchen.

I balance the tray as they lead the way down the corridor to the closed door that marks Alec's bedroom. It's a little past seven, and I'm pretty sure he's already awake. He's never been one to sleep in.

I don't know what else he told the kids last night, about us. He always puts them to bed himself when he's home, and yesterday's ritual lasted longer than usual.

Nerves make my stomach tight. *Do you still love mommy?* The question had shot ice straight down my spine. He's been holding back for weeks, even when he's given me his nights and evenings, his concern and his smiles. And I can't shake the feeling that it's because of his past.

Sam pushes open the door, and Willa starts to sing. Her

brother immediately joins in. I follow behind them, singing quieter, and watch as a light flicks on by Alec's bedside.

He pushes up into sitting. The duvet falls from his bare chest, pooling around his waist. His hair is messy, the way I'd come to love, the way it only is when he's in bed.

He smiles. "What's this?"

I place the tray at the foot of his bed, and the song finishes. Sam immediately climbs beside Alec, and Willa points to the pancakes.

"We didn't have enough candles."

Alec's gaze flicks to mine for a second before nodding. "That's okay. Let me get them all…"

The kids cheer as he blows out the tiny flames. I hand him the orange juice and perch on the far edge of the bed, watching the kids crawl across the sheets. I better keep an eye on this tray or something will get knocked over.

Alec pulls Sam back to his side and looks at me. "You helped," he says.

I nod. "Happy birthday, Alec."

He smiles a little, but it doesn't reach his eyes, and the nerves in my stomach tighten into a little ball. "Thank you. What a surprise, you guys. I think this will be the best birthday yet."

"When do we have to go to Grandpa's?"

"That isn't until this evening," Alec says. "Your Uncle Nate will be there, too, and lots of Thanksgiving food. More than we can eat."

"I like Uncle Nate," Willa announces. "Will Aunt Connie be there, too?"

I look down at my nails and try to swallow the guilt, waiting for Alec's response. "I don't think so, honey. She'll probably be celebrating with her husband's family. I think they were going away for the weekend. But I know she wants to come by and have dinner with you guys next week. She told me just yesterday."

I look up at him. "She did?"

Alec nods, but his half smile is wry. Right. She wants to hang with the kids, not with him, and maybe not with me. We haven't spoken properly since her party. I've tried to text a bit, and she's responded, but it hasn't flowed the way it usually does. I'm trying to have faith that we'll be okay, but right now... I don't know.

I don't know anything, and I'm getting tired of that, too. Of being in this constant state of limbo. Ever since I left the ballet troupe, my life has been one long exercise in uncertainty.

But today is a good day.

Alec's birthday, Thanksgiving food, and happy kids.

"Isabel," Willa says. She's munching on one of the blueberry pancakes, no syrup, no honey. Just holding it like a cookie. "*If* you marry Daddy," she starts, making sure to emphasize the first word, "could you have a baby? I want a sister."

Alec leans his head back against the headboard with a quiet groan. "Willa, we don't know the future," he says softly.

"I know," she says happily. "That's why I said "if." What do you think?"

"Well, I do want children one day, so... maybe?" I say.

She nods, looking somewhat mollified. "Okay. Maybe. Just please make it a sister, because I already have a little brother."

Alec runs a hand over his face, and I try not to notice his agitation. It's the same as last night.

"Okay, I'll try to keep that in mind," I say, "but it's the babies who choose what they'll be, not the parents. No way to affect that."

"I know," she says again. Then she nudges away Sam, who's trying to grab her pancake. "When is your birthday? Do you want pancakes in bed, too?"

"December," I say, and glance at Alec. He is running a

hand over the back of Sam's squirming head, but his eyes look distant.

"Oh. Christmas," Willa says.

"Early December, actually. But yes it's pretty close."

"You're turning twenty-six?" Alec asks me.

I nod. "Yeah."

"Twenty-six," Willa repeats. "Forty-one. And I'm eight." She pauses for a beat before continuing. "So, you were thirty-three when you had me, Daddy?"

"Thirty-two," he says.

Willa repeats the numbers slowly. She uses one of her hands, counting up to four fingers before putting it back down. "You're both old."

That makes me laugh. "Yeah, we're both much older than you two, that's for sure! Come on, do you guys want to eat properly? We have a ton of pancakes out in the kitchen."

Sam launches off the bed. Willa follows, holding on to Alec's right hand and dragging him along. He's in pajama pants, something he doesn't usually sleep in… and peeking out from the pillow he just left is his laptop.

Right. He had been awake and faked it for the kids. Small things like that make me like him even more.

He brushes my hand as he walks by. "Thank you for helping them," he murmurs.

"Happy birthday," I whisper back.

For tonight, after the Thanksgiving dinner, after the kids fall asleep, I'm planning something else. Something that most definitely doesn't involve pancakes or candles, but it does involve a surprise and a bed.

The apartment we walk into a few hours later reminds me very little of Alec's home. Both have that same classic structure, with the crown moldings and prewar details, but that's it. That's where the resemblance ends. This place doesn't feel lived in. It's almost museum-like, with the china cabinets lining the far wall of the living room and the edges of Persian rugs are perfectly laid.

I've heard from Connie that her father rarely stays in the apartment the entire family once lived in. After she left for college, and he retired, it became a place only visited on major holidays.

Sam walks close beside me. He has a starched shirt on, the collar crisp against his neck, and a pair of blue chinos. It almost looks like his school uniform.

I know my role here. I'm to help with the kids, but as I glance at Alec and spot the tenseness in his jaw, I wonder if it's not to help him, too.

His brother had flown in from London. Nate's the first to greet us, swinging Sam up into his arms and ruffling Willa's hair. She pushes him away in response, and he laughs.

"You used to love it when I did that."

"No, I never have," she announces.

He chuckles again. "Well, you were younger then." He and Alec hug in that one-armed, half-assed way that grown men often do.

"Connie's not coming?" Alec asks.

Nate shakes his head. There's a wry expression on his lips, and his gaze flicks quickly to me before returning to Alec. "No. She said Dad didn't invite her."

Alec lets out a soft groan. "His stubbornness will be the death of me."

"She's standing her ground. It's cool to see," Nate says. Then he gives me a proper hug. "And you brought the lovely Isabel. It's always nice to see you."

"You, too," I say. In some ways, he's very much like Alec —the suits, the confidence, the Connovan composure—but he's the smiling one, the charming version.

Alec walks ahead with the kids to where voices rise. Nate and I follow, walking past a giant grandfather clock that ticks with rhythmic sounds.

"I know this family can be a lot," Nate says. "Constance, Alec, our father… maybe even me."

That makes me smile. "Maybe?"

"I'm willing to concede that I *might* have a flaw or two, yeah. Don't tell my siblings."

"I'll take the secret to my grave."

He nods. Runs a hand over his jaw and looks ahead to where Alec is now talking to his father. The nervousness that has been living inside me for days, a silent and unwelcome partner, reaches a new level.

I've never met this man, but I've heard plenty about him.

"Alec is loyal to the bone," Nate says, "and he doesn't do anything lightly. But he's not one to open up easily. Never has been…"

I nod. "Yeah, I'm learning that."

Nate chuckles. "I think he's worth it, though, if you stick it out. Not that I've ever dated him. I'm stuck with him for a very different reason."

That makes me chuckle. So Nate suspects we're dating, then? Alec must have told him. My laugh bubbles over stronger than I'd anticipated. Heightened by the anxiety and the somewhat uneasy atmosphere, no doubt, which makes the men in the room turn.

David looks like an older version of his sons, separated by decades and a few inches. His hair is gray, his eyes steely. He glances at me briefly before looking back to Alec.

Right. I'm just the nanny to his grandchildren… not as his son's date. Because I'm not his son's date. Nor am I Alec's girlfriend, or partner, or any kind of word that would signify a future. Not yet.

The dining room table is laden with beautiful decorations. It looks like it could host a family of fifteen, rather than the six of us who are currently here. Something about it feels so decidedly different from the Thanksgiving dinner I'll be going to tomorrow at my parents'.

The sounds, the setting, the constant questions, the emotions, the arguments that will ensue.

We sit down around the table. I'm seated on the end of the table between Sam and Willa, ready if either needs me. Alec is on Sam's other side and Nate is opposite him. Which also means David is on the other end of the table... in my direct line of sight.

But the kids behave brilliantly. It's like they know they're at their grandfather's, and different rules apply. The three men discuss business as we cut into the turkey, into sweet potato mash, and gravy. Staff regularly refill our glasses and keep the plates on the table overflowing.

It isn't until we're halfway through that their father asks the question.

"Why is your sister not here?"

Nate and Alec exchange a brief look. "I don't believe you invited her, Father," Nate says.

"She has a standing invitation. She knows that," David says.

I have to bite my tongue not to interject.

"She has a husband now," Alec says. "She might be inclined to spend the holiday with his family... especially after you decided not to come to their wedding party."

David leans back in his chair and crosses his arms over his chest. He looks from Nate to Alec, thick eyebrows drawn down low. "Unreasonable," he says. "She never acted like this before she met the Thompson boy."

"Gabriel," Alec says. His voice is unusually sharp. "That's his name. We don't have to like Thompson Enterprises to respect the man Connie chose."

David looks at Alec for a long moment. He chooses to

ignore the comment, but I can see that he's fazed by Alec's sharpness. "Did you tell her to come?"

"I told her she was welcome," Alec says. The distinction is clear.

Their dad shakes his head and reaches for his glass of wine. "She hasn't called me in weeks. I don't know when she stopped prioritizing her own family."

Irritation swells inside me. She *always* prioritizes her family and Contron. Arguably to a fault.

"Maybe she's waiting for an apology from you," I respond.

The table goes so quiet you could hear a pin drop. Only Sam is still eating away, using his fork to scoop up potatoes.

"And who," David says, "asked *you*?"

Nate shakes his head. "She's Connie's best friend. And she's not wrong."

Alec has gone perfectly still. He's staring at his father, and from his profile, I can see the tenseness in his jaw.

But I'm annoyed, too, and I can't quite let it go. "Yes, I am Connie's friend, and I have been for years. She married someone you don't approve of," I say. "That's okay. Kids shouldn't live for their parents, but from what I've seen, you've forced all your children to."

The words just pour out of me. It's the frustration, driven by my own uncertainties about Alec and me, and about me and Connie, and I just need to stand up to *someone.*

But in the deafening silence that follows... maybe it shouldn't have been Alec's dad. And yet, I can't find it in me to regret the words.

David's face twists with anger. But Alec lifts a hand in his dad's direction before the older man can speak.

"No," Alec orders. "You don't say a single harsh word to her, or anything else not appropriate for the dinner table. We'll continue this conversation later. Just you and me."

David looks at Nate like he's expecting backup. But Alec's younger brother only shrugs. *You got yourself into this one.*

"Fine," David says. But his voice exudes displeasure. "I suppose we'll just keep eating, then. Where's the server with more cranberry sauce?"

Silence settles around the table. I run a hand over Sam's back reassuringly, only to meet Alec's. He's already put a large hand there. His fingers curve over mine, squeezing once, hidden behind Sam's form.

"That sounded mean," Sam says. He's chewing his turkey and looking around the table with bright eyes. "Isabel is Daddy's girlfriend, and she's nice. We play superheroes."

I want to bury my head in my hands.

Nate chuckles behind his glass of wine.

And Alec, he just looks straight at his dad. "Later," he repeats. There's no brokering with the tone of his voice. He's with family, but he's also Contron's CEO, and the man his father always schooled him to be.

Dinner doesn't last much longer.

The kids' patience runs thin, and Nate suggests we go into the den. I end up on the floor between the children, trying to put together an old puzzle we've found with an image of a seventeenth-century ship. It's a little hard, but the kids don't seem to mind, at least not yet.

Nate comes in to join us.

"Ignore him," he says. "I've been trying to do that for years."

I put a hand on Willa's head. "It's hard when he's disparaging people that I… care about."

Nate nods. "I know. Look, you shouldn't have to work while you're here, too. I can show the kids the creepy doll collection Mom used to have. Take a few minutes."

I smile at him. "Thanks. I'll just use the restroom real quick."

The kids rush away with Nate, and I'm left alone in the

dark wood-paneled den with my thoughts and silence. I push the puzzle to the side and rise. I could use a glass of water, too. It might help the headache that's starting to throb in my temples.

That's when I hear the voices coming from beyond the closed door. It must lead to the study... because I can distinctly hear David.

"So you're sleeping with the nanny," he says. "Congratulations, you're a cliché. That's fine. Just don't let it get to your head like it did out there."

I lay my ear flat against the door.

"You will not be rude to her," Alec says. His deep voice is angry, so angry, it seeps through the tight control he usually maintains. "And you're not going to talk ill about Connie in front of her niece and nephew."

"Christ, listen to yourself," David says. "This is still my house, and you're all still my children."

There's a tense pause. "We're all grown up. You could try treating us as such."

"I've always treated you as an adult."

"Yes," Alec says. There's a dryness in his tone. "You have, haven't you? Try extending that privilege to both Nate and Connie."

"Who are you to lecture me on fatherhood? Your children are still young," David says. "Connie gets a Thompson for a husband, you start sleeping with a gold digger. It's like both of you have lost your minds."

I inhale sharply.

"What did you just say?" Alec's voice is venomous.

"Look, she's what, twenty? Think, son. She's working as a nanny, and she has you as her employer. Surrounded by everything your money can provide and knowing your wife's no longer living. You're an easy target. You don't think I met similar women after your mother died? I know what it's like. But think with your head, not your dick," his dad says. "She is pretty, but not wife material. Not like your mother was, and not like Victoria was."

I push away from the door. My heart is pounding, and I can't think, can't hear another word. There's no way I can handle hearing Alec agreeing… And I won't be in yet another place where I'm not wanted.

I'm done spending years fighting to be the one who's chosen.

CHAPTER 36
ALEC

"Not like your mother was, and not like Victoria was," Dad says.

I haven't felt anger like this for a long time. It closely resembles how I felt after Isabel was mugged, but it's different, because this time, I can see the culprit.

And he's right in front of me.

"Take my advice," he continues, "and don't let your guard down."

I run my hand along my jaw. "And what, exactly, has following that advice given you?"

His eyes narrow. "What?"

"You've been alone since Mom died. She was wonderful. I remember her, too. I was thirteen when she passed. But that was almost thirty years ago. So, I ask you again. What have you gotten, by keeping your guard up?"

Dad crosses his arms over his chest. "I raised three children by myself, and I made Contron one of the biggest companies in the country. That's what I got. No distractions and no entanglements. Or would you rather I'd remarried; got myself a trophy wife, and you ended up with three new siblings to split the ownership of Contron with, huh? Because that's what you're going to give my grandchildren out there if you're not careful." He shakes his head. "I can't believe I'm having the safe sex talk with you, at forty-one. Happy birthday, by the way."

"You got *nothing*," I hiss. "That's the real answer. You had the memory of Mom, and you devoted yourself to the company and handed us off to nannies. That's the example you set... And it has left you on your own. Alone, except for Lauren, but you can't even make something real there, either, can you?"

Dad's eyes widen, but his voice turns nasty. "And what do you know about Lauren?"

"Your affair with her is over a decade long," I say. Our COO had been a staple at Contron for as long as I can remember, and she remains fiercely devoted to Dad. Why is that hard to see, considering he's kept her at arm's length with this psycho-babble for years? *You see, I can't offer anything more stable because you might be a gold digger.*

"That's none of your business," he says.

"Just like my relationship with Isabel is none of yours," I fire back. "God, you know *nothing*. She's the last person who would be a trophy wife. She's the least—*she's* the one who'd be sacrificing things in her life by being with me. She'd have to answer questions from everyone about the age gap and become a stepmother at twenty-five. Maybe some women would gladly sign up to that in exchange for a cushy life, but not her. If you knew *anything* about her, you'd know she's not afraid of working hard." I raise a finger in his direction. "Any of the things you said to me in here, you will *never* say to her, or I swear to God, I will never talk to you again."

Dad shakes his head. "You're threatening me over a girl you've known what, a month? Two?"

Fuck. Being with me, *really* being mine, would mean dealing with all of it—the Contron expectations, the business travel, the strained family relations, and the eventual inheritance battle over the appointment of the next CEO.

It means having this man as the father-in-law.

That realization sends a surge of venom through me. "Dad, you're not getting a seat back on the board."

He gives a shocked cackle. "You're denying my spot because of a fight about this new girl of yours? If that's where you're at, I can't believe I ever made you the CEO."

"No. I decided that as soon as you asked me, but I entertained the idea to humor you." I cross my arms over my chest and level him with the stare he taught me so many years ago. "The company is moving on. You should too, and your interference within the executive team is not welcomed. We don't need your input. You're harming, not helping."

"That's presumptuous," Dad says.

"No, it's the truth. If you want to mend the relationship with your daughter, you will call her. You will set up a lunch. And you will make it clear to her that while her choice of a husband surprised you, you respect her ability to make her own decisions. You will also praise her for the work she's doing for the Connovan Foundation. You've told me privately that it's off to a good start, so you'll tell her. To her face."

Dad's eyes narrow even further. "But that's not all you want me to do, is it?"

"No. I want you to take your prejudices, your emotional immaturity, and whatever else sparked your reaction to my relationship with Isabel and shove it up your fucking ass," I say. "I'm not a neglectful father or an incompetent CEO because I may fall in love and marry again. And I wasn't a bad husband to Victoria because I'm choosing to move on. And if I were you, I'd realize the same thing about myself, and maybe ask Lauren out on a proper date. If she's still willing after waiting around all this time for you to have an ounce of courage."

Dad's face is red. I don't know if it's with anger or with

shock. It might be both, and I know he's reached his limit. The man can only handle so much until he explodes.

"Courage," he spits out.

"Yes. Your wife died," I say. "Well, Dad, so did mine. There's no worse experience. But I'm learning that life has to keep going, and we have to keep living. Mom would have wanted that for you, too."

———

We don't stay long.

The kids want some dessert, and we eat it with Nate in the living room while Dad sulks somewhere in the apartment. My brother gives me a few curious looks.

"Later," I tell him after the third time he looks my way.

He nods, letting things go. In a few days, Nate is flying back to London, but he'll be back soon enough. He mentioned that his friend Dean got engaged, and he's been asked to be the best man.

I've tried to be better at remembering things. More caring. For a long time, not caring was the safer option. Maybe it still is. But that doesn't make it the right one.

Beside me, Isabel is mostly quiet as we head home. Mac drives us. He's off tomorrow for Thanksgiving and will be away the entire weekend. Isabel asks him about his plans, and they chat about his son and Mac's impending trip down to DC.

When we arrive, there's a cake in the fridge, and this time, the kids take their time blowing out my candles. Forty-one. Not once had I thought about aging, or reflected on my age, until I met Isabel.

And now, she's standing next to me and laughing with my kids, looking so magnificently, incandescently, wonderfully alive with youth and possibilities.

It isn't until later that evening, once the kids are in bed

and the apartment is finally quiet, that I have the chance to say what I've needed to all afternoon.

Isabel is sitting on the edge of the kitchen island. Her dark eyes are unreadable, her features calm like the untouched surface of a lake. I've always loved her graceful composure. I think it's what struck me, the first time Connie introduced me to her new friend, even before I noticed her beauty. It made me wonder what lies beneath it.

I step in between her thighs and wrap my arms around her waist. "I'm sorry for how he spoke to you."

"Hi," she whispers. Her hand brushes back my hair, her skin is cool against mine.

"I'm sorry about today," I say again. "Sorry that you had to be on the receiving end of it... And I'm sorry this isn't more simple."

"Your dad's attitude isn't your fault," she says.

"Maybe not. But exposing you to him is." I take a deep breath. She smells perfect, like home and warmth.

"I would've met him eventually. Well... maybe," she says. Her hand threads through the hair at my nape, her slim fingers playing with the strands. "Happy birthday, Alec."

I rest my forehead against hers. "Thanks. May it be over soon."

"You don't like being celebrated?" she asks. "I guess I'll skip the blowjob I had planned on giving you in bed later."

Damn. "If you've already gone through all the trouble of planning that..."

"Yeah, it took so much effort."

"Mm-hmm. I will accept it, then."

"You're very generous," she teases.

"That's my middle name."

Her fingers twist beneath the collar of my starched shirt. "But only if it won't interfere with your bedtime, old man."

I groan. "Don't start."

"Hmm. Because you won't be able to keep up?"

I tighten my grip around her waist in sudden warning. "I'll keep up," I say. "Doesn't matter how old I get, I'll still want you."

But you might not want me.

She rests her cheek against mine and takes a deep breath. I feel her body soften beneath my hands, melting against me. It's the best sensation.

I run my hand over her hair. "But sweetheart, I am old, all jokes aside."

She pulls back. "Forty-one isn't old."

"No. But it is compared to you."

Isabel frowns. "Fifteen years isn't a lot."

"Not compared to twenty, perhaps, but that's the only direction that's favorable." My voice sounds bitter. "Look, nothing about this is fair to you. I know that. You're twenty-five. You have years ahead of you, years of exploration, and adventure, and figuring out who you are and what you want. My limited time and two kids don't fit into that."

There's a defiant spark in her eyes. "What are you saying? That I'm too young?"

I shake my head. "No, that I'm too old."

She's shaking her head before the words finish leaving my mouth and scoots back on the countertop. "So I'm not too young to fuck, but I'm too young to properly date?"

The crassness of her words makes my jaw tense. "No, but think about it, sweetheart. *Really* think about it. How would you introduce me to your family? How would you handle endless questions and comments and little remarks? And do you want to be a stepmother? Because I'm a package deal. I know you like the kids, and you're the best damn nanny they've ever had, and I could watch you with them forever… but a nanny can quit. A stepmother can't, not like that, and you're *twenty-five*."

She frowns. "Don't make this about me and what's best for me."

"But it is," I say. "It always has been. You're the one who will be sacrificing here. I can't leave New York, can't leave Contron, can't leave my kids."

"Why is that a problem?" she asks. Her body is strung taut, a wire ready to snap. "Tell me why. Explain it to me."

How can she not see it? It's been clear to me from the very beginning. Isabel is mine… but not to keep. No matter how painfully it hurts to imagine her walking away.

"You want kids. You told me that, and of course you do. You'll be an amazing mother. Let's say you want them in five years. Earliest. You'll be thirty… and I'll be forty-six. Fifty-six when they're ten, and sixty-six when they're twenty."

Her hands push against my chest. "I can do the math, too. Do you think I haven't run the numbers in my head?"

"I'm sure you have, but experiencing it will be different." I shake my head again and think about my dad's words today. He won't be the only one having those thoughts. *Gold digger. Trophy wife. Can't be a love match. Married the nanny…*

She'll be followed by those assumptions wherever we go.

And she's so above it, so beyond it, the thought of anyone thinking something negative about her because of me cuts like a knife.

Isabel gives me another shove, so I step back. She slides off the island, crossing her arms over her chest. "This is about what your dad said today, isn't it?"

"Not at all."

"You're lying," she says. "I heard you two talking in the study. Him saying… saying I only want you for your money, or your status, or this apartment. As if all I've ever wanted are some pretty things."

"He's an asshole," I say fiercely. "Don't listen to him for a second."

"But you think like him, don't you?"

"Of course I don't. You don't have a gold digging bone in

your body, and even if you did, it wouldn't matter. If you were mine, I'd spoil you until you begged me to stop."

Her eyes widen. "But you think others will think it. Is that it? You're afraid of what others will think? What the… the moms at St. Regis, at the fundraising events, will think? What Connie will think, too? Headlines about the Contron CEO hooking up with the nanny?" She takes a step back, and her eyes flare. "Have you bought into that clichéd narrative too?"

I take a step forward and grip her shoulders. Her eyes flick up to mine, and I hate the shininess I can see in them. Hate it with a passion. "Listen to me," I say. "I don't give a fuck what other people will think. I did for a great many years. But if there's one thing I've learned, it's that it doesn't matter. It's wind. It's noise. It's nothing compared to what we know is the truth."

"Then why did you mention it?" she says. "Why does it bother you?"

"Because it will hurt *you.* You'll have to suffer people's assumptions, their side-eyes, their questions. I might already have ruined your relationship with your best friend… But I can't ruin more things for you. You deserve the world. You deserve *everything*, and I want to cut anyone down who's ever hurt you."

"But that's you," she whispers, and a tear slips down her cheek. "You're the one hurting me. With your hesitance, and your vagueness, and your overprotectiveness. I just don't believe any of it."

I blow out a breath in frustration. "This is the only thing I've thought of for weeks. The math of us, and the kids, and what your friends and family might think. And what *you'll* think eventually."

"What do you mean? What will I come to think?"

"The age thing might feel small now. I don't think it will in a few years."

"That's not true. It's never been true." She puts a hand on

my cheek, and it's not cool anymore. It feels shockingly hot. "Either you don't see yourself clearly, or you don't trust me very much. What makes you think I'll ever see you as too old? Or resent the beautiful kids sleeping in the other rooms right now?"

"Because I've seen it before," I mutter.

Her eyes widen. "What?"

"I've seen it happen."

"With Victoria?"

"No, with my mother. She was only eight years younger than my dad, but she was so… full of life. And that dimmed when she had us, and when he was gone for weeks at a time on business trips. I can't see you go through that. You deserve so much better."

And I can't have you resenting me.

It would kill me.

Isabel's hand slips from my cheek, and her voice hardens. "You take what you want. I've seen you do it for years, read about it in the newspapers. Contron is bigger than ever with you as the CEO. You don't make excuses, and you don't hold back. So why now? Why here with me?"

I close my eyes and offer the only truth I have left.

"Because I can't be responsible for causing you pain. With work, the company… I don't care about them in the same way I care about you."

Because I love you, I think. *And it's breaking me.*

She looks at me for a long moment, and then she shakes her head. Another tear slips down her cheek. "No," she says. "I don't accept that reasoning. You don't get to say that you're pulling away because you don't want to hurt me. We all hurt in life. That's inevitable, but we do get to choose. That's what I did for years. I chose the pain and soreness, all so I could experience the joy of that life, too. And maybe I'm willing to do the same thing with you. Maybe I'm willing to accept the risk of getting hurt… but I don't think you are."

I open my mouth to speak, but nothing comes out. No words at all. I don't know how to make her see how much this is tearing me up inside, the thought of her having to justify being with me to everyone around her, all the time.

For years.

But it's also killing me to think of her doing it all with someone else. Having someone else's baby, moving out of the city, and gracing someone else with her kindness and her love.

"I think you're terrified," she whispers, "of getting hurt again. Of losing someone you love, and having difficult conversations, and handling your kids' questions about us... and the perceptions of those around us that you married your nanny. I think this is all about you. Not about protecting me."

"Isabel," I say roughly. "It's always been about protecting you. This job, the physio, the car service... I want you to—"

"The job?" Her voice sounds half-broken. "What do you mean, the job?"

"A part of me wanted to take care of you. Always have." I rub a hand over the back of my neck and sigh in frustration. The impulse had been there longer than I cared to admit. The graceful lines of her, the soft smiles, the kind words. She'd always spoken to me like a person. Like someone she wanted to get to know, and not just Connie's brother or a stranger passing by. And my hands ached to hold her then, just like they do now.

I'd just done my best to bury the impulse.

"But you just won't," she says. "Or you will, and in your mind, looking out for me is ending this now. Because that's what you're saying, isn't it? That the age difference, and your way of protecting me, and... and... people's perceptions..." She swallows hard, and while her eyes shimmer, her mouth is set. "I'm done being in places where I'm not wanted, or working to get someone's approval. If you'd rather not try something real, but stay safe and miserable, then fine. That's your choice, Alec."

You're wanted, I want to say. So much I don't know how to think about anything else.

She pushes past me and heads in the direction of her bedroom. Her long hair swishes across her back with every quick step.

"Isabel," I say.

But she doesn't turn around. Her steps hasten, and I'm left with my fists clenched, regretting every word.

Even if I meant them all.

CHAPTER 37
ISABEL

I spend Thanksgiving Day with my family.

It's my day off, and it's wonderful to be surrounded by the warmth and laughter and delicious food. Mom chastises me for my rusty Spanish after I make a single mistake, and Seb nudges my shin under the table. He winks, and I smile back. He's usually the one bearing the brunt of the language corrections.

I stay overnight at my childhood home, after board games and too many desserts, lying on my back on the couch. My sister is dead to the world on an inflatable mattress beside me, in the apartment I once called home.

I wasn't here a lot, even then.

Always up early, out running or at the studio. And late at night, when I was catching up on homework, I'd sit at the kitchen table while the family slept. Only the faint sounds of sirens and laughter from the streets below kept me company.

Some things don't change.

I shouldn't be awake now. Shouldn't be checking my phone, but I do anyway.

He hasn't texted.

I was half hoping he would. That he'd be awake right

now, too, lying in the bed I've become so used to, in a dark bedroom. Staring up at his own ceiling.

I squeeze my eyes shut tighter to avoid crying. I don't want to. Not when I've cried so much about dancing, and my hip, and my prospects. Not when those things are finally looking up. I have a potential new job with two other former ballerinas to dance again, to dance for fun. Life is good. *It's great.*

But I can't get over the look on Alec's face last night. He seemed anguished, and frustrated, and more worn-out than I've ever seen him. Like he was carrying the weight of the world. *Put it down,* I'd wanted to yell. *You don't have to carry it all.*

Fifteen years.

Fifteen. I spell it out in my head, the difference that had him so tormented last night. It's greater than any age gap in my family, true. But my aunt is seven years older than my uncle and no one batted an eye when they got together. Would people really care that much? Would my parents freak, like Elena had said?

Maybe they would. At first. But life is long, and emotions calm quickly.

I look at my sister. In the faint light shining through the window, she looks younger than her twenty years. She'd told me to ignore what people around me might think and just focus on what I want.

But I want to be wanted by the man I love.

And if I can't have that, I don't want to settle for anything less.

———

I feel anxious, sitting at the smoothie place I once frequented so often. Connie should be here any moment, and I'm nervous to see her.

I tap my toe in a familiar rhythm against the floor. It's an 8 count, the one I've used my entire life to learn choreography. Never failing. Always consistent. Five, six, seven, eight... and off we'd go.

She'd answered my text right away. Said that she would be happy to meet and talk.

I want to make things right. I want to make so many things right, and it's time I'm proactive about that.

I spot Connie from my seat by the window. She's hurrying across the crosswalk, her long beige trench coat open and revealing the dark-emerald dress she's got on underneath. She's also sporting thigh-high boots.

The view makes me smile. She looks fierce, fearless, and cool. A businesswoman through and through. I've always loved how different we are, in ways that might seem fundamental, but have only ever been surface-level for us. She's never been anything but an inspiration to me.

Connie smiles when she sees me. We hug, and she sinks on a seat across from me. "I can't wait for the Berry Blaster and the oat cookie," she says. "I've been craving them for weeks."

"Yeah, we haven't been here recently," I say. Our regular Saturday yoga and smoothie ritual had been disrupted by my nannying job, and then put on hold after the fateful party.

She shoots me a small smile. "Yeah. I'm glad we're back here, though."

"Me too."

We order and talk a bit about her work, and Gabriel, and the trip they've planned for New Year's Eve. She asks me about my work prospects, and I fill her in on the dance studio idea. *By former ballerinas for aspiring ones.*

Connie lights up at the idea. She asks me about investments, business plans, and timelines until I have to laughingly tell her that the concept is still in its infancy.

"You look great," she says. "Happy, when you're talking about this. It's wonderful to see."

I nod. Use the straw to stir my classic Green Supreme with a single shot of ginger. "I wasn't for a while there, was I?"

Her smile turns wanes. "No. You weren't really yourself after you left the ballet. It was... I didn't know what to do to help you through it."

"Neither did I. It's hard to believe it was only a few months ago."

"Yeah. A lot has happened since then."

I tap another 8 count with my foot, inaudible against the table leg. "Yes it has," I say. "But I never meant for any of that to hurt you. That was the last thing I wanted."

She looks down at her smoothie. "I know that. I always knew that, even when I was initially... upset. I reacted more strongly than I should have, and I want to apologize for that. Maybe it gave you the impression that I was angry at you, but I wasn't. I'm not."

"You're not?"

"I was surprised and taken aback and concerned," she says. "For both of you. I know how he can be. He's my brother and I love him and respect him, but he's not great at emotions and intimate relationships. God, I don't know if anyone in my family is. Including me." She runs a hand over her hair and takes a deep breath. "But I didn't want him to hurt you, or you to hurt him, and I didn't want to have to choose sides. I've decided I won't. No matter what transpires between you two." She holds up her hands, and her eyes are determined. "I'm Switzerland, or Sweden, or whatever it is."

"God, yes. Of course. I would never ask you to choose me over your brother."

"I know you wouldn't, and he wouldn't ask it, either, but I've decided to just take that out of the equation. I won't choose anyone over anyone." Her smile turns a bit crooked. "I hope that you won't either. That whatever happens with him, you'll still be my friend?"

"Of course! Oh my God, Con, I didn't think you'd ever... definitely."

"I was worried about that, too, during these weeks." She shakes her head and laughs a bit ruefully. "Gabriel kept telling me to just talk to you about it. And I was going to, but I needed a bit of time to... put words to my feelings."

That makes my heart clench. Of course. Alec is exactly the same, and why wouldn't they be? They were raised in the same household and by the same father.

For all of Alec's easy communication about us, about desires and wants, he must be deathly afraid of expressing his emotions. And I understand. It's not something I'm well-versed in as it comes to intimate relationships. But I have siblings and parents and aunts and cousins who do nothing *but* talk about feelings. I've had plenty of practice.

And he's had none.

Nor has Connie.

She takes another deep breath and her expression turns chagrined. "I hate to admit it, but I was a little bit jealous, too."

My eyebrows shoot up. "Jealous?"

"Yeah. Not of—God, no." She chuckles slightly, and I smile, the tension between us starting to drain away. "No, but about your closeness. I've tried for years, with no success, to get my brother to open up, and I wanted to be there for you while you were upset... but instead you'd found each other." She shrugs, and her voice turns careful. "That's not very noble, perhaps. Not rational, either. But it was how I felt that first week. Like you'd bypassed me. And you'd kept it a secret!"

I laugh. "It was so hard to! I wanted to tell you, because I tell you everything, but I couldn't!"

"You could've," she says. But then she chuckles again.

"Okay, maybe not. I'm not sure how I would have reacted if our first convo was you being like 'I think this guy is pretty hot. He's your brother.'"

I hold up my hands. "Which is exactly why we didn't tell you. I'm sorry you had to find out that way, though. It wasn't what I wanted. Nor Alec, I know."

She nods. Spins her smoothie around. "I get that. I heard you were at Dad's for Thanksgiving... and that it didn't go well. I'm so sorry about that."

"Nate told you?"

"Yeah."

"Well," I say. "You shouldn't apologize for that. Alec does that too, apologizes for your dad or for circumstances that are neither of your faults."

She laughs feebly. "A habit, I assume. With Alec it's basically ingrained within his personality."

"To apologize?"

"No, God knows he rarely does that. No. To take responsibility. He'll do it for everything, for everyone. Like, the buck stops with him. It's a great trait, but maybe it goes too far sometimes."

I nod along with her words. "That's exactly it. It's driving me nuts, because I think he believes that if he can't ensure... sorry, do you want to talk about this? I don't want to make you feel weird or anything."

She shakes her head, and a lock of auburn hair falls over her forehead. "No, no, go ahead! I feel like I may have some actual insight this time, which I never did when a fellow ballet dancer asked you out before. And for the record, I'm always okay talking about my brother's flaws. His sex life? Absolutely not."

I laugh. "Good to know. No details."

"Not even a teeny one," she says. "Okay, now shoot."

It's not so easy to "shoot." "I don't know where to begin, really," I say. "It's like he believes that if he can't ensure that things will go one hundred percent perfectly, they're not worth doing? I don't think he believes that when it comes to his work," I say quickly, "but maybe with relationships? Like if he can't be certain that people won't look at us sideways for being together, or that I will never... be hurt or leave him, or even die, then it's not worth it."

Her expression softens. "Yeah," she says. "I can see that."

"We do have odds against us," I say. "I know that. He's older, and he has kids already. There will be some adjustments. But I felt like I wanted to try."

"Wanted? Past tense?"

I shrug and try to keep the emotion out of my voice. I'm not sure I'm succeeding. "Maybe, yeah. If he doesn't... want this enough to give it a shot, then where else are we supposed to go?"

Connie puts a hand over mine. "What if—"

My phone rings, lying facedown beside us on the wooden table. I give her a smile and reach for it. "Sorry, it could be the school or something with the kids."

"Of course, take it."

But it's not the school or about the kids.

It's the newly formed Seattle Ballet Company, and they've heard from esteemed choreographer Antoine Dubois that I'm rehabbing an injury but looking for work.

And just like that, life throws yet another wrench.

CHAPTER 38
ALEC

The work day is bleak.

It's only been a few days since the interaction in my kitchen, but I haven't had a chance to talk to Isabel properly again. She had the rest of the Thanksgiving weekend off and spent it with her family. When she returned Sunday evening she'd closed her bedroom door right away.

I stood outside it, wanted to knock, knowing I shouldn't.

The look in her eyes on that awful evening haunts me. Every time I close my eyes I see her face, her eyes angry but sad, and that tear slipping down her cheek. It's the proof of everything I wanted to avoid.

Isabel, hurt.

Me, hurting her.

I rub a hand down my face and try to focus on the emails filling my screen. My assistant does a great job filtering most out, but too many messages still seem to trickle in, each demanding a slice of my time.

Those demands have felt never-ending for over a decade. My time is not free to dole out the way I'd like anymore.

But that doesn't mean I can't still make things right. I

might not know what's the best course of action to take with Isabel, but I do know what I need to say to Connie.

My assistant confirms that she's free, and I walk across the floor to the office that bears her name. *Constance Connovan.* I remember holding her, right after Mom had died, when Connie was small. Wondering if she was the lucky one because she wouldn't remember our mother, and because she wasn't feeling the suffocating sadness at the time... Or if I was fortunate because I had the memories, even though the life I knew had collapsed. And I had known, beyond a shadow of a doubt, that it was my job to protect her.

Connie is sitting behind her desk. She's not a toddler anymore. She's my grown-up, married sister, brilliant in business and great with clients. Her expression is neutral, but there's a hint of something soft in her eyes. Maybe she's not so angry with me anymore.

"Alec? What do you need?"

I brace my hands on the vacant chair across from her desk. "I want to know how to fix this rift between us," I say. "If you want me to say I'm sorry about Isabel... I am. But not in the way I suspect you'd want me to be. I don't regret anything, but I am sorry that you found out the way that you did, and that it upset you. That was never my intention."

Her eyebrows rise. "Oh."

"You were angry with me. If you still are, that's fine," I say. "But for what it's worth, I'm sorry."

She nods and taps her fingers against the desk for a few long moments. "Nate told me about the Thanksgiving dinner. What happened. Well, as much of it as he knew."

I grit my teeth. "Yeah."

"What *did* you tell Dad? I know what happened at the table, but not after."

"Well." I run a hand along my jaw. "I know you and Nate joke that I'm the favorite. I doubt that I'll be after this."

Her eyes widen. "Really?"

"Yeah. I told him to shove his prejudices up his ass." I chuckle as I say it. Connie's face goes slack with shock, and that makes my chuckle deepen. "What?" I ask her. "Didn't think I could get mean?"

She blinks a few times. "No, no, it's just... um. It's you telling off Dad, and it's you laughing about it. Just laughing, period. Been a long time since I saw you do that."

I don't know what to say to that. Luckily, an answer doesn't seem necessary. Connie runs a hand over her hair. "Thanks for saying that, by the way. About Isabel. I appreciate it. I wasn't angry at... now that I've had time to cool off, I actually think you might be a perfect match."

Now my eyebrows rise. "Sorry?"

"A perfect match," she repeats. "Your personalities, your goals, sensibilities... I can see it. The two of you. Not that I try to picture it or anything," she adds with a smile. "But it's not the craziest thing in the world."

Her words feel freeing. They sweep away some of the weight on my shoulders. "You approve?" I ask.

"Absolutely, as long as you make each other happy. But I think there's a good chance that you do... and judging by your laughter and improved mood these past weeks, I think the answer to that is yes. Isn't it? Does she make you happy?"

I look past my sister, to the view of a rainy New York outside the window. This one is easy to answer. "Yes."

She sighs. It's a soft sound, like she's happy just to hear it.

I look back at her. "But that doesn't mean I'll be able to make her happy in return."

"Has she told you that?"

"Doesn't matter," I say. My voice hardens as I lay out the bitter truth. "Con, the facts aren't great. I'm fifteen years her senior. She's in a transitional phase right now, and she could go *anywhere*. Take any job, see any city, travel. Study. She might want to go to college now. The last thing I want is to hold her back. The alternative… If she chooses to stay with me, she'll effectively be a stepmother, Connie. She might be your sister-in-law."

Connie nods slowly, her face serious. "Yes. I've thought about that too."

I nod back. Thank God for my sister, and her logical, forward-thinking brain. We're cut entirely from the same cloth.

"As for the sister-in-law thing, I think we'd both love it. Don't worry about that. Her being a stepmother, however… I don't know if that is what she wants." Connie's eyes turn curious. "But have you asked her how *she* feels about all of this?"

"Yes."

She nods. Curves her mouth into a wry smile. "All right. But have you *really* asked her?"

I narrow my eyes at her, and a suspicion takes hold. I'm certain I'm right. "You've spoken to her."

"Yes, we met up on Friday."

"What did she say?"

"Well, what she said is between the two of us," Connie says. "Just like what you and I talk about stays between us."

I glare at her. "Con."

She shakes her head. "Doesn't matter how much you stare at me, I won't budge on this. But I can tell you that you're not necessarily on the same page about this."

I throw up my hands. "She says it doesn't matter, all the obstacles between us, but I know they do. How can I put it all on her, knowing how heavy it'll be to carry?"

"You need to trust that she wants you enough to handle it," Connie says.

I shake my head slowly. It sounds like an impossible order. Trusting her isn't an issue. It's the idea of having her… and losing her. Of seeing her kind eyes turn apologetic, or pulling away.

It's about her leaving my life.

"Didn't you make this calculation before, with Victoria?" she asks.

I grip the back of the chair again, my hands tightening around the frame. The words are easy to think. They're harder to say out loud, to confess to someone, especially someone who knew Vicky.

"It wasn't like this before," I say.

The admission seems to amplify in the quiet room, expanding against the window glass and filling the voids of the built-in bookshelves. It's getting harder to breathe. Guilt is an acidic taste in my stomach. But my words are the truth.

That's why I don't know how to handle it.

Connie's face softens. "Oh."

"That doesn't mean I didn't love Victoria. I did. We were a great fit. She was funny, and ambitious, and we wanted the same things. Came from the same world." I shake my head. "We were a team. I loved her, and losing her was... It was the worst thing I've ever experienced."

"I know what you mean," she says quietly. "I saw you together."

This with Isabel isn't as straightforward, and it's not something I planned, not the way Victoria and I were. Isabel took me by surprise. Caught me off guard... and she's made me feel alive again.

I look back outside Connie's window, my gaze landing on an office building in the far distance. I can just barely make out the people, dozens and dozens of them, at their desks. Each is framed by a pane of glass.

"I *need* Isabel. And I don't know what I would do, how I could go on if I ever lost her."

Connie gives a slow nod. "I wish I could tell you that'll

never happen. It's my instinct, but I know that's not... well, true."

My voice grows rough. "It's not. Anyone can go at any moment. It was true with Mom, and then again with Victoria."

"We all live with that risk," she says. "I know it's marked you in a way it hasn't most, but the alternative is not loving at all. To let Isabel go now and to never know what you two might have been... to live your life with the question of *if*. And I've never known you to be the kind of person to back away because of uncertainty."

My gaze slides back to hers. "When did you get this wise?"

She smiles crookedly. "Somewhere over the years, I grew up."

"Hmm."

"I have one more thing to say," she says. "You've taken responsibility for me and Nate for as long as I can remember. For Contron, and even for Dad, saving him from his own impulses. You're a great father to Willa and Sam. And as the CEO, you've made this company more profitable and a far better employer."

I lift an eyebrow. "Is this some form of pep talk?"

"No," she says with a smile. "It's tough love. Because you need to *stop* with some of it. You can't be everyone's big brother, and you can't solve every potential problem. Just like you needed to let me go my own way and make my own mistakes... you need to let Isabel make hers."

I take a deep breath and force it out through gritted teeth.

"Stop thinking *for* her," Connie says, "and listen when she tells you the age gap isn't a problem for her. Just be there in the moment and don't try to solve it. Not everything is a problem."

I run a hand over the back of my neck. Damn, I really

hadn't listened at all when Isabel had protested. I'd heard her words. But I hadn't believed them, not really. Not when I know how easy it is for love to slip out of your hands and disappear into the ether. How simple it is to lose someone you love.

All it takes is a single phone call.

But what comes before that phone call, well…

It could be glorious.

And loving Isabel *will* be glorious. Calling her mine, *making* her mine, and giving her the world. Truly letting go and giving in.

To kiss her in public, to take her to dinners…

The fantasy of her in a wedding dress comes rushing back. It's too soon in every sense of the word, but I see it clearly anyway. Her walking down the aisle, her brown eyes smiling, and her long dark hair in an updo.

It won't be simple this time. I can already feel it, the hold she has on me.

"You're right," I say.

Connie smiles. "I was taught recently that it's worth taking risks," she says. "It's paid off pretty handsomely for me, so I have to pass the knowledge along."

"I can't believe I'm getting advice from a Thompson," I say.

Her smile widens. "You know, you and Gabriel would get along, if you buried your swords."

The way things are going, that might very well become a reality. All bets seem to be off these days. The world has changed beneath my feet, or maybe it's exactly the same but I've finally become aware of things I spent years missing.

I head toward the door.

"I don't think I should tell you this…" She stops me, her voice holding a faint warning. "But she just received a job offer."

"I know," I say. "The new dance studio idea."

She shakes her head slowly. "Another one. To dance again for a ballet company… in Seattle."

My chest constricts. It's immediate. Knowing that time is even more limited than I thought. I need to speak with her today. To clearly lay it all out and let her make the decisions from now on.

"If that's what she wants…" I say. "Well, we have a company jet. I can visit her."

Connie smiles. "Go get her."

CHAPTER 39
ISABEL

It's an exciting day. Diane and I have found a studio space with a year-long lease available. It has huge sunny windows, old wooden floors, and just the right amount of dust in the air. Not particularly big, and we'll have to repaint and put up the barres ourselves. Lockers for the dancers to leave their belongings in. And maybe do up a little staff kitchen area. And… ideally… we would upgrade the AC system… and the speakers…

It needs some work.

But I've worked hard before, and this time, it won't be for a performance. It'll be for teaching, inspiring, for the joy of it, in a way it has never been before.

I leave my bag in the corner of the room. The space was a gym before, and the wall on the right has windows lining it. The floor is scuffed from the rough handling of machines and weights, and the air still smells faintly of rubber and cleaning agents. The building maintained this gym for its residents before the rising operating costs forced them to reconsider. That's why the space is available for rent now, and we were fortunate to find it so quickly only because Diane's brother lives in the building.

I cross the floor. It's been a long time since I've been in a studio. I came here in my workout clothes, wearing a thick parka overtop, just in case I got some alone time. And luckily, Diane has left, and I have the keys.

The building's superintendent has allowed us to hang on to them for a full week before we need to make a decision about the lease. Apparently the idea of a ballet studio in the old, prestigious apartment building has greatly appealed to the co-op board, and they thought it would be an elegant solution.

I shrug out of the jacket and toss it on top of my bag. I look at myself in the mirror, the familiar shape, the one I've studied, obsessed over, and perfected for two decades of my life. A tool to be shaped. A tool to be used.

My hip is better. I've been following the physiotherapist's advice to the letter, but it's not there yet. It might never be at the level it needs to be for me to perform again at the highest echelon of professional ballet. And if it is… that could be another year. *Two years.* I'd be almost twenty-eight.

I always knew my career would have a short shelf life.

I shrug out of my sweater and toss it away, leaving me in a thin camisole and my leggings. While stretching, I'm luxuriating in the bright space, taking in the huge mirrors. There's much more room than at the gym in Alec's apartment.

Am I brave enough to sign this lease with Diane?

The movements take over. Ingrained in my muscles, set in my bones, I don't need to think about what to do next. I string together a set of stretches and the first, second, and third positions, practicing my foot placement, feeling the familiar creaks and cracks in my body after a few days of stillness. Limberness doesn't come naturally to anyone. It's a skill, just like everything else in life.

After my talk with Connie, I made a decision about what I needed to do. What I must say to Alec… as soon as I gather the courage to.

I understand that he needs time. But I need clarity, and he's not giving me that. Not with his talk of not hurting me. If he genuinely thinks we won't last, if this isn't worth a shot…

It hurts.

It hurts more than the burn in my thighs as I move across the floor, practicing dance moves that I know better than the back of my hand. But I've known pain before. I have survived it before, and I will survive this, too.

I thought I finally reached a point where it wasn't just about survival and winning. A time when I could focus on thriving instead, on deepening relationships I'd neglected, on learning to embrace joy again… on finding love.

I spin in the empty space. The floor definitely needs to be sanded down, and I feel its unevenness through my thin ballet shoes. But all of this has potential, so much that it's practically seeping through the floorboards and the scuffed walls.

Potential for new friends, and a new job, and a new life. A revival. I could build this studio into something wonderful. I could teach here. And maybe I could even study part time, find something I like…

There is potential.

And for months, I haven't seen any.

I perform a pirouette, and then another, but switch to jumps before my hip twinges again. It feels amazing to move like this again. To have the space to dance fully, across an entire studio.

Maybe Alec and I aren't meant to be.

Maybe that's another thing I need to accept.

The ache in my heart doesn't like that thought. But maybe… maybe I'm strong enough now to handle this heartbreak, too. I survived the first one, with a loss of a dream, a career.

I can survive another.

"I could watch you forever," a voice says.

I spin toward the half-opened door. The studio is on the second floor of the prewar building; it does have a doorman, but no one should have been able to bother me.

But there he is.

Alec leans against the doorframe. He's in a suit, his left hand in his pocket, and his eyes are locked on me.

"Hey," he says. "Didn't mean to scare you."

I wipe a hand over my forehead. "No, it's okay. How did you know where to find me?"

"Katja." He takes a few steps into the room and looks around. Raindrops cling to his hair, and I glance out the windows. I hadn't even noticed it had started to pour outside. "This is the space you're considering renting, to start the studio with your dancer friends?" he asks.

"Yes, but nothing is signed or decided yet."

He nods and turns back to me. There's a slim cardboard box in his right hand that I hadn't noticed earlier, and we're both quiet for a few long moments.

My heart races at the tension in the air.

Alec's lips curve into a half smile. "We haven't gotten a chance to talk properly. Not since Wednesday night."

"No. Things have been busy."

"I hope you enjoyed Thanksgiving with your family. Was Elena there?"

"Yeah, and the rest of my relatives. They were all horrified by our mugging story," I say. "But my parents were very grateful after Elena told them about you."

Alec nods, his face turning serious again. "I'll call the police station again tomorrow. I want an update on the investigation."

"Thank you." I shift from one foot to another and glance back at the nondescript box at his side. "Is everything all right? Nothing has happened, with the kids, or—"

"No. I'm here to see you." He closes the distance between us, and a furrow appears between his brows. It's the expression I know so well. My hand aches to reach up and smooth it away. "I heard you got a job offer."

I wrap my arms under my breasts. "Connie told you about Seattle?"

"She did," he says. There's a heavy seriousness in his eyes, an intensity that I've always longed for. Now it's making me feel nervous. "If you want the job, I won't stand in your way. But I can't let you make that decision before telling you how I feel."

My breath catches. "Oh?"

"I realized I've been looking at us the wrong way."

"You have?" I whisper.

"Yes. Entirely wrong. I've been so caught up in the potential pitfalls, the ways we might not work, that I forgot to say the one thing that matters the most. The only thing that ever mattered." He hands me the box, and I finally see what it is. It's a Kindle. The latest model. "Open it. Turn it on."

I slide the device out of the box with trembling hands. "What is this?"

"I wrote my own scene," he murmurs. "My own fantasy. There's a highlighted part, too."

I press the button and watch as the screen flicks to life. There's only one book in the library. It doesn't have a cover, and when I select it, a page full of text appears. My eyes immediately find the highlighted part at the center. It's only three words.

I love you.

"What?" I breathe.

Alec's eyes are warmer than I've ever seen them, but just as serious. "I love you," he says. "That's what I forgot to mention the other night. What I should have said every night for weeks, because I've known it for just as long."

"You love me," I murmur.

His lips tug into a smile, and the skin around his eyes creases. "Yes, sweetheart. That's why I've been turning myself inside out about everything. Your family. The age difference between us. The kids... None of it would have mattered if I didn't feel this way. It shocks me, just how strongly I feel. It's out of control, and I can't make it stop, and even if I could... I wouldn't want to."

He puts a hand beneath my chin and tips my face up, our eyes lock. "You are the most beautiful, unexpected, kindest woman I've ever met, and I'm so glad you danced into my life. If you're going to ruin me, then, Isa, I'll let you. There's no one else I want to hurt for."

My mouth parts on a soft sigh. "I'm not planning on ruining you."

His thumb strokes up my cheek, and his smile turns rueful. "I'm glad, sweetheart. But you can. Maybe that's love, when it's true and deep. It's the ability to give someone absolute joy... and absolute misery. And that's what I'd feel if I lost you."

"Alec," I murmur. "You won't lose me."

His smile stays in place, and a new warmth enters his eyes. "I might. But it would be a far worse fate to lose you before I could tell you that I love you. To lose this, right here...

"You've brought magic back into my life. I've thought about it, this past weekend. The things that lead us both here. There were so many obstacles in the way of you and me ending up together. So many mistakes, and twists in our paths. What are the odds of you moving in next door to Connie, and the two of you bumping into one another... Victoria passing away, and your hip injury extinguishing a dream. And if the kids' previous nanny hadn't quit when she did..."

His thumb moves in slow circles along my jawline, and his voice grows hoarse. "You and I never would have met if not for all those things," he says. "Maybe we are an accident, or a cosmic mistake. Unplanned and unexpected. But it's the best thing that's ever happened to me."

I swallow hard. Tears are welling up, and it's only a matter of time before they spill. "Does this mean you're willing to try?"

His smile widens into the most glorious expression, the one I've seen more of lately. "Try? I want to do it all. I want you with me every day. I want to spoil you. I want to take you out. And I want you in my bed every night. There's no end of wants I crave with you. And I can't remember ever wanting this much, this fiercely, but now that is all that I feel." His hand cups my cheek, and his warm breath ghosts over my mouth. "I want to make you as happy as you've made me."

"You do," I say. My voice comes out a bit wobbly, and I grab the lapels of his suit jacket with both hands. "I want all of that, too, and I want it with you. But I don't want you to change your mind again. To get into your head, and start thinking about what people will say or the age difference or all the things you mentioned the other day."

He kisses me instead, his lips brushing over mine once, twice, and then a third firm time. "Does this mean I'll ever stop wanting to wring the necks of people who look at you sideways for being with me? Or that I won't be afraid you'll come to resent the age gap someday and leave me? No, of course not."

I slide my hands up and lock them behind his neck. "I guess I'll just have to stick around forever to prove you wrong."

His fingers move down the sides of my body. "Good," he murmurs and settles them at the small of my back. "I've never felt this way with anyone before. It's like you've embedded yourself inside of me, under my skin, and diffused in my blood. You're essential."

Warmth races through my body, spreads into my limbs like molten honey. It fills up the hollows I didn't know I had.

Outside the window, the rain shifts into a heavy downpour that beats against the glass.

Alec's lips brush mine. "I want to give you everything."

"I don't need everything. I just need you."

He smiles. "You have me. But I'll give you all the rest, anyway."

I lean against him, our bodies touching at every point, and whisper the words against his lips. "I love you, too."

Alec kisses me deeply, taking my breath away, before lifting his lips an inch. "Say it again."

"I love you," I breathe.

He grips me steadily, but we fall anyway, sinking to the uneven wooden floor. He hits his knees and tugs me against him. "Sweetheart," he murmurs. He runs a hand down my back and kisses me with a fierceness that has none of his usual slow finesse. He trails his lips across my cheek, my neck, the scruff on his chin making me shiver. "I love you," he murmurs into my skin. "I didn't know how good it could feel to say that to someone again. To mean it with every cell in my body."

I run my fingers through his hair, the emotions are making it hard to speak. My eyes are blurry. "I love you, too. I have loved you for so long…"

His mouth traces the edge of my camisole, lips over the skin of my chest. "I want you in my life forever," he mutters. His voice is hoarse, his hands on my waist are tightly wrapped. "I want… I want all of it. I didn't know I'd missed that, too. The wanting. It makes me feel alive. *You* make me feel alive."

I tug his face up and we kiss again. It's an all-consuming kiss. Every nerve ending of my body is firing. I'm feeling too much, and all of it is concentrated right here, in the tight space between our bodies. Nothing else exists.

Alec stretches out on the floorboards and pulls me on top

of him. His hands trace my back, up and down, and he doesn't stop kissing me.

I hope he never stops.

"I love you," I whisper again. His hazel eyes are dark and smoldering, and locked on mine, but warmer than I've ever seen them. "I've never said that to a man before."

He brushes my cheek with the back of his hand. "I'm honored," he says.

I feel light, like I could float away at any moment, and also wonderfully anchored to the man beneath me. I trace the faint lines at the corners of his eyes, his high cheekbones, and the thick hair that has the slightest hint of gray. I caress his cheeks down to his lips, and wonder at him being here with me. Lying in his suit on an old floor and looking up at me as if I'm his entire world.

Maybe we'll float away together.

I flatten myself firmer to him and kiss his neck. He shudders beneath me, and that's when I feel his hardness, pressing against my stomach. His hands dip lower and slide over the thin fabric of my leggings.

I brace my hand on his chest, pushing up a bit. "You're hard?"

Alec lifts an eyebrow, but he's smiling. "I'm not that old."

"I know you're not," I say with a laugh. "I didn't know the 'I love yous' would turn you on."

"Mm-hmm. Well, they did." His hands tighten their grip. "I always want to be inside you, sweetheart. It's my favorite place."

Heat creeps over my cheeks, and I look over at the half-closed door. Diane won't be here all afternoon.

"Well," I say, and kiss him again. "Good thing we have this room all to ourselves…"

CHAPTER 40
ISABEL
TWO WEEKS LATER

He lies relaxed beside me, his eyes closed and his breathing even. With his hands behind his head, he looks like he could be asleep. But then I tighten my grip, and he groans.

"What do you want to have for dinner tomorrow night?" I ask.

"Italian. Indian. Any of the I's."

I trace the ridges along his cock, following the outline of a vein. The skin is silky-smooth and surprisingly hot beneath my finger. I'm lying on my side, with a perfect view of the naked planes of his body and the tightening of his jaw.

"Mm-hmm. Pizza. The kids will like that," I say.

"Yeah. Let's do—argh. Shit."

I'm rubbing my thumb back and forth over the sensitive spot below his head. I love doing this. Teasing him. Watching his face for every little reaction.

And I love having him like this in bed, all to myself. His body is amazing. The broad shoulders, the dark hair smattering his chest and lower stomach, and the masculinity etched in every line. There's something about the faint hint of gray at his temples and the strength of his body that turns me on like nothing else. Not to mention seeing him lose control… and being the one to make sure he does.

"What was that?" I ask sweetly.

"You're evil," he mutters.

I stroke him from base to head, reveling in the way his breath catches. "I thought I was good."

"Oh, you are. You're my good girl. Edging me like this." His voice is a bit hoarse, but it's sincere, and I know he means what he says. The dirty talk isn't from a book anymore. It's real, and it's ours. "You're making me so hard."

"I love your cock," I whisper.

He smiles. "You know I always love it when you verbalize what you want, but that? Yeah. I could hear it all day."

I tighten my grip around him. I really mean it, though. In the weeks since we'd officially become a couple, I've become even better acquainted with it. And with Alec. It hasn't been easy, around his schedule, the kids, and the early mornings. But we're both surprisingly creative when we want something. Happiness has settled around us like a cloak, and I hope we never shrug it off.

"I've gotten used to the thickness now," I say. My hand strokes from base to head again, slower than I know he likes, and he groans in frustration. "And the length. I don't think I'd even like a more regular-sized one now."

Alec's eyes meet mine. "Good," he growls. "Because this one is all yours."

"That's right."

"Just like you're all mine." His gaze drifts down my body, following every curve of my near-naked form. I'll never get tired of it. The weight of his desire and the way it engulfs me like a warm embrace. It makes me feel good, and beautiful, and powerful. And safe. Safe to be whoever, to do whatever. Safe to explore and to be myself.

My hand tightens. "I've been thinking," I say.

His eyes are closed again, and he's breathing shallow. "Yeah."

"It's almost time for me to move out."

His eyes snap open and lock on mine. "What?"

"We're dating now," I say. My voice still comes out a bit shy. It's hard to wrap my head around. *Alec Connovan's girlfriend.* Connie knows, but we haven't been out to dinner with her and Gabriel, yet, or gone to any events together. Tonight is our first time all on our own. She's watching her niece and nephew, and the penthouse is entirely quiet for the first time since I've moved in.

"Yes," Alec says. "Is this because you think it's what I want? Because I don't."

I smile at him. "So when I start working at the studio in a few weeks, and you have to find a new nanny? Where will they live?"

"I'll find a rental or something nearby," he says. "Or you move in here, with me, into the master bedroom. I want you sleeping here every night."

I stroke him again, slow and hard. "I want that, too," I say. "But I want my own place. It's too early, however much I love you, to move in together completely."

I'm afraid it'll kill us before we've properly begun. We need time to settle into a new routine, for me to find footing in the new studio I'm a part of creating, before Alec and I move in together. And when we do, I want it to be official. Not me just slotting into his life, but the two of us building one together.

The idea of *us* makes me feel so happy my chest aches.

"Mm-hmm. I see what you mean, even if I don't agree." He groans and leans his head back against the pillow. "Okay. I'll help you look for an apartment nearby."

"This is a very convenient position to have you in when I want to get my way."

"Oh, you could ask me anything right now and I'd say yes."

I smile at him. "Where do you see our future?"

He groans. "Okay, not what I meant."

That makes me chuckle. "I want to rebuild my career, have a small place that's actually mine… and date you. I want to be here for family dinners and get to know the kids more, and I want to go with you on business trips so we can get some alone time. I want to be your girlfriend. That's what I want."

Alec nods. "Yes. That's… yes. That's what I want, too. Except with you sleeping here every night."

I tighten my grip, and a breath hisses out of him. "Many nights I will," I say. "But not all."

"I guess," he grunts out, "I'll find a way to survive."

Chuckling again, I lean over him, my long hair falling across his legs. "Tell me what kind of future you see for us."

Then, I take the swollen head of his cock inside my mouth. He curses, and I hold still, letting him rise to the brink of eruption but never crossing over. I love doing this. I only discovered it a few days ago, and now it's my favorite thing to do to make him fall apart.

He likes doing it to me too… but I'm left too weak to stand after, and that won't do when we have a date night planned.

Alec takes a deep breath. "Right. I see…. I see… you with me. You find your footing. Your dance studio becomes… *argh, fuck*. Okay. It becomes very successful. You love what you do and I love watching you be happy. When the time is right, I finally convince you to move in with me…" His breathing catches and his stomach muscles tighten, and I lift my head again. Watch his cock twitch and hear him groan.

"Devil," he mutters.

I chuckle and put him back in my mouth. *Continue,* I say, a hum around his girth.

He obliges. "You move in with me. The kids love you, obviously. By then, they really want you to move back in too.

We go on a beautiful trip somewhere. I ask... shit. Okay. I ask you to marry me." He's looking down at me with dark eyes, sweat beads on his brow. And he looks completely serious.

A warmth starts low in my stomach.

"You say yes," he says hoarsely. "On our wedding day, we... well. We do various versions of this. After the ceremony."

I want to smile at that one. I nod instead, my head bobbing along his length.

"And then," he murmurs, his hand brushing my hair back and his eyes warming, "I get to spend the rest of my days making you happy. We can have another kid or two, if you want. We do lots of this... God, the thought of trying to get you pregnant makes me—" He cuts off with a choke and drops his head back again. I pull my mouth off him just in time to stop him from coming, and he curses in frustration.

I smile at him. "You done?"

"I was done ten minutes ago," he mutters. He reaches for his cock, so swollen now it looks painful. "Come here. Tell me what you thought of my plan while I'm inside you."

He sits up and grabs at my panties. I lift my hips and let him peel the garment down my legs, and revel in the hoarse groan that follows. "Yes," he mutters, a thumb stroking between my legs. "So wet for me, sweetheart."

"Always," I murmur. I bend my legs, bracing my feet on the bed while he aligns himself, and then he's pushing in, so slow that both of us hiss out a breath. He's on his knees, and it gives him the perfect leverage to go hard, with slow, heavy thrusts that make my world narrow into nothing but sensations.

"Tell me," he says.

I lift my legs, stretching them up past my head. His eyes flare, and his hips piston faster. There's a special kind of turn-on, being like this. Bent over in half, with both watching, and feeling him lose himself. It usually brings me right to the edge with him.

"I like the sound of that," I say. It's hard to breathe right. "I love you, and I love the thought of being with you forever… and getting married one day…"

He groans and lowers to his elbows, his hips snapping against mine. A lock of hair falls over his forehead, and I brush it back. His skin is hot to the touch.

"You're mine," he says. His lips hover just over my own, and his hand strokes my hair. My body is dancing along the crest of an orgasm. Just barely, but it's there, the snap of his hips propelling me on. "Tell me you're mine."

"I'm yours," I say and wrap my arms around his shoulders. He groans against my neck and erupts inside me. I feel the force of it, and the sharp jerk of his pelvis against mine sends me barrelling over the edge along with him.

His breathing is fast. So is mine, and we just breathe together, our foreheads touching. I don't know where I end and he begins.

"And are you mine?" I whisper.

He smiles. "Always, sweetheart. Always."

It takes us longer than it should to get into the shower. To get cleaned up and pull ourselves together in order to do what we had planned. The whole reason Connie and Gabriel are babysitting in the first place.

I sit on top of the counter in the master bathroom and watch him do up the buttons of his shirt. His hair is still damp from the shower we shared. I haven't even tried to dry mine. It's wrapped in a tight knot at the back of my neck.

"If we get there fast," Alec says, "we can leave just as quickly."

"That ashamed to go with me?" I ask with a wide smile.

He sends me a dark look. "Please. If anything, I want more time with *you*, and less with that crowd."

"We'll get in, make a donation, and get out," I say.

He does up the last button. "Yes. You look fantastic, Isabel."

My smile widens. I'm just in a black slip dress, ballet flats, and minimal makeup. But I feel beautiful, my cheeks still flushed from the warm water and something else, something cozy, a feeling in my chest that hasn't gone away for weeks.

"Thank you."

He puts a hand on my knee, his thumb rubbing a circle. His eyes are warm. "My pretty girl."

"You look good, too." I run my hand over the collar of his shirt, fixing the collar. It doesn't get old. Getting to touch him like this—intimately, proprietorially. This man is mine. "You always do. Handsome, intriguing, eye-catching…"

Alec's eyebrows lift. "Eye-catching?"

"Yes. Everyone notices when you walk into a room."

"I think you're talking about *you*, Isa."

I run my fingers through his hair to brush it back. "No. I'm talking about you. That's how I felt for years, from the first time Connie introduced us. Do you remember when we first met? It was in the hallway outside her apartment. You were arriving, and I was leaving."

Alec's eyes soften. "I remember. That was five years ago."

"Mm-hmm."

"I must have looked haggard," he says. "Must have been only months after… I had little to no sleep that first year, with Sam."

"You did look tired," I admit. "A bit rough around the edges, maybe. But you stole all the air out of that hallway. We shook hands. Do you remember?"

He steps between my legs. "I do."

"You do?"

"Of course. I shouldn't have noticed you in that way, but I did. Even as far gone as I was… I did." His lips tip up into a half smile. "And every time we bumped into each other after that, I couldn't help but notice you over and over again, and feel like a creep. For wanting to get to know you. For feeling the attraction."

I grin. "A creep? What does that make you now?"

He wraps his hands around my waist and leans until our foreheads touch. "I have no idea, and I don't care. I only care what you think of me."

"I think you're the best person I've ever known," I say. "But I also think you're stalling. We're both ready to leave."

He groans and closes his eyes. "This is not the date night I wanted us to have."

I chuckle. "I think it's perfect. And as soon as it's over…"

"Mm-hmm. We'll come back here, and we'll be all alone." He lifts me off the counter and I slide down his body, landing on the balls of my feet. "Let's go, then, sweetheart. Let's face the wolves."

St. Regis's annual Christmas fundraiser is the event of the year. They'd called three separate times to confirm Alec's attendance. He's that big of a donor, apparently.

Mac drives us. Both he and Katja have handled my transition from being an employee to Alec's girlfriend surprisingly well. Katja spoke to me for a solid hour about how much she liked me and wanted the best for me, while Mac had told me that he was happy for me. *Working relationships can be hard,* he had added. *I hope you two can handle it.*

We'd been alone in the car at the time, and I hadn't been able to resist.

They can be, I said. *But they can also be worth it. Don't you think?*

He didn't respond to that, but he did glance down at the coffee cup and sandwich resting in the center console. We both knew who prepped them for him. She didn't need to tuck a little cookie into his lunch packs, or make him freshly brewed coffee as often as she did.

I suspected we both knew why she did that, too.

Alec offers me his arm when we enter the fundraiser. The

school rented a penthouse space a few blocks away from campus, and the decor is spectacular. Snowflakes hang from the high ceilings, and music plays from the hidden speakers. The place is already packed.

I shift closer to Alec. "What are you planning on bidding on?"

"Bidding?"

"The school sent out a list of all the blind-bid items available for auction. They were described by kids and accompanied by a drawing. It's a cute idea."

Alec chuckles. "That's how they plan to raise money?"

"Oh, yes. I read all about it in the newsletter. Forwarded it to you, too."

"I should have read it."

"You're busy."

His mouth grazes my temple. "Never too busy for you. You smell good."

"Mmm. People are watching us."

"Let them," he says.

We each grab a glass of champagne and take a turn around the elaborately decorated room. There is a row of tables in the back, displaying the auction items. Little bowls in front of the framed kid-drawn artwork are filled with folded notes containing people's bids.

A group of women approaches us. I recognize the one in the middle immediately from the last time we attended a St. Regis event. The woman who made the comments about me and Alec. The mother of Willa's friend, who had wanted Alec to come to her networking meetups disguised as dinner parties.

"Alec," she says warmly. The other women smiles at him, too, but their eyes all slide to his hand resting on the small of my back.

"Ladies," he says. "Excellent event, as always."

"Thank you. So happy you could make it. Checking out the blind-bid items?"

"Yes. There's something that looks like it could be a lawn mower over there," he says with a nod. "The kids are imaginative."

"It's a great idea, isn't it?" The woman's eyes land on mine, and her smile stretches just a bit wider. It looks entirely fake. "I see that you're accompanied by your children's nanny tonight again."

Alec's arm curves more firmly around my waist. "No," he says. "Isabel is my girlfriend."

CHAPTER 41
ALEC

"That's it!" I hear the sound of Isabel's voice, encouraging and upbeat, and the patter of feet. "Just like that. That looks wonderful, girls."

I lean against the doorframe. Isabel is teaching three little girls, one of whom is Willa, the different starting positions in ballet. The studio is bright and airy, with the faint smell of fresh paint lingering in the air.

Classes haven't officially started yet. Willa is Isabel's first student, the guinea pig, and so far she seems to love every minute of it. She even convinced two of her best friends to join in her second lesson.

Isabel is dressed much like she was the first time I saw her at the old Dance Academy, twirling through a sea of dust motes and illuminated by the rays of the sun. Her dark hair is in a high bun. Her arms are bare, her long legs in tights. She is fluidity personified, in a pair of satin shoes, showing the girls the different starting positions in ballet.

Neither she or Diane had let me invest in the studio. I'd offered. Twice, actually, and Isabel had said no. I understood why. Freedom is a beautiful thing, and it's been a long time since she had it.

I want to help, but I want her to soar on her own wings more.

I'd inherited a company. I know how hard it is to make it yours; and there's a part of me that envies her, a chance to start something from the ground.

It takes the girls a long time to notice that I'm watching. Willa is the first, catching sight of me in one of the giant mirrors.

"Dad!" Willa calls. She's beaming from ear to ear. "Look, we're doing the third position."

"I see. It looks great. You too, girls."

"Can you stay to watch?"

"Yes, of course," I say. "But I only think there's ten minutes left."

The girls look at each other and immediately start whispering. Isabel laughs and nods. "Yes," she says warmly. "We can try."

Apparently they'd asked her before if they could try spins, and she'd said it would have to wait until the end. The girls struggle. Isabel is patient, helpful, and not nearly as stern as I would have expected. It shouldn't surprise me. She's always had a caring touch.

Afterward, when the girls are sitting down to put on their sneakers, Isabel comes over to me.

"Hey," she says.

I wrap an arm around her waist. "Hi, sweetheart."

"It went great." Her voice is buzzing. "So good, actually. I really like teaching."

"You're great at it," I murmur against her temple.

She sighs. It's a happy sound. "My old teachers would roll over in their graves if they saw the techniques I've been using. Well. None of them are dead, but you know what I mean. They taught me a lot, and they were incredible, but I don't want to be like them. I want the kids to know that dancing is fun. That there doesn't—oh, awesome girls! You're all ready to leave?"

Willa nods and looks up at me. "Can we drop off Dora and Elsie?"

"Yeah, and we've already cleared it with your parents," I tell them both. "Come on, girls, let's get you in the car."

"There are snacks waiting for you," Isabel says. The girls race ahead, and we follow at a leisurely pace.

I brush her hand with mine. "Grand opening in three weeks."

She smiles. "Thanks for reminding me. I'd *just* been able to forget it."

"Don't be nervous. You and Diane know what you're doing."

"Yes, but we don't know if the classes will fill up, or if there will be… actually, you know what?" she asks. There's a wide smile on her lips, and it lights up her features, making her brown eyes glitter.

God, I love that expression. Ensuring this woman is happy has become my vocation. Maybe it's not Contron. Maybe Contron is just an occupation, but this is my passion in life. If I do nothing else but make her and my kids happy, I've lived a good life.

"What," I ask.

"I've decided that it doesn't matter what happens. I'm still happy I tried. And if this doesn't work out… I guess I'll find something else. Become an oil painter. Learn to race horses. Become a marketing executive."

"Go to business school and join the family business," I say.

She laughs. "God, can you imagine? Absolutely not. I'll leave that to you and Connie and Nate. I love you, but we're not working together again."

"Is that criticism?" I ask, but I'm smiling too. She's officially no longer my children's nanny. I'd understood her concerns. Honored every single one. I've hired a new nanny, a woman in her sixties without a single degree in child psychology but with twenty years of experience. Isabel had joined me for the interview. I've also talked to Willa. Explained that it's not the nanny that keeps me away, but my work.

Hearing Isabel tell me of Willa's words had been hard. Hard, and heartbreaking, and important. I've vowed to make sure both Willa and Sam will always know they come first.

"Me? Critiquing the great Alec Connovan? I would never," she says. Her smile is crooked, and teasing, and I want to kiss it off her.

"Are you guys coming?!" Willa yells.

Our walk has slowed to a crawl.

Once we're home, it's only an hour until the doorbell rings again. Isabel is still in the shower and I head to open the door. Two kids flock at my sides as I pull it open.

"Hi!" Connie says. She's smiling wide, her arms extended. Gabriel is at her side with two large grocery bags.

Willa grins at Connie. Sam tucks close to my leg, but he's peering out at both his aunt and his new uncle.

"Hello," Willa says. "What's in the bags?"

"So, I got this idea," Connie says. "How about we make homemade pizza? I brought the dough and all the ingredients. You can each make your own, and you get to choose the toppings."

Gabriel's eyes meet mine. They're amused. "Neither of us knows how to cook," he tells me matter-of-factly. "We might end up getting pizza delivered."

"There's a place down the street," I tell him. "One Hawaiian and one margarita, and the kids will be golden."

He grins at me. "Thanks for helping me out."

"Anytime."

Connie frowns at us both. "No, we're cooking. It's a great activity. Okay, let's find the fridge… Sammy, can you show me the way?"

The kids hover around Connie and Gabriel for ten minutes

before they fully relax. Willa loves Connie, and Sam has the disposition to be happy just about anywhere after he gets over his initial shyness.

Isabel comes out of my bedroom a few minutes later. She's in a beautiful green blouse and black jeans, and her hair falls softly around her shoulders. Connie and her hug, and she's pulled into the kitchen, to where Connie wants to have a private word before we leave.

Seeing them together is odd. Shouldn't be. But it's reconciling the two worlds—Isabel as Connie's friend and Isabel as mine—and I know it'll take me a little while. I suspect it will also take a bit of time for Isabel and Connie to get used to the new dynamic too.

But somehow I'm not worried about that. We'll solve it.

Gabriel hands me a beer he must have swiped from the fridge. "You might need one," he tells me.

"Most likely. Thanks. And it was great you two could come over and babysit tonight."

"Anytime," he says. "Connie wants to spend more time with her niece and nephew, and I like kids. Odd to think we might have some one day."

I slide my gaze to his and he chuckles. "Not yet, don't worry. That wasn't me implying anything."

"It is odd," I say. "Having kids. But then you have them, and it's the most natural thing in the world."

He hmms in agreement. We stand side by side and watch as the kids examine the wide array of toppings Connie has brought. It's far too many for the four of them to consume. The scene makes me smile. My little sister, ever the overachiever.

"Nervous?" Gabriel asks.

I take a long pull of my beer, and answer him. Eventually. "It's going to be interesting, yes."

"I know something about meeting the girlfriend's family," he says, "and them not being too impressed."

I huff a chuckle. "Yeah. You do. I won't apologize, though. We needed to vet you properly."

"Of course you did. Which is what they will probably do to you," he says. "But it's only a first meeting. And if it goes terribly, it means you have nowhere to go after but up."

I touch my bottle to his. "How inspiring. You should be a motivational speaker."

"And resign from Thompson Industries?" he says. "You'd like that, wouldn't you?"

I shake my head. "Do us both a favor and sell the solar company that's dragging down your books. We both know it was a bad purchase. I also know someone who could utilize it more wisely."

His mouth drops open, but his eyes glitter. "Hands off, Connovan."

I chuckle. "Bring it on, Thompson."

Connie looks over at us. She looks surprised, but then her face softens into a smile. "Am I hallucinating, or are you two enjoying yourself?"

"Don't bring attention to it," Isabel stage-whispers, "or they'll stop."

I roll my eyes at them both. "We need to get going," I tell my girlfriend.

She turns to Connie. "See?" she asks, but they're both grinning.

We leave the kids to my sister and brother-in-law. Connie wishes us luck, and Isabel smiles in her direction. "It'll go great," she says confidently.

In the elevator riding down, I double-check my appearance in the mirror. I'm clean-shaven. My hair brushed back. Neat, yes, but there's no hiding the traces of gray at the temples, or the creases around my eyes.

Soft lips press against my cheek, and Isabel's hands grip mine. "Relax," she whispers.

"I am relaxed."

"Mm-hmm," she says smiling. "I'm not worried, so you shouldn't be."

I raise an eyebrow. "I know how parents think."

"Yes, but you don't know mine. Not yet." She threads her fingers through mine, and we walk through the lobby and out onto the sidewalk. It's been weeks, and it hasn't gotten old. Holding her, touching her, freely in public.

Being part of a couple again. Being a part of a couple with *her*.

We stop by the curb to hail a cab. Mac has the weekend off. It had been Isabel's idea. *Give him the evening off on Saturday. Katja is free, too, and I… I just have this feeling.*

She'd asked me while sitting on my lap, her hands locked around my neck, and I wasn't in a state to deny her a thing. Apparently, she suspects something is going on between my housekeeper and my driver.

I pull her close while we stand on the sidewalk. "And you're sure," I murmur, "that you're fine with their reaction? Whatever it might be?"

She puts a hand on my cheek. "Alec, I've told them about you. They know how we met. They know we're together. And they know your age."

"Right."

"You told your own dad to fuck off a few weeks ago," she says brightly. "What makes you think I wouldn't be willing to do the same if they object?"

I frown down at her smiling face. "You shouldn't have to do that because of me. You shouldn't have—"

She kisses me, pressing soft lips against mine. It's a very effective way to kill the argument. And when she lifts her lips, she keeps them an inch from mine. "Alec," she whispers again. It's a chiding tone.

I rest my forehead against her. *I know.* She keeps reminding me that it's not my job to save her. To solve everything. To give and never take. It's a hard habit to overcome.

I don't know if I'll ever crack it, or will ever stop wanting to give her everything. But I can learn to trust in her… and take her word for things.

"They're going to love you," she whispers against my lips. "And if they don't, it's still you and me. Isn't it?"

"You and me," I murmur. My hands tighten around her waist, over the thick padding of her winter coat.

"Mmm. And what does that mean?"

I drag my lips over her cheek, to the curve of her ear. "I want your parents to like your choice of man. But if they don't… I won't let you go. Not for anything, sweetheart."

Her hands tighten on the lapels of my jacket. "Oh," she whispers. "I like that."

"Good." I press a kiss on her cheek and raise my head. Resolve makes my spine harden. I've faced my share of tough negotiations before. I can face this one, too.

The cab drive to Brooklyn takes a while, but we're not in a rush. We finally pull to a stop outside a small apartment building. The street looks charming. Ordinary. Homey.

A woman sits on the steps leading into the building. She's got short hair, and she's talking on the phone.

Isabel waves at her as soon as we exit the car.

It's Elena. She grins at us and gets off the phone. "Hey!" she says. "You guys are early."

I glance at my watch. We're right on time.

Apparently Isabel is thinking the same because she laughs. "We're on schedule, but maybe we shouldn't be. Are Mom and Dad ready?"

"I have no idea. I've been out here for twenty minutes talking to Avery."

"Things going well?"

"Going great," she says. Her eyes land on mine, and she smiles. "Hey, rich guy."

"Hey, stand-up," I say.

"Evaded any taxes lately?"

"Bombed on stage lately?"

Her grin widens. "I knew you could take a joke. Okay, let's get going. They're really eager to meet you, you know."

"I'd like to meet them, too."

"Oh, you don't have to be polite with me," she says. She brushes off her jeans and looks between us. "They'll love you. Maybe not right away, but of course they will."

I raise an eyebrow. "And I'm not too old for your sister?"

Isabel nudges me, but she's smiling, too. Looking at her sister.

Elena shrugs. "Of course you are. But why should that stop either of you? I'm too unfunny to be a stand-up, Isabel's too injured to perform, and bumblebees are too heavy to fly, and all that. But here we are anyway, doing all of it. Now come on, let's go upstairs."

I keep my hand at the small of Isabel's back as we follow her sister into the narrow hallway of the building where both of them grew up.

Maybe love is hard. Maybe it's destined to chafe, to hurt, to break. Maybe love comes with risks… but that shouldn't stop any of us.

And I won't let it stop me any longer.

EPILOGUE
ISABEL

One year later

I stand in the darkness, posed to strike. The silence is punctuated only by soft breathing and an occasional cough. The music starts to play. Beside me I can hear Diane's indrawn breath, and to the right, I see Christa's leg tremble.

The music starts.

The curtain parts.

We spin as one, erupting out on the makeshift stage in a flurry of motion. I catch sight of the audience, in that brief, quick way where their faces all blend together into one. But I know it's the kids we teach and their parents, and some of my friends and family. Everyone who has an interest in seeing our showcase. But right now, they're all one entity. It's a relationship I'm used to. Audience and performer... and the magic created between us.

The kids performed first. They'd practiced all term for this showcase, and while this day has been filled with nerves, we've made sure they all had fun. Today is about joy and progress, and we won't be keeping a list of who stumbled. That's not the way we do it here at our academy.

It was the kids who asked for us teachers to perform as well. *Please. Can you three dance together?*

It had been a far-fetched dream, and then a fun idea, and in the past week, a passion project. Diane, Christa, and I had stayed late three nights in a row, perfecting and training and falling back into the kind of hard-core practices that had once been a part of all our lives.

And I loved it.

I love it now, dancing with the two women who have become incredible friends. First Diane, and a few months later, we'd recruited Christa too. We'd all bonded over the process of turning a profession into a hobby, and somehow, back into a profession. We're teachers now, not performers, and that has its own special kind of magic. To see the girls and boys we mentor discover a sense of belonging, and joy, and self-confidence in a skill that I love like the very air I breathe.

The music shifts, and we line up again on pointe. Start twisting, and then we're spinning, one fouetté, two fouettés, all holding the same tempo. It's always been a crowd-pleaser, and I hear the indrawn breaths from the audience.

Many of our students are here today, and that includes Willa. But Sam and Alec, Connie and Gabriel, and even my parents and my siblings are here. They insisted when they heard I was performing.

It's touching that they came.

Once, my performances had been nightly. They're not anymore. The people in my life know that, too, what it means to me to be doing this again.

I lose myself in the choreography. Diane's face flashes before mine, and Christa's, and we take our final positions, and then the music ends.

The audience erupts in applause.

It's not as loud as those I received most nights for years, but it's far more warmer. Someone whistles, a kid shrieks in excitement, and I hear whooping.

Next to me Diane relaxes, and I follow suit, turning to the audience. Our students, their families, and our loved ones.

Willa comes running up to me with a giant bouquet of fragrant red and pink roses. She's smiling wide. Her hair is in a tight bun, and she's in ballet clothes, too, from her own performance.

"That was amazing!"

I hug her close. "Thank you. You were phenomenal as well up there."

My family follows closely behind Willa. And Connie, and Gabriel, and they're all telling me how wonderful it was, as if I'd just performed the prima role in *Swan Lake* at the opera house.

"Guys, guys," I say through my laugh when Connie hands me a third bouquet, "it really wasn't that special."

"I don't know, I don't think I could have done that," Gabriel says.

"You were beautiful," Mom says. Her eyes are glistening, and I know it's because of more than just the showcase. It's for all of this. The ballet studio, the job, all the kids filling this very room right now.

The way my dream has turned into a life I love.

Alec hands me a single red rose and pulls me close. "That," he says, "was extraordinary."

"You've seen me dance at home a hundred times before," I tell him. It's overwhelming, this response. My cheeks feel heated from the joy in the air.

"Maybe, but it never gets old. I love you," he murmurs against my temple. I lean into his side with a soft sigh. That never gets old, either, hearing that. The support he's given me this past year, the steady, all-encompassing nature of him, feels like a part of me I can't believe I ever lived without. He's the person I want to talk everything through with, the man I want to sleep next to every night, and has the driest wit I've ever known.

"I love you too," I tell him softly. "And I love my life."

He smiles against my temple. "Move in with me," he murmurs.

I look up at him. "What was that?"

"Move in with me," he repeats, his arms tightening around my waist. "Live with me, sweetheart. We can redecorate."

"That's the first time you've offered redecorating."

"I realized it might not have been implied before." He tips my head back, the people around us forgotten. His hazel eyes are sincere. "Whatever you want, sweetheart, you can get. I want you to keep loving your life… and I want us to start building one together."

My lips turn up into a smile. He's been hinting at this ever since I found my own place, just a few blocks from his. I spend a ton of time in his apartment, too. Entire weekends. Weeknights. But it's been important for me to have something of my own… especially while I was rebuilding my life. Starting this studio, finding my footing. Learning who we are together.

But I know that now.

"Do you know what?" I ask and smooth a hand along the rough stubble on his jaw. This man, as infuriating as he is intelligent, hardworking and honest, who loves deeper than anyone I've known. "I think I'm ready."

His eyes widen. "Is that finally a *yes*?"

"Yes," I say, smiling, "that's a yes."

He kisses me. In front of everyone, including our siblings, my parents, my business partners. And afterward, he lifts me, and I can't help but laugh. Sam hears us and laughs, too. Then, Connie is asking *what's happening*.

Willa rushes to my side as soon as her dad puts me down. "Isa? Daddy?"

"What happened?" Connie asks again. Her eyes are bright, too curious, a big smile on her face.

"I think I'm ready to move back in," I say and put a hand on Willa's head. "If that's okay with you all."

Her face turns into a frown. "Yes. Of course. You should never have moved out. But I thought you were getting engaged!"

Connie laughs. "Me, too!"

I glance at Alec. His face is serene, a wide smile across his lips. He wraps an arm around my waist and looks at our family.

"That's my next move," he says warmly.

―――

Want more Alec and Isabel? Join my newsletter to read two extra chapters about what happens a few years later…

Link: https://BookHip.com/GXRKJCB

BONUS SCENE

Read on for the bonus chapter about Alec and Isabel, previously only for newsletter subscribers.

Revelations

Extended epilogue for
The Perfect Mistake

REVELATIONS

Isabel pushes closer to me and kisses my neck. The warmth against my skin makes me shudder, and more blood rushes south. Shit. But I can't help but want her, when she's lying on top of me, and the word *love* floating around in the air.

God, it's only been a few days, but I've missed her. I slide my hands down over the lush length of her body and grip the firm globes of her ass.

She lifts herself up with a hand on my chest. Her dark eyes glitter with delight. "You're hard?"

I raise an eyebrow. "I'm not that old."

"I know you're not," she says with a laugh. "But I didn't know *I love you's* would turn you on."

"Mhm. Well, they are." I tighten my grip on her ass. "I'll always want to be inside you, sweetheart. It's my favorite place."

A flush creeps up her cheeks, and I love the sight. I love everything about her. And love the way we think alike, as she looks over at the closed door. "Well," she says, and lowers back down to kiss me. "Good thing I have this room for another hour…"

I groan against her lips and tug her tighter against me, our hips touching. The friction against my cock between our bodies is delicious, tantalising, and not near enough to satisfy. She rolls her hips against mine, and I groan.

"Sweetheart," I mutter. My hands stroke over the thin fabric of her workout ballet leggings. Does she really mean…?

I kiss her, brushing my tongue over her lower lip, savoring her warmth and taste. This woman has seeped beneath my skin and into my veins, and I want her like nothing else.

I fit my hand around her waist and tug her upwards, letting me kiss down her jaw and neck. Down to the curve of her collarbone, and the thin fabric strap holding up her camisole. God, I could get used to seeing her in these dancers' outfits. Somehow it's *almost* as wonderful as her naked.

She rolls hers hips against mine again, and I groan. If that's what she wants… I slide my hand down and find the thin clasping of the leotard between her legs. It's a three button snap, and I release it with a soft pop. It snaps up, leaving only thin tights and underwear between my fingers.

I can feel her warmth through it.

I stroke her slit through the fabric, and she shudders against me again. The sound of her soft sigh makes me twitch. My cock aches behind the tight zipper of my jeans, and I remember her detailing the fantasies about quickies.

I kiss her cheek. Her jaw. Her lips.

Isabel grips my shoulders tight and rolls us. I follow along immediately, and she settles beneath me on the wooden floor, still in her camisole, her hair loosened beneath her face, and mouth swollen from kisses.

I find the elastic of her tights and tug them down along with her panties. They only make it to her knees, trapping her legs tight together, and leaving the most beautiful sight between them.

A physical ache pounds through my body at the sight of her pussy.

I love her. The words are a steady beat in my veins. *And she loves me.*

She *loves* me.

I touch her with my left hand. I just need to. Smooth my fingers over her hipbone and down across to her slit, and the clit I know so well by now. We both sigh when my hands make contact with her bare pussy.

She's so warm, so soft, and I'll never get over touching her. Stroking her and circling her clit and feeling her grow wet beneath my fingers.

I run my thumb over her clit, back and forth, back and forth.

Her back arches softly. "Alec," she breathes. "I've missed you these last few days. I've missed this."

God, so have I. So much.

I brush against her clit again and kiss her jaw. Her cheek. Her lips. "I know, sweetheart," I murmur. "I've missed every part of you."

"I love you," she says again. Her hand slides into my hand, grips tightly. "I love you so much. I feel like I've loved you for years."

I groan against her lips. Every fiber of my being needs her, and as close as we are, I want to be closer still. I want to bury myself inside her and never leave; I want to hold her close and never let her go.

I push two fingers into her tight warmth, and she moans in my ear. She's wet. Wet and I want her and she wants me and my chest feels light with feelings. So many of them at ones.

Gratitude that she walked into my life.

Overwhelming need to have her close.

And love like I haven't felt in years.

So much love for the gorgeous girl lying beneath me, her arms holding me tight, breathing hard against my neck. My cock feels swollen, constrained behind the jeans.

I reach down and try to undo my belt buckle with one hand. Isabel helps me, and together we tug down the zipper. The sudden freedom from the restriction makes me groan, and I pull out my cock.

Her fingers tighten on my shoulders in urgency.

I feel all of it too. I brace on one forearm and use the other to guide myself between her slim thighs. Trapped as she is with the tights only pulled halfway down her legs, it's a squeeze, and Isabel mewls in my ear when I brush the head of my cock along her pussy. She's warm and delicious and I find the notch of her entrance.

I sink in, and she groans in my ear at every inch.

With her legs closed together and mine on each side of hers, the fit is even tighter. I close my eyes against her temple and focus on breathing.

Fuck, it feels so good. Being inside her always does.

"I love you," she murmurs against my ear. Her voice is breathless and shaky, and I know the fit is snug for her too.

I feel like I'm on the edge of coming already. Hearing her say those words… I know I'll never tire of it.

I move slowly inside her, in long, deep strokes. With every thrust, the tight squeeze robs me of breath. The friction envelopes my entire cock, from base to head, and makes it impossible to think. I kiss down her jaw and suck her earlobe between my teeth.

Her hands trace down over my back, stopping at my ass, like she can pull me even deeper. She grinds her hips against mine.

My balls tighten and I groan.

Not yet.

I stop, still buried inside of her. Force my breathing to even out and ignore the urgent encouragements she whispers in my ear.

"Alec," she says, arching her back.

I lift on to my elbow and trace the neckline of her camisole with my finger. "I didn't even get this off you," I say.

She rolls her eyes. "I can show you my tits later. Will you please keep moving?"

I grin. "I'm savoring the moment."

"Mhm."

I lower my head, press my lips against hers. My hips give an involuntary flex and I struggle to resist the overwhelming urge to pound into her, to give my cock the friction it craves.

"I love you," I say. "Fuck, so much. So… I can't…"

"I know," she whispers, and my hips move again. It's a much faster pace this time. "I know," she says again, and buries her fingers in my hair. "I want you so much."

"You feels so good… I'll never get tired of your pussy…"

She runs her nails over my scalp. "I love you."

Energy starts at the base of my spine and I lower my head to her neck, and mutter her name against her warm skin, and then the pressure explodes inside of me. It radiates through my limbs and emerges through my cock, and I come inside of her, my entire body shuddering with every pulse of release.

She grips me tightly. I can feel her heavy breathing in my ear, and her softly murmured words, things she's rarely said. *I love it when you come inside me. I love when you fuck me like this. I love you so much.*

I try to hold most of my weight by my arms, but she pulls me down, and I relent, fusing our bodies even tighter together.

I feel like I've lost ten years of my life. My heart is pounding, and I'm oversensitive, and feel better than ever.

She smiles up at me. It's a wide, brilliant, beautiful smile.

"I love you," she whispers again.

And I know without any doubt that I've been given the greatest gift.

THE STORY CONTINUES...

Nate Connovan returns in the final book of the series. The woman he's loved for years is about to walk down the aisle to marry his best friend.

Until she changes her mind right before the wedding. She disappears, only to show up in London a few days later. New job. New country. *New life.*

She's in need of a friend. Except that friend shouldn't be her ex's best friend... and it should *definitely* not bloom into more than friendship.

She's totally off-limits. But you know what they say about forbidden fruit. It always tastes the sweetest...

This hero-falls-first, forbidden, ten-year-age gap romance is coming soon!

ACKNOWLEDGEMENTS

Whew. It took a real village to write this book, my longest yet, and most definitely the angstiest.

My author friends, who have listened to more voice notes about this book than anyone should have to, advised me on plot and character, and guided me through writing slumps, thank you. This can be a lonely job and you've made it so much brighter.

I tried to learn as much about the challenging world of professional ballet as I could while writing this book. Thank you to everyone who's shared their experience online, answered questions on Reddit, and otherwise helped inform this book. Isabel's love of ballet—and her stepping away from it at a professional level—mirrors an experience I suspect many can relate to. Writing is a dream come true for me… but it meant giving up a career I thought I wanted more than anything. What we spend our days doing greatly affects our identities, and it's always a challenging thing when they change, even if it's welcome.

And of course, anything I got wrong about ballet is my fault and mine alone.

Thank you to Becca for the brilliant plot coaching. To the amazing beta readers, Andie, Andra, Alexandra, Amelia, Cal, Julia and Nikki, thank you for your great insights and opinions. It really helps me refine the stories I tell.

Andie, your editing always makes my books stronger. I don't know what I'd do without your help.

Thanks to Yoly for the beautiful ebook cover, and Books & Moods for the stunning discreet paperback cover.

Above all, thank you to every single reader. Thank you for continuing to pick up my books and spend time with my characters. It will never stop being a gift.

OTHER BOOKS BY OLIVIA
LISTED IN SUGGESTED READING ORDER

The Connovan Chronicles

Best Enemies Forever
Gabriel and Connie

The Perfect Mistake
Alec and Isabel

One Wrong Move
Nate and Harper

The New York Billionaire Series

Think Outside the Boss
Tristan and Freddie

Saved by the Boss
Anthony and Summer

Say Yes to the Boss
Victor and Cecilia

A Ticking Time Boss
Carter and Audrey

Suite on the Boss
Isaac and Sophia

12 Days of Bossmas
Christmas anthology

The Seattle Billionaire Series

Billion Dollar Enemy
Cole and Skye

Billion Dollar Beast
Nick and Blair

Billion Dollar Catch
Ethan and Bella

Billion Dollar Fiancé
Liam and Maddie

Brothers of Paradise Series

Dark Eyed Devil
Lily and Hayden

Ice Cold Boss
Faye and Henry

Red Hot Rebel
Ivy and Rhys

Small Town Hero
Jamie and Parker

Standalones

How to Honeymoon Alone
Phillip and Eden

Arrogant Boss
Julian and Emily

Look But Don't Touch
Grant and Ada

The Billionaire Scrooge Next Door
Adam and Holly

ABOUT OLIVIA

Olivia is a hopeless romantic who loves billionaires heroes, despite never having met one. So she took matters into her own hands and creates them on the page instead. Stern, charming, cold or brooding, so far she's never met a (fictional) billionaire she didn't like.

She picked up the pen in 2019, and she hasn't put it down since. With over a million books sold, Olivia writes fast-paced, swoon-worthy stories filled with banter and spice. Join the heroes as they meet, clash with, or stumble into the ambitious heroines that make them fall, and fall hard.

Join her newsletter for updates and bonus content.
www.oliviahayle.com.
Connect with Olivia

- facebook.com/authoroliviahayle
- instagram.com/oliviahayle
- goodreads.com/oliviahayle
- amazon.com/author/oliviahayle
- bookbub.com/profile/olivia-hayle

Printed in Great Britain
by Amazon